Miklós Szentkuthy

St. Orpheus Breviary, Vol. II
Black Renaissance

Translated by

TIM WILKINSON

Edited by

ERIKA MIHÁLYCSA

Endnotes by

TIM WILKINSON &
ERIKA MIHÁLYCSA

Contra Mundum Press New York · London · Melbourne

Szent Orpheus breviáriuma: Fekete reneszánsz is published by arrangement with Mariella Legnani and Mária Tompa

Originally published in Hungarian as *Fekete reneszánsz* in 1939.

Library of Congress Cataloguing-in-Publication Data

Szentkuthy, Miklós, 1908–1988

[Fekete Reneszánsz. English.]

St. Orpheus Breviary, Vol. II: Black Renaissance / Miklós Szentkuthy; translated from the original Hungarian by Tim Wilkinson

—1st Contra Mundum Press Edition

350 pp., 5×8 in.

ISBN 9781940625263

I. Szentkuthy, Miklós.
II. Title.
III. Wilkinson, Tim.
IV. Translator.
V. Mihálycsa, Erika.
VI. Editor.
VII. Birns, Nicholas.
VIII. Introduction.

2012946494

Table of Contents

Startling Dryness: Szentkuthy's *Black Renaissance*

by Nicholas Birns

The era in which Miklós Szentkuthy lived, an era which spanned the many lurchings of Europe toward barbaric self-destruction, the monstrous despotisms of Mussolini, Hitler, Stalin, and their epigones, gave a sense that Europe's seeming achievement of civilization was in peril. Indeed, one might say that European civilization was narrowly perched on a cesspool of barbarism into which it might relapse at any minute. Walter Benjamin famously remarked that there was no document of civilization that is not also a document of barbarism. The implied posture of Szentkuthy's narrator in *Black Renaissance* ramifies & complicates Benjamin's aphorism. He seems to be saying, there is a difference between civilization & barbarism, but that civilization is still on a trial run, still having its kinks ironed out. In *Black Renaissance*, the second volume of his massive treatise-cum-*roman fleuve* called the *St. Orpheus Breviary*, Szentkuthy explores two infrequently examined but constitutive ironies of European civilization: that its sources are the only partially compatible legacies of Athens & Jerusalem (a paradox perfectly captured in the very idea of 'St. Orpheus'), that it originates equally in the Byzantine East and the Latin Catholic West, and that the very centuries in which European culture was solidified were also centuries of instability, barbarism, and histories that the mainstream Eurocentric generally prefers to avoid. What is perhaps associated with this is the observation, made by many postcolonial scholars, that Eurocentrism as we know it is something only for export, to a New World 'Creole nationalism' that needs a rhetoric of European superiority to intimidate the indigenous and non-white migrant populations. As someone situated in the heart of Europe, Szentkuthy can afford to regard the contradictions in the European legacy. Equally, thinkers in Europe who distance themselves from the nationalisms of their countries, like Heine, are often seen as toothless and overly cosmopolitan, the antithesis of a thinker too rooted in nationalism such as Herder. On the other hand, the unquestionably well-intentioned 'good Europeanism' of the later Nietzsche may well be seen as hyperbolic at best, however salutary it is in warding off vulgar interpretations of Nietzsche's late work. The contrast between the two attitudes — of nationalism on the one hand, & 'Europeanism' or cosmopolitanism on the other hand — is, as David van Dusen aptly points out, at the core of Szentkuthy's writing:

> It is not accidental, then, that [Szentkuthy] was thrilled by the expression of the 15th-century polymath, Nicolas of Cusa — who is later echoed by German Romantics like Novalis, English Romantics like Coleridge — that the essence of things is a *coincidentia oppositorum*: a 'coincidence of opposites.' Szentkuthy is himself such a 'coincidence,' & for what may appear to be a perfectly banal reason. Early critics hissed that he was 'non-Magyar,' and with them, Szentkuthy regarded himself as a 'European' — by which he meant to say, and more on this shortly, a *contradiction*.[1]

Van Dusen is pointing to Szentkuthy's literal ancestry — that his father was from a German family, his mother from a Jewish one — and also the general cosmopolitanism of his outlook. Szentkuthy is incredibly cosmopolitan, and none of his highly-marked and specific attachments negate this aura of cosmopolitanism. He accepts and foregrounds the inherent cultural contradictions in the European heritage — the clash of Greek and Jew, East and West, passion and reason, elucidating their glorious beauty, & their apodictic discomfort.

1. David van Dusen, "All That Exists Is the Only True Luxury: Miklós Szentkuthy's *Marginalia on Casanova*," *Los Angeles Review of Books* (May 2, 2013).

II

The first paragraph of *Black Renaissance* throws down the gauntlet to the reader:

> Saint Dunstan was a radiantly handsome young man, and his intelligence, his intellect, & his cultivation were just as far-reachingly radiant. That duality, the feminine charm of an Adonis and the mastery of the entire culture of those days (from Ireland to India), provoked very great & fateful inner battles within him. There was also another 'permanent crisis,' in his soul & politics, namely, a struggle of old Celtic Christianity, luxuriating in pagan elements, & of the Roman, imperial modern Catholic, almost legally mandated state religion, for more than once he had a more regal role than that of the kings in 10th-century England. And a third dizzying swing of the pendulum playing out in his soul, embracing virtually every possible role in itself: the role of emperor & dictator in contrast to hermitism, the solitude, art, his unquenchable love & yearning for romantic forests.

We must ask: why Dunstan? We understand the 'Saint' if we have read the first volume of the *Breviary, Marginalia on Casanova,* where Szentkuthy juxtaposes the libertine and the saint, the ascetic & what *Marginalia on Casanova* called the 'wandering' of the eponymous hero. Like Nietzsche,

Szentkuthy does not embrace historical Christianity, but unlike Nietzsche, he does not see it as superfluous either. But why Dunstan? As Szentkuthy says, Dunstan was a real historical figure in 10th-century England, someone who was in effect prime minister for a lengthy period of time, and who was the leading figure in the English (Anglo-Saxon) church of his day. The homosexual and Celtic elements are Szentkuthy's own innovations (albeit based on some historical evidence) and make Dunstan into a more sensual and rebellious figure, one whose relationship to the Christianity he so zealously espouses is filled with struggle & contradiction. But why choose this saint? After all, though reasonably well-known, he is not a household name, and lacks either the aura of the famous or the novelty of the totally fictional.

The answer is simple. The key date in Szentkuthy's eccentric historiography is 1000 AD — the year Hungary converted to Christianity under the leadership of its king, St. Stephen, and as guided by Pope Sylvester II. A later volume of the *Breviary*, the one that marked the resumption in 1972 after a twenty-seven-year hiatus, is titled *The Second Life of Sylvester II* and explicitly takes up the themes already evident in the Dunstan episode — as the Dunstan episode was appended to the edition of *Black Renaissance* Magvető brought out in the early 1970s, the two were written more or less concurrently. When as readers we encounter Dunstan, we should also think of Sylvester II. The key date is 1000 AD, and the elemental readerly move in the first section of *Black Renaissance* is to judge whether a reference made is to something before or after 1000 AD; if you measure things as they are before or after 1000, then you will get their place in the Szentkuthian *Umwelt*. Dunstan is then important for being (in Szentkuthy's view) a fervent though divided Christian just decades before 1000 AD. As an Anglophile, Szentkuthy was on the hunt for English-Hungarian connections — for instance, that Prince Edward, the father of the last Anglo-Saxon claimant, married the daughter of Saint Stephen & was exiled in Hungary for a while.

Szentkuthy is making the point that one cannot see England as the core of civilities and Hungary on the periphery, that England was going through cultural convulsions and contingencies at the same time as the Hungarian state was being formed. Szentkuthy is indicating how contingent & even inchoate the now-established cultures of Western Europe were, & that to see Hungary as 'behind' them is a misperception.

But these English connections also had a modern valence for Szentkuthy. As *Black Renaissance* explicitly avows, the portrait of Dunstan was modeled on the fusion between the Anglo-Saxon and Celtic sensibilities found in the work of Szentkuthy's great elder contemporary John Cowper Powys (1872–1963). The remark made of Dunstan's milieu, "In that Christianity there was more paganism than people might imagine, but there was nonetheless more Christianity than people might imagine" (1), is a quintessentially Powysian observation. Equally, the two other key historical figures in the first part of *Black Renaissance*, Tiberius and Theodora, are also borrowed from an English source, the historical novels of Robert Graves: *I, Claudius* (1934), for Tiberius (Tiberius was Claudius' uncle and his reign occupies a major portion of the novel), and *Count Belisarius* (1938) for Theodora. Szentkuthy admired and actually met Graves, and his use of Graves and Powys is not only important for his work but also underscores the way both of these British writers represent an alternate yet still important part of modernism to the Joyce who was such a towering influence for the Hungarian novelist, as attested both by his first novel *Prae*, and by his much later translation of *Ulysses*.

But Szentkuthy was also, plain and simple, an Anglophile. Indeed, one is almost tempted to write a book about Hungary entitled *Anglophile Nation*. In his autobiography *Confessions of An Original Sinner*, John Lukacs — who, since he considers himself an American writer, does not have the accent on his name as does his namesake Georg — reveals himself not only as an Anglophile — growing up in 1930s Budapest, where he spent his adolescence — but as someone as up-to-date with the English scene as the lead reviewer for the *TLS* would have been, even as the storm clouds of war gathered all around him. Tiberius and Theodora are not only Gravesian but, above all, *British*.

But why Tiberius & Theodora in the first place? It helps to remember that the date 1000 AD is cardinal. Tiberius was the Emperor at the time of Christ, and Szentkuthy's evocation of him takes this into account, as does all fiction on Tiberius, up to the late twentieth-century novels of Allan Massie

(*Tiberius*) and Anthony Burgess (the highly underrated *Kingdom of the Wicked*). Both personalities are appealing to Szentkuthy in other ways — their mixture of power & sensuality, conscientiousness of governance & cruel authoritarian caprice — but the temporality is the key: because Theodora, the empress of the Eastern Roman Empire, is halfway between the time of Jesus & Hungary's conversion to Christianity, she is thus in the middle of Hungary's relation to Christian time just as Hungary's Christian conversion in 1000 is in the middle of the story of Europe's vexed relationship to Christianity as seen from a twentieth-century vantage-point. This long reach of temporality is both enabling and transgressive. One sees this instance in this glorious quote from the first volume of the *Breviary*:

> The whole Orient makes its appearance: after the Renaissance asceticism of Italy the peeling, ghetto-like Balkans, and on top of those two stages, now for the very first time, a third: Constantinople, Smyrna, Baghdad; Europe's adolescent apple — the enchanting East.

In this tableau Hungary is mediatorial both in space & time.

For all the daring and speculative erudition of the Dunstan-Tiberius-Theodora section, there are shoals around which the reader has to navigate. At his best, as in *Marginalia on Casanova*, Szentkuthy not only gives us an opulent tableau of the past, but screens it through a filtering, interceptive authorial sensibility. With the Dunstan-Tiberius-Theodora section, though, this filtering often seems missing & we just have an intelligent, sensitive person saying things that are extravagant, & of course temporally splayed, but as comments about these figures, what Szentkuthy says is little more than routine. Moreover, they are designed to appeal to initiates, people who already know & sense the significance of history. Indeed, Szentkuthy's mediations on Graves and Powys are almost like an erudite and avant-garde affection. They are fired by enthusiasm and the delectation of books he admires and the distant historical worlds they reveal, but which mean so much more to the specialized than to the general reader. In addition, one feels a fundamental ambiguity in Szentkuthy toward history itself: he is fascinated by history, its minute facts and hidden crevices, its lost sensualities & occult intricacies, but there is also an element in him that, like Joyce's Stephen Dedalus, feels that history is a nightmare from which he is trying to awake. Thus, there is nothing in the first two volumes of the *St. Orpheus Breviary* to indicate that the past is better than the present, or to deny that the opulence of past ceremonies is also tinged with a sense of melancholy distance and bitter aftertaste. Szentkuthy's purpose is thus not simply to write "the story of Dunstan" or to celebrate tenth-century England, even as a mirror of contemporaneous Hungary. But there is enough of an emotional commitment to the material to make some readers, who may not be archivists or antiquarians of this sort, uneasy.

The reader who perseveres to the second Brunelleschi section will nevertheless be far more satisfied, as the density, granularity, and specificity Szentkuthy has established with respect to history is turned within itself and applied, more interestingly, to aesthetic perception. Thus, for all the apparent awkwardness of the first section, there is a method to Szentkuthy's approach, and the reader, again, should not give up. But the first section does indicate an important truth about Szentkuthy: for him, subject matter is, against all appearances, important. In this, he resembles figures like Pater & Huysmans, two writers who also took on Europe's long transition from antiquity through the Middle Ages to troubled modernity, but for whom those ages are always mediated by style. Furthermore, Szentkuthy does not really have dramatic situations or characters in a way that not only, obviously, Proust and Mann do, but that drier and more essayistic writers like Musil and Hermann Broch also have. Szentkuthy does not really believe in the individual person in the psychological sense, & his portrait of Dunstan has some of the speculative impersonality of Broch's graver and more tormented Virgil. Yet he is intensely interested in the person as historically regarded and situated; if anything, in most of his books he is a kind of wildcat biographer. During the period of harsh Communist censorship in Hungary, he turned to straight biographical fiction, as someone like Boris Eikhenbaum turned to biographical work on Tolstoy once the Stalinist monolith could no longer tolerate his earlier formalism. With such, biography functions doubly, both as a seeming endorsement of official Communist historicism and as a subversive emphasis on the individual life creatively framed, adhering to no metaphysic, whether historical *or* subjective.

If we see the Szentkuthy of the Dunstan-Tiberius-Theodora section as more a biographer than a historian, we might find the exercise less historical *&* more æsthetic. Yes, Szentkuthy is at times professorial, getting the genealogy of the third-century Emperor Elagabalus exactly right, but failing to dramatize this compellingly for the non-uninterested reader. In the first section, at times, there are hints that the historical material is nought but extracts from a Monteverdi opera; but we do not have Monteverdi as a Jamesian center of consciousness, just erudition that, even if intelligently discerned, is not necessary, or in the first place artistic. But Szentkuthy needs, as an artist, to go through what for some readers might be an arduous journey, and the reward is there in the next section, centering on Filippo Brunelleschi.

III

The framework of *Black Renaissance* is measured in five segments, five hundred years apart from each other — Tiberius/Jesus, Theodora, Dunstan/Sylvester/St. Stephen, Brunelleschi, Szentkuthy (us). For Szentkuthy, the Renaissance is the most glorious of all these contexts, because of its beauty and cultivation, its daring and transgression, and its pluralism and heterogeneity.

Yet Szentkuthy's treatment of the Renaissance avoids the potential pitfalls of the medieval section, with its over-enthusiastic indulgence in period detail that might alienate the non-'fan' reader. His treatment of Brunelleschi is steadier and deeper, and above all more æsthetic than historical. His technique is signaled by these remarkable paragraphs:

> In the frescœs and statues of your villa I want to bore to the very deepest of the inner meaninglessness of history. I want to formulate all my disappointments with startling dryness. Don't worry! The connoisseurs will in any case never notice my pessimism in the picture — my disillusionment finds expression in such abstract formal tricks that my confession behind it will never be suspected. That transport of the dead is an unforgettable historical lesson — all of that on an island: in a chosen nest of limitedness and narrow-mindedness. (142)

Szentkuthy's habitation of (his fictive) Brunelleschi's voice exemplifies the way his depiction of art is at once vivid and always at one remove, summoning an incarnate presence that is yet always laced and filtered through the rigors of perception. Witness this description of Lake Garda in Brunelleschi's day, supplied by the authorial overvoice:

> The blue of the lake, which is never blue but either white as milk or foggy or a transparent ultra-green, combining mirror, lizard, & Madonna: never endless but simply and clumsily empty: that lake is also before him, sobered-up, cooled. (Is the masquerade I am making of Sixtus too simplistic? It could be — I must trust that the accumulated variations of sensitive whimsies elsewhere will compensate for the monotony of mania.) Is there anything lovelier than a balcony room opening onto such an empty, white lake? Two beds with quilted coverlets, the large baptismal font of the washbasin, the oh-so-narrow Latin hardly-door, the balcony, a sunbaked straw armchair, grids in the big nothingness of water, sky & air, then nihil, auroral mist, more mundane than all of Gardone's women put together. (155)

Whereas the first section tries to formulate meaning in history, the black Renaissance of Brunelleschi finds at history's heart naught but its inner meaninglessness. Brunelleschi, in his design and applicability, will not alienate his customer, who will not on the immediate level be able to see the pessimism the artist has ingrained into his creations; for them, the surface prettiness will be all. But Szentkuthy's articulation of what Brunelleschi (never in fact) might have thought, the true coruscating loveliness is that of the blanched, etiolated white lake, an æsthetic so perfect it *becomes* mundane banality, even if the hedonists who use it do not notice. Life and death, inspiration and boredom, mingle into a whorled, indelible composition. "Startling dryness": this syntagm could indeed stand as Szentkuthy's æsthetic credo. His writing is essayistic, often even pedantic, yet its goal is not to be magisterial but startling, even abrasive. We look to the spectacularly disruptive for æsthetic effect — in Szentkuthy's own era, Dada, Surrealism, Futurism, and Expressionism. But Szentkuthy's cerebral, deliberate dryness has its own startling quality, perhaps all the more in that the superficial observer will have trouble seeing how startling it is unless they really plunge into it, whereas the one thing even the most doltish student of Dada, Surrealism, et alia can see is that there is an intent to startle. Szentkuthy demands intelligence from his readers — yet an intelligence laced with æsthetic awareness and the ability to sense loveliness and fascination where it might least be expected. The Brunelleschi passage also astonishes in its ability to juxtapose minute detail with a renovating emptiness that seems to make all detail unnecessary, inessential, yet also more inexpressibly beautiful. There is in Szentkuthy's aesthetic description often a sense of stimulating and provocative assemblage standing on top of what is impossible or absent:

> In truth, in treeless, unwooded Venice those Tintoretto Susannas, Danæs, and Catherines substituted for the yellowing foliage, as the large, ivory-tinted linen curtain through which the afternoon light leant against the paintings made them even more waxily languid. (161)

The paintings of women by the great Venetian artist substitute for nature — and yet, what nature could hold a candle to them? Still, they are undeniably substitutes. Szentkuthy makes an æsthetic virtue out of his temperamental refusal of comfort & autochthony.

The third section of the book accelerates this realization by breaking out into direct poetry — styled as a Monteverdi aria, this section releases the pressed lyricism that has accumulated in the previous hundred pages of exposition, and lets the imagination run wild, excavating and sounding out sepulchral chambers of consciousness and experience. This section is just where it should be formally, like a scherzo in a Beethoven symphony, changing the pace and allowing the reader to register the full formal dimensions of the entire work. The fourth section, focusing on the Palazzo Grimani in Venice, intensifies the focus of the Brunelleschi section on architecture, while also encompassing the contestation of the Mediterranean arena between Arab, Byzantine, and Western European influences, only belatedly overlaid by Venetian maritime prowess. The final section, with its long monologue of a tutor to Princess Elizabeth (the future Queen Elizabeth I) resumes the Hungary-England analogy, as well as indicating the English Renaissance, with its asymmetrical excellence in literature but not in art or music, as another kind of Black Renaissance in its unbalanced jaggedness.

Clearly, however, there is an allegory of art and power, and we must again remember that Szentkuthy wrote in the age of the great totalitarianisms. Van Dusen intriguingly calls Szentkuthy someone with Nabokov potential (taking into account his striking ability in writing in English) but who chose to stay home even in a *dürftiger Zeit*. He was not a dissident in the literal sense (and remember that, in the latter years of the Kádár regime, the ambience in Hungary was enough for Miklós Haraszti to call the country a "velvet prison," which, whatever its exactions, was relatively better than the iron cage of its other Soviet-bloc neighbors). But he was someone whose career and oeuvre were impacted by living in a Communist country; had he lived in the West, he would not have set aside the *Breviary* for so many years, though who knows what distinctively Western distractions might have made him veer away from it in a different mode?

Yet Elizabeth is not addressed as a potential tyrant such as her contemporary, Philip II of Spain, but merely as a sort of captive audience who might have ears to hear — much like Hugo von Hofmannsthal addressed Francis Bacon in his Chandos letter. She is an impressionable young woman whose tutor knows he is supposed to profess Christian doctrine, but who in fact lets her know of the Szentkuthian Christian-pagan mixture that, it is implied, will be the true, animating spirit of the "Black Renaissance" of her reign. Elizabeth as addressee also brings in a feminine element, & the sexual tension between tutor and charge adds a *soupçon* of excitement to the former's labyrinthine instructions:

> Don't forget that only *one* saint functions for the human mind: realism, understanding by that the unceasing prying into reality, the excited groping for its criteria — and the greatest enemy of that is the idol, a Greek or Persian myth. Not because there are no gods and there are plants, but almost the reverse: there are no plants — *sed numina turbulentes adsunt*. Yes, ritual intercourse or the carving of phallus stones is such a hair-raising and ludicrous simplification of the divine reality of love as the number 5 is to a storm of five apples, five maidens, five seas, and five muslin shirts. It is incomprehensible that even clever evangelizers hounded the 'modeling,' the materiality, & the sperm-curse in Greek deities, yet that gallery of gods is the most pedantic store of ghosts of indifference to reality & denial of reality. (277)

There is one saint — reality, but reality is so multi-textured as to be infinite: a sprawling monism; the key to it is to acknowledge the graininess and variegation in the One rather than literalize them in a fetishization of the Many.

We might ask, though, why is this novelistic? Why did Szentkuthy clearly think of the *breviary* books as novels? After all, he could have remained on the expository level and still been thought a genius, and if the choice of mode might have stanched the potential for sales, nothing Szentkuthy was ever going to do was going to be truly commercial.

He does not so much depict characters as animate historical personalities. Is it the speculative element, what these people might have thought, what these juxtapositions of historical consciousnesses & sensibilities might have been?

To this end, let us look at the stunning conclusion to *Black Renaissance*, the last words of the tutor's digressive and hortatory exposition:

> The essence of the heresy known as the 'the other' is that it is always just a single portrait in a flash of a single historical second. Something that, in any case, cannot resemble Pharaoh's horses & the tired-scented fruits of cypresses going back millennia — it is a solitary wonder that has no premises, its conclusion unknown. (281)

Szentkuthy explores sensibilities, seeks a momentary spark, an *Augenblick*, of awareness and understanding which for him is the only true real, more psychological roundness being a false synthesis (since he seems to have had a Karl Kraus-like suspicion of Freud). The novelist thus makes clear he does not believe in the sort of characters who have traditionally been at the center of fiction: the figures with detailed biographies & thoroughly rendered inner lives at the heart of the fictions not only of an Hugo or a Tolstoy or a Dostoyevsky but a Proust or a Joyce of a Woolf. Why then call it fiction at all? Why does he not give up on the genre utterly?

Is Szentkuthy's text a counterfactual lament for possibilities latent in history but not actualized? Is the tableau given life by the authorial perspective within its manifestly modern and Hungarian concerns? Is this why Szentkuthy devotes his life to fiction even after giving up on character and psychology? Why take this long creative road with only authorial sensibility and biographically illumined personalities — rather than characters — as companions? Or is the central and only character Europe itself, riven, melancholic, at war with itself in a way even its brilliance cannot fathom, tethered to a history that at once nourishes and divides it?

> Whether I look at the shepherd or at the women, what happens to them in the *Song*? Her love is better than wine; she is comely like tents & curtains; like Pharaoh's horses, the hanging cones of cedars of Lebanon, clusters of camphire, and bundles of myrrh; the gaze swaying out from her eyes like doves ... If ever there was something that is not a face, not human, not a portrait, it is that. (280)

In this culminating passage of the book, the conflict between Western and non-Western, Greek and Jew, male and female, nature and culture, inner and outer, and the desirer and the desired is paraded, but never resolved.

In the book's final image, the tutor of Princess Elizabeth directs her to look for, and be looked at, as a scintillating shard of insight rather than a full manifestation of subjectivity.

So should we regard the possibility of an answer for the European dilemma that is the occasion for such serene agony on the part of Szentkuthy: — "it is a solitary wonder which has no premises, the conclusion unknown" (281). History can provide the background for this; but the mystery is always, elusively, elsewhere.

1. *Vita* (Life of a Saint)

Dunstan (924–988)

Saint Dunstan was a radiantly handsome young man,[1] and his acuity, his intellect, and his cultivation were just as far-reachingly radiant. That duality, the feminine charm of an Adonis and the mastery of the entire culture of those days (from Ireland to India), provoked very great and fateful inner battles within him. There was also another 'permanent crisis' in his soul & politics, namely, a struggle of old Celtic Christianity, luxuriating in pagan elements, and of the Roman, imperial modern Catholic, almost legally mandated state religion, for more than once he had a more regal role than that of the kings in 10th-century England. And a third dizzying swing of the pendulum playing out in his soul, embracing virtually every possible role in itself: the role of emperor and dictator in contrast to hermitism, solitude, art, his unquenchable love & yearning for romantic forests.

He was descended from the family of the kings of Wessex; if you like, a Biblical or Donatello David — if that serves you as a reference aid: a male, Old Testament, pagan-mythological Artemis; an adolescent nymph as created by Thomas Mann, perfumed with Freudian psychology. It would not be a fault, of course, if those character traits were handled with a muffle, but for a more obvious understanding of the divine reading ("Black Renaissance") this condensed intonation of ours is also necessary.

He received his religious education in Glastonbury, the setting for J.C. Powys' monumental novel *A Glastonbury Romance*, and what is decisive (for both Dunstan & Powys): from Celtic Benedictine monks who had fled from Ireland and who had fused together the above-mentioned old pagan Irish myths with old Judaic and early Christian legends, and the motley, kaleidoscopic pantheon of the early or imperial Romans. In that Christianity there was more paganism than people might imagine, but there was nonetheless more Christianity than people might imagine. For pedagogical aims, therefore, on the left side of a highly simplified stage would stand Stonehenge's gigantic prehistoric altar or temple stones, as stormily, all bones and dissection of the sky, as Constable painted them (1836) — whereas on the right side, Roman temples with Greek orders in which Christians were already saying mass.

In the huge baptismal basin at Glastonbury the noviciates always 'bathed' in new and freshly consecrated water, spiced with a few drops of martyr's blood and a few drops of the waters of the River Jordan (possibly with Mary Magdalene's scent and a relic of her "night and cold creams"). They stood with candles (including Dunstan), in halo-light headgear reminiscent of wandering apostles, wound around by disintegrating mignon-paper ivy leaves, flowing blond locks of hair — reviving snakes under the Madonna's trampling feet: angelic face, musing, Hadrian's lover and Good Shepherd, wavering breasts, cardinal's skullcap, a discretely protruding belly with the Oriental pasque-flower of the navel, candle in hand, a pigeon-quivering test idol of light, dropped out of the heavenly nest of *"fiat lux"* — his arms & thighs: adventurer delta-gambolings, straying velvet *canali giocosi* of heat sources.

Dunstan was the best Latinist and the best Hellenist in the monastery. He knew Tacitus off by heart — the politics, style, sex dreams (those are certainly unavoidable, and we should neither bless, nor excommunicate, even less analyze them), the life of Tiberius, characters in life and literature, the diversity and the secret common denominator of divinities, the rationality, love, & 'statelessness' of decadent Greeks, the intellectual utility of old age as yet unknown to him, his siding with politics as opposed to paranoid 'ivory towers,' — and he nevertheless learned from them the (at first *con grandezza*) surrealist consequences of solitude — do read with zealous attention the "Anthimus" chapter in the divine lesson below: "Anthimus in the Empress' Park," for example: poetry, philosophy, Garden of Eden, solitude, imperial majesty — is anything more needed? Is that not a pipe-dreamer's dream?

It would be senseless to talk about truly, generically classicized mystery or Passion games in Glastonbury, because everything there was a pantomime of games, dances, dramas and stained-glass-window-puppets, nobly mixed up with everything mixable from the Old Testament and essential-intuitive Celtic foolishness through Greek Legenda Aurea down to the four pretty-protagonisted Holy Gospel books. In the darkened, *one*-lamp church on Maunday Thursday evening Dunstan was the despairing Christ on the Mount of Olives (the altar a whole mound of leaves, Dunstan in his pain lies on his stomach as in a Dürer woodcut) who in his passion sobs the words of Euripides' *Iphigenia* into the hayrick, as if "Lord, Why hast thou forsaken me" were the next to come in the wail: "Who knows what kind of destiny befalls him? The ways of heaven are unknowable. No one will either dis- or recover them, and man cannot evade Evil's hideaway. The ship of fate has a single funeral port: the Unknown."

Naturally, he became a professor at the Glastonbury 'university' at quite a tender age, and expounded on Lucretius' native Roman-language work; he proved ultimate meaning & interpretability precisely from the word's un-interpretability, transparent truth born peremptorily out of absurd nature and nonsense history. With his students he descended daringly (some of them were nuns) to the bottom of such 'theses' — embodying a more precise version of Samuel Beckett — as can be seen in the Table of Contents to our "Brunelleschi" chapter: 1) disenchanted æsthetics, disenchanted logic, — 2) conflict of the struggle for complete *truth* and the struggle for perfect *form*, — 3) toward unsurpassable relativism, — 4) both reality & its interpretation are nonsense, — 5) there are only directions without a goal, 6) hatred of names concealing facts, — 7) there is also a romanticism-free, stone-cold sober irrationality, — 8) physical Eros and spiritual Eros lead equally to fiasco (oh, that is not what a girl student felt under the drapery of the candidate's brushing garment). Only a rationally certain, all-solving Absolute can be behind so great a nihil — and what's more, Dunstan unraveled it rationally, and the nun, deathly pale, was led on Dunstan's arm to a father-confessor after she had changed dress and perfumed herself — that was compulsory for female students on those certain days of the month.

In the Middle Ages, as is truly common knowledge, mathematics & music were incestuous twin subjects, which of course was not the slightest bit of a detriment to music's sensual and emotional passionateness, and still less to the blissful, indeed salutary rigor of numbers — a listless afterscent of that is, perhaps, the *musikalische Mode* connected to the name of Arnold Schönberg. Dunstan was an excellent musician, a singer with the voice of a female soprano. On the day of the Beheading of St. John the Baptist the dance of Salome was also performed (why on earth not, when in the East a dancing *Christ* was also known and that manner of worship of course found its way to even the most westerly shores of Ireland "within minutes" on Roman ships and roads), with Salome being played by Dunstan on the shores of a lake, because the dance figures were mirrored in the green basin and thus he could best illustrate the musical themes' simple inversions, retrogrades, and the simple inversions of their retrogrades.

On the other side of the lake the male & female students noted down musical scores, graph-like lines and cardiogram choreographs, onto parchment rolls spread out left and right of their thighs, with connecting arrows in green, red, and blue, but all that went with great difficulty: Dunstan was just too good-looking (in those days there was no question of priesthood or a monastic life; for a long time Dunstan remained a worldly person). After the dance 'Salome' lay on his belly in the grass, legs drawn up (the triangle for Pythagoras' theorem perhaps being the model), his hollow barely-stomach panting from weariness like polyps or flatfish in an aquarium when they breathe or whatever else they do. The Buddha-bowls, the calices, of water lilies were never so drifting while fixed as the eyes of girls regarding Dunstan's *corpus Christi* and begging him almost in chorus to sing. Dunstan sat among them (oboe? lute? flute? guitar or Vivaldi mandolin?), and the unsuspected confession aria sounded from his Adonic-hedonistic body with shockingly unexpected tragedy:

> My Ego-fate is darkest, its face & reverse but a poltroon;
> Like a scruple-dry soul, it drifts between life and work:
> Startled by work in life, my fate in work is: being —
> My epitaph be this: "no heavenly work, nor earthly life."

Now that we are at the subject of Dunstan's musicianship, one must pedantically record another anecdote from Dunstan's subsequent life. By then King Æthelstan ruled in England — Dunstan survived many kings — and at that point in time England also strictly recognised the appeal of the Synod of Carthage in 392, according to which Christian newlyweds should abstain on the first night, because the *jus primae noctis* was the due of Our Lord Jesus Christ, who was the First Heavenly Bridegroom (husband) not only of favoured saints and nuns, but of every Christian woman. When Æthelstan was wed, his wife spent the night in a separate bed, in a separate room, and Dunstan sang and made music before the closed door; inside, just one lady-in-waiting attended the queen (for protection). While the music was playing, and in the intervals, Dunstan and the entire courtly household heard such ecstatic vocalizations, sobbing, sighing, and laughter, as though Dunstan's songs had supplanted the queen's consort; in the morning Satan was seen frantically escaping in the form of a fiery horse. Drunk on rapture, the consort only sent the heavenly flute player away from before her door a week later; then Lent ensued, but we have no record of how the rest of the forty days were accounted for.

A third musical legend: when, under the influence of various vile informers, spies, back-stabbers, and the truest holy-intended saints, King Æthelstan kicked out Dunstan (perhaps out of certain justified feelings of guilt?), the most beloved of his men at court, thus fell seriously ill in his grief, and instead of extreme unction, had himself ordained as a priest in his bed by his elder brother, the Bishop of Winchester, and, once his health was restored, and having grown disgusted with life in high society (perhaps out of certain unjustified feelings of guilt?), withdrew to Glastonbury. The Danes had long since battered the place to ruins, but then he had craved for just such a milieu. There he composed music in the vein of Gesualdo, Duke of Venosa (1560–1613), murderer of his wife, his wife's lover & his second infant son, madrigalist of *danse-macabre* chromatics, hysterical dissonances, tonality-shredding, orgiastic-murderous harmonies, sadomasochistic groanings and shriekings. A tawdry psyche dog's-bone worthy of an Aldous Huxley, but even something of that kind is unable to spoil our most justifiable musical 'enjoyment.'

But he did more than make music among the ruins. He cast bells in white-hot forests of flame like a beautified Vulcan; he carved crucifixes (having himself bound to them for an hour), produced censers, and from those he had veils fluttering to the moon & stars, and he painted pictures the likes of which one has seen in Irish illuminated manuscripts (the Book of Kells! from which James Joyce himself was born as it stands in the books), where St. Luke's head is daubed a barbarian calf-mask, big-eared, with single-cross, bird-winged, fish-finned, peacock blue, lute-hammed thighs — modern-day Surrealism is but an impotent phlegm mausoleum set against Dunstan's one thousand everlasting drawings.

After the Dunstan portrait limned above, what is wanted here is a period or earlier *coulisse* of English history, though often that backdrop was the main protagonist in the drama and the kings and Dunstans were themselves the *coulisses,* occasional decorations — in what in the first place? In the truly splendid, bloodthirsty battles of Old Celtic, pagan-flavoured Christianity and emperor-flavoured, new, Roman, Anglo-Saxon Christianity. The Irish and the Scots formed an autonomous Church, of which papal (imperial) Rome was sorely aware: Romans snooping among the Irish and Scots brought shiploads of abominations of the Celts, which is to say, distortions of Catholicism, to the Pope's long 'customs inspection' tables for heresy — from the identification of Orpheus with Christ & Adonis, the Yahweh-Logos hogwash, the semi-erotic, semi-philosophical cult of Holy Wisdom-proto-Eve-New Madonna — *nowadays,* of course, those are just dead smiles in dead books on the history of religion.

The Celto-Roman dispute was not theoretical: Rome stirred up its Anglo-Saxon 'jurist' Catholics against the 'mysticizing' Catholics of the Celts; burning down of churches, burning down of royal palaces, overt slaughter on open meadows — everybody knows. It will be good to forget forever in the grave, or grasp the sense once and for all (as Dunstan had taught) of those brayings of the Bloody Ass.[2] Of course in that braying contest it was always still-imperial Rome that won — its most colourful symbol was when, in the company of papal legates, hetæras, 'Great British' pirates, truly well-intentioned nuns, and absolutely modern-style diplomats, an Anglo-Saxon king went to Rome: into the eternal enclosure of monasticism. As a gift for the pope he carried stumps of the timbers of incinerated churches along with routinedly churned out, nondescript Venuses of late Roman descent, psalters daubed full of Picasso clowns, and magdalen priestesses celebrating mass, et cetera — he puked in his cowl due to seasickness. By the time he reached Rome, under the influence of his booty, his entire retinue had become 'Celtic' — the king indeed remained a hermit.

In the course of Dunstan's life, six or seven Anglo-Saxon kings ruled. Æthelstan is known the world over, celebrated in the most terrible and ludicrous, tedious and cannibalistic epics because he had Pharaonic pyramids erected from the bodies of butchered Celts, with skilled corpse engineers — incidentally the greatest masters of early Romanesque-style cathedrals (that statement, like everything in the *Breviary*, is not meant sarcastically). Æthelstan's Celtophobia was not altered in the least by the fact that he adored Dunstan, in a manner that came dangerously close to the 'friendship' of Emperor Hadrian & Antinoüs; anyway, Dunstan was not Celtic, but an Anglo-Saxon aristocrat — it was only his fantasizing spirit that turned him into a (crypto-) Celt. After his career at the university of Glastonbury, on account of his descent, he automatically ended up in court, where he naturally swam in the political milieu with its intrigue-textured, diabolical agenda. *Auctor et actor*, leading player, court writer, painter, musician — a star flashing now here, now there, in the twists and turns of Eros, a butterfly, *nympha medica*. There is something reminiscent of Goethe in this period of his life — the parallel service of sober state ('the establishment') and *Midsummer Night's Dream*, but what with Goethe is a provincial, stupid rococo child's playroom, with Dunstan is "*Venezia Incarnata*" — Venice embodied, that is, the merging of a city of poetic magic and world politics.

David-Dunstan played the harp to Saul-Æthelstan in darkened boudoirs; the week's psalm merged with the half-snuffed lamp, "*amor amicitia*" — and yet? Behind the curtains and flush doors there were non-contracted eunuch singers, their eyes and ears were by then ere a dagger in the envied singer's heart. They knew when they ought to squeal to the king about the highly suspicious 'virginal' wedding night of Æthelstan's wife and Dunstan's *Pierrot Lunaire* music. In no time Dunstan became a discreet-insolent and polite-brazen diplomat at some summit about Norse imports *&* exports: the traders were already honing hands against not only Dunstan but also the king. When Dunstan, following his artistic bent, was working on a golden crucifix, the papal nuncio rushed in (after due peeping and with a snooper's more than sexual sense of gratification), cast the statue of Orpheus that was serving as Dunstan's model into the light well (or rather squeezed it, as he had difficulty in poking it through head first). The crowing old maids — quivering-aged, tower-periwigged stalagmites gone blue, martyr-turkeys — held a formal council directed against all the young ladies at court who were in love with (naturally unreachable) Dunstan, and "they accepted the young politician within their circle as a woman at their unspeakable magdalen gatherings." He gives seminarists Ovid to read! He carries on a confidential correspondence with Celts, Danes, and Normans: he covets Æthelstan's throne! He is a sorcerer who made a pact with Satan: assuming the likeness of Æthelstan, he pays frequent visits to the queen's bedchamber! At that, Æthelstan had him lashed at with a scourge. That is how he retired among the ruins of Glastonbury, as mentioned earlier.

Maybe a word or two has already been said in this rather absent-minded prayer book (a feature we may safely put down to gazing heavenwards) concerning the range of things with which he occupied himself. Now the gist is this *one* thing: at the end of his Glastonbury hermitism and partly voluntary exile, news of Dunstan's saintliness, his senatorial statesmanship, his art, his protection of the poor, his organizational genius, his training for a bishopric, spread across half, perhaps the whole of England, and Rome would no longer hide that light under a bushel. The papal nuncio made an appearance among the ivy-riddled ruins — imperial triumphal procession, consuls, censors, tribunes, *non*-operative slaves, and then cardinals, lilac saints, scarlet lawyers, and carmine-hued theologians, who led a repentant, music-making, confession-writing Dunstan straight before the by then regnant King Edmund. From then on, Dunstan became an adherent of the Imperium Romanum — a legal church! a military church! a dogma church! a banker church! a king-making & king-deposing church! a church that builds the propaganda citadels of ascetic monks! Who for all that did not forget in his heart his poor people and his artistic artificership, as the somewhat anachronistic Imperium Romanum would be ultimately destined for the service of the two essentialissimost things: the good of the poor and the everlasting Paradise of art & learning.

Let us take out our schoolbooks and declaim what we have boned up on: King Edmund reigned for six years (940–946), King Edred for nine years (946–955), King Edwin for four years (955–959), over which period Dunstan was chancellor, prime minister, war minister, semi-official deputy king and auxiliary king, like protocol mistresses in courts far and wide across the world. But then with Edwin came the Parcæ-tripping, Harpy-scruffy reprise, the replay: Dunstan's imperative flight & forced banishment. Its cause can be summed up briefly as follows:

King Edwin was one of the so-called "voluptuaries" who occur rhythmically in history, the kinds of people who have no other need, beyond the emetic effect, to filch from Dunstan's library the life of Heliogabalus (Elagabalus), who as emperor (218–222) had made his grandmother his lover in his 14-year-old holy thistle youth, shot a statue of his *pseudo* father (the emperor Caracalla) into the sky and up among the gods in an enormous perverse orpheum (in the air it immediately pulverized into pollen dust), afterwards being declared emperor (old Granny, of course, continued to enjoy Elagabalus' physique, albeit through abnormal technicalities).

The new emperor passed himself off as a woman, compelled the Roman Senate to worship a black stone phallus: an alluring parliamentary scene — he worshipped snakes and monkeys on the island of Lesbos, married his mother, murdered and stole myths wherever possible with his swarm of well-paid divine bagmen. In the end that representative of Rome, worthy of a film by Salvador Dalí, was assassinated — his mother was hauled out of bed on what happened to be her wedding night as if she were an endless sheet, and after a whole barracks had enjoyed the *jus primae noctis*, she was chucked into the Cloaca Maxima, glistening white like a stinking camisole in the slow and surging excrement, mimicking Phallus' high priestly processions. So lived King Edwin.

In one of the above-mentioned little genre paintings Dunstan, wearing high almost papal garb, burst in on him — the king ran (totteringly) at Dunstan's heart with a long, sharp poniard; in a state of inebriation, the disporting district dames and queens of hearts had within a moment ripped all the clothes off Isaac- and Elijah-visaged Dunstan: they wished to draw him into the confidential circle of their sex-tangent divertimenti. Dunstan (Moses dashing the Ten Commandments against a wall?) raced out, flung open the door, trotted precariously across a makeshift gangway plank — the corridors of the palace of lust were pitch black, but the royal crown & robes were hanging on a hook under Venetian-taste moonlight — and thereby concealed his nakedness.

That was how he galloped or blindly groped into the bishop of London's palace, where under the chairmanship of the archbishop of Canterbury and the bishop of Winchester the whole army were just then debating Edwin's dethronement (Dunstan proceeded to occupy the bishop's seats of Worcester, London, and Canterbury after them). The dethronement did indeed take place at the site of the above-mentioned intimate-most *divertissement,* whereat King Edwin (in the due order of events) died of a heart attack — his concubine (his wife? his too-closely related kin?) and grandmother's people attempted to fabricate all sorts of wounds into the corpse in order thereby to gain patriotic distinctions for succeeding to the throne, but the clergy and military kicked them into a corner (making them skid on the polished floor). Granny was highly disappointed that no blood flowed, and meanwhile palpably endeavored to win the love she felt for herself — after all, there have been as many 'Elizabeth Báthorys' brand 3, 9, 11, etc., in the world (and twice as many in the world's dreams) as there is rubbish. Dunstan was no longer present at the drawing of the consequences that outdid their premise in foulness: he immediately set sail for the continent. In a famous pastoral letter he had just forbidden the drubbing of serfs when Edwin's widow was flailed to death on the stepped terrace of (rebuilt) Glastonbury Abbey. In line with the recipe of mannerist and de Sade-realist painters ("Damn this world," a cultivated onlooker muttered, "where every thing, every blessed thing, is now just a recipe thanks to Dung-beetle God, and now a novelty, a surprise, and a wonder!").

When Edgar acceded to the throne, it was as though the palaces, cathedrals, souls, bodies of all England had turned white, and a recalled Dunstan became now the Archbishop of Canterbury and a fervid reformer (he gave Brothers, too, voting rights at elections for bishoprics). Dunstan was king — the most powerful lord stood or sat before the judiciary as an equal of the poorest of serfs, whom (we are in the tenth century as of yet...) he endeavored to make less poor. Edgar had the reputation of a holy man, owing mainly to Dunstan's political good offices: if the Archbishop of Canterbury was England's first economist, the army's commander-in-chief and diplomat-sorcerer (and not the king), let the latter, by way of compensation, be the angelic Catholic chevalier hero of legends. Dunstan's cause started out swimmingly, but in the meantime a blemish marred the 'nun-king': it started to become conspicuous that Edgar paid too frequent visits to the nunnery, in which orgiast Edmund's lady courtiers had been locked up for penitence. 'Saintly' Edgar had to rely on Dunstan for everything, so he even tolerated that (nay, thereby he even enhanced his holy repute!) when those spiritual exercises that he carried out with the sisters received their natural appraisal, Dunstan forbade him to place the crown on his head for seven years, and he was only allowed to take the communion bread if he had lacerated his hands previously by pawning a crown of thorns (his *head* was unworthy of that first stinging Judæo-Roman 'tiara').

Dunstan constrained priests into all manner of crafts — they became cobblers, carpenters, musical copyists, illuminators of initials, building foremen, and goldsmiths (to the present day Dunstan has remained the patron saint of goldsmiths): they were lined up along with the armorial bearings of their crafts at the coronation of King Edgar as emperor (seven years had passed by then) — a papal, indeed Byzantine move, on Dunstan's part! The kinds of words that rang out from the altar were: *Edgarius Cæsar, Augustus Angliæ Albionis, patricius patronus consules* (in the plural) *Brittaniæ, basileios saxonicos,*[3] Christian Censor of the isles, Emperor of all Seas, Jordan and Genezareth.

After the coronation (& after murderous wars), he sailed around England — that was where Handel's *Water Music* was played — think of the Doge of Venice's promenades (Palazzo Grimani! Palazzo Grimani!), betrothals with the sea with a ring made by Dunstan (I am continuously shouting out Palazzo Grimani because the Doge's palace was under restoration and covered in scaffolding — homework of abstract architects) — think of Cleopatra's voyage on the Nile with her lovers ordered from Madame Tussaud's Waxworks in London, of Exekias' Etrurian cup:[4] Dionysus, grapes, dolphins, the late 6th century AD, Edgar's sailing vessel afloat.

But an æsthete pastry like that is nevertheless "plug ugly" (in the encyclopædia entry: "a utensil made of a dense mass of material that obstructs a passage; name of hard-bodied fishing lure") — *one* thing is important: the moral.

When circumnavigation was not an Art Nouveau-swanking gondola fantasy but a disgusting Roman victory parade custom (ugh!) ripe for extirpating, according to which 'holy' Edgar's ship was impelled by eight conquered kings (crowns on their heads!) as slave oarsmen when, in periods of dead calm, the sails were wrinkled up like the bellies of decorticated multiparas.

After Edgar came the child Edward II,[5] but by that time already those dilettante plastic kings were of diminishing interest to Dunstan: Edward's stepmother, of course, wanted her own natural son to be made king, and she had recourse to the simple trick (and reckless Phædra pleasure) of publicly doing a Madonna circus act with baby-Jesus Edward (people bowed down to her — Stepmother's Day was celebrated every day) while secretly she seduced Edward boyo into a love frenzy — and in the meanwhile? She expelled her natural son (here's the continuation of the trick) from her quarters in the harshest possible terms, lest anyone intimate her ultimate goal. When she judged the time was ripe, she carried out a punctiliously planned sex-murder on her stepson, Edward: Dunstan's equally numerous political and ecclesiastical antagonists openly accused him of *knowing* from the very first moment about the stepmother's erotic and *coup d'état* stratagems — but Dunstan's authority was by then untouchable, and he crowned the sex murderess' natural son, Æthelred II,[6] and had the murdered Edward venerated as a saint in Britannia Romana. Out of gratitude the stepmother fulfilled the Archbishop of Canterbury's wish and travelled to Rome incognito (or as it happened — that being the point of an incognito — nowhere). Above Æthelred's head the blood-stained, vengeful Furies of Greek tragedies danced their maddening dance — he was forsaken by all; Dunstan cautiously nursed him, but to his dying day the boy remained a victim of somnambulism, phobias, and depression — his endless suspicion forced him into the dopiest games of political patience, of course insofar as Dunstan permitted it.

When a person has whiled away fifty to seventy years of life with a Sisyphean flipping of a box of matches on the legless table of Fate, a great many things become clear on looking back, to be sure. Dunstan sensed the approach of the end of his life; in the vigil for Holy Thursday — our Lord Jesus Christ's ascension into heaven — he entered with his closest priestly entourage the crypt of Canterbury cathedral, where no difference can be seen anymore between devotional lights in little bowls and the street lights of Andromeda clouds beyond the Milky Way galaxy, he pointed out his burial place among the illegible gravestones of anonymous friars, placed his archbishop's insignia on one of them (for perpetual decay, as was customary), prayed (according to one priest, along with his clothes he also took off God in the negative dressing room of death), then without staff & assistance, he mounted the wobbly steps to his room and lay down in bed, all without the faintest trace of theatricality.

In one of the darkest corners of the crypt, however, in the garb of a penitent sat what may have been the ninety or one-hundred-year-old ancient queen mother, whom (whether that was in the life of Edwin or Heliogabalus it makes no difference) we derided as 'Granny,' presenting her — rightly — as martyr to the love she felt for herself. When Dunstan set off upstairs with his train, after the selection of his burial site, on the steps (why was that stupid, tottering brick so peculiarly dreadful?), the aged queen mother, her hands barely trembling but with lachrymal sacs dropping almost to the floor, full of poppy seed or cream under her eyes, & 'a hundred' rings on her fingers (spectral algæ — those rings, from first to last, had been fashioned by goldsmithing Saint Dunstan) — with that hand she handed over a letter to the last priest in the procession, "Queen to Archbishop," (the title's lilt could be an advert for an American perfume or fabric), to be instantly handed over to Dunstan. The letter:

In disguise, I have heard all your lectures, from philosophy to music, from pagan literature to Lenten conferences. It is ridiculously easy to go about the world in disguise; in our real clothes it is practically impossible. Whether you know it or not, a whole intellectual & aphrodisiac harem listened to you in silence, seeing in you a new Orpheus, with fatal love. You were already wise as a child; you are not surprised for a second by the near-absolute identity of the most intense thinking and the most intense love. You were a poet even when young, in all your gilded-Apollo joints; the lily-flame of poetry burned in me as well, palpable to you or myself alone. As I write this to you my ladies-in-waiting are eavesdropping by the door: they believe I am conversing with my body, always with a first communicant's thirst for god; as a matter of fact, when I play I'm in the habit of tossing my rings onto a little glass table (the sound of hailing) and now, too, I have slapped them down there in a row, but so as the pen should be wielded more easily in my hand as I write this.

You taught me Greek — the root word "orph" connotes depth-of-life darkness, death-smudged mystery (a Joycean jest: the homophony of the root word "orph" and a musician with Orph in his name). That is what you mean to me in the present day. Orphée was also the name of a raving-mad prophetess — I searched for you, my feminine puberty-Pulcinella, with the purity of belief on the island of Lesbos. With that sort of paradox too, you go about undressed, Archbishop. In many places fish were saints, prophets, instruments of lust, animals suggestive of the primary causes of primitive life — were you not that for me, in music lessons, on lakesides, my dear Eucharist? Should I race to you to confess this analogy of mine?

Orpheus is revered with orgiastic rapture, you taught. So we paid our reverences where no one could see. You & I were giant, conclusively decisive proofs that the Dionysians (of course only if endowed with a big heart, great poetry, a great love of flowers, and great love of wisdom!), the great Dionysians & love, goodness & gentleness, are not in opposition. Even if you never (how superbly-woefully never) brought the poems of Sappho to life — in the imagination —, you certainly knew more searchingly than that dolt Aristotle what was going on in our organisms that remain forever foreign to us. Orpheus-Jesus tamed the wild beasts, saw souls in blades of grass, and wanted to take all of them with him to heaven — today, on Ascension Day, I saw you for the last time, merry young man,[7] happy playboy.

Even now, I am your Eurydice; you are the Orpheus of Canterbury now, too, but you did not come after me into my inferno; I remained alone, and the difference between the old Inferno and Paradiso became blurred inside me. You protect seamen, Stella Maris — if somebody is in mourning, you are always there, the constant consoler, in the likeness of nipples popping out like frog's eyes over black mourning corsetry; artfully you lay our darling Celtic Joyce's wandering rocks on a regular chess table, so that no ships should run aground (only mine!). The amusing trouble with mythology is that with it, everything, really everything, can be different: Orpheus can be Christ, or a barbarian abuser of corpses — according to your teachings, the mænads tore him apart because he steered clear of their religious services. How many times I would have turned into a mænad for you, Archbishop, even mate in blood (not yours), but I won't toss such trifling deep-psychological small change into your rattling cathedral collecting box for gathering Peter's pence.

Chewed off by mænads, your head & body were tossed into the sea — a map of the blue and red veins mounted on nude photos in modern shop windows, in endlessly self-repeating painters — your lute was swimming beside you with strings shredded into loop springs; the whole arrangement (*kylix*) swam onto the island of Lesbos, and there songbirds flew up from the skull and musical instrument, robin redbreasts (your cardinals), nightingales (your carillons), blackbirds (your requiems for kings), song thrushes (your hermitage in the depths of the forest). The Muses gathered your bones together. In all likelihood you will die before me; I will put my Jewish doctor to steal something from you, though with him that is always disproportionately expensive.

In the neighbourhood of Smyrna your cult was carried out by *women,* no man was ever allowed: we, your female students, were that new Smyrna. That was what took us (as many reasons as causes! I have to chuckle!) to the pecker-swapping confraternity divided up among the women. You spoke about an Eastern denomination that Jesuitizes with dance; you also danced on the even nimbler ships of the Argonauts, and — in music theory classes — presented the various rhythms by dance. Your Excellency may perhaps have forgotten about these in the times of your chancellorship of the empire and of Canterbury, being more Catholic than the pope in your British pontificate. Yet you also declaimed poetry that spoke about Orpheus' ritual, existential, lyrical, and neurotic suicide: can that be forgotten? Oh, no doubt.

Some time before, you fabricated the archetypes of Early Christianity, Cluny monasticism, penance, contrition, and fasting out of Orphic priests — excluding, trampling on, cursing pope and bishop —, resting solely on individual, interior, free religiousness: that too is not exactly redolent of archiepiscopal '*haut goût*' (penetrating stench of game).

The reason for the impatience of my Narcissan patience games was also an Orphean theogonic table: the Night — in the fashion of poet Vörösmarty[8] or Mozart — the primal principle lays the world-egg out of self-love, from which Eros is born — that, too, can be tailored into an orgy or altar Caritas-cut, my Archbishop most politicke, diplomast gynæturbator.

Otherwise, we learned from our world history lessons that Orpheus, while travelling through Egypt, frequently read Moses' hieroglyphic manuscripts with the pharaoh's wife (or was it perhaps his mother?); what a shame that in the last minutes before you die, though I see you are hale & hearty, you do not have time to lecture to *me* on the Orphic Torah. Salve.

On his own wishes (the special voracity of pregnant women), and stirred by the early Christian allusions of The Woman's Letter — the letter is still extant — Dunstan read the *Revelation*, and on the blank reverse sides he wrote his notes in squashed round-hand, pre-Gothic lettering. For example:

1. The eternal battle between nature & the supernatural is undecided to the present day — great theologies can perhaps only ever be *crisis* theologies. — 2. Morality is condemned to death, logic is condemned to death, vegetation is condemned to death: three negative Graces. — 3. Heresy: eternal titbits for those of a romantic nature in who well-nigh depraved intellectuality meets a just as depraved sensuality.

2. *Lectio* (Divine Reading)

(I) TACITUS

Tiberius and waters.[9] Rivers. Lakes. Seas. But first & foremost islands. Islands of exile; little islets of Greek snobbery; and islands of delight. Sometimes of voluntary solitude & guilty conscience. Bays & riverbanks. Tiber and Tiberius. How fitting the name, how fitting the Triton. Tiberius' marble statue before me is always *watery*, muddy, glittering with Nile-bottom or a shower in the Paris *Concorde*.

Roman waters: adolescents splashing in the swimming pool; bathhouses of perverse repute; old *roués* among sun-kissed statues of Apollo and terry towels smelling of sweat. I can never imagine Tiberius as a senile sodomite of that sort; he is always adolescent, an Oxford student, rough with sirloin-red cheeks. Sporting even in his debauchery, Spartan even in his procuress' slyness, or in his neurotic, baroquely-embellished death fears, stoic as the reliefs on Trajan's column.

9. Detail from a letter by Monteverdi (1640) in which he recounts to an English friend how he was looking in the works of Tacitus for a subject for his new opera. The section of the letter presented here comprises three parts: casual fragments of impressions of Tacitus' text, Byzantine topics, and finally (since priesthood became the culmination of his life), portraits of two theologians.

The contrasts of water: glistening port, swaggering health (Floridian or Californian) — and the mystical elementary material of the earliest life. But Tritons are Cantabrigians, not Freudians.

In a French film magazine I saw two photographs juxtaposed: a 'white' and a 'black Venus.' The white was a naked girl — her breasts, stomach, & hips were all empire-psyche, full of classic translucence, slimness and rustling parabolicity, with a sensuality more elemental than anything. Next to it, what a clumsy lump of wood the thousand breasts, resembling a bunch of bananas, or the puff-ball hips of an Astarte. Then on that body an Anglo-Saxon head. Eyelashes and rouge. Beside that the 'black Venus': that was Tiberius! A bronze statue that in reality was only dark *green* and could stand in the middle of a well. The wind splashed water on it, so it seemed black.

That sparkling bronze-bald, hollow bronze-ringing, bronze-liar belly with the puritanical, Euclidean, fingerprinted umbilicus in the center: for me it is Rome, the glittering sobriety of '*ius*,' the bitterness & perversity of humanism — though it is the undulating helmet of the female womb, it is a memory of Tiberius' boy lovers. Yet I am also fond of the true portrait, that quintessentially non-Jewish, adolescently-fringed London head *par excellence*, with the toga pulled over it. Like a vestal virgin or the mother of the Gracchi. He roamed in Tiber-bank gardens.

The gardens of Rome! Here they are more gardenlike. Were there any gardens in Egypt? In Babylon? Bungling jungle: tigers, deities, and some sort of cabbalistic monumentality. Semiramis is powerless; her garden appeal is nil. In China? The landscapes in the paintings are lovely — the smoking, tea-steamy Buddha-nothing and pages, silks of true, intoxicated analysis. But too nihilistic or too realistic. Full of bad resonances of fate and impression. Japanese? Undo the cherries, dear, since there's no help, undo the cherries...[10] The Greeks? There I can only see chalky walls, the sand and white of Arabian villages. A Greek flower? Nonsense. An olive tree? Of course: white, silvery, cold, abstract, with some nauseating fragrance. As if Diogenes were to perfume himself in his barrel. In short: every fishpond surrounded by lilac bushes is nonsense, except for the Roman ones, the Tiberius, Sallust, Lucullus variety. Parks: full of urbanity, half-credited formal deities, in a scrumptiously swinging balance between Rousseau and Voltaire. English gardens? French gardens? World-rule syntheses? Persian oases? Teutonic druid-laube? Sicilian orange-fireworks and Senecan sanatoria? Marble and cypress, lakes and gravel paths, carbon dioxide-rivaling trout and the quartz mask of Divus Augustus in wonderful harmony.

Tiberius rambled in such things. How many gods he'd had: whisking fish, shades, and blades, bubbles or peeled-off lipstick that retain the shape of the mouth. Fishes, fishes! Trans-illuminated roses, or just another green undulation. Delicacies at the banquet; gourmandize. And the tragically simple sigils of the Christians — a semi-political, semi-death-poetic omen daubed on the wall by fanatical cellar peoples. The 'true' gods are, after all, somehow gods: Jupiter, there, at the turn in the road, between two naked calla lilies.

An undressed woman or boy is not naked; they are still all body, all Turkish-delight-sticky humanism, anatomy, copulation, and disease. But a calla is the *shell* of a nude without the nude; vestal porn. But what is the echo of this bureaucratized Juice-Pitar in Germania, Tiberius considers among his dancing fish diadems, whom a pair of Greek gibe-Platonists have enticed to the black Narcissus sin of contemplation. Three demonic steps of the worship of Jupiter: in Hellas, the mythic moving-spirit of a snob-æsthete world; in Rome, a gentlemanly lawyer of a *Rechtstaat*; in Germania, tossed there by centurions, a tough-as-nails, pasta-hard-muscled, tragic, gigantic, diabolical Falstaff.

The gods migrate like birds, and even the halcyons of Spanish élan look like harpies in marshy lakes. Fish, deities. But the most exciting gods are the cæsars. The *divus Augustus*. Tiberius: *ultimus deus, divus nullus*. Yet the world is god. Here everyone is a pantheist. God is the boy for whom he is waiting. A bunch of Greeks spoke to him about doubt, though nothing of the sort exists — we believe in everything. From what are religions born there? From nature: from fish, from callas, from eclipses of the moon, from boy hetæras of the thermal baths. And then from death: the Carraran marble ghost-deity of *divus Augustus* is indissociably connected to death. A god: because he is absolutely dead. The whole apotheosis is attributable to the fact that the Romans were the first to notice that if a Roman dies, then he is dead.

This deification is a spiritual embalming, mythicizing mummification. How often Tiberius shuddered at the thought of that: he got goose flesh, and his chilled blood rustled through his skin like the sestertius leaves of birch trees in the moonlight. Death masks. Is that a pose? An Oriental influence? Death? Neurasthenia? Delirious humanism? A thirstily slurping, resigned pseudo-theology? What is this deification? The being-statue of a statue? Oh, we have plenty of scales, gamuts of them, *les gammes, les gammes*: a statue, the living body, the dead body, a wax mask, the gods. Those all prowl about in the park, that is all obviously reflected in Tacitus' sentence when he writes that Tiberius visited the gardens by the Tiber.[11] *Sine ira et studio.*[12] But with Delacroix *et les paradoxes de Saint Augustin*; the little hypocrite. Yet riparian solitude is different from that by a lakeside or mid-sea. A river is all lapping, evanescence, time & onward, non-returning, history's lyricism, death's menstruation. The unattainable, unique. At times slower than the great proconsul river of Isis and Osiris, Serapis and Anubis in Egypt, on Anthony's Dionysian theater stage; at other times enigmatically, camiknicker-chafingly, cash-rubbingly like this Tiber, with dolphins snooping under a pseudonym; a boyish, babbling, Puck-like river. Tiber-Tiberius. There is no god, only wordplay. The sole thing that is a better religion and more philosophy.

What about lakes? Fakir water, lotus-Onan water, Chaldean water, Jewish Dead Sea, Dodonean water, Delphic water? Isn't life typically a rushing *river*? Isn't it pan-

Tiber-pan-Tiberius? Isn't life typically a monotonous *lake*, a sterile lake, a stagnant stretch of water choked with seaweed? 'Soul' and death: that is, stagnant water. Stagnant water reflects; stagnant water is choked with seaweed. That's it — stagnant water is 'soul,' stagnant water is death. But then Tiberius sailed on fast boats to islands, and then the sea came, the salty infinity, the azure, more azure, even more azure, the most azure, the very most azure. And the very, very, very azuremost? By now that is his senile mouth: his cracked, chapped, flat-toned flute-mouth on the body of some smuggled-in Matisse boy or aristocrat. The blue of the gentian-whelks of the Adriatic and Tyrrhenian Seas always becomes more intense, perpetual enhancement, as if its horizon were continually racing like the edge of wine while it is poured into a glass. Here he is: Old Tiberius, already unable to distinguish a tinge of conscience from a tucked-up boy — an old body in the Capri spring. Skin-and-bone hands & mimosa shrubbery. Blue-purulent eyes and white spume shivering onto a rock. Lengthy wheezy coughing & dark green leaves which flutter as they sprout; the wind casts them around Tiberius' sporulating lungs with a crack like a juggler does knives. Solitude.

Solitude at night, in a confined room, in a curtained-off bed. But solitude on the springtime island, exposed in the space of spaces, above seas & hills, stars & triremes, Greece and yet more early summers. That, too, is solitude. *Paradoxon insulare*. The eyelashes of that Parisian, petal-chested, and Modiano-wombed girl[13] (a Tiberius pendant) are like triremes. Like the caterpillar-keyboard of oars at sea. Or the black bone of Tiberius' god-fishes. Sex is not good for marveling at, not for myth or anti-myth, not for psychology or the proliferation of the herd, but for games. And not bodily games either: the body is something a lot clumsier. For intellectual games. Tiberius games. For a Tiberius portrait. In Capri Tiberius *plays* and has *played* sodomite adolescent physicalities. Boy with boy: oh, *principium identitatis*. I am unable to separate the emperor from that female portrait. Neither from the watery-green bronze belly nor from the palm tree of ice made of pliant glass. Where is the boundary of academic *'sérieux'* and Giraudoux-style buffoonery here? A pedantic question. Where is that unearthly strength of a senile, demonic-Shakespeare Tacitus, that with him for the first time a river will be a river, a mask — a mask, Capri — Capri, a boy — a boy, an old man — an old man? The simplest words become filled with themselves like the sails of the treacherous warships of Ravenna & Byzantium fill with vigorous winds.

The two types of Tacitus: that of the late *Annals* & that of the early *Histories*. At the end of the *Annals*, admittedly, a Stoic philosopher (at least the semblance of one) and a Cynic feature on one page: the two passport-portraits of the *Annales* and the *Historiæ*. The *Annals* is stoic: classic melancholy, Satanic pessimism between colonnades. A Stoa Poikilé.[14] The Histories are cynical: Tacitus is a 'dog,' yelping, mongrel, Grecian, romantic, moralizing, *la Rochefoucauld*, replete with Augustinian stylistic tricks and ever-so-big novelistic flair. Spanish literature. The *Annals* are cubist in the most globular sense of the word. In the *Histories* there is still a lurid adolescent streak: to give a Spenglerian background to the occasional event — Byzantium & Trebizond are not *just* Byzantium and Trebizond (that is reserved for the diabolical declaration of the *Annals*) but '*the* East,' just as York & Urbino are not British and Latin cities but '*the* West.' The broad perspectives & elevated horizons give the book a downright pubertal dew. The titles are also splendid: one is the horse-mad Hippolytus: *Historiae*, 'history,' as if anything of the kind existed, either as reality or as literature. The great Indian source of illusion.

The other is that of monomaniac Phædra, of the tragic, sick, green-blooded, green-livered, green-bowelled Tacitus, more puritanical than a puritan: *ab excessu divi Augusti*. Any conception of nymphs and faun-perspectives is foregone here in this puritanical title. There is no 'history'; literature is out of the question. And here, in the yellow-fire of gossip, the finest marriage or May sodomy is realized: the love, the identity of Tacitus & Tiberius — whether literary or concubine, it doesn't matter. Because old Tiberius, in his Capri sin-hermitism and picture-asceticism, is identical to old Tacitus' Acherontic intellectualism, his historical lovemaking, his portrait-perversity over events.

The sea rocks a light skiff that bounces like a rubber ball between Sorrento and Capri, bringing an aristocratic lover — a delicious golden virgin, an asparagus-flavored innocent. Another boat transports coarse material in bulk from Naples: sailors, gladiators, actors. Perhaps an "erotic sociology" (excuse the phrase) would save the world... And this is Tacitus' study of sources, the most *irate* of *ires*, the most studied of *studia*. Yet Tacitus states that this is a "regal" habit in Tiberius — to pollute freeborn youths.

Regal: which is to say, at that time: some scruffily colonial, disgusting Eastern import stinking of fairy superstitions & devil cults. A Syrian, Judæan, Silician, or Cypriot affair. What a fresh color and piquancy the word "regal" has here. The emperor and consul: the shavenness, the *suum cuique*[15] morning, the tile-touch of civility. The 'king'? That is the brigand faun-bristles, faun-beard, faun-jungle, cheap pomp, sham-myth, low-caliber democracy. What sort of world is it where a king is a synonym for the small, the Papuan clown! Tiberius reached the lowest degree of depravity: he had "regal" habits, Tacitus says. To be sure, there was sharp, rational-ritual distinction between Greek & Persian, intellectual sodomy, and "regal" gluttony for boys. There is an eerily haunting elegance, irony, and evocativeness about the fact that Tacitus can make pronouncements like "Neapolis (Naples) ... is a *Greek* city." The suggestion that the Greeks were Rome's Jews is all too true. After all, they were intellectuals, erotic, and — *pour comble de gloire*[16] — also had a dreamer's anti-state view of the world.

Tacitus' chapter on Judæa is very good. The disdain mixed with horror of Gnæus Pompeius Magnus when, after a thousand bloody theater *coulisses* of the Temple in Jerusalem, he found nothing in the Tabernacle, or rather to express it with theological scrupulousness: he found *Naught* — that is Tacitus' horror at our own God. Nevertheless, Tacitus is so much a cosmetician of the nirvanas of "*homo factus est*"[17] portraits because that kind of horror stands or sits in his lungs like winged snow on Swiss trees. What about the relationship of fashionable humanism to Tacitus?

That is Pilate humanism, Pontius Renaissance: "ecce *homo*" — that is his dogma, his conclusion, the sole intellectualizable part of him. The rest is: portrait, battle, god, the indifferent detritus of life. Never had so many *people* stood by so many *people* as in Tacitus: the way the relief-gauze of the world-conquering imperium wraps round the sick foot of Trajan's column (so that the poor little darling should not ache) is the way in which the destructive swarm of human worms evoked in his work leeches around Tacitus, to death. Not out of humanism, not out of literature, but out of otherworldly *ira et studio*. There are times when he dithers between blind statistician and visionary poet: if one takes a pen in hand (*penna desecrata, verbum nefas*),[18] that is the pen's habitual reflex: swaggering in ink. He distractedly relates stories about the gods, tales of Eastern temples. He rests his elbows on ships' railings with the somewhat snobbish Germanicus, and muses on the preening enactments of *1001 Nights*; or along with the more romantic and more Amazonian Titus, he is dumbfounded in the temple gloom of dead-rouging and necrophiliac Egyptians. But those are just *moments musicaux*, and Tacitus is tone-deaf, heroically, divinely, and victoriously tone-deaf. The zither is a slur like 'king,' with its Greek-inflected name and baboon *raison*. *A*-zitherer, *de*-zitherer, *non*-zitherer Tacitus.

We shall never know the secret of that portrayal. Of that puzzling mixture of non-writing, of that utterly Stone-Age-clumsy inability to write — and of style, sentence, and word composition. Because that is not literature: it is a primitive, beastly communication. Yet style nevertheless: the culture of words, nevertheless. An 'objectification' of Tacitus? Is Tiberius good? evil? old? Does Tacitus portray complicatedly or simply? Maybe he just portrays, but for us it looks complicated? Is his portrayal complicated as a result of clumsiness or out of his nuance-mosaic making?

Naïve questions that are blown away by the Latin wind like sheets of paper by a draught on opening a door. Tacitus is also unanimous with Tiberius in matters of morality. In vain did the emperor degenerate into a 'king'; in vain was the writer a puritanical republican. Tacitus has one morality: his style, his literature. That syntax morality and ethic of composition — that is also Tiberius in old age! Some playing about between animal breeding and intellectual hallucinations. A budding hyacinth and an agonizing Seneca; skeptical lust and stubborn netherworld; a pessimistic body and a despotic soul. A drawn battle. The reality: tragedy — a keeping at arm's length of the tragedy that would be Naples, "a Greek town." For Tacitus there is only the moment; that is why he is a historiographer so that he can wind up the momentary horror & the momentary lesbianism to suicide, & in the moment, in that absurd earthliness, in the Capri-*hic* and Naples-*nunc* morality is meaningless: it is so tight, so ecstatically bottled up, so screamingly hidebound, that it is impossible to interpret or evaluate. Tiberius' head: on it, the shades of a villa's trees; in it, patinated, dense chlorophyll.

Minute points, indentations, as if the whole head were a mimicry of a dream, a mimicry of a cypress: not sinful, not songful, not lecherous, not anatomy. Just some color, an inner pressure, some phosphorous tickling in the brain — god, number, ephebe. The majestic mask of determinacy: Tacitus-Narcissus looked into the Atlantic-mournful mirror of history and got that Tiberius echo thrown back. The most insane lyric, the most Circe of an incantation. There is no trace of this in the other pictures. Claudius is the sacral idiot, an already mummified-cretin even in life, all gravity and statuesqueness.[19] His movements are those of manikins carried around on long poles in processions: they are dead, but roll about every which way around a single rigid axis. Inflexible painted eyes; idiocy like Byzantium. One cannot laugh at that idiocy, there is no mental shading in it: for all he cares, music halls and analysts can starve to death. That is institutionalized insanity — insanity as a forum, as an orientalized legal paragraph. While Tiberius constantly plays in dark-green shades of water, Claudius is a greyish yellow, ashen yellow, oblong Pompeian Greco. Nero is an actor, but on a fairy-tale scale. He is a butterfly and flutters, the very playfulness of the elements that glitter like an innocent firebug and is as lethal as poison. Maybe the prototype or patron saint of electricity: a moth and death at the same time. Nero has no body, no flesh — he is just a rainbow over thousand-colored Rome, from which red droplets fall on Seneca's papers. He is the colorfulness of the world itself, *in abstracto*: a Hindu Maya, a diabolical illusion; the first radical non-human: a metaphor, a daubed principle. Tiberius is Tacitus' Narcissus-lyre; Claudius — a Byzantine manikin; Nero — the poetry missing from Tacitus' opus, and the impossible poetry of the opus of the Creation ... so what about humanism then? So far not one of them is a man! How could they be when they are all portraits!

And Otho?[20] No one died more exquisitely than him. Otho: Nero embodied. If Nero had not been a Shelley-bird of being, an immaterial mirage of Paradise, but a man and indeed, as a result of some curious but conceivable accident of fate, Roman emperor, then I swear he would have been precisely like Otho: as fat, as drunken, as gluttonous, and like him even in his morals — under Stoic circumstances he would have been a stoic himself, even a hero, and what is more: one of the best. Otho has a tragic fate: to take immateriality to the bitter end in matter; to agonize the absurdity, the mystery, of happiness into humanity. His suicide is more beautiful than Seneca's.

What about Vitellius? He is the theatricality of demos, black melodrama. But he is also the apology, the eternally irrefutable apology for this most sacred of genres. Perhaps he is the human-shaped human ... his death is spine-chillingly Matthew Passion in nature.

And I find extra pleasure in all that irresponsible-unphilological banter that the Latin language does with me, or I with it. Around me doddering cardinals sacrifice their entire lives for the true meaning of each and every Tacitus *nomen,* and cross-eyed literary Medici-henchmen would bundle out all their dead from the ground at the slightest hope of unearthing a battered statue of Tacitus underneath. Me? I indulge myself in the shallowest sonic and other associations.

Tramisso: if instead of *trans* I read *tra-*, it's rather as if instead of the doge I read a gaudy harlot; instead of a Romulus wolf, a scatty dachshund; and instead of empire, I were to find a Dantesque party-partisan Italy. That *tra-* is a plebeian corruption, a flaky, street, tramp modernity. *Capreas*: scrawny goats, almost golden fleeces sewn into some transparent *crêpe,* glinting roe deer, shining silk. *Interluit*: all the brutality of lues, its liquid underhandedness, a quagmire-Gothic of venereal disease. Every disease is at one and the same time a Gothic clamor and Proustian intrigue. *Ambiguus*: for me there is no word so expressive of double-entendre and duplicity, the reality of every alternative, dualism, or tormenting dilemma. Two snakes are twisted up in that double 'uu' with bifurcating, Janus-maniacal heads. That word is all riddle, hopeless chaos, a living blazon of the human dread of choice. Sticky and discontinuous, hissing like the salamander of philosophy on Eve's body in Paradise.

"*Speciem* venturi simulans" — I have read a hundred times in the works of medieval doctors about the *species impressa* or *expressa* and I was always left with a sense of some loathsome emptiness, professional meaninglessness, after the word *species*. Here it was first given reality. Appearance, aspect, mien — it means all that! Something clarifying and something mendacious. *Saxa*: from that puzzlegrass, rushes and willow trees come to mind, not rocks. White-leafed, cobweb-flowered. How lovely those flowers that resemble leaves. *Solitudo maris*: that is very poetry, Italian literature, all the music that I ought to write, the eternal vibration, the Nike-profile sentence and harmony amid the noise of words. It is like a saying, the Bible, Richard II's abdication. Ah, *laissons*... *Pubem ingenuam*:[21] in pubes there is all of adolescence, unpoetically, motherlessly, in the hands of diagnosis-ticking, doltish doctors. A despondent, 14-year-old body, skin and bones, among medicine, sadistic nurses, chemistry officials: that is pubes. And in the 'es' ending is every ill omen and croaking augury. 'True' Latin words unfailingly end in *-us* or *-a* — the rest are demonic. *Stupris pollueret*:[22] Narcissus' first sex-poetic and fear of *tabes*; and all the many fine lotions de Clyanthe, lotions Arabes, lotions de Cléopâtre in women's hairdressing salons: one can hear how they softly bubble from the bottle into the palms of Figaros and onto the hair of Poppæas.... Poppæa! On account of whom I began reading Tacitus in the first place. *L'incoronazione*! *Nec formam tantum et decora corpora*:[23] in relation to beautiful boyish bodies that is the geometrical, ice-crystal word: *forma*. That means every hill and valley of delightfulness on the skin, the deadly nerve-Saturnalias in the aged Tiberius' body, and in the eyes of adolescents barely budding from the March showers, all that troubadouring and loss that the bodies of graceful women and graceful gigolos signify: "*forma*." With a short "o" & a short "a" to close. Old Tiberius' marble statue, with a million cracks and discolorations, the entirety of changes over an entire life — all depend on that one thing, that Latin yelp: *forma*. What about *decora*? The grace is thereby not something physical, vital-animal, but fictive, decorative, crafted — all business, theater, fashion. The word "*forma*" is like the formula of a philosophical curse on gigolos, while "*decora*" is of the workshop, mechanical. Overlooking the barbaric rhyme: ora-ora. *Imagines maiorem*:[24] that is the *coup de grâce* for gigolos — if the Mephisto injection of "*forma*" or the business mask of "*decora*" have not killed off the human in them, then the "*imagines*" will do so for sure.

The picture of the ancestors as sex appeal: tatty oil paintings in unheated salons, gravestone statues on a dark side altar of a godforsaken church, family museum for bald senators. *Imago* is also a ghost, not just marble: a duplication of an individual with all its madness & cunning. *Les amours de Tibère*... Psychology itself is loafing around there. Maybe Tacitus would call that, too, "*more regio*"?[25]

(Vol. XII.8) Old Tiberius. Old Tacitus. Old Seneca. Is it possible to pose the question either of humanism (which is a game), or of man, *homo* (which is a hair's-breadth less of a game), without the question of aging? Man and aging are consubstantial things. Youth is a terrible dream, and there's no way of telling what the biggest trouble is with it: the fact that it is terrible, or the fact that it is a dream. Manhood — 'activity': can one pronounce a more damning verdict on something? Only old age is life: only Tiberius lived on Capri, only Tacitus in Tiberius, only Seneca in his vast villa and flabby Buddhism. Youngsters are to be avoided; they are nullities. Men should be persecuted: they are minuses. The elderly: they are everything. Read and put on fat. The three kinds of old age. Tiberius is the experience that saw so deeply to the fabulous bottom of life that he was unable to express it by gesture or word.

Those paradoxes that sophists, church-founders, and psyche-salesmen writers assert about the infinite complexity of life are all elementary-school platitudes as compared to life's genuine confusion. Tiberius knows that better than anyone else. His whole loneliness, his grim silence, his Hamlet-senility is nothing but an endless submission to the remoteness & unfathomability of realities. Duped interviewers like Suetonius can blabber about Tiberius' shameful swinishnesses, but is anything of less significance than those maladroit *cochonneries*? Why did he not write articles about Tiberius' skin hanging on his neck? That would have been more sensational. Tiberius could see through people's games — so plainly and clearly that he did not fall into the stoic or literary vulgarity of trumpeting that insight to the world.

Capri was nothing new to him; he had spent long years on Rhodes. There he had made the acquaintance of the two dubious muses of the islands: the tragic gloom of his own human individuality, and the mentality of the Greeks jesting from Thanatos to teahouse. Rhetors, sophists, pederasts, and Alexandrian poetasters clung to him like midges to flypaper, but no one was more majestic, more aristocratic and haughtier in his contempt for those pornographers than the emperor, mossy as he was from mushrooms and the depth of the forest. Was that cynicism? blaséness? tragic resignation? All together, they are: invincible, triumphant old age. So was Tiberius hypocritical? A sadist? As much, perhaps, as anybody who came into the world through the side door of a bloody womb.

Anyone who can for a second, pessimistically, disconsolately, indeed more than likely charitably, delight in his own child's demented howling would probably do the same if, all of a sudden, he were hauled to the top of an empire like a raggedy flag on a mast. In any case, it is infantile to bring a children's room din of defenses and attacks into the proximity of old Tiberius. They say that he had very large eyes with which he could see perfectly even at night if roused from his sleep. *C'est lui*. He had night vision; that is to say, when and where the world was going on in the sloughs of unconsciousness. These are then the black victories of schizophrenics: those eyes opened with the mute-tragedy of knowledge, with the consistent lunacies of *savoir-faire*. In vain do erotic scenes glitter in garish colors in the hall of the Io Villa; in vain are the most succulent *frutti* sons of Italy stripped and dished round by zealous slaves: Tiberius is a melancholic onlooker, a disparager of life, who knows that mysticism

& philosophy are the misery of amateurs. Like those state-licensed and morally permitted voluntary clowns who used to accompany the bigger funerals with jokes. While well-paid wailing-women with their Lenthéric streaks of blood and chalked-tear wrinkles hollered for taxi-metered spells of time, those little plebeians guffawed at the theatrical horror of the deceased. Seneca was also like that, *in prima analysi*: a *histrio*. That is one kind of old age: the best and most intellectual. The other is Tacitus: the romantic corpse dissector, an æsthete crow. Or if you prefer: a free wailing woman. He bawls, calls out thief and fire, doctor and god, at the sight of the ghastly comedy of empire, the world, all humanity. That is also magnificent old age, an unending accusation, representational disparagement, portrait jungle. Statue-crammed cathedral façades come to mind — the whole thing is a laic, negative, devilish church façade where rows of tragic buffoons are lined up; the Amphitheater of the Antichrist. Finally, there is Seneca's old age, a meditative, hypochondriac blend of the "ripeness is all"[26] type of sensuality & cowardice forced to monumentality.

What an overweight head; the whole thing a Himalaya of the adipose. A perpetual deposit for inducing a stroke. Perpetual puffing and blowing, the skin insensitive to any dribbles of spit. It does not matter what his thoughts are worth: he is thinking old age. Chaotic solitude, theatrical litigation, cautious philosophy. Tiberius has primacy. Why was he at one point in time in Rhodes? Exile? Disgust at the world? A diplomatic trick? Pleasure hunt? Philosophical treatment? All of those things together. Capri & Rhodes: old age and youth, two islands. Two kinds of Greekness: one more honest and one more sublimated. Rome & Hellas. Tiberius and the Greek eidolons, specters, dead souls. What did that Roman man (no Greek man lived) have to say about the vignettes of death on Attic vases in Rhodes? Those soldiers with beards like blinkers & resembling the silhouettes of insects, lugging the corpses of slain companions, through whose mouths a diminutive soldier is seen flying out: the soul. What did Tiberius have to say about this Greek sorcerer-phantasmagoria — the 'soul'? Or about the snake, which to the Greeks signified a soul?

Tiberius had a tamed pet snake that he fed himself: whether he used it to fatten a phallus, death, or some exotic frill, it would be hard to decide. Like every cynic and someone beyond religions or this side of them, he was superstitious and hypochondriac to the core — he laughed at Olympus, but fainted on seeing his own shadow. So what did he have to say about those Ascot Thoroughbreds that raced in memory of the death of Patroclus?[27] For him the Greeks in Rhodes were: mystery and sophism, insular superstitions and insular lies for the brain. Angel-winged Eos with Memnon's cadaver. Tiberius had only seen such half-Egyptian, half-Assyrian curly locks as on that Memnon vase on one of Otho's coins.

Tiberius was smarter than my fellow humanists in Rome or Florence. They see in Greeks only harmony and justice, statues and Plato, whereas Tiberius saw the *carcasse mirages*

& lies: that was the idyll on Rhodes. The heroicized corpses, the way they had been depicted by the Spartans about half a millennium before Christ (*"auctor nominis eius Tiberio imperante per procuratorem Pontium Pilatum supplitio affectus erat,"*[28] Tacitus-Lucifer writes): with a snake writhing behind the throne, pigtailed puppets, amphoras with interminable ears, and Egyptian Lilliputians.

Is there a more terrifying sight than the Harpy tomb at Xanthus,[29] on which smirking women are making away with souls? Their breasts are hilly like the 'after' shots in cosmetics adverts in consumer magazines — they have huge, cubistically simple insect wings with the most rudimentary striping; their ghoulish grins, their marvelous hairstyles are like chain mail. Their buns have nothing to do with their wings, their breasts nothing to do with their chests, and their chests nothing to do with the corpses — Capri was an *island*; it may well have been reminiscent of Rhodes; a Hermes psycho-pomposity strolling in a palm-beach straw hat (*&* those are *not* Offenbachian attributives) as the dead body is offered to a doughboy-featured Charon. Psyche: a Rhodian nightmare, the most lethal poison.

The midnight Dionysiads: the togas and chitons on the priests and the women with their thousand, million, ten million folds, the sole harvest of lines in the world; the torches; the un-Dionysiac Dionysus like a *privat-dozent* dervish — that was Rhodian Hellenism for the groping schizoid. Hecate's death-mugs, obese pooches at their heels, and jet flames bigger than man. In Capri it was another world.

From the outside. Rhodes still unsettled him, like a premonitory thrombosis. Nor were Hypnos' enchanting nudes posing outside. The odd Corinthian column sprang up in the air — and Corinth itself was floweriness, graceful & foamy palm, slender female legs, the buds of ankles, roses of knees, the fruit of hips. The stones were greyish-green, as if they were underwater. The capitals of columns: heads, tousled hair, abstractedly trampled flowers. Corinth *anthos*. That is my first and most significant commentary on Seneca: only by Tiberius can I stay. On Rhodes he would still diligently drop in on the schools of the sophists, he was erudite, bookish, an intellectual. On Capri he made do with sagacity and the mind among Corinthian palm marbles; in the darkness of the depths of the forest, with an intelligence resembling a leaf that flickers from a single ray of sunshine. That was his notorious senility, his insanity! That is what Seneca tried to break up and pester into thoughts & morality. It didn't suit him all that well.

Seneca was Spanish born, from Cordoba; his father even managed to die there. On many occasions Seneca stood closer to Messalina than her nipple-pastellers or her compass-drawn lovers. Nero dazzled Seneca by showering him with palaces and gardens, yachts and women — he showed little haste in abstaining from such. Instead he wrote bombastic tragedies, and half of his pessimism was little more than his baroque style, his penchant for paradox and *bon mots*.

Tacitus' entire romanticism is lurking and straining in Seneca; the baroque of the era around Philip II. I am fondest of that passage in the *Moral Letters to Lucilius* where he praises old age.[30] His comparisons never give the feel of a poet but of an ordinary frequenter of the empress' soirées; old age is like a ripe fruit on the point of rotting, like a boy who has just passed his catfish-flavored youth; like the last sip, which voluptuously completes the hitherto only sketchily-outlined drunkenness. Only old age truly knows the value of one *day*. A whole life.

Indeed, if anyone, I live for the day, not the hour or year. That is the sole unit, the sole life, and also the sole genre: from morning to evening. Not love, which may also endure tomorrow; not god, which may also haunt one tomorrow; not life, which may also resurrect tomorrow. It was old Tiberius, not the Syrian procurator, who felt that mythical-artistic unity of a single day so much that after every feast he had himself buried, surrounded by yellow candles bent into the shape of ram's horns, tousled hetæras similar to headsprings, & drunken guests suddenly packed into black. Evening is death; the moon and stars are virginal lanterns of the other world. *Bebiōtai. Bebiōtai.*[31]

Yet old age and death have nothing to do with each other. Death flows from a tree that unfolds in spring — it is an arrow from the young muscles of Artemises, the scent of violets and pasque-flowers, meadow anemones. So it hardly befits adipose-colossal Seneca. He was likewise an island dweller: he passed the days of his exile in Corsica. The grave-digging philological racket of the Renaissance is still buzzing around me, but this flea market has been yet unable to resurrect even so much as a single Greek or Roman. Maybe for that to happen a tardy musician is required? For Tiberius & Seneca to be not books but people? Every detail has to be pictured: the ship of exile, the color of the sails, the thickness of the ropes, the papers tossed into the sea, the slave monograms cut into the oars, the Corsican trees, the Cordoba cradle. Why? When his books are the essence, the thoughts are what count? This is not the place for me to argue.

I am unable to live without people. Gossip, necromancy, charlatan relics, books, hallucinations, every cheap and exalted means is equally good for something dead to live. A detailed biography? Naïve, well-meaning humbug. Seneca's life? In one *moment* his blood pressure, scraps of memory, details of his milieu that happen to strike the eyes, evanescing facial modulations, words that were dropped, each more insignificant than the last. It is no longer even a detail, not even a nuance. But this alone is the being-life of life. Of course the farther away a person is, the more inhumanly classical & paper proverb he is, yet the more exciting it is to conjure him up from behind scholastic triteness. It is at such times that a sham romanticization follows, a "*Versuch einer Mythologie*,"[32] the spurious picturesque. Let it come at any cost; let nothing else come. After all, that is life itself, some untrue, illusory thing, mottled confusion, polyphonic absence. If I were to write a biography of Seneca, I would begin with an analysis of modern-day Cordoba.

Would I be lying? Do I have more of a golden mouth than St. John? Is there not something baroque in his stoicism of style? An Arab ornamentation and Catholic resignation? Is it an accident that Seneca, in the 9th of his moral letters to Lucilius, drops the remark: "the wise man's life will be like that of Jupiter, who, amid the dissolution of the world, when the gods are confounded together & Nature rests for a space from her work, can retire into himself and give himself over to his own thoughts."[33] Is that not oriental mysticism? And can I make it life-like in any other way than to charge that adjective "oriental" with a thousand particulars, Cordoban mosques, Jesuits, harems, eunuchs, and Quran exegetes? After all, that is the simplest, most superficial nature of the word.

Anyone who does not sense these trivial plastic associations in the pronunciation of the word "oriental" is not a 'speaker' but a mathematician. With its awful frivolity and demonic maternity it is the only word that resembles life.

Do you suppose, my friend, that when, at the end of my previous marginalia, I gave you a taste of a little impressionist counter-philology, it was just empty neurasthenic fidgeting inside me? It wasn't. For me Tacitus is the ultimate reckoning with the fact of *man* & the fact of *cogitation*. Cogitation is: language. Seneca and Messalina. Maybe the entire sick horror at richness that is reflected in the letters to Lucilius did not originate in the wake of the hunting lodges & manors showered on him, but on account of Messalina's clothes, make-up, and jewelry. After Cordoba, therefore, Paris. Once again the ghastly piquancy of resurrection *ex nihilo*. The whole Messalina, the whole relationship of Seneca to

Messalina is from a scrap of a sentence: "For just as other things have for us an inherent attractiveness..."[34] Or about poverty (with a wink at Assisi from afar): let it be our domestic woman friend. "Inherent attractiveness": to shudder anew the shiver that snow-white Messalina, rising from her marble basin, aroused when her *fleur-de-Paris*-style black lace kimono was thrown around her — let people see what they saw, cover up what she could. "Other things": to create from that an entire woman, with an entire life, an entire birth, an entire death. Messalina's Chinese knot of black hair. "Woman" friend: from a feminine case-ending, every love. The biggest laugh is that this may be a more philological than poetic instinct. Old age is beyond women. But in any case Messalina was a woman for oldsters. Annæus Seneca permeated by a portrait of Messalina is mentioned in Book XII, chapter 8 of Tacitus' *Annals*, where mention is made of a grove of Diana's. If I was so loud-voiced in calling my margin to Tacitus a show-down with man, am I not now staging a show-down with the broader scholasticism of superficiality? Diana and Messalina? Marriages and perversions? Eunuchs and Assyrian fertility superstitions? Love and carnal lust? Before me I still have Tiberius frolicking with an abducted boy in a concealed swimming pool; as if an emerald-colored squid were to reach out from the depths of the water after the corpses of lily-white seagulls floating on the surface... the emperor's gouty legs, the backs of white louts, big black fish, irresolute giant water lilies, waves making love with themselves — what a delicious Pompeian game. A good

Suetonius anecdote, a good Picasso tapestry. And afterwards, this cold blue sentence: *addidit Claudius sacra ex legibus Tulli regis piaculaque apud locum Dianæ.*[35] Love is not known in Tacitus — what a redemptive, reassuring thing. There are Dianas: in whistling & purling groves. There are marriages: matrons under contract, profit-seeking adoptions. And lust. Nothing more. Wisdom is ignorant of love. Here no apology is fabricated for lust. Diana, but what kind of Diana? Also known as the Trier Arduinna, that barbarian-Greek hybrid! With her bony, angular elbows, in her bulky tunic, with her bulky dogs, beside a bulky tree. She hunted so long for the tusked and grunting wild boar until she herself turned into one, and to this day she thrives upwards in the north: an etherealized lump of a girl, a heavyweight virgin. In the erotic anything goes. Nothing in the world is less of a picky instinct than the amatory.

Tiberius' mother, Livia, is perhaps the most gorgeous woman I have ever seen. Are you familiar with her statue? There are thousands of busts in the world, but none of them is a bust of such burning simplicity as that: just a head. There are portraits, enigmas, stylized skull-motifs vibrant with psychology, in which either the hairstyle or the pose dominates, but this is the very head, a tragic and arrogant part of the body, just as the Creator intended. That straightaway makes it manly, dryly energetic. So symmetrical, so incredibly uniform both to the right and to the left of the nose, that it has already become a permanent law, a republican order, but still the mirroring proclaims the entrancing duplication of a kaleidoscope. From the ears to the chin are two straight, vertical lines; essentially nothing oval. The face is a *castrum*, a military camp, not a mask. Above it a mass of tiny whorls, curls, Græco-negroid coils. But only at the ends of the tresses. Naturally parted in the middle, the locks flow smoothly, with barely a wave, over the temples. Citadel bones & small Assyrian undulations. And yet again: a straight nose, and lips like one of Amor's bows, a diminutive kiss-lizard, a slender erotic puzzlegrass. With what primness and unearthly coolness the lawyer Amazon and concubine are divided up in that face, the Livia and the Livulla Livicella. Do we ever write any other sentence than that: someone is a hybrid of Artemis and Phryne? Yet this is a game that with some individuals is truly melting-soft. Not here, though: here the two elements are strictly divided, doled out. How is it that the rather slender brow stirs not only a non-animal but a directly divine impression, more compelling to veneration than a diadem? Is that a heraldry of female sobriety, virginal restraint, an earth-cold *mater*?

For someone to have a mother like that! And the huge eyes: notwithstanding the fact that intense Dead Sea curses menaced in them, they were not poetic, 'spiritual,' or oriental eyes, but the conches of reigning, subterranean self-discipline. Woman starts and ends with Livia. Here virgin, mother, concubine, Lesbos, & boys are unequivocal things. This statue of Livia is a conquering of sex without a fight, without asceticism; at one and the same time a prosaic, dry solution & secret. This is where Tiberius' capers in

Capri start. How nauseating Greek sculpture is beside this 'Grecian' head. What a clumsy little distinction between 'man' & 'woman' as against Livia's face. These two responses merit the name response: Livia's ice-cold, Bengal-light appeal head, and Tiberius' sensual mathematics on the island. Livia's head is going to shine like a blue star at every Eastern wedding against every Jewess, every psycho-pomposity, every Persian sultan. It is the Occident personified, 'barbarianism,' a Roman, Germanic, Saxon woman in whom sadism and dream clasp in fragrant embrace (incomprehensibly to the East).

This Livia looked on love in the same way that Rome handled its little satraps in Asia Minor, the glass-pearl politics of Syria & India, a Jordan valley rag of virtues and 'soul.' You came by a worthy son in Tiberius: he sits there under the flowering jasmine bushes & amuses himself by setting on his own breast infants stolen from their mothers. Let the menfolk stay alone and not seek a partner or person in women? Not share pleasure with women? Nor with men, not because man is any good or better — that's tripe, Tiberius is well aware of it — but because they are not women. Not women: that is such a lot that it is worth suffering even such a fleabite as another man. Lust is always tragic. But there is also something in it of a vengefulness against women, a kindred vengefulness of the one that radiates from Livia's head. And that vengefulness cannot start early enough.

I wish to take leave of love, of the whole sexual circus. *Poenæ procurationesque incesti.*[36] I would like to cite every possible form of love to this Tacitus *cour des adieux.*[37] Every now and again, in my weaker moments, I indulge in the illusion that I am an idle impressionist, which is not the case. A ponderous, pedantic systematizer rather. A botanist. There are times when I keep quiet about it, other times when I flaunt it *ad absurdum*. Incest. Diana, Messalina, Livia, Tiberius. Woman with woman? Woman with man? Woman with horse? Woman with a god's statue? A woman on her own? A woman in labor? Is that not a pitiful series? Aristophanes or Sophocles? (Myth or Freudian barrel organ?) Horse-god or registrar of births?

How many things people have made out of sex. Out of boredom? Desperation? When it comes down to it, is it a simple or complicated matter? Important or trite? I would like to abandon it once and for all. Never to encounter it again. Or its saints. Its noseless syphilitics. Or the multipara. Its record-breakers of abortions. No, no, there is too much impossibility in all that. Yet there is no one who has had the luck in love, so to say, that I have had. Among my not inconsiderable number of lovers there has not been one who would not have given up her life for me, and yet they showed heavenly loyalty in tolerating my cheating on them. They even encouraged me. The redhead, the raven-haired, the blonde, the brunette: a stoic and cynical rainbow. How did Seneca look at Messalina in his Corsican *temps perdu*, and at Agrippa when he was recalled? The senile *dilettante amoroso* who, one tradition had it, was in correspondence with St. Paul? There is nothing more charming than when a stoic explains that, to be sure, there are occasionally things that alarm him, causing fleeting melancholy or evanescent ecstasy.

Of course, there can be no question of one's mental balance being upset, perish the thought, just… "something natural, an insuperable instability for the rational mind." What the philosopher trotting homewards from the beach on the bay of Baiæ felt in the dimly illuminated, dusty tunnel at Posillipo, that little chill of fear and spleen and eventually airy cheer in the sunshine — feelings of those sorts must have been chafing & frolicking in his breast in front of Messalina-Medusa. When he writes about his impressions of the beach he explains at length that anyone who could get steamed up by twittering birds or heave-hoeing galley slaves, is still restless from inside — the word is almost on his lips —, that person still has stuff that needs to be "analyzed away."

That tang of *"gout de névrose"* fragrance on the respectable toga is nice. It is quite certain that those kinds of fidgety dreams and embarrassed worries were abounding in Seneca at the time of his Messalina interviews. If one did not sense that throughout the moral letters to Lucilius, and in his other works, they would be worth nothing. However we might twist things around, intellectuals are excluded from love. Seneca from Messalina. Maybe he didn't even want her, but it would have been futile even if he did.

Intellectuals are affected so exclusively by external appearances, they can be nourished so solely by the epidermis, that any contact or relationship is impossible. Messalina may often have asked Seneca for mundane advice as a joke or out of coquettishness; he was permitted to crouch beside the mirror, among the slips & castrated chiropodists, until the current beau was shut out. Meanwhile the woman would simulate all sorts of amatory moans, whisper dock and tavern language in order to tease her *"iuventutis Romæ pulcherrimum."*[38] How insulting and humiliating that was to Seneca … Only the tunic-jacket of the ensemble is used for this cocktail costume. It has the flare of the newest tunics and is worn over a separate skirt. Designed for sizes… That soft-frilled neckline will make you look fragile and crisp at lunch. The skirt is wrapped, and the kimono sleeves have a switch of shivering. Designed for sizes… Women do not kill with their virginity; they do not kill out of a thirst for lust. The horror of Messalina is not the lovemaking. Those are non-entities. Deathliness kills in fashion, in the Gorgon-spirited vanity of dressing; Seneca never forgot that. Is that why Tiberius chose sucking babes over his sclerotic breast? *Hic amor, hic salta?*[39]

(Book XII. 63.) *Namque artissimo inter Europam Asiamque divortio Byzantium in extrema Europæ posuere Græci…*[40] When I read Tacitus' lines about Byzantium, I almost get the feeling that he, too, senses the thrill, the excitement, & the ascetic modesty that I always experience when I think of Byzantium.

Byzantium is, I suppose, the topic that is most sought after and also the most unworkable. In Byzantium all the human and mythological contrasts and self-contradictions that so excite psychologists & historians crop up with such fantastic coarseness, such vulgar pointedness that, out of art's ancient Vesta modesty, one is ashamed of handling it.

If I were, perchance, disposed to show you the most profound secret and bluest wound of my life, I would have to refer to that (I love those red-tape phrases) — to that sick, religious modesty & humility of mine in the face of reality.

Every humanist poet and Florentine or Venetian musician accuses me of being an esoteric, abstract, mystic, reality-denying stylite, who both in his mathematical analyses & in his star-scraping manias avoids reality, the mundane, the bittersweetness of actuality, ordinary kiss, ordinary death. Me abstract! Me not ordinary! Every moment of my life is a magic suffocation in actuality; every cell of my blood lives on the ephemeral; and when my eyes eventually close on my deathbed, I am *not* going to shoot out the arrow of my soul at Plotinus' symmetrical æsthetic targets, but at the rags, the momentary sounds and colors of the room of my death-chamber. The only difference between my cult of reality and that of my fellow artists is that, being truly familiar with every frightful particle of reality, I fear it, I am awestruck in its face, & for the time being I haven't the strength to be able to render it with its own dreadful tang and savor of reality. They write marvelous little skits about some snack or other, a hypocritical ceremony, a creepy-crawly city council, or a *condottiere*'s pensioning-off; they produce brilliant sketches of dead old biddies and frisky squirrels, reclining periwigs, & a thousand flowers, after which they contentedly rest their heads on their crummy pillows — "Hoo-hah! What a neat way of presenting the reality of the world that is!"

Those people picnic beside chasms and at the bottom of valleys from which even the sadness of the *de profundis* would sound unduly frivolous and profane. Reality is a dark, inscrutable, tangled entity: the chromatic & sonic realities of a moment, the tiny flippancies of politics, its phosphorescing heroisms are far more complicated matters than scholasticism or advanced mathematics. Don't let anyone who does not sense that babble on about reality, or gossip about my alleged 'abstractedness' and my insanity. My abstractedness is a consequence of my infinite sense of responsibility, and my cult of actuality, surpassing as it does every composer of cabarets and politician of the hour, every tea-partying forty-something dame or newsletter-scribbling chronicler. One cannot set about the big Arcanum just like that, with the intoxication of youth, or the impotence-mask of old age, which some scoffingly call "experience." As to whether it is in any way an artistic goal to express reality with such mystic precision, I never spontaneously raise that question to myself, at most only if it is provoked by small disputes.

Artistic goal? I have no artistic goals. I have an organism, a compulsion to live, eyes, ears, the internal ready-endings of nerves, and at the same time pure intelligence, a dazzling broad-based *raison,* like a gigantic Spanish hairpin that climbs with arabesque curlicue from around the nape of the neck to above a Latin storm of ringlets. Have I the temperament of a founder of a religion or an artist? Of what interest is that to me? I know that reality is a huge excitement; I know that I go around with a heart of Atlantic euphoria and a brain of Euclidean enlightenment into the sensation paradise of reality, & finally, in the way of a third axiom: I know that I need to create some connection between reality and my passionate-intelligent individuality for my own salvation, for my own narcosis. As to whether that relationship is mathematics or opera, religion or philosophy, nervous disease or hallucinating cowardice — those are such trifling questions besides the three principles that even to raise them is ridiculous. But my companions feel comfortable in that ridiculousness. I know them well, the amateur mystics, the mercantile mystics, the philologizing mystics; the sincere cynics, the pseudo-cynics, and the tragic cynics who are still burning inside; the petty realists; the barrel-organ classicists; the aborted prophets — I am outside them all. That is no merit of mine, even if occasionally, in moments of depraved vanity, I feel that is so.

The reason I like (I think it is quite needless to say, without realistic grounds) that little snippet of Tacitus about Byzantium is because I sense in it my own modesty trembling before reality. He speaks about Byzantium, about that *intellectual* indecency, like someone who is disturbed in the face of such a big bluff, such whorish romanticism. A footnote is tossed in about an oracular prophecy, then fleshily frisky fishes, and that's it: all done. *Posuere Græci.* One cannot lay a finger on Byzantium, although there would be no experience of Europe without an experience of Byzantium. Byzantium is the caricature, the absurd degree, of the paradox, the patent absurdity, that is 'Europe.' As if one were suddenly to introduce a thesis in the history of philosophy in the form of a *danse macabre* on a lowdown catafalque-stage. One instinctively jostles away the woman who offers herself too obviously, even though she may be the one and only one for whom it is worth living. That is how Byzantium offers herself; that is why Tacitus gives it a wide berth, why he fears it. Byzantium is a pulp novel incarnate, Europe incarnate, and artistic excitement incarnate.

Yet it is still impossible. Who can hit the tone (in a musical, pictorial, or literary portrait of Byzantium) so that it contains all the normless-kitsch juices of its history, and all the same not be a vulgar circus of contrasts, but an elegant work, enflaming coolness. The Greek statues and Virgin Mary dogmas, Platonic debates in the gardens of sophists and wild convocations in the circus, boundless despotism and fairy-tale democracy, emperors who are Apollo or Antichrist and meanwhile also stupid peasants, blind manure-mongers; a mix and clash of Greeks and Latins, barbarians and Jews; a perennial opal of *cortigiane* and nuns; the frenzy of ascetics and abstract stratagems of ecclesiastical diplomats; a theologizing of world rule and a politicizing to smithereens of theocracy: bursting with contradictions that are far too raw, far too glaring for one to be able to lay a finger on them. Yet for all that, *this* is Europe, this Byzantium is my autobiography, my great confession. I have no other sin than Byzantium, no other illness than Byzantium. Indeed, I can have no other virtue but Byzantium.

Posuere Græci — we know what Tacitus habitually implies by that. Either the hocus-pocus and sophistication of Rhodes, or Capri fornications. What would he have said about Byzantium if he had been able to live though its red currant-mosaic centuries? If he had seen Theodora on the catafalque and heard the requiem that I wrote last week out of all sorts of exhumed Byzantine musics to mark her death? What splendid game: secular songs, hit tunes, & tangos are full of liturgical elements that have trickled down into them, whereas sugary Tin Pan Alley melodies hang around in the masses, the Kyries & Agnus Deis. If I didn't harbor an insuperable horror of Byzantine crass-nudity for the foreseeable future, then I would no doubt write an opera about Theodora's death & funeral. And not about Poppæa's coronation.

Up above, on high, the red-headed strumpet. There is always something ghoulish about biers that are already high *in excelcis*: when one can barely see something at the fringe of the corpse. What, one wonders, is up there, apart from strings of candle-wax on black walls? Perhaps the deceased, already invisible on high on the Avignon castle-wall edge of the catafalque, is like an enchanted tropical palm after rings of Northern Polar ice and snow? But who can get up there? The paid mourners loaf around at the foot of the Babelian bier rising up into the cupola, like weary soldiers under the walls of an unconquerable fortress. No drawbridge or ladder. A single gateway, a single window. In the human brain a dead body is always associated with earth, with a bed, with ditches, with down below, with lower down, with falling.

Now it is up so high, *in summo meretrix,*[41] that it can no longer be seen. There was as yet no syphilis at that time, either, & people knew the "*Gradus philosophicus Angelorum.*"[42] That is the Byzantine curse: to drive such dirt-antitheses before me from moment to moment. I need to wrestle with that antithesis once for, after all, that is the axis of my life, of Europe, of art.

The mosaic of the coffin is green, so over the catafalque a pale green mist seems to be hovering, shot through with dust by a reverberating sunbeam. Cummulium of scents. Down below, the wax of the candles. Wax — that is perhaps the raw material of my Monteverdi body. Wax — that is a Roman writing desk when the thoughts sink into the material like a woman's inebriated head onto a pillow. That, too, is writing! That digging in the mud of wax's primeval flora. Wax: the stuff of seals. Red & black seals: fused together with a flame, with politics, with cadavers. Sealing wax is the blood of history. Wax is the body of death masks, the sculpture of death, breaking waves of precision. Wax is death in so many ways! Death is a written table; death is a seal, whether a donation or an execution; death filling up the cold channels of a lifeless body. Wax is the sweating and transparent anatomy of candles. Of very slender ones, whose flame is a lisping point, and of very robust ones, the candles of Russian corona chandeliers, squat like the challah bread of peasants. A slender candle, of course, is everything: *arpa bizantica*. Much fake fruit that is not for eating is wax. And, horror of horrors, deadlier than even death masks are the many mannequins in a waxwork: the prima materia of grand guignol. Wax is also the hexagonal cloister of bees; I always feel as though in honey I were nibbling a seal or a death mask with my morning milk. The whole of Byzantium is a kind of "wax thou art, and unto wax shalt thou return" construction. The apotheosis of wax is truly in place in that setting. Wax is an unguent, and Byzantium is a city of unguents. An unguent is cosmetic and hypochondria: a typically false entity, quite apart from being an entire death. Unguents never cured, never beautified; what cures is health, what beautifies is beauty. Still, humans love rubbing salves on themselves: applying an unguent or ointment is arguably the most symbolic human gesture. The service of the exterior, of appearance, of illusion. The sharp expression of living for the mirror & only for the mirror, until one's dying day. Of naivety, of superficiality. Theodora, invisible haughty hetæra, is herself sticky with unguents that dissolve like the feeble grease between Icarus' feathers. Maybe Tacitus' revulsion at the reign of Nero is nowhere better expressed as when he notes that Poppæa, Nero's wife, was not cremated in the Roman fashion but embalmed; she was titivated Egyptian style for the underworld. Unguents: in puritanical Tacitus' eyes that was tantamount to defiling a dead body. Undeniably, one senses that nausea: the boudoir-world of unguents, jars, rouges, and perfumes, instead of the hygiene and pathos of fire. As if the deceased were able to look at herself in the mirror. *Corpus non igni abolitum ut Romanus mos, sed regum externorum consuetudine differtum* odoribus *conditur.*[43]

And it is perfectly logical, what is more: natural, that after that had been done, Nero himself mounted the platform to praise his wife's beauty: *laudavitque formam eius.* The embalming had turned Poppæa into a mundane corpse; he could not have spoken about anything other than her beauty.

Many a verse-monger and bearded æsthete has dealt with death and beauty together in one pack. That opposition is the same kind of Byzantine contrast — endlessly alluring, and since it touches such instinctive strata, it cannot be raised to an intellectual or artistic level. It must be lived through mutely, alone, avoiding every expression — the way all the other matters that can be lived through at all should and could have been done. But the funeral of Poppæa is a good scene because at least the morbid character of the relationship of beauty & death, its non-religious, non-philosophical, non-artistic aspect is dominant. It is rather good in German as well: ... *mit einer Füllung von Spezereien einbalmiert.*[44] *Spezerei*: that is spices, cloves, nutmeg, marjoram & ginger; by now we are in the world of cookery, slap-bang in the middle of recipes and gourmandizing, *cent façons de préparer les morts.*[45] That is how I like female beauty the most: when it is not a matter of æsthetics, not an ideal or a matter of art, but of the disconsolation of a primitive female vanity; when it is technology and when it is unguent; when Senilius cautiously paints rouge on dead Poppæa's lips, wavering between obscene jokes and hymns to Charon. The same was done with Theodora, the wax angel, the wax fairy, before hauling her up to death's masthead.

At three o'clock in the morning it occurred to one of the corpse bedizeners that he had forgotten to brush over the lashes on the empress' left eyelid a second time with green mascara. As it was, one was green, the other (on which there was only lacquer) was black. What was he to do? Was it worth pulling himself up the scaffolding with ladders and ropes to the top of the 50-foot high catafalque to correct a blemish that no one could see? But it would be noticed when the body was lowered later on. Yes, the mistake had to be made good, and quickly at that, because in the morning the pope would be arriving with his whole entourage.

He rouses his wife and together they make a rummage for the verdigris mascara. They can't find it. Half-naked, the wife runs next door, where one of her woman friends lived. She, a person of 'independent means,' has some — though maybe not of the precise shade of green as the empress'. The neighbor is reluctant to hand it over, finding the affair eerie, even ominous. She pleads to be taken up to the catafalque. A truly dumb wish. The cosmetician has to negotiate with the priests, eunuchs, and soldiers who are keeping vigil. In the end, the supreme keeper of bodies permits the flaw to be corrected. Ladders & ropes are produced — dawn is in the offing, a whiff of sea salt with a tang of seagull feathers is on their lips. A lot of people are mooching about in the street, dozing on folding chairs so as to be well-placed to view the procession 18 hours later. The breaking of a tiny plank or the absent-minded blow of a hammer doing repair work on the tribunes sounds as a rifle shot far away in the unhindered sunrise-silence. The cosmetician makes it up onto the catafalque. Around ten people hold the swinging ladder with ropes, poles, and hands to stop the cosmetician from falling into the forest of candles. Even so a few candles are upset, each knocking over another five or six, like dominoes. A bit like stripping an altar on Good Friday. The hairdresser is just setting out to do his painting when a priest rushes out of the sacristy & bawls up to him, *sotto voce,* that the mascara had not been consecrated. On a string, he lowers a mug belonging to the woman of independent means. It swings like a bob on a plumb line and again knocks three candles over; crowds are jostling at the gate. Apparently the pope's boat, the coat of arms of Ravenna on the sails, can already be seen from the pier head. Is that possible? They are arriving earlier! The cosmetician up on high is saying his prayers, close to fainting. What if he was left up there. Like a stylite on his column. And if he were to jump down among the pope's retinue. He does what every living person has to do in thought with a dead body, because it was impossible not to: he prays to the dead person, then for the dead person, imagines himself being dead, thinks something appallingly obscene in relation to the dead body, and finally runs through in his head the possibility of hell; eventually doubt and animal fear end in a muddled and dull jumble. The eyelashes are green, albeit a very different green, but then the sunshine bursting into the cupola would even things up. The empress was not just a strumpet in her younger days but also an artiste and actress. That will forever remain appealing when erotic attraction is not connected to psychology but to the circus trapeze & theater stage. That is a priceless of the empress', too.

There, around the catafalque, everything is *just* formal: there has never existed a world more content-free, more averse to content; that is why it was so fine. Eros was represented by a deceased actress, whores rigged up as hired wailing women, & eunuchs made out to be 'angels.' But not lyricists! Not sensual, oriental women! ... The netherworld? Ecclesiastical diplomats; canonists; deranged hermits in the desert who recognized no faith or god beyond their own lunacy and pessimism; hooded soldiers and courtesan-nuns. But not believers. And paint in place of beauty, perfume instead of flowers. Church instead of gods, democracy instead of people, philosophy instead of truth, law instead of morality, hierarchy instead of order, 'Byzantium' instead of Byzantium. That is not good out of fun and perverseness but for fairly ordinary practical and fairly high-class intellectual reasons.

A prostitute, a eunuch, a prostitute, a eunuch: that, too, belongs to the Byzantine bedrock of vulgarity. I need to delve into what is behind Tacitus' reticence. What is a eunuch? Some intellectual — a scribe, writer, philosopher, household *raisonneur*, palace sophist. That aspect is unquestionable. After that, 'angel.' Not virgins — angels. Wouldn't it be interesting to write a "*Dialogus Eunuchi ac Virginis*"; I wouldn't mind that, even if it were to be in the manner of Erasmus. Who would come off better — the *moral* virgin or the *biological* one? 'Angels': white robed; not belonging to either monastic or secular orders, they are the sole ones who represent some sort of unification of symbol and reality in Constantinople.

They are equally surrounded by a buzz of erotic gossip and by the incense of religious respect. But they are not just sophists and ambiguous mock angels. They are singers! Or not singers so much as voices. I am familiar with those even today; I know that Palestrina locked himself up for days with a she-capon in the cloister-garth of a monastery in San Gimignano, & fantasized on it as on harp. They were not people but living musical scores: anyone who has not heard them does not know the meaning of music.

Those castrati are the greatest opponents of my instruments. Is it not they who are going to win? Palestrina with his eunuchs and Monteverdi with his sound machines and sound catapults. But thank goodness, the *human, Homo ordinarius* and *medius* and *communalis,* was left out of both. If a few idiotic and soapy hormones are scraped out of us, we shall at one stroke become 'angels' and be purified into sounds, music. Their erotic role is obscure, but insofar as one can guess it, their chief merit consists in unifying fairly contrasting features of Socrates and Phryne, Seneca and Messalina. On the one hand, they were the great connoisseurs of every intellectual margin, of the mental and spiritual onward-vibration of love; on the other hand, the repositories of perversities. For love is only usable in these two forms: as a fermenter of thought, the yeast of hurtling deliberation relating to life, as a drunken rapture of reflection — and as body technology, neuro-mechanics, much the same dexterity as is required for lace-making: a thousand long threads, at the end of each of which is a small bobbin so as to let the threads be twisted more easily and precisely. The eunuch is aware of this: love as an *intellectual* revolution, and love as a coolly calculated counterpoint of *nerves*. They physically represented degrees of castration (there was a whole medical scale in that!), in accordance with greater anatomical precision: all those shades that we, poor epigones and dilettantes, are obliged to substitute with coarse shades of the 'soul.' In short, they were 'psychology' *avant la lettre* and, I believe, will for evermore be the sole possible and, at that time, magnificent form: with their bodies. (It's a good thing, my dear Cambridge friend, that you already know me a little, otherwise I ought to explain, as I have had to so many times before, that I am neither a materialist nor a gourmet.) Eunuchs are situated somewhere on a line between the Narcissists and sodomites: they give new, classical formalism to the uncertainty of sex. Both a man and yet not, love and yet not; slave, scholar, rival, angel; nullity & demon; a provocative secret of life in its entirety, & bad joke, a sadistic punch line in society.

They had to process around Theodora's cadaver — that is indisputable. Theodora's dead body was Europe's, the procession of the eunuchs was an embodiment of the round dance around the cadaver of European thought. Every people plucked something else from the souls and bodies of the castrati: a Gallic peasant responded differently from an Attic young man, a Persian ephebe differently from a Jew. When the concepts of proles and the sacrament were as yet unknown, when marriage was not yet a theologizedhumanized rite, such sexual experimentation took place fairly easily, whereas nowadays we are familiar with little more than sanctity & perversity. That's all how it should be, of course; a good variation on the surely, and forever surely, variable theme of sex. I'm putting that badly: *it's not* a theme, it's the core.

Sex has only one imaginable definition: *variazioni eterne senza tema alcuno.*[46] Why did Roman women in Juvenal's time like those castrati? Why did Cleopatra? What shame that such questions are lost in a quagmire of piquancy, pursued with the stupidest fanaticism to the point of murder, even when raised by meek pedants like me and you (since, oh dear! or Hallelujah! that is irredeemably what we are!). Maybe what was seen in them was *l'art pour l'art* loveliness in the way each such body becomes a pure instrument: previously undreamed-of fair F-sharps and black D-flats, in the same way as they secreted a beauty for its own sake that can never have anything to do with an ordinary sex life. Either-or: either sex or beauty. The two can only unite in idiots, though even they don't know what makes a picture beautiful or, on the other hand, what physical joy is.

Mais laissons les idiots et voyons les nuances:[47] there were eunuchs who under Roman law had nothing to do with the castrati, & the latter in turn had nothing to do with *thlibia,* and those nothing to do with the *kazimazia* — and so on, and so forth ...[48] What instinct is at work with those surgical interventions of such antiquity? Is it to make life more delightful, or to destroy through a cruel inquisition the ludicrous physiological blunder of sex, that most foolish of superfluities? Sex-heresy and sex-finesse, sex-hatred and sex-enhancement: just drift about there, in the basilica, around Theodora's feet.

She was always fond of tight-fitting silk stockings; she is lying in them now too. Skin cancer did not disfigure her legs. Apart from a couple of heretic cliques that she fostered, just about everyone was happy about Theodora's death. The workers painting mile upon mile of black fabric were yodeling and dead drunk in their jubilation. As Rome did, so did Caucasian brigand kings & hordes of Persian pashas.

First & foremost, though, the paid mourners, the wailing women. Offhand, the Roman attendants, secretaries, & soldiers did not know what should be done to gain favor if that were not with extra wailing women. Footmen rushed far & wide around the city, and at great expense gathered together a bunch of girls & *'artistes'* from all the dives, low-class music halls, operetta fleapits, circuses, and Chalcedonian funfairs so that they should weep for the empress on behalf of the Duke of Siena, the margrave of Campovenere, or Baron Lussofiore.

Zealous henchmen scraped those dames off theater stages, or much more compromising and intimate places, and within two minutes had daubed their cheeks and arms with vermilion and mauve; they ripped off their garments, if in performing their 'art' they happened to have anything on, & in place of those promised them ghastly satin two-pieces; that was how, inebriated & filthy, they went to wail for the empress. The better part of those semi-lunatics were unaware that Theodora had died. The 'recruiting' lackeys duly hung round the necks of the brandy-breathed wenches, like a school satchel, a sash with the armorial bearings of Siena, Campovenere, or Lussofiore. Need I send you a sketch of my two choruses? I have it here. The labored lamentation of the drunken mourners, punctuated time and again with guffaws and tavern refrains — and on the opposite side of the stage the chorus of eunuchs, an abstract Palestrina-pastiche, if you wish, or a caricature as you like, the land of my heart's desire.[49]

What did Anthimus do during the funeral — what could he have done? — he the Monophysite heretic[50] kidnapped by Theodora into the most clandestine gardens of the imperial palace, whom everyone thought dead, above whose fake relics mounds of Syrian & deep Chinese, pseudo-Christian crypts had been raised, whose spirit had appeared in Rome, unexpectedly, during the exarch's sweetest dreams, who was unable to write a single letter, but whose Stonehenge volumes of writings filled entire libraries on their own? What did Anthimus do?

For this Anthimus was an absurdly perfect embodiment of every human pipe-dream. What was his 'true' ego, the happier or more logical, the more determined or more bird-chosen: the one that he gave vent to in councils, between political hypocrisy and anonymous fanaticism, sophistry and starless clairvoyance — or the one that lived here, locked in for decades in an intimate *1001 Nights* between solitude and flowers, negligee-crowns and dreams on which you could play as on a keyboard? Is that not my life? Is that not "*Romantik überhaupt*"?[51] Not the most intrinsic life? A duality of active intellectual revelry and paradisiacal sensory solipsism? Those are always the most exciting states of mind — withdrawal after the greatest struggles. The mind is already burdened to the point of madness and to the point of the onset of spring with the pictures and tastes of experience, & now it takes all of that away into a completely self-serving, luxuriously anarchic solitude, letting dream and thought, fermenting salvation & monumental nonchalance make of it what they can.

If only through some mythical stenography or pictography it had been possible to record all the thoughts, pictures, and palpitations of mood that Anthimus thought and felt over the course of 20 to 30 years, locked into Theodora's park! What fiery nuances of irresponsibility and intensified logical responsibility! Council and garden, council and garden: the one dogma, the other a flower. To think through the thought to the very end, to the most 'trans-sophistical' tatter, and sniff through, compose, live the blossoming flowers down to their very last cell.

Don't I, too, want that? How stupid the clanking semi-grammatical, semi-legal antithesis of flower and dogma, life and intellect, dream and morality, must have seemed during thirty years of contemplating the park. Language? How could he ever have stooped to that! How all those little, teensy-weensy 'rational' objections that are supposedly able to compromise the chaos of the soul, the romanticism of nature, and the mysticism of free associations, must have sunk for him out of existence. How much everything *was* there, without argument, name, or object. The ultimate, absolute solitude: only that is worth anything. Every true monumentality is singular, incommunicable, absurdly turned in on itself. A soul, if wise and intensive, steps into an ever newer relation with the world every millisecond: that equilibrium, made up of a million elements, that continuity of composition beyond the poles of nonsense of 'mind' & 'fantasy': that magnificent opus — that alone is what is worthwhile, exciting. But then every element of it is so absolutely subjective, so inexpressibly just-individual and just-momentary, that there is no language refined enough, no mathematics complex enough, or no dream surrealist enough, to come close to it; there are a million elements here, but they are all anonymous & unanalyzable, totally unknown in social life.

Still, they are positive and monumental. Is that an illusion? What if it is? Who cares about such superfluous practical aspects of word formation as 'illusion' or 'disillusion'? Anthimus meditating from the luxury among flowers, empresses, slaves, harlots, & books in Theodora's garden will be a perpetual symbol of that absurd opus, the radicalism of solitude. The sole 'religion': to demand a god and heaven where every wrinkle, the root of every desire and thought of the mind, is visible, where moods exist as imponderables that change with dizzying rapidity as everlasting forms. "*Deificatio hysteriæ*," says the pen, the mouth, the pseudo-socially castrated brain. Let it say that. If they 'say' so, then it is superfluous anyway, for if it were significant in the least, it couldn't be said. The insinuated mysticisms, every romantically written-down mysticism, or if not written down, known as a form of life, is just a vulgar & ultimately disillusioning parody of Anthimus' type of solitude. Seen from the perspective of Anthimus' solitude, extreme rationalism and extreme irrationalism are of absolutely the same standard or lack of standard. Anthimus has nothing to do with mysticism — his essence can only be defined negatively, if indeed that is a definition.

Apropos of mysticism: much as my favorite figure is this Anthimus kidnapped to be among goldfish & Sun-cracker amphoræ, I am just as fond of old Guillaume de Champeaux,[52] who withdrew from the scholastic storms around chairs of learning to the abbey consecrated to St. Victor in Marseilles. He is not as absolute in his retirement as Anthimus, but his gesture is just as moving and enviable, even if it does not enter into an *"antidefinita indefinita"* like Anthimus, but into a more concrete mysticism, not to say prosaic, bourgeois irrationalism.

Beside Anthimus, the circuses of the people's assembly are: imperial laity, a hagio-bushy hetæra, masses, & Greek sophistry — in other words, a wide, crudely orchestrated theater stage, a species of *theatrum mundi*. I see William of Champeaux differently: he has only one counterpart that he leaves there — a young, stubborn, bleeding Abélard, casuistic with ascetic snobbery. Two kinds of divorce from the world:

Anthimus suddenly abducted by the empress; he does not even know what is happening to him, whereas William of Champeaux, by contrast, gradually worms his way out of the world: his old, blasé body falls from the stammerer Abélard like an aged fruit from a young branch.

How could Anthimus have been abducted? At a late night sitting of the council? Torches barely light the circus. Theodora knows that an attack against Anthimus is going to be carried out that evening, so she has an idiot slave of hers disguised as Anthimus — let him be killed. Her own actors and comedians make up the slave in Theodora's bathroom; the real Anthimus sits as a model as if for a statue. The slave at times sniggers, at times whimpers as if water were pouring out from his skin; at times he rips off the disguise and sets to boxing the mirror. Meanwhile Theodora takes a leisurely bath, a paradoxical Susanna as she quietly splashes about. She surrounds herself with light bubbles as if she were planting them, looking now at the real Anthimus, now at the decoy.

The real Anthimus is very haughty: when Theodora (after lengthy, giggly underwater hunting for the soap) asks Anthimus whether he feels any sympathy for the alter ego who was due to be killed that evening, he answers that he didn't, but envied him rather, because it was a great merit & sacred virtue to die for something so theologically unique as he was. While she is scratching monograms with her as yet unmanicured nails in the mauve bar of soap she has found, Theodora asks Anthimus whether, in that case, the candidate for the Carnival cadavership was in point of fact not already a relic, a living, moving, mystical item — *aussi une nouveauté de Byzance mondaine.*

Verily, Anthimus affirms and meanwhile drafts his tirade about the *Ambigua Reliquia*: that the slave was a mythical entity, firstly because he was going to be killed in place of him, Anthimus, and secondly, because people would think he was the body of the real Anthimus — and that belief made an object just as real as if it truly were his body. In her perfume-drenched basin, Theodora does not know as yet what will become of this Anthimus after his mock-death: an exotic gorilla in her grounds with whom the slave girls will cavort after they have annoyed the eunuchs to distraction? A diplomatic trump card that at some dramatic moment she could flourish under Europe's nose? A lover? A domestic god who would compensate for every sin: like scented water with which urinal drains were doused. What if the true one were murdered and not the alter ego — the way it customarily happens in Chalcedonian popular theaters? But then, there was also a variant whereby Theodora could kill two birds with one stone: she would not only save Anthimus but also have the young pope, whom she loathed, disposed of: that is, not a stupid slave disguised as Anthimus for a nocturnal council, but the young pope himself as he arrived for the Council.

The pope resided in a secluded villa by the sea — one afternoon, out of the blue, the empress arrives unannounced. The pope is resting on some kind of lounger, paying scarcely any attention to the secretary beside him who is reading through, explaining, and preparing files for him. Sails crackle from afar like sargassaceæ under the soles of children's feet; overhead birds are chirping, their voices falling on the pope's clothes like dandruff from trees running combs through their May-time hair. As if it were not afternoon, but daybreak; everything is pale blue and white — it is weird to have to think of nocturnal councils and black Monophysite bogeymen at a time like that. For a second the secretary leaves off reading. The twittering of a single bird is heard: as if it were confused, feeling giddy and, in the manner of a falling star, veering with a snicker in a huge disoriented curve into the sea.

Down below, a sedan chair; a woman thin as a wisp of straw descends from it. Even the pope raises his head from the almost horizontally set lounger. He shades his eyes with one hand. A lot of meandering steps had to be climbed to reach up to him across the rock garden. The pope and the secretary exchange glances. That is how it started. The empress arrives, in a light beach ensemble with a fluttering cape and a broad Chinese parasol. The pope is also in a state of undress, in that indefinable papal undress in which his holiness and mission are nevertheless asserted: monastic even in his *déshabillé*.

Women had no effect on the young Roman, of course, not even this 'hagiolatrous' equestrienne. He has a snack with the empress; neither of them touch food of any sort, with the pope clutching his crucifix and watching, the empress twiddling her parasol among the pebbles and chattering. A tasteless scene, can't help it, but that is how I want it to be all the same — a toning down to grey, without literature or art. They talk about the location of Byzantium, about relationships between men and women, about apocalypse and the chances of diplomatic compatibility, about the pope's mother, and about Theodora's grasp of languages. Meanwhile a couple of slaves & soldiers take over the villa. The secretary is by then a captive. They had an easy job: there was barely anyone in the house.

The pope hears nothing; he dishes out compliments loud but inwardly curses that Babylonian parvenu. Garish fruits glare on the small table: mute, accusatory strawberries, splenetic tree leaves, most likely *"in lydischer Tonart."*[53] The empress spots an apple on a nearby tree. She will bring it down for the pope — she, the empress! "What typically Byzantine bragging gestures," the pope thinks. Disgusting. "Your Imperial Highness, I shall call for a servant to pluck it." "God forbid!" the empress says with somewhat overdone fervor. "I myself shall pluck that apple for Your Holiness. *Je me pique.*"[54]

Of course, it is child's play for her to clamber into the tree; she had been an acrobat, a dressage horsewoman & trapeze tart; the operation was all the simpler with the beachwear being so loose fitting. The Roman casts a slightly anxious look around; there is something doltish in this worldly idyll. He distractedly scoops into a bundle the manuscripts lying beside him; he wants to say something serious. Should he be worldly or pedantic? "The issue of hypostasis therefore...," he commences the cut-and-dry sentence, forcing a French-salon smirk. It won't do. "Be careful! You'll fall!..." he starts a jesting remark with the austerity of a John the Baptist. That wouldn't work either; don't force anything, leave it. By then Theodora is among the boughs and from there laughs back: "Adam & Eve: *reprise à Byzance*. I hope you will accept the apple from me?" Embarrassed, the Roman mutters something. Rome is a different city. It was madness to exchange even so much as a chopped phrase with Byzantium.

The empress is swinging before his nose, but he sees nothing other than a huge black flotilla; pitch-black as soot with blood red, vermilion, and carmine sails that attack Byzantium and... *ceterum censeo esse delendam.*[55] Ridiculous! Council? Scholarly debates? In the place where she is empress? The mystery is, how the world could come to this? What then are a heretic's ribs worth here? Ascetics, monastics? An English lord's pack of retrievers is more pious. By now Theodora completely disappeared in the foliage. Was she, too, a woman? The pope meekly prays his Angelus, though it is not as if he needed to fight temptation. Not a bit. The very idea is laughable. Theodora is not a sin, and his Angelus is no virtue either. Theodora is simply a bluff. Colorless humbug around the body, with not the faintest thing to do with piquancy. In contrast, the pope's prayer is sobriety, mild moderation, humming, at the moment tuneless and topicless intelligence.

With a single bound Theodora is back on the ground; she falls, ripping foliage and branches, like an unexpectedly wrenched-off swing or a bird's nest overburdened with gigantic eggs — "*Voilà!*" she says and hands the apple to the pope, disheveled and flushed. The pope is barely able to conceal his nervousness; he intones almost aloud the anathematizing Latin words that were to be sewn with taboo letters and in six-feet high strokes on the topsail of the first warship (black? white? yellow?) against Theodora and the entire Eastern Roman madhouse: "*Dementiam pictorialem ac syphilitica umbra Parisi proto-rubeam accidens mihi carismaliter promisit ...*"[56] (are Byzantine wines so strong? He has only taken a few sips, purely out of formality, with the meal). Nevertheless, he smiles clumsily, and, precisely because he very much wishes to avoid any evidence of greed, bites too amiably into the apple.

Theodora watches: amid the foliage, she has injected with a syringe a strong sedative into the apple. The stuff of a cheap thriller? *Fiat.* The pope has to fall asleep, so that he can be carried away and disguised as Anthimus, to have him murdered by the pro-papacy party's hit men instead of the real Anthimus. These voluntary hit men are counting on the pope later rewarding them for killing the leader of the Monophysites. They know exactly what to ask from His Holiness: a dog farm in Ravenna; the Duchess of Urbino's hand in marriage; a shapely sum of investment capital in a Sicilian bank.

Theodora smiles: now they will murder the pope himself. By then he is asleep — the sleep of Adam. Meanwhile Anthimus was already packing somewhere to make his escape, giving instructions to the slaves as to what needs to be added to the one trunk and what is missing from the other. A fine picture, my friend: an ascetic, young pope asleep in the garden on a height overlooking Byzantium. To his right the booming, wire-taut evenness of the Sea of Marmara with its sharp blueness reminiscent of freshly torn paper; to the left, the twittering of a single bird: its voice flits about here and there among the leaves like a top between the lengths of cord stretched between the sticks of two players in a game of *diabolo*.

Oh, darling face, persecuted faith-Adonis, sleep until a beastlier death overcomes you: let the sinful sacrificial host on the plate of the sea disclose to you the battle won by dogma, let the vagrant throat of the songbirds cover up the idiotic intrigue of murderous girls. I wonder if anyone caterpillar-peeping at the corolla of your dream could see who you really are: Orphean larva? Would he suspect from your peaceful profile that you lived from Christ for Christ's flock, that in vain did the hetæra scatter her cheapskate tricks in your eyes, you opened the gates of your dream with an Angelus? Would that ignorant wanderer, cheered to fairness by your fairness, believe you to be an ephebe who, paid off with the myth-coins of two birds & a pair of women, is now resting after the affairs of the body? Or would he believe that you are the new Adam, and that the world had spun round, and here was the most antique age of antiquity — seeing Adam, the heavy relic of sin? Yet how useless the cracked hypothesis: by your ready-to-die body every god, from however provocative and advantage-filled heavens, is bashful — and history also keeps mum with closed lips, because in the face of dreams history is forever nothing; intruding love keeps mum with its blind navel flower: the body's grave-anchoring solitude commands silence here, too. Whither are you going, dream's Western cargo, pope of Rome? Will your Christ, from whose Jewish trope you are grown, wait for you on the other side — or will your limbs, numbed out of a hideous irony of fate, knock even there into botched-up statues of Hermes and Apollo? Perhaps there will never be a miracle, and there is only gymnast Theodora offering an apple for your unhungry lips — maybe not even that, but dumb oars of eternal Naught hurling you into a grey damnation? ... That is the pope sleeping under the empress' washy grease-paint and disguises, in point of fact the death of the West in the arms of the East: the symbolic death of Latin intensity and pureness in the embrace of Eastern romanticism and chaos. Instead of pope, I could have said Paris; instead of empress, Istanbul.

... That is why I am unable to tear myself away from the figure of Guillaume de Champeaux withdrawing into 'hermitism' — there everything is Frenchly pure, even though by that purity one is not, of course, to understand an inane boot-tree talking about the "crystalline *raison*" of the Latin peoples. Just think of the cityscape of Paris, and it will immediately become clear to you that Latin clarity is a very complex clarity and far from reducible to the transparent structure of an Ovidian sentence.

But it certainly lacks the culture organism of Byzantium. Guillaume was a "Parisian theologian," I read in a dull biographical synopsis. And when I read those two words, "Parisian" and "theologian," I felt an urge to proceed with them as the students of the retiring Guillaume did with the words of the Holy Scripture: they came to a halt at every conjunction, page-, or sentence-filling attributive (although attributives are paradoxical goods: if there are a lot of them, then we are truly impoverished), and they analyzed them symbolically, or at least with that enforced huge background (the two converge).

Typically, that symbolic exegesis started first in Alexandria: all over-scrupulous philology goes over, unnoticed, into that kind of mythology — the triumph of positivism in hermeneutics (hermeneutics?): even typos and printing errors become gods, physically, with idol-like concreteness. Pathological over-precision in the interpretation of words leads to the reeling off of a thousand shades of meaning, each bringing with itself the scent of a different historical age, the geographical atmosphere of another people; that is how mystical Bible exegesis is born (when genuinely religious temperaments are involved), or (if it is only hypocritically or pusillanimously religious temperaments), the history of ideas. In that kind of thing, naturally, the attractive and repulsive forces are completely uniform — Bible and literary interpretations of that sort will forever look like inflated humbug, but at the same time, they will forever remain the sole exciting and worthwhile intellectual nurture. "Parisian theologian."

Paris: whether at this point I am forcing a total Paris picture or whether it intrudes naturally into my consciousness is something a thinker can never decide, because for him spontaneous and forced are unequivocal, ultimately convergent things. The main point is that it is a great pleasure to evaluate every attributive independently for a while, irrespective of the noun it qualifies, even to the point of absolute contradiction with the noun — and just when it has inflated to the fullness of refuting the noun: then, and precisely then, to release from it the lethal adverb-gas and deflate it back into god-fearing civil marriage with the noun, with which noun it is incidentally possible to go through the same game. Paris: at the moment it knows nothing about theology & theologians; it is just the city, an "*énorme grisaille*," as someone once said. There is something alarmingly schematic and cheap in contradiction-mongering; but then perhaps it is always necessary, *de natura*, to have something primitively semantic and thus vulgar, cheap in thinking (if it can be called that).

I preface my remarks with this small note for internal use because I can enjoy Paris only with such contrasts. For instance, grey and colorful. Grey: its sky, too, is grey, its stones, whether the stones of burgher dwellings, or divine Gothic stones, are grey. The perspective of long streets is lost in greyness; so is the shared texture of the tiny, sparse leaves & thin but dense branches of a tree; the multitude of people bustling on the streets and squares — in the city there is something porously antique, dust-covered, ascetic and monotonous: desiccated, sadistically calculating. But all the same, mottled: nowhere else is there so much shading, so much stone & map 'psychology' within the grey as there: so many surprises, aphoristic sparks, so much eternal restlessness, nervous shivering and electric drama pervading every bay-window lock & gatepost; nowhere else is there so much mundane hoarding, crazy vaudeville, and red miniatures.

Byzantium does not even dream about such refined, Western paradoxes. "Parisian theologian": but Paris strives to stamp out the theologian — if an attributive has any content (and what sort of content 'Paris' is we both know full well) it cannot be, in point of fact, an attributive. Paris is big and small. It gives an equal impression both of a Latin peasant family's farmstead, and of the world's almost boundless Babylon. Nowhere else are those two experiences so excitingly intertwined as on a boulevard stroll: the houses are Latin 'tower-huts,' I can't define them better than that — *naïve* elements, *naïve* windows, *naïve* roofs: if a child had to come upon those on his own, that is how he would mold them. Windows and doors: 'apertures' and nothing more; house roofs: 'covers,' nothing more. Thereby they convey an impression of the infinitely abstract (grey!) since, after all, they are barely-realized concepts; but for the same reason they are unclassifiably sensual, for they are identical, to the point of excluding any non-essentials, with the core-human, indeed well-nigh animal, vegetative activities of 'opening,' 'entering,' and 'covering.'

This duality of abstraction and sensuality is one of those Latin, and primarily French, features, on account of which, as I have already mentioned in passing, phrases like "crystal-clear *raison*" should be accepted only with the greatest reservation. In any case, that duality (village vs. world) is present in a single Latin house that characterizes Paris: the house is rickety, a blood relation to the antediluvian wicker baskets for animals, but at the same time it is slender and tall like a blade of grass or bamboo shoot. All élan, Gothic to out-trump Gothic, "slim fairies grown more slim in endless mirrors of lakes and all these glassy realms of heaven ...,"[57] as a compatriot of yours writes somewhere. That Latin counterpart between material breed and abstract angelic verticality is unknown in Byzantium. Paris' ambiguous monumentality crops up somewhere around this topic. Apropos of verticality: there is no other place in the world that is more able to make such a refined use of flatness, horizontalness, the gravitational secret of sea level than Paris. Steppes, oceans, ice fields, deserts, grey November skies — those are all relatives of Parisian streets. They almost grow giddy, stagger at their own flatness and perspective-opiates. All that, of course, while no enormous dimensions are seen. No one knows whether Paris is a small town or a big city — if it grew through accretion or was born out of a theatrically uniform "*grande vue*"?

Classicism is very much a Janus-faced matter: Paris is formulaic, theatrically griddish and engineered, but at the same time also a Venice — in Paris inscrutable games of perspective substitute for the waves of the lagoons. *That* is where my Guillaume is a theologian, even though Paris is so acutely Paris-like that it cannot hold a single speck of dust that is not Paris.

He is tired of the university, as well he might be, for who were the people around him? In my library I have the books of all his fellow professors; a dark line on the wall, I could say. Guillaume fetched up in the redeeming climes of hermitism from a blind booth of intellectual marionettes; Anthimus from the circus ring and bitch-politicking. A huge difference. The outcome was also different: with Anthimus the indefinable solitude ('Pan' and 'nothingness' will feature in massive doses, if one is to give it a name), whereas with Guillaume (I say this with the greatest sympathy) it is from bureaucratized mysticism and a concrete way of life that Hugo from Germany, the Scot Richard & the Frenchman Adam, formed their own St. Victor character.[58]

Among intellectual techniques antithesis-mongering is about as inelegant as cataloguing is ponderous. Yet what else is my life? Always a burning *antagonism* between two poles — a perpetual mirroring of every single object, phenomenon, & moment: a self-consuming *inventory*. One pole, if I wished, could be Augustinian demonism, a Catholic tragedy of ultimate principles; the other, if I had the necessary arrogance, would be the first true and fully responsible realism:

the first concrete synthesis of religious pantheism, analytic art, and total science. But I am neither Augustine nor a realist. I am a coward: the very personification of absolute poltroonery. Thinking in terms of opposites only serves to protect myself, well in advance, from intellectual attacks from both right and left, from below and above; I anticipate all objections. Likewise, a catalogue is only good for this — a childish tactical trick vis-à-vis a vindictive outer world and death; I must at all times keep everything in sight as a cowardly king does every last soldier, or Harpagon every coin of his money, otherwise they feel they could be attacked from the rear or robbed.

After this eye-pleasing confession, let us look at my volumes: the figures around Guillaume. You, too, are lonely, so am I; we are all interested in those last seashore stakes that tie a ship to the world for the last time before it sets out on a voyage into solitude.

The first item in the catalogue: Eccartus of Alexandria. A southern figure, Saharan, with Arabic colors; a combative, sadistically inclined small Saracen, more suited to one of Frederick II's Antichrist academies in Sicily than to theology in Paris. A short, paunchy man.

Guillaume made his acquaintance when he still had fairish-sandy ashen hair straggling around on his head, but by the time that he had the final quarrel with him he was bald as a slippery bone knob. He had an elongated, parodically pagoda-like head, with a hairless brow of Tibetan or Gobi bleakness. He had very thin skin that moved independently of muscles and bones; his barely noticeable thin, feminine lips also fluttered and wriggled in his face like a diminutive pennant at the end of a tall spear in the wind. They were snappish, pedantically sensuous, lynx-like positivist lips. For him god, virtue, history, prayer, philosophy, and roughly all the rest of the things in the world boiled down to textual exegesis. As if that Arabian, Bedouin carnage and Mohammedan fanaticism smoldering in his autumnal red leaf-like body (fire and puritanism out of an *Arabia deserta*), had crossed over into such vengeance-philology.

Learning for him was nothing but insatiable *ressentiment*: 'truth,' a permanent compulsion to kill; 'precision,' a sanguineous vivisection. An elemental pessimism was at work in him, a loathing of every hypothesis & metaphor — he found the human brain so ludicrously crippled that he considered it suitable only for the most extremely limited tasks. He was manifestly exasperated by the brain's sickliness, & whenever he irritated himself into such vicious, brigandish positivism, he did that out of spite, against a fate that had spooned out such an incompetent dollop of mush into our tiny skulls. But it could be that he was not guided by such considerations and I am unduly dignifying him — perhaps he was just hidebound without any gesture of disillusionment.

He had a malicious look: if he regarded a person that must have given one a sense like someone playing overbrusque *marcatos* or crude *fortes* on an instrument — his eyes bored into one awkwardly. There was not a hint of affection, of social grace, of the aloof and yet broad fire of solitude in them — they were alarmed eyes, self-consciously challenging out of cowardice, for fear of being found out. They flickered to & fro without radiating an honest neurasthenia or a childish liveliness of observational power: low-protein, insubstantial balls of ball-and-socket joints. His nose was the nose of a cadaver: in its form there was that intolerable (*par excellence* non-aristocratic) slurring of the r's, which the elderly Guillaume de Champeaux recollected with gentle humor in a letter that he wrote to Hugues de St. Victor. That nose was crooked, paper-thin, polypous, with a deeply pendulous tip — the kind of nose that Bellini painted in his portrait of Sultan Mehmed II.[59] It is no accident that it was he who at a funeral explained to Guillaume how splendidly Villon describes the nose on corpses: "*... le nez couchchchché*" — he stuttered into the mortuary's afternoon prandial pause. Guillaume's relation with him was murky like that of closet homosexuals: although Guillaume was anything but an Eccartus-character, he nevertheless liked best to show him his works in progress. That was partly out of a self-tormenting penchant, because he liked to see his dreams trampled on (that was his training in objectivity, which he was to recommend later on), and partly because in some peculiar manner Eccartus Alexandrinus was nevertheless drawn to 'freer' writers; as if he had a mystical substitute ego with which he liked people of the opposite type to himself.

He had, for instance, a verse translation that he had rendered from Turkish. Besides, Eccartus always kept immersing himself in politics, & in Guillaume's eyes those political excitements, the ephemeral polemics somehow (God knows how) æstheticized, slightly modernized, the scholar: on the channels of frivolity, poetic 'flightiness' could also sail in. There were times when Eccartus put Guillaume on the rack, and times when he rewarded him for trivialities. I think I have made that theologian, the first item in my catalogue, fairly appealing in your eyes — you will probably beg me for his works.

If that figure points to Gothic monkeys and buffoons on church towers, then the other one, likewise a version of positivism, is reminiscent of Romanesque bear cubs, dumpling lions, and dough-shaped Cerberuses. Joannes de Illyria.[60] Eccartus is an urban, decadent, southern Spaniard — in Joannes there is something of the perennial peasant: squat, slow, lazily malevolent, tenacious, elaborately ritual, morosely conservative. For all that, much more complex than the Alexandrian. In point of fact, a constant battle of two opposing mentalities is raging inside him: one is down-to-earth common sense and overwhelming simplicity, the other, the eternal mysticism of Teutonic thinking, its hocus-pocus of words and perspective, the obsession with a "*Versuch einer Mythologie*." In his theology he attempted a fusion of the most dismal philology and the most romantic history of ideas — in no one was that struggle more sublime.

Here the 'positive,' the bit of data, was not the occasional "*piqûre de vengeance*" in some antagonist, as it was with Alexandrinus, but a requirement of peasant shackles to the soil, of tortoise sluggishness — yet like a wily, materialist serf who is forced to scheme stratagems, he always observed currents that were alien to him and subsumed those with hard slavish tenacity as well. That was not very difficult because, as we know, a peasant has just as plentiful reservoirs of neurosis, hysteria, and all kinds of sensitivity as any citified bag of nerves.

This Joannes, wavering between the land-tilling, northern French 'Calvinist' peasant *&* German *'Geistes-Morphologie,'* was an uncommonly interesting version of the 'analytical brain.' As if it were just as feasible to reach the subtlest elements of philological shades of meaning with a technique of limited legal and economic calculations as it was with poetic ease or urban intellectual nervousness. Maybe he was the sole person at the University of Paris in whose books there was something we could call *style*. He gave definitions a new sensuality, finding appropriate words by deliberate archaism. To define! — that was Joannes de Illyria's passion, and his definitions do not resemble any intellectual pursuit to which that name has been hitherto attached. His ultimately grotesque sentences are masterpieces of abiding peasant punctiliousness and an insatiable German hunger for plasticity. No one could write a portrait of the styles of various prophets in the way he did in *Elucidationes Prophetarum*.

He showed particular genius in adding color, exoticism, and precision to his style, by mixing in cut-and-dry official, legal, and obsolete commercial expressions: thus he spake about literary *molds, herited* traditions, *negotiation, propriety* (for property), *injunctioning, inflationary* spirits, *admixture of additives, desiderates, formulaic stipulations, stock* of material, *exercise* of one's art, *prolongation, apologues,* the *inhibitory* and the *prohibitory, assuagement, conjunctive* forces, *demeanor, tenancy, lyricity, confinement, idiosyncrasy, cathectic.* Plucked out like this, one can barely sense the "distinctive savor" (that, too, is a Joannes figuration) of these words — you will have to read the *Elucidationes.*

Peasant common sense, peasant word magic; German word-elasticism; antiquarianness resulting from a gourmandizing of nuances; antiquarianness resulting from a defiant conservatism; gentlemanly eccentricity or English 'hobby-horsicalness'; mandarin bureaucracy; positivist nostalgia for mathematical formulæ; an anti-romanticism of tragic resignation; an unexpected, hysterical slide into inorganically picked modernity, fashion — & on top of those, who knows how many other elements make up that style. His favorite term was "anywise": on the lips of the Mecklenburg lump that sensitive "*je ne sais quoi*" had an altogether acerbic charm. He was fond of quotation marks: that, too, was a sign of segregating individualization, of the mania in which he burned up. Imagine these two lunacies: the meaning of the portrait absurdities & the "impelment" (this word of mine, too, derives from Joannes), of the absurdity of synthesis.

His favorite intellectual maneuver was a highly precise determination of the imprecision of imprecise entities: from fragments, textual scraps, the driftwood of thoughts he did not create random wallpaper but drew up a precise inventory & thereby brought the matter to a close: he did not restore or combine the ruins, merely segregate them with geometrically severe fencing, as when one sets various Art Nouveauish scraps of prehistoric carpeting onto regular panels of snow-white cardboard. He evinced a certain affinity for a simple form of paradox whereby attributive & noun were in opposition: melancholic blitheness, romantic sobriety, oral tradition bearing bookish marks, pessimistic peace of mind, etc. Those he delivered with shiny-eyed gusto to his students, and one did not notice that they were perhaps too embryonic to be 'nuances' — such near-Celtic-flamed fervor of definition did they flourish before the seminarists' pallid-pensive brows. Besides, with his gesticulations (a surviving contemporary biography recalls them in a separate chapter) he gave a thousand tiny refractions, fine convolutions, and suppleness to what, in spoken words, may have seemed very rudimentary. You can imagine what an ambiguous situation his students were in when it came to tutorial debates: none of the more profound thinkers knew whether to categorize him among the ultra-conservatives or the anarchists. As I said, that only caused difficulty to the more profound thinkers; the more superficial ones, without a second's hesitation, classified him among the narrow-minded archaists.

But Guillaume (who at one period of his life was mad keen on him and until his death carried the marks of his style) knew that, whatever the mummy-like backwardness of his apologies, in his extraordinary polyphonic style a greater anarchy inhered than in a thousand revolutionary leaflets.

The source of the anarchy was conspicuous: the constant defining, ultra-individualization, the underlining of the particularities of the particular. He was a superb analyst of genres. The result? The profiles of genres got blurred: that history was a "lyrical gnome," that dogmatism a "historical elegy," certain prophesies "dramatized catechism," certain prayers "sophistic confessions," and so on — the contour-mongering madness resulted in countourlessness. But perhaps only his students saw it so acutely.

One of his students summed up his entire life very interestingly in a funeral oration that was probably never delivered. A good deal later, some time in the 15th century, someone appended to the codex the title *De Joanne Gallico, tragico et maniaco*. Truly, it was those three majestic attributes that made him unique among the professors of the University of Paris. Gallico: he did indeed practice French theology (for all his winks at clumsy German *Geist*), and in his whole personality he anticipated, however droll it may sound, the maid of Orléans. What that peasant girl did with Charles VII, Joannes de Illyria did with theology. Jeanne d'Arc was also half-peasant, half nerve-ornament, and Joannes was no different. The person of Charles VII is the embodiment of mythical aristocratism, fantastic heraldry, inexplicable madness, an imperial chimera foreign to the French land, illness, individuality, nihilist dream. The peasant girl wishes to pull down to the ground the show-off lily of Acheron — into the nation, into the seemingly ephemeral, into unmythical, blind

Rheims. For a few moments she even succeeds: decadence cavorting in unfamiliar heavens breaks its neck into peasant patriotism.

The tragicomedy of the scene will forever excite Europeans: the king, a hundred times more Gothic than the cathedral, like a Breugelian scarecrow or Don Quixote in a slimming mirror, with elongated embroidered flowers, a scepter more slender than a conductor's baton, goatee-shaped chin, and blue blobs of aspic accidentally stuck on his face which, for simplicity's sake, were taken to be eyes by contemporaries. Well, then: theology in Paris was exactly like that before Joannes leaped in and stamped on it the *amère* crown of France with his boorish tyranny. A somber, puritanical, Calvin-flavored rationalism of that kind had seldom occurred in the history of erudition — that was one of the forms of asceticism.

This leads to the other feature, the tragic. Joannes was always alone, rendered so by his childish narrow-mindedness and restless universality. One could not say if his poseless hermitism was the defiant opposite of the 12th-century Paris bustling around him, or on the contrary, its symbolic crystallization? A contradiction: after all, Paris was mundane, hysterical, and fragrant to the point of martyrdom. An embodiment: after all, Paris was dry, cruel, self-seeking and closed. Joannes was a marvelous sight, passing through Paris, in processions, at toasts and in dispute among the foreign professors. His other companions either pilfered with shameless greed, in its raw state so to say, everything that jabbering young Italians, baroque Byzantine fops, or wild-eyed Spaniards drugged-up on morphine brought to Paris from their own universities — or they understood not a single word of what was said, so scratched themselves and passed scathing remarks. Joannes kept quiet, weighed up the possibilities in his mind, sensing the charlatanism of southern & Oriental thinkers together with their sickening idealism and thirst for truth, but he never made friends with them.

These guest professors used to go home saying things like "De Illyria is boring, a reactionary ex-cathedra bear." That was his tragedy. And maybe if one looks through his works (so the caput of the funeral oration mentioned above), when it comes to it, they are much more fantastic things than Spanish or Byzantine romantic theologians. The work of that self-tormenting Puritan (what a grubby tower cell he lived in at the university!) was: precious, baroque, góngoristic. He has compositions that for a while passed for works of Arabian, Syrian, & Egyptian authors — in much the same way as it would have been, had it been believed that Jeanne d'Arc wrote *Rule Britannia*.

The interesting thing is that he passed on something of this tragedy to a student of his, Guillaume de Champeaux, and albeit Guillaume lived under Joannes' influence in his whole style, until this dying day, Joannes never noticed; indeed, if his former student ever came to mind, he dismissed him as a poseur and heretic. Perhaps justly, since however decisive an influence de Illyria exercised on Guillaume, the student would have suffocated sooner or later if he had been forced to line in the professor's seminary. In life, though, things are ordered in such a way that one clings with a much deeper, self-contradictory, truly undiminished fidelity to those men whom, after profound tussles of conscience and intellect, one feels bound to quit in order to fatefully tread one's own paths, than to those with whom one allies with natural facility, at a shared level of cozy agreement.

(II) BRUNELLESCHI

Young Monteverdi's interest in Brunelleschi is linked to a stroll in Venice. His father once went near the Chiesa di San Moisè to visit a patient, and left little Claudio in the square in front of the churc — he would come back for him in half an hour.

Claudio could not have enough of the beauty of the façade; he had once heard something about it to the effect that it was "crowded" and accumulated senseless Spanishness, but he could see that those words, when all was said and done, had no meaning there. True, the neighboring house had flat walls, and the church was full of flourishing protuberances, but those were rather for touching, and the rendering of a bunch of baroque thingamajigs with the word "crowded" was valid more for the blind who worked only with their fingers (it may even have originated from them) — the eye could hardly believe any of it. Claudio raced to the right in order to inspect it from there; then up onto the bridge, down the steps to the lagoon; he could not have enough of the perspective games; he even darted over into the next street so as not to see it and that way perhaps enjoy it more. He lost his way when hiding in one such side street and all of a sudden found himself in front of San Salvatore.[61] The main gate was open; a breeze was blowing the red curtain into big bulges; little Claudio could squeeze through without having to pull the seemingly hundredweight of drapery to one side with his tiny hands. He was just able to reach the font of holy water, but his fingertips could barely touch the water because when he traced the cross on his forehead, all he could feel was his own familiar warmth, no whiff of the water's musty cellar odor hit his nose. He slowly crept inwards, and after the initial customary church murkiness & tomb mustiness (*divinissimo gloriose imperatorium illustrissima optimo maxime celeberrima unica div. reg. sien. venet.* MMCCCCXXXXIIII.), he landed in a strange enchantment of lightness: in a yellowish-grey and alchemical atmosphere coming from very high and from afar. He looked up. An oval cupola of unknown shape circled above his head with the speed of a swelling soap bubble.

In the egg shape there was a perpetual carbuncle composed of some mystic, wild yeast; he fancied he could see vases going round between the knees of potters. Their color was also alluring; a sick butter-yellow & candle-tallow grey; without any fresco, sketch, or internal division — only the lower edge was drawn with a dark greyish-green shading into quite black.

Three cupolas came like that, one after the other, & when little Claudio, his eyes twisted up above the crown of his head, tarried beneath them, he felt the same magnetic upwards giddiness that a person feels in looking downwards from endless towers: there was something nauseating in the twisting of the cupolas, in the color of withered grapes, the relentless alternation of black and white bands, the floating obscenity and unctuous nude-likeness. What was that? Was that simplicity? Puritanical form? Pure structure annihilating everything Gothic and baroque? Was that (he added fearfully, as if he were uttering the name of the Antichrist in a spirit-summoning séance), was it — Florence? He immediately sensed the discomfort that he had felt in front of San Moisè. In the way that the 'Spanish madness' had shrunk there into mignon, jewel-like, medallion-idyllic harmony (like a flower which, by virtue of the cleanness of the weather and the magic prismatism of the dew, appears to have a million components, although it remains just a naïve dot in a meadow, its thousand pollen- and vein-reliefs notwithstanding), here the opposite happened: these candle-colored, revolving ovals in pursuit of one another, the naked and distant cupolas, the black pillars supporting them and the movements of arcades more arrogant than the face of Colleoni,[62] were not brought into harmony, a transparent mood of arithmetical crystallinity, but into the realm of violence, a Byzantine ascetic's pose, dark Syrian sadism, and eternally reverberating cabalistic diagrams.

That is what Florence would be — he stammered to himself with superstitious certainty, feeling the muddle of animal longing and frantic fear that a child feels in front of the first woman he desires. He knew nothing of Florence, only the name Brunelleschi, about whom his father had spoken more than a few times.

At that time he did not as yet suspect that something other than Venice could be so heart-stoppingly, stomach-churningly different. He staggered out one more time, his head swirling, under the three cupolas: there was something wonderful in the fact that those three globular forms followed one *after* the other, in a straight line, above the squared base of the floor, and they did not intertwine into a grapey, Byzantine-Slavonic cluster of circles like the three Graces on their every statue: they were not carried along in a collective circulation by that profusion of curves, embraces, & hint of rings that emanates from such a cupola like a gentle but constant eddy: they revolved separately, self-seekingly, in cold isolation, the snail dynamics of their independence cooled and enhanced by the consecutive soberness of the straight line. How nice the three degrees of glimpsing them while passing underneath: first of all the lower, drawn outline with its huge dash, its vaulted freedom, its mirror-spaciousness reminiscent of lakes in a park — then a step further on already, the wall of the cupola leaning inwards and running round and round, as if one's eyeball were the lost stone of a catapult speedily swung into action, and due to the rotation I were to become flattened into the form of a pebble; then finally, when one has ended up right beneath it, one glimpsed the pinnacle of the cupola, a tiny geometrical bud where the outside light spatters in. At that point Claudio saw *nothing* of the neighboring cupola any longer, and he had to move on for everything to start all over again. He had never felt that in the Byzantium of San Marco's: there the globular spaces of the cupolas streamed into the lower regions of the church to such an extent that he had occasionally had the impression that beneath his feet was not a floor, but hemispheres inverted to the vaulted cupolas like glasses, as if the upper ones were being mirrored in dark water.

Here though the church was strictly double-storied: for a start, the world of columns and semicircular arches, and above them, quite unexpectedly, alien, like a marvel without any forewarning, the abstract-magical world of cupolas almost not made of stone, nor even belonging to God. San Marco was a single big dark gold bough, an antediluvian fern with not a stem or flower or root anywhere, only tautological vegetation; here the column part was a trunk, the cupola an *exotic* flower, an incomprehensible transparent marvel on the black body of the trunk. Naïve Claudio sensed in it something that was almost mockery, cynicism, heresy.

Hardly had he met up with his father than he immediately began pumping him about Brunelleschi; at first he thought he had also made the cupolas of San Salvatore; he asked for woodcuts, gossip, everything. His father promised that that very evening they would take a stroll over toward the Jewish quarter, and then he could point out one or two things in connection with Brunelleschi. Claudio settled down in his room with an even greater chaos in his head than before.

What could Florence (because for Monteverdi, as we have already said, Florence was both a proper name and the name of Brunelleschi's city) have to do with the Jewish quarter in Venice? He sought out woodcuts of Florence in his own books but found none. But time passed quickly: before he had even put his books back on the shelf his father called in.

... Brunelleschi spent his childhood in the house of three aging women; his parents neglected him. The architect, reticent to the point of gloominess, always referred to them as the "three Parcæ." The young child did not make the acquaintance of adult men or girls; only the three crones. He actually made polychrome statues of them; virtually no one knows about those, they are in the possession of a wealthy but totally reclusive Venetian Jew; Claudio's father only knew about them because the old fossil was once a patient of his. He was now taking little Claudio there, so he could see the group of statues for himself. Claudio could scarcely contain his excitement — he would never have imagined that the "Renaissance" would irrupt into his life in this way: magically revolving cupolas, a secret treasure of the Jewish quarter, & old dames.

The first of the Graces was the embodiment of puritanism; young Brunelleschi lived like in a Carthusian monastery. One knows this and that about the families of such wealthy traders, at whose home every column is marble, every spoon pure gold, and the lady of the house does not sleep in anything but Belgian lace schmattahs, whereas the way of life, timetable, recreations, and relaxations pass by with such dreary mechanicalness from one day to the next that one feels one is constantly at a funeral. There was never a smile, never a superfluous word, nothing but measured paces — everything was just a number and a business profit turned into an abstraction. That is how he got to know the cold demon of money, the involuntary fakirism of bank materialism within the pomp: the lady of the house was always calculating — never greedily like an avaricious second-hand dealer's wife about the bridges, nor even calmly like a feudal count doing his totting up with nonchalance, but with a cold unemotional obsession the way only women can, and even then most likely when the possibility of love has deserted them with a twilight flutter of wings.

How many times did young Brunelleschi creep into the black bank boudoir of the first Parca in order to examine the invoices, bills of exchange, and letters of credit: he understood not a word about them, of course, but he did know that those numbers were sources of life and death: due to those numbers the palace was so Veronesean-illustrious, and owing to those very same numbers every female in the rooms, every single one, was world-weary, dead and menopausal. In that way, already in his childhood, Brunelleschi became 'materialistic': to his dying day he was afraid of money, got goose bumps if he had to walk in front of a bank because he knew that the life-consuming prime mover of life was there. Naturally, he himself was never able to handle money; he was poor and had no business sense, but he inquired continually about prices, currencies, and credits as his most feared enemies, who had filled his superstitious, cowardly imagination once and for all time.

Later, as he began to reach puberty, the banker woman got bored of the boy, in whom to her deepest disgust (which of course was not betrayed by so much as a twitch of the face) she deemed to discern artistic inclinations, and tossed him to his sister. By then Brunelleschi was already a morose, lonely adolescent with a phobia for money, who had been unacquainted with freedom or play in his life, and had learned from the ladies to despise men, the majority of whom slid into the filthy world of heroism, politics, and dreams without having grown to love the ideal of the fortune-minding woman. For a while his artistic disposition, keen on carving and painting, rebelled against the ladies' puritanism, but he soon perceived that they were so absolutely the stronger that willy-nilly he, too, started to turn up his nose at, and, prematurely blasé, to disdain and deride art.

It was an excruciating, ambiguous youth, and if, on a very rare occasion, quite by accident, he found himself among painters, he looked down his nose at their blazing imaginations from the background of bank branches, and, being a stranger to them, walked out on these unfruitful individuals with their "naïve dreams" (it wasn't money but, as I said, the *number* that had power); if he pined away in the female tabernacles of interest rates he felt he was, nevertheless, the child of the brush and burin as he remained forever a nonentity in business. The mistress of that house was the first of the Parcæ in the sculptural group in the Jew's possession.

Deathly pale; down-turned lips; violet eyes in big, black troughs; disheveled, black clothes; spreading Buddha belly. The symbol of the sick trader, who in desperation, out of unbounded cowardice & hypochondria, counted from dawn to dusk: her menopause-tortured eyes may have glowed with some distant benevolence, but it had long been driven out by loneliness and fear originating in living without male company. Young Claudio was gripped by the uncertain rapture of feeling adult when he saw that it was possible to seek in the rigor of Florentine arcades and cupolas not only symmetries fallen from heaven, but also invoice-melancholy old dames: in the vaulting of San Salvatore there was maybe more of a banker woman's suppressed hypochondria than any Greek philosophy of art. The wrench into humanity was splendid child's play, and Monteverdi, make no mistake, played with it until his death, not troubling much to make a secret of it.

But who, I wonder, just who, was the second lady (the Second Muse of the Renaissance as he now formulated it to himself in childish hypertrophy)? His father stopped by the rail of a small bridge; it seemed he did not wish first to show his son the Three Graces (that was how the secret Brunelleschi statue was referred to by those who knew about it) until he had sketched out to him a brief portrait of all three...

The second woman had been silver-haired, a white head of curly, short locks, which angelically jumped all over the place: very much the eternal child, but without any true glee. She was demented, no doubt. She was always cocking her head to the right and left, like a seal popping up from the water & inanely orientating itself. Apparently life ran high in her quarters: guests came and went, a heap of gondolas rocked in front of the gate like clumps of autumn leaves that have fallen into the water; music sounded, a ball was in progress — yet none of it was driven by *joie de vivre* but by some jiggling pack of idiocy, a hurry-scurry, an agonizing snobbism.

What in the first house had been money darkened into abstract *pavor*[63] was here social life, the dreadful self-torture of parvenus, the complex, marrow-wasting arithmetic of "keeping up." Menu plans, seating orders, collecting of ranks: all that with a suffocating speed, crazed impatience. It took the wœful-wild boy less than three days to realize that as a matter of fact there was no difference between the first Grace and the second: just as some abstract scheme had there been the be-all-and-end-all (the bogey of 'value') of life, here too something similar was the case: the mathematics of rank, irrespective of the individual, pleasure, or life. In vain was the first Acherontic banker a conscious, provocative anti-snob, and the second a grinning heraldry-nut: they remained the closest of siblings in the *female* conspiracy of the culture of *abstraction*.

The Mercury who so joylessly, barrenly put on herself the make-up of the rotten feudal order had an appalling influence on the lonesome adolescent. Whereas the first 'Auntie' had been a big, paralyzed, underwater frog-fetish, the second was a white-peruked puppet with a painted smile squirming to and fro. Despite her barrel hips, she was all zigzags & mercurial restlessness: yet it was always possible to feel the wire; she was a machinery that would start to bow and scrape in front of any scutcheon-scrap that drifted by like the figures of certain clockworks when the hands reach midnight or noon.

At that time of his life Brunelleschi often thought of suicide. What was the point of living? He felt nothing in his own body but the great predominance of its *vegetative* part and the redeeming anguish of individuality — yet he saw that only *abstraction* was worth anything: in the world of combinations of money or combinations of armorial bearings, no one cared about the person. Then the puppet died, and that big woman colossus who would suddenly grow quiet and flash a smile in bed scared him off his own death: he saw that in death it is precisely we ourselves who die — to our skin: even a fly on our skin lives on.

That was how he ended up with the third Grace. In point of fact she was a variant of the second: a mystic snob, a parvenu bloated into religious stupor. Whereas with the first one fatness only manifested in a paunch that drooped inorganically (an unfastened belt slackened hole by hole); with the second it was permanently creased into a huge chain of hills and valleys running across the whole body (it might have taken weeks for it all to level out flat in the sarcophagus), in the plumpness of the third this vagrant tomb-shape finally reached its classicism: the whole woman was a single gigantic ball of flesh, with even her hair flattened very smoothly from her brow to the nape of the neck, so that the snow-white body (naturally sometimes punctuated by a rash of pimples) might retain its perfect sphericalness. Here there were no belly and hands, heart and speech: there was one sole sphere function, nothing else.

This woman in her younger days had been a court lady of the pope, now in his 87th year; later on the heir to the Spanish throne honored her likewise; afterwards the Duke of Milan married her, & when Brunelleschi landed up with her she was in the third year of her widowhood. In her soul, life & household there was nothing but those two shadows: the pope and the king of Spain.

Brunelleschi made her acquaintance when the second Muse (the most pleasant of the three) was already seriously ill. When the third saw that all hope for her sister was gone and she was already wheezing unconsciously on the bed, she did not wait for death ("After all, an unconscious body would have no use of me sitting beside it, would it? It would have no *razón,*" she added in Spanish, as a heart-wrenching souvenir), but went home with the greatest indifference because the King of Naples, in heading to see the Pope, had quartered himself in her house. Although recovery was not medically impossible, she had already ordered the flowers, & foreseeingly had one of her dresses dyed black.

Brunelleschi, still a child strictly speaking, had never felt such deep loathing for a person, a woman, or life in general, as when he accidentally witnessed the flab-spiritualist's undressing; in point of fact she considered that the dress she happened to have on would be the most suitable to wear for the eventual funeral. It was somehow possible to tolerate the amiable fool who died, even to have some affection for her, but one could not even look at that fanatical lump of dough. It was to her that Brunelleschi passed. A new element made an appearance in the house: superciliousness and theater Catholicism, diamond-studded crucifixes and cornelian Magdalenes, a domestic chapel fried in incense, mundane liturgies, & confession cenacles. That is where Brunelleschi learned from a skivvy that Jewish blood flowed in the veins of the three *Parcæ*.

Young Monteverdi, who in his boyhood thought much more dramatically and more ariatically than later when all the arts preoccupied him, was already picturing glum adolescent Brunelleschi in vivid colors & words, as he appears at the Monteverdi family's Whitsuntide children's theater — he pictured late-arriving midnight guests in the house of the first Parca, the catacomb banker woman; everyone was sleeping, only little Bruno (let us call him that for short) is awake, listening to the drops from the flaming torches on the rear balcony as they were suddenly snuffed upon hitting the waters of the Canale; he goes down to the door and indeed a small group arrives in the moonless, starless night: an extremely delightful young married couple, virtually children; an aging humanist character (he had a book!), an armored stalwart and a wizened little Shylock draft.

Bruno does not awaken either the lady of the house or the valets — he places the guests according to his own fancy: the young wife in his own room, the geriatric Jew in the attic.

(... In vain did I wait on my cramped balcony for moonbeams & the entrance of stars: its driver had perhaps chased the Plough to the cypresses, & along with it, a star-hungry sea had perhaps driven the moon to be the new Venus or shell. But scarcely had I started to dispute with the selfish elements when like a fairy-lake swan you came toward me, barely tested *sponsa*,[64] and brought in your hands, instead of star spangles, the whole world. I had known Atlas, the Babylon of muscles, tortoises, and many elephants who carried the world in the palms of their hands and on their weary backs: but such an ephemeral girl who in the gleam of a single strand of hair, the silk curve of a single little slipper, draws for me a Fate-opium secret: who could conceive such a happy miracle? Oh, at last, at last: the calculated light & shadow of branching multitudes of candles casts a planet's gossip-sketch on a flower, and the ascetic bed of my little room is glorified with fragrance by this gift-apparition ...) Truly, this is Bruno's most beautiful night — the young husband he locked the young husband in a room in the tower since he was dreadfully sleepy anyway, so let him rest in peace.

Toward the morning, knowing that the lady of the house is already up, he creeps into the crypt of her bed-room and recounts about the guests: a bit tipsy, he lyricizes about the little wife, forgetting about the Jew bunged into the chimney. Then comes a big turn of the tables: the married couple were poor relatives, they would have to be thrown out; the humanist is a fool; the soldier — awfully dangerous; but the rheumy second-hand dealer was to be put up in the best room (and I must learn for good: every human face is just a goy lie; the love of girls is buffoon virtue; book learning is madhouse lunacy, & the many heroic swords are also gratuitous whimsy. I must learn to loathe the sea because its azure nooks and crannies are just a proletarian romance; I must detest the dance of constellations because it makes me thirsty for dreams, and dreams are a thousand plagues. And O, my greatest pain is that it is no big struggle to trade in my poetry. Did I not feel it so boundary-hard, when the garrulous torch brought in that little bride, that I will never have the strength for true joy; and what for others is body-candle-fusing destiny, for me is just the lyrics of an interlude — if for others it is play, for me it is just the threadbare shadow of a game. Come, then, my crone witch-teacher, you have no idea in what fertile soil you showered your money scholasticism: how tight the ointment of cursing sits on my kiss-cracked lips, and how speedily the wines poured out for nuptials foam a "*Prosit!*" for second-hand dealers. Because my sole treasure, my shadow, my face, is eternal foreignness: the dark acidity of my blood is always only 'anti' & 'counter' — for me, whether I slap money's helmet on my head in this battle and call the antagonist poor matters so little; my fate is to kill — names do not reach me …).

So young Bruno ended up with the third sibling. In vain did the woman ready her mourning dress in advance: the King of Naples arrived at her place on the day of the funeral, so naturally she had to stay at home. In the king's escort there was a young man, or rather child, who had just as decisive an influence on Brunelleschi's whole life as the three Parcæ, or rather summed up those macabre influences in an unexpected form.

That mongrel Spanish-Arab boy was the royal court's fortune-teller, stargazer, and mathematician. Bruno almost passed out when he saw him because the Sicilian Adonis could not be told apart from the young wife with whom he had once been so happy and whom he had had to eject from the house. After the banquet Bruno & the boy went down into the garden and started talking. Bruno had imagined stargazers to be quite different: big, bearded old clowns, wearing trumpet-high fur caps, who were blind to all earthly matters, and spent their barren time at night with all kinds of hocus-pocus. But this one? That was the way Frederick II must have envisaged the anti-Jesus of the anti-Gospels.

He was a thin, bony boy with golden brown skin, black hair, &, unexpectedly, blue eyes. His whole handsomeness was sharp as a knife. He had no sense for poetry (as immediately transpired from the first greedy gout of adolescent dialogue) or women. The three old biddies put together were sentimental troubadours as compared to this boy. His thinking was a Semitic Sahara; his body (almost preposterous) European beauty. This duality, contradictory for the child's head of Bruno, profoundly unsettled him: he perceived in one and the same individual every physical adornment of his midnight love and the aridity of the old crones who had cursed her away. He learned from the boy that he was going no further with the King of Naples because everyone, from the king himself to the last lady in waiting, was persecuting him with love. (... what a foolish bevy the royal household was, pushing lips full of desire toward desire-blind lips — blind people, not suspecting the otherworldly Rule of Reason in which beauty had molded itself. If my cluster of locks is the prey of twigs and birds in the deep bell-void of cypress shadows: it is not a love line into which my hair curls, but celestial cycles and geometry, primordial proportion, which cannot be conquered by earthly girl or woman, only fair-unknowing Yahweh or blind Pythagoras. As to what secret business excited Fate when a mask of beauty slipped onto my only-numbers being — I have no idea. Maybe as a lesson, so that one sees every now and then: the fairest beauty is nevertheless — an imago-less rule; the most voluptuous marriage is 'barren' mathematics. That is how I became and remain an Arab number-Adonis: my *virgo*-stimulus — the youth of knowledge, my Narcissus reflection in the conquered world: pure geometry...) (In this way something absurd presents itself to the narrator, of course: he has to draw the portrait of the driest form-maniac, the most self- and world-agonizing Florentine via the child's mind of a Venetian romantic musician — the development of a funerary, anti-æsthetic soul, born almost of vengeance, in the language of Monteverdi's adolescent lamentations and æsthete *ariosi*: the assassination of the baroque in an apology of the baroque.)

Young Bruno and the 'Arab' spent a lot of time together: the boy was the greatest love of Bruno's life. During their excursions, the Arab brought down birds with slingshots, strangled kittens, dissected flowers — Brunelleschi had not seen such cold-blooded destruction before. He saw that he could rip a person (himself, for instance) to shreds with the same cold-bloodedness. (... Alas! Could you have guessed that while, head hung down and dusty with indifference, I plodded toward you and after your horse at the deer hunt: it was not an image of antlered deer that pranced in my soul, but the elasticity of your muscles that attracted me as wild apertures communicated their strength among distant oaks. But I was hideous, cowardly, and sick of the world: there would not have been a more insolent heresy on Earth than if I had approached your cold beauty with the mutilated desires of my abortive body. "Did you see the glimmer of the blood of its ankle?" you asked me in a shout, and while I forced out a crippled "Yes!" from my tightened throat: I was not getting drunk on the blood of perishing roe deer, but clambering the lotuses of your blue eyes, like a caterpillar pupating to a cocoon in the fall.

But what did you know of that? Even if you did know, you scorned it and threw it away like bits of gravel pricking the soles of sandaled feet. Or did you perhaps see my yearning with your malicious eyes, & while you laughed as you tore the wings off budgerigars, you mocked the feathers of my love to my face, sparing my real body out of pity? That's how it was — like that; what was the dreadful gymnastics of a dying squirrel on the spacious screen of tree branches beside the mournful tumbling of my death? It was me you plucked to shreds in every petal; it was me your rabid dogs devoured; it was my blood you sprinkled in a peasant shithole; and it was I who became, in the heifer interlarded with arrows in a faithless corner, like a misshapen icon, because of your youth: a Saint Sebastian of love...

Later the Sicilian properly taught astronomy & mathematics to young Brunelleschi, yet even outside the lessons he would only speak of those. So for Bruno a new disappointment was added to his disappointment in love: with the best will in the world he was unable to understand the Arab's lectures. He still adored him for his good looks, but out of envy he hated his knowledge. At that time, no other subject preoccupied him but Abraham's wish to sacrifice Isaac. Isaac was always the Arab, always bound and wounded in impossible poses by desperate Brunelleschi in his pictures and versions in clay — that was his way of gaining revenge.

He even showed those sadistic Aretino figurations to the mathematician, who with aristocratic nonchalance suggested a whole gamut of even more cunning exaggerations for the altar: as he carried out his own idiosyncratic calculations of the permutations & variations of algebraic symbols for the human limbs and instruments of torture, Bruno's lyrical love & lyrical vengeance proved very shabby in comparison. Quite aside from the fact that that was terribly exasperating for the young sculptor, he nevertheless used that subject to enter a competition for the design of the Gates of Paradise to the Battistero of San Giovanni in Florence. Like every mania, Bruno's, too, lost its positive or negative sign over time: the Arab boy was at once a subject of murder and love, ideal and disgust, together with mathematics. How many were the times they sat together at the edge of the woods beside their quarry, gazing at the stars, the sculptor myopically screwing up his eyes in superstitious fear, the Arab with ironic clarity like a straight line. He acquainted Bruno with the infinite, absurd distances. Right away in that concept of distance Bruno felt a curious paradox, which occasionally stood out in the thoughts of the stargazer and was possibly the most decisive influence in pushing him in the direction of becoming an architect. One of the stars was so remote that the light that we see now shows the state around the time of Christ's birth — if Bruno were now in the place of the star and had the eyesight of mythical acuity, he would be able to see Jesus in the manger. That scene, therefore, was potentially present in the infinitely distant stars and lights running at their tireless speed: as pure light, as vision projected by a line of beams into space, as a floating perspective.

The other constellation was already so far away, according to the Arab, that its light had set out when man was still as hairy as a bear — maybe there was not even separate man and woman. He wrote those calculations down in a book: Brunelleschi expected bulky tomes, but the whole thing was only three pages. Alongside that, every other text was ignominious. So there was a star that was witness to a still sexually undifferentiated world; how differently he now saw his coolly lecturing, hundredfold fair friend. Finally, there are agglomerations, clouds of millions and millions of stars, the light of which had dawned in a prehistoric time when plants, animals, and minerals were just a single wriggling bubble and even mere spermatic preludes of man were lacking.

This is where the paradox was most acute for Brunelleschi: on the one hand, the antediluvian world was in labor in anarchic colors before his very eyes, while, on the other hand, the fact that the Arab adolescent had intimated those worlds by way of numbers, geometric diagrams, and engineering design dizzied him to his dying day.

To each more elegant equation & numerological turning-point, the world linked a bigger chaos; to each more mystical chemistry of Creation — a more transparent, one might say, more symmetrical formula. The distances, the number, weight, and light intensity of the stars all so intensified that those unimaginable, preposterous masses became: *abstract*. The boy was also able to corroborate that impression scientifically (insofar as Brunelleschi, barely understanding mathematics as he did, was able to discern): he converted the infinite masses to forces, the forces to geometrical properties, so that, at one & the same time, he was able to see the world-all as *material*-madness suffocating the universe & as transparent *geometrical* equation or idea.

The stars always featured as points, as sources of light: at that time Brunelleschi dreamed with much more frantic love about points than about the boy. The point was a symbolic marriage of mass and nothingness: of pure location, of the *locus mathematicus* and matter, of the chaotic-vital whatsit of the Creation, the *materia bergsonica*. It is worth citing these reveries from Brunelleschi's notebooks because an architectural consequence derived from each — a precise counterpart of even the most fantastic stellar arithmetical memento can be traced in (not just read into) one column or cupola contour or another.

Brunelleschi swam in relativity, in doubt; but that astronomical relativity was regular, it had a strict algebraic composition; indeed (this is again very important), he sensed the radical *instability* of all material existence and every intellectual inference, yet he felt the *fixed* nature of the mathematical formulæ and of the transparent geometrical models to be inseparable; only an arithmetically and geometrically extremely harmonious structure was able to make the eternal density of sophistication & illusion of being perceptible for him, and the other way round: only those logical diagrams could suggest for him the secret, the obscurity, the shapeless irrationality-kernel of the universe, the stars, and therefore of the atoms of atoms.

It was then that the average classicism which renders order with order, and the average romanticism which represents chaos with chaos, failed once and for all for Brunelleschi, or if you prefer, in Florence, indeed in the whole Renaissance: this young sculptor saw, with demonic narrow-mindedness (under the influence of the Sicilian astrologer ephebe, of course), a hyper-meaningless and hyper-geometrizable world, and perceived them to be eternally correlative. It is the expression of that duality that became commonplace in the Renaissance, above all in Florence: in images, immense architectures encompass a relatively minimal group of humans — Christ's christening is covered with the most opulent refinement of engineering perspective by twenty-nave basilicas; for the advent of the Holy Spirit, anti-graphic, non-Euclidean geometry is made graphic in an exciting scale of provocative contradictions; and Salome is only able to press her perverse kisses on John the Baptist's lips when a ten-story palace rises behind her hips, which an Einsteinian curving of space signals in a complicated model. Perspective, the drafting of projection, are the areas where relative and absolute, world illusion & precision of *raison*, meet in a mirroring that is inexpressible in words — monomaniacal Brunelleschi tapped that source of paradox, which yields both boundless thirst and boundless satiation, to spring forth, and he drank from it until his dying day (maybe the two sketchbooks of Jacopo Bellini indicate that mental state most tangibly).[65] Great architecture, therefore, was not born out of stone, soil, and decorative or practical need, nor was it a continuation of Stonehenge. On the contrary: it was born of the systems of lines inspired by abstract astronomy, out of the relative, or if you will: out of the void.

Philologically, there is nothing more intriguing (*hic salta!*) than to read side by side the notebooks of that Arab boy (who, by the way, died in Verona at the age of 27 — some say that he was poisoned by Brunelleschi), at present in the archive of the city of Palermo (under the mark *Phil. Nat. D.* XVI. a-f), in which, with a bit of discreet license with the history of ideas, one can already divine in distorted form the most modern theories of the electron and models of an expanding universe — and the Florentine diaries containing the works of Brunelleschi's younger days plus the *canon juvenile* compiled by Coppa. One of the sentences of Ibn Athl-n'Othech (whence the oddly sounding latinized name of Io Atlantica for the young Arab, who happened to be half Spanish, as we have already mentioned) runs as follows: "Space can spread by itself, and the cosmic fogs are only to be considered as bundles of straw that float in space and are driven on by space waves. It is thereby shown to us wither world space flows, in the way in which the smoke of opium betrays what kind of draughts are moving about in a room, & in what direction..." All the signs unmistakably indicate that the initial plans set down by Brunelleschi in the *canon juvenile* did *not* seek to place stones in space but sought simply to depict the internal modulation of space — indeed, just as the role of stars and of world 'space' was reversed: stars were just a mathematically abstract state of space, & space became a quasi-living body here as well: column, roof, wall, & cellar became nullities, and it was precisely the nothingness in-between that became architecture's sole theme. The first Brunelleschi sketches, with their circles, angles, & spirals can barely be distinguished from Kandinsky's off-the-shelf mumbo jumbo.

In one of the drafts, for instance, one sees nothing more than a recumbent parabola, the two branches of which fade into nothingness; faint traces of green chalk can be seen in the space between them, so that it is fair to assume that Brunelleschi envisioned a lake here, one of whose banks would be closed by a sharp oval frame, whereas the part left open is in the act of falling, probably in the form of a broadening waterfall, to a lower level of the park — and passing obliquely above that water parabola is a folding screen bent in a zigzag, a thin, tall plate, in every fold of which is a floating statue. That's all.

Fortunately Futurism was unaware of that codex, otherwise tragic Brunelleschi would also have been rolled in the tar of being a 'forefather' of the new -ism. The boundless openness of the parabola with its ever-further-opening or, still more, the folding in the air, left and right, of the folding screen shows that it is not meant to be a building or a shelter but an X-ray shot of the anatomy of space. The second drawing is indicative of the same: on one side are twelve tightly juxtaposed, undulating semicircular niches, opposite it likewise, but in the latter series the wall is pulled by roughly one third further over, so that it starts later and then stirs up its half bubbles in the air a good deal further.

A floor runs along the length of the wall, water before the second; above the wall accompanied by water, supported by a thin lance, is a flat lamina roof, whereas there is nothing, only open sky, above the wall accompanied by the floor. Here too the tendency is explicated *ad nauseam*: not to create a well-delineated structure, but one that merely pops out of space by accident, only in order to immediately fold back into space.

All these are, it should be emphasized, when it comes down to it, the products of childishly vulgar inspirations and adolescent misunderstandings, but we should also emphasize that, after all, even the soberest old fogeys of the Renaissance also moved around that selfsame infantilism. However well we may have learnt the lesson from the history of ideas that the Renaissance was not a revolution but only a variation on Gothic and an insignificant presto-prelude to the baroque, a mere "intermezzo from Florence" and a "*pastiche éphemère*": if one looks at Brunelleschi's spiritual development, that will unquestionably appear a frightening, bloody revolution even today, a self-tormenting hysteria of abstraction — one only has to stroll with open eyes along any of the streets in Florence.

Brunelleschi was also accustomed by Io Atlantica to the idea that the infinitesimally small is followed, both logically and physically, by the infinitely large, without any transition, and *vice versa*: the orbit of the universe is echoed by the orbits of the electron, and the infinite mass of all the Coma Berenices and Umbra Ledæs — by the weight of a sliver of negative material, an almost fictive photon. We have not one but a whole bunch of drawings where, again in that same inveterate enfant terrible manner, he seeks to express that minimum-maximum vibration.

Take one plan for a fountain, for example — which has the added historical interest of being prepared for the Pazzi family: its ground plan is made up of three circles that intersect in cloverleaf fashion, their marble wall is eight feet tall and completely smooth — above, in the center of each circle, stands the slim figure of one of the Graces (in their own *calcule* thinness they better express the abstract life of the three old crones of his childhood than the naturalist caricatures in the Jew's possession). Behind the first circle & parallel to it, in conspicuous proximity, rises a huge semicircular wall, as if it were the projection of the shadow of the small leaf of a cloverleaf.

The second well circle also has a wall projection — albeit no longer as rigorously parallel (it is oval rather); additionally, it is not so close, for it bends away from the well. The folding screen transposition belonging to the third circle is curved only at the point where it starts, its other end is quite straight, running away from the well almost into infinity — also signaled by the fact that it does not end on the same plane, but horizontally, with steel rods running parallel in space, the way in which at the end of a cloth the strands running in one direction often fray in the air. The well is narrow, massive, closed like a stone-deaf atom — its projection being world space itself: this endless screen is as much its mathematical shadow as it is the uncategorizable opposite, a refutation of the small fountain. In a letter Brunelleschi cites Io Atlantica word for word, then passes a remark from which his entire anguished adolescent world glows out.

The quotation (eerily accurate down to the punctuation marks) runs as follows: "... since space is the kind of thing we ourselves have constructed for ourselves, so its waves & curves or, if it comes to that, its non-waviness & non-curving depend exclusively on whether we wish it to be one or the other, or on whether we would rather possess a flexible or a non-flexible space ..." The remark, thrown in subsequently in agitated handwriting, is this: "Five minutes ago he was proving to me with the positive noise of the formulæ that streams or bends in space are just as real as currents in the sea or the curving of the skin of apricots. And now this fancy doubt ..." The exciting bit starts from the drafts of two frescoes which illustrate that frantic wavering between complete relativity and complete absolute — the world as an arbitrary but manageable fiction, a subjective formula, and the world as a once-and-for-all-time ready objective reality: the two poles juggled into each other by the Arab boy.

One of the pictures is the Temple of Janus, the other the Birth of Eve. The former depicts a very long basilica without a façade that runs into the depth of the picture, at the end of which stands a Janus figure on a low pedestal. The adolescently feeble and fairly overcomplicated jest results from the fact that everything visible on the left wall, either as geometric rigor or miniaturist naturalism, is repeated on the right-hand wall as in a distorting mirror, tripled and elongated; what was kaleidoscopic becomes monochrome, a boy becomes a girl, what was Venus is now bearded — a great madhouse of Gothic relativism. Underneath is a comment: "... well, perhaps the natural law is just a metaphor of my nightmares, which can be exchanged for another at any time, should changed fashion so desire — though perhaps the natural law is everlasting & something that does not exist in me but in the objects of the world, inside, like a skeleton within flesh ...?"

The Eve fresco speaks about the same thing. Eve separating from Adam's body is nothing other than a transformation of the real Adam into a hypothetical Adam — the possibility that Adam is not full-blown reality but a whimsical idea, a fiction, temporary in the most far-reaching sense. Eve herself is not even a woman in this fresco (perhaps the Arab boy's pre-sex world view was also working in Brunelleschi), but Adam repeated in a pale silhouette form: the major key of certainty played in the minor key of uncertainty.

But that this *'abstractio pathologica'* can be derived from unbridled vitality just as much as from unbridled schematic geometrism — that piquancy is gloriously illustrated by a letter of Brunelleschi's. One of the snobbish members of the Pazzi family sent him Book I of the *Histories* of Herodotus, entitled *Clio*, for him to illustrate with a cycle of pictures. That was the first commission for the young artist, who for the time being had not trained himself to be anything other than an anti-artist, and his joy over the first task manifested not so much in the finished works as in the lyrical voracity with which he detailed his struggle with the subject to the flexible snob.

"... I shall without fail paint the rape of Io, the daughter of the king of Argos, by the Phœnicians.

Should I paint it? Was the vision of the whining traders, a truly red notion of the Red Sea, the automatic identification of Io the Argive with the mythological Io, the taking of the abducted women to Egypt, the throwing of the amassed Greek and Persian, Jewish and Nilotic forms of art into a motley funfair: was that indeed artistic vision, I wonder, & not simple *joie de vivre*, the finest and most deceptive dowry that we brought with us from the dark of the womb? Everything that I see appears before me in some frantic, suffocating, and idolizing clarity.

I am the slackening of oars at shore, the by now impatient bargain sputters in my mouth, the makeshift bridge on which the king's daughter descends onto the second-hand merchant's boat buckles in my knees, the cloud that surrounded Io is my breathing, I am the golden red, warm-ruddy light in which I condense all this: the Mede, Persian, and Assyrian reflex in Greek culture; that is my only instinctive instinct, sex, divinity, eating and drinking being just pale experiments beside that — I see the past with such sharpness and liveliness of detail that I am on the verge of swooning when I come to feel, nevertheless, that I am not Io, not a second-hand dealer, not a Red Sea, but a Florentine would-be fool. And now comes the table turning: it is clearer than daylight that this detail-lavishing, religious, mantic seeing of the past can be expressed *not* with accumulative, romping Gothic miniature but, on the contrary, with a simplicity that is beyond simplicity: with such a degree of absurd reduction as its veil intimates and flourishes around degree zero like the rings round Saturn. For what reason? Because only the *elements* can act on me, the burning, single-element core of substances — and because that can only be a tragic, resigned, defiant, & vindictive art, given that it perpetually remembers that it must forget its sole *raison d'être*, the *living identification* with all other & long-past lives, and leave them unsatisfied, until one's dying day. That is terrible.

That Io, in a momentary clearing in the time jungle of millennia, never knew, nor can she ever know, that much later a Florentine boy would live through her flesh, shadow, price, and kiss in the ship's hold with such intensity that he would give up everything to really become, for one moment, Io, for it would merely have taken a 'transcendental click' to become her. And I shall die, I shall be reduced to nothing, the sense of my whole life, this maddening closeness of fantasy to the reality of flowers, women, and ships will be even more definitely barren and senseless. And art will have to express that, in the form of vengeance-mourning: that boundless melancholy filling in all my passing hollows — that the essence of my life is radical barrenness. The Red Sea? A layer of red varnish on the wall, nothing more. That is a basic element, *aqua aquissima,* the intoxicating essence of water, water where it is the most watery and thus sensual art, lecher and not philosophical — and besides that defiance: with one gesture the tidal flood which stimulates one to a million analyses of detail turns into an inferno of nothingness. Everything but analysis: that lousy evasion of detail, that most Judas kiss on reality. So what is the minimum of the minimum that will be a worthy partner in my fresco of that maximum of imagination into which I tumbled on my first reading of *Clio?* A red plane; out of the ship, just the fish contour; the oars and sails are superfluous; from Io, whom Jupiter surrounds with mist, I am unable to subtract the idea of mist, so she will be mist: I shall paint a nude on one margin of the picture, but only in the form of a grey fragment of a shadow; a few jugs, strings of pearls, and bales of silk will stand for the traders. In other words, the whole will no longer be a picture but, if you will, an Egyptian hieroglyph, or the formula of Gothic armorial bearings.

But is there a more life-fermenting art than heraldry? One that is both more resigned and more evocative? The court ladies have all escaped, only Io and a few others are left on the boat. Can't you hear the women screaming, the sailors whooppeeing; can't you see the grimaces & clothes of every single Greek girl, the pattering of blondes and brunettes between the hawsers; or the chained-up galley-slaves in the water, who are applauding the unexpected comedy with the clanking of their chains? Under a tall baldachin the solemn and stupid king of the Argives, as he would like, at one and the same time, to somersault into the water after his daughter, and to retain his statue-stony dignity — you see all that; you and I would like *to be* that above all else — instead of which I will only send you a statue of ten running women, ten identical women, with an identical stride, because the running is what, after all, is the gist of the whole game, and since the analytic picture is the crummiest compromise between extreme reduction & full reality.

Believe me, Pazzi, my friend, it is a sublime and eerie moment when an artist gives up analysis for good, i.e., in point of fact everything that excites him. But for anyone who likes reality above all else, analysis is just a momentary adolescent illusion: his despair will soon drive him into suicidal puritanism, into that strict world of substance hallmarking

& allusions in which Arab abstraction and European greed for life are indistinguishable. Classicism? Renaissance? Selection? Simplicity? What rotten hit tunes. What is at stake here is a lot more funereal, more disconsolate: the eternal impotence of fantasy — that is my *rinascimento.*

I shall also paint for you Gyges and Candaules, possibly one of the finest subjects. If I paint red the curtain that hangs behind the queen's bed, there should not be any difference between it and the Red Sea — a wave of the waters and a wrinkle of the velvets, horizontal water and vertical curtain are insignificant differences in the resonant community of red & the 'object.' But if that is an exaggeration, in the end it is of course possible to portray all sorts of curtain variants. Not long ago I was in a theater; nothing else appealed to me than the curtain that started by the ceiling & reached down right to the ground, right down to the soles of the musicians, completely filling the room both to the right and to the left — all the while being less than the narrowest architecture in the world: yes, that was an 'absolute' curtain. The Gyges story, by the way, is as elementally simple as I now want all things to be, not in its pictorial parts, but in its moral content. The very nakedness of the woman.

This becoming-nude is not erotic, not spiritual, nor gourmet; it is a nakedness far from æsthetics, far from everything: the nudity of nudity itself, denying Venus, Praxiteles, Hippocrates, and mankind. Can you guess what I am thinking about? This woman is not a wife, not a lover, not a source of religious inspiration, not a birth machine, not a matter of metaphors, not a body for the king but 'beauty,' in such an asexual, indeed, an-æsthetic barbarity that it could be a symbol of that minimum-madness that has overtaken me. In the nakedness of Candaules' wife, a most fakir-like *abstraction* & a hyper-*corporeality* more poisonous than opium finally encounter one another: she, and only she, can be the Janus-faced patron saint of the Renaissance. That, true enough, is the relationship of men and women *à la manière du pauvre* Brunelleschi: there are no genital bodily capers, no Christian marriage, no physical beauty, no child & psychological goldfish scramble — what is left is only the formula. Perhaps that bores you rigid, my dear friend, that I go about expounding the death program of simplification with such verbosity, but the birth of any thought is mucky. Near the door there's a chair ...[66]

This fragmentary sentence speaks to me more tragically than a trumpet at the Last Judgment. It is as if St. John were to say: *in principio erat* chair. No object drifted in space so solitarily and in such royal singularity as that chair. A chair: long before the Creation of the world. To paint a chair like that! Who could express the infinite surplus and richness that inhere in that cosmically orphan chair as against an overcrowded, perfume-stenchy boudoir? If the woman is the barbarian anti-Eros, then this chair on which she will place her clothes is hyper-Eros itself. It stands near the door, writes Herodotus, & in this thoughtless little adverb glows all amatory intimacy, all refined Bengal lights of being-inside within-*gynaikeion*. "She will put her clothes on it ... as she takes them off, one by one": there is more pornography in that specification than in all the French dives combined.

That is the important thing: the re-dedication of the turning of objects into objects again. The convergence of rite and the banal reflex movement. What is undressing? An entire human life. The drama of nude and shirt: the drama of the eternal animal and eternal culture; of sensuality and of being lowered in the grave, of poverty and royal mantle; a drama of instinct and mask, matter and spirit, atheism & *civitas dei* ... But no, no! If I carry on like this, it's a rotten trap: let the simplification to extremes of the most naïve movements be not ritual simplicity, let it not be suffused with religious, lyrical, or philosophical 'meaning' — let it not have 'significance' — let not the nude be 'life,' & the shirt, 'civilization,' because symbolism is merely lousy baroque, a source of nausea. That is the eternal risk of heraldic simplicity, its dancing on eggs: its meaning is either too broad, too ritual, hence is drowned in hideous bogs of 'eternal humanity' and 'mythical completeness' — or too tight, scarce to the point of meaninglessness — which is still the nobler of the two. The 'chair,' therefore, onto which Candaules' wife puts her clothes, one by one — let it not be the "eternal chair," because that already makes it a cesspit myth, but a momentary seat, by chance a chair right now — by all means don't let the simplification be a common denominator.

If Plato conceives the idea of a chair, that simplification will be ceremonial, sacred, transfigured simplicity, complete with the vaudeville-flimsy sorcery & posing of the 'essence':

that is to say, a simplisticism worse than the stage setting of a thousand closet religions. The way I picture it, the simplicity of a solitary chair is the simplicity of being cleaned out of everything: not the philosophical exhibitionism of pointing to the 'essence,' but the poverty of a dispossessed person, the skeleton of despair, a stripping of leaves, the tragicomedy of the object's being-object.

Oh, my friend, don't believe that those differentiations are the idle finesses of a play-meticulousness: no, I can declare with the triumphant melancholy of self-conceit that in those 'unhealthy' struggles a robust health of art is born. Somehow I sensed that mathematically in advance: if my frescoes and buildings are going to accomplish the *non plus ultra* of simplicity, then the thoughts from which those done-to-death cortiles were born will needs be full of sophistic folds, qualms spinning between abstractions. Just as I am convinced that the essence of the visual arts is sadistic simplification, so I am convinced that the essence of thinking is grubby sporulation, total morass: thinking like that can never be simple, as its essence is impossibility, the inability to accept the world, a wriggling negative ...

How grand the alternative that the woman sets before Gyges when she learns that he had seen her naked: either he kills her husband or himself. Gyges kills her husband. Here nakedness triumphs without Eros and sensuality; a murdering sword is flourished without hatred and vengeance. That is my world: that is the only purity that I feel is pure. Before you or before God, dotard Brunelleschi would yet like to recount what two kinds of morality were at work in him: one highly strung, *pleureux* to the point of simplicity, at times perhaps even evangelical — and that second, psyche-trampling, value-denying, animal-apologizing one, where deeds are born from stinky motive-dungs, they are not driven by a Christian will or its stoic ally, they do not run into filthy nets of goals, all the while avoiding the empty & mendacious dynamic of "instinctive life" as well — they are simply deeds, functions, and algebraic deductions that neither classical intelligence nor romantic spontaneity can appropriate. When Gyges killed the king, he did not shed any tears; he neither grieved nor gloated, but had a pile of golden and silver goblets and vessels cast, and he laid them in a row on the Delphic shrine as a sacrificial gift.

Do you know what that means for me, Pazzi? One thousand gold tankards: in place of psychology & morality. Can you sense those three magnificent tones in that Asia Minor scale: the nude without sex; the bloody deed without anger; and finally, vase madness in place of 'spiritual life' or the hurdy-gurdy of instinct? Do you know that I filled thick notebooks with sketches for you in order to assemble a series of Gyges-style goblets as a stone ornament for the garden of your villa, the book of Renaissance morality engraved in stone, a new Ten Commandments of *de*-humanization? (Morality, morality — Brunelleschi indeed swims in it with perverse pleasure: I am a moralist, a moralist.) Imagine a high wall; on it not a trace of decoration or articulation; up above, on its edge, thirteen huge monotonous vases with an inscription of the kind, "Gyges in place of psyche." Or a skirting and intersecting constellation for the walls, with amphoræ of various sizes & colors at their feet and on their edges? You may choose, I have prepared a vast range of versions — circles, spirals, a recumbent 'S' from triangular walls, from miniature vases & from vases three times higher than the wall. There are tube-thin vases and bagpipe-bloated ones, plate-flat and lasso-eared ones — Brunelleschi gets inebriated when he thinks of such combinations.

Imagine their shadows; or the whiteness of the sun on their whiteness; imagine their dialogues with mirror-flat or frothing waters; their shadows among cypresses or frayed lime trees. Can my youth have a more agreeable and more expressive work than this Delphi furnished by Gyges? A marvelous place, that Delphi — partly made up of vases, golden whims, & cornelian dressing cases, or in other words, inanimate objects; on the other hand, of a jabbering prophetess, a mysterious elegiac couplet-automaton, and nonsensical hocus-pocus. In Florence nowadays man is made of body and soul, according to a consensus between high scholasticism and petty bourgeoisie: at Delphi the human 'body' is lost in the great, mute triumph of the inanimate objects, the vases, and the human 'soul' logically runs on in Pythia, i.e., in opium chaos, in sleep, in ridiculous madness & pathological falsehood.

To Delphi, Pazzi, quickly to Delphi! Did I not map out Delphi to you before when I said that my life is made up of two parts: the extreme purity of architecture and the extreme muckiness of thought? What is architecture within me if not Gyges' expiatory vases? What is thought within me if not the mendacity and madness of the Pythia? Delphi is the capital city of pessimism, I say; let us hurry there, dear Pazzi, if you want some sort of *Rinascimento* with me. By the way, if you don't mind, I would like to paint an enormous picture on one of the vases. A portrait of you and me: Myself as Adrastus,[67] you as the young son of Crœsus.

I'll tell you why.

Adrastus was a royal scion, the son of the king of Phrygia, who unwittingly killed his elder brother & fled to the court of Crœsus, going to Lydia in order to do penance. His entire life was consummated with that fateful conscience of guilt feeling, it was contrition itself, the darkness of memory; in vain did the expiatory smoke of Lydia envelop his yellow body, it remained forever a senseless death. How well that role suits me! Just like wandering Cain. I see him as on the right, a condescending, mundane Crœsus, on the left, a naked priestess accompanying him with a polite smile toward the penitential altar, but he is barely able to stand on his feet, his dark blue hair falls to his chest, his whole body is the shadow of a *métèque*.[68] Because that is the main thing: he seeks the expiatory sacrifice in Lydia, on foreign soil, like a foreigner looking for medicinal baths or the climate — Lydia was probably the nation with the most famed industry for forgiving sins. But Adrastus, it seems, did not succeed in freeing himself from his soul — he is the unchristenable original sin, he is Brunelleschi. And his partner, Pazzi, the king's son? Don't take it amiss, my dear patron — he, too, is betrothed to death. Crœsus dreamed that his son, Atys, would when young be killed by a spear point. I perpetually see around your body a sword and poison, those little cosmetic instruments of politics and history.

Crœsus keeps the boy far away from weapons; he bestows on him a harem and wife, so that he becomes a weakling more translucent than alabaster — his whole body no more than a cobweb with a few pips at the bottom for others. Don't think that is a satirical caricature. No, it is simply taking youth's healthy, natural repletion with death *ad absurdum*. How splendid are those death-condemned figures — the morals-metic and the Thanatos-gigolo. Incidentally, I was driven to wild associations of ideas by the fact that the Phrygian penitent happened to be the nephew of a man by the name of Midas — imagine all the barren gold, the autumnal boughs or Byzantine mosaic backgrounds behind the penitent's figure. Adrastus accidentally kills the youth on a hunt. I almost climbed a wall in my artistic delight when Herodotus writes that they set off with "carefully chosen young men and dogs."[69] Young men and dogs! The king's son alone is slim as a whippet skeleton, and there he is in the middle of the pack just like a woman, like Artemis herself. What a picture! On the left the harem's pushy ladies, Lydian snakes, Lydian fishwives, Lydian minxes, Lydian sibyls, and beside them, indeed among them, mixed up in them: the ticklish waves of canines; and you, young Artemis-Pazzi, as it were, swim in that sea of harems and dogs, a stray fall leaf in the billows of a swollen river.

The background & upper part of the painting is a forest — with wild Germanic foliage, not with the barbed-wire cell-nature of Tuscany. Quite far off, in a small clearing of the Germanic superstition-flora, my own bent figure can be seen — Adrastus sharpening an arrow, which will later kill the inebriated prince. Whether I imagine your fate as becoming a victim of politics or as painted by me on a vase — both are equally lethal. Death here is not something lyrical or tragic; it is not autumnal or a Gorgon joke, neither Christian nor Greek scholarly scam, but an uncommentable point, nothing more. Everything inside me that evolved under the influence of the three old dames and the Arab mathematician has your loan of Herodotus to thank for its final crystallization.

Herodotus is not history and not epic: Herodotus is picture and morality. If the catalogue of my plans wears you out, throw it away; but, o my patron, I am obliged to lay out on the counter the selection that I can offer you.

I would like to paint on the ceiling of the domestic chapel the excavations carried out by Peisistratus on the sacred island of Delos. For on Delos that Greek potentate announced a grand "purification," as prescribed by celestial portents, and he dug up the dead from the area around the temple and had them transported to quite another region. What a topic! Resurrectionless resurrection, the hellish parade of "I don't believe in the resurrection of the body" — all in a marvelous Delian landscape, a heap of dug-up dead bodies amid palms & parrots, carried in the arms of slaves like the abducted Sabine women; Hellene floozies on Saracen shoulders, Greek sages in the arms of Persian soldiers, Thracian despots on the backs of Jewish stall-keepers. Is that picture not to your taste?

In the frescœs and statues of your villa I want to bore to the very deepest of the inner meaninglessness of history. I want to formulate all my disappointments with startling dryness. Don't worry! The connoisseurs will in any case never notice my pessimism in the picture — my disillusionment finds expression in such abstract formal tricks that my confession behind it will never be suspected. That transport of the dead is an unforgettable historical lesson — all of that on an island: in a chosen nest of limitedness and narrow-mindedness.

That penultimate judgment will be a caricature of metaphysics & the philosophy of history.

One could also paint the scene at midnight: the corpses would glisten amid huge shadow spokes under the firebrands of torches, but I want it at noon, with a lot of flowers, blue water, sun, and ruddy birds. After all, that is Ægean death. Apropos of history's radical meaninglessness: can you imagine what joy it caused me when after those lines I read the alternative about the Spartans, whom we all knew as a bunch of cold militarists & bureaucratized ascetics — that Lycurgus' laws[70] were either suggested by the Pythia or imported from Crete. Pythia is pure insanity, morphine delirium — Crete, on the other hand, is pure primitive world, the dominion of bull-loving Pasiphæ & the child-gobbling

Minotaur, simply an awe-inspiring paradise of primordial animals. *That* is virtuous Sparta: a marriage of hysteria and the aurochs![71] Is that not worth reading about? To cap that, I can suggest another subject & present its outline in draft form: the construction of the mausoleum for Alyattes,[72] King of Lydia. That was initially built by Lydian trollops, high-class courtesans, women of the street, in accordance with the country's ancient custom. Would not that be a superb counterpart to the excavation of death on Delos? The living host of gorgeous women as they build a mausoleum for the king.

It takes some guts to distinguish here democracy from aristocracy, riff-raff Eden from theocratic despotism, to find your way between living demi-monde & dead king, religious philosophy & lowdown market. Did the hetæras pass into political mythology, or was it the king slipping down into the bordello? Nobody can tell, & it would be pointless to think about it. One should not wallow in romantic antitheses. The point is rather that one is at last allowed to sketch a great many architectures here in the way that I learned from the Arab stargazer. Each and every semicircular arch springs up from the hands of a harlot: the most abstract forms from the most abstract beings. I will rest here…"

The Pazzi to whom Brunelleschi wrote this letter was a friend of Sixtus IV. Characteristically, fate so willed that Brunelleschi should end up with a Pazzi and not a Medici, and the pope whose shadow fell on him was not a Dominican but a Franciscan. The Pazzi family were upstart peasants, the Medicis by then almost faded aristocrats. Of course, it's all rather a matter of style — the Pazzis must have been lordlier lords than the Medicis, only in their temperament there was something pushier, fresher, & more robust than in the Medicis with their greater readiness for the *fioriture* of decadence.

Who was Sixtus IV? A Franciscan: that meant decent politics, morality, and intellect, of the kind that was very much to Brunelleschi's advantage — Sixtus IV is none other than a macabre Brunelleschi profile: world politics, the swaggering *theatrum catholicum*, projected onto a wider plane. In a more cleanly season, even their bodies were similar in external appearance. Monteverdi was never able to tell the two apart — he was well aware that the colonnade or codification of dogma, the commentary on Herodotus or the chances of excommunication, were insignificant external accidents: the essence was the hungry constraints fighting inside a person's body, and what was decisive were the obsessions inhering in the insoluble curse-chemistry of the nerves; in particular, those manias were identical in architect and pope like two peas in a pod.

Life for young Monteverdi consisted solely of two parts: the mute "*an sich*"-blind treasure of objects,[73] atmospheres, and inflorescences, and of people, whom he pictured as little foci of manias, pathological and irresponsible points of selfishness that fate slings into the senseless external world, where they try to mold the plastic *senselessness* of the world to suit their own immeasurable *selfishness* and madness in a way only they are able. Every person is a will which, when it comes down to it, does not know what it wants, and every object that that will would employ for the 'perming' of its own selfishness-pattern in all likelihood wants to be anything in the world except the means or target of an irrational human will directed toward it. Self-serving, uninterpretable objects and foolish, aimless instinct-buds could not have found better tailor's dummies than those two forlorn figures for their double panorama.

What a superb statue is Pollaiuolo's tomb of Sixtus IV in Rome! The thin lips like a cicatrized scratch on the stem of a plant, a protruding, pointed chin, a thin hooked nose, the brow raised in a thousand wrinkles, the orbits round the eyes spreading into cynical, disappointed rims: as if the head of an infant that, out of obstinacy, had died of starvation, were thrust into the feeble, disillusion-defiant sheathe of the tiara. Because those revelers in abstraction, vigorous pessimists, and Florentine 'malcontents' are always reminiscent of children — of children in whom the senseless monster-nature of man exhibits itself most frighteningly, children who are tireless recreators, over and over again, of the sweet tetralogy of phobias, selfishness, ignorance, & utterly consistent vengeance.

Because it is unquestionable that Brunelleschi's Renaissance is the vengeance of an affronted child, brutishly looking neither left nor right, and that Sixtus IV's theology, as it is, is underscored by a spot of muttering rancor. Brunelleschi's heraldic device might be a blood-red embryo or infant in a pitch-black field: disconsolate egoism and ecstatic ignorance of the world shine out from that insignia. Sixtus IV experienced the problematic nature of the relation of faith and knowledge as profoundly as an illness (and all thought is that). But whereas the great syllogism-decorating Thomists were able to dress up *evidentia rei*, experience (that is to say, a drowning man's touch experiments on the fabled straw), and mystical or quasi-mystical intuition into one greater common harmony, that did not in the least work out for young della Rovere:[74] he saw the woeful gap between positivism and faith, and for that reason (and not at all with enlightened hauteur, not likely!) drew a black line between *res* and celestial *principium* with tragic defiance. That was the "Franciscan pessimism," which on so many occasions seemed unruffled plain common sense, although with him one of the barely maskable forms of despair. But is that bitter resignation not the tastiest background to Assisi's hymnically pampered birds?

Though della Rovere was the Minister General of the Franciscans, by the time he was elected to the papal throne, he strolled down from the hills around Lake Garda like a warbling Papageno: anyone who looked at his face from close up would have been able to see the traces of the battle that tormented the whole Scotist philosophizing — the battle between the hysterical inner atheism of the *real* world's positive objects, and the *fictions* of Platonic frames and abstractions, lying about there as an alluvium of the history of philosophy, i.e., the passively breeding lies. *Evidentia rei naturaliter a-theistica et mundus conceptualis abstractionum naturaliter* mendax *est.*[75] The world: godless, by definition anti-Christian; thought, by the same token, *de natura*, the mendacious moon itself with its elegant harlot contours. This invisible *mendax-meretrix* moon-sickle was always more visible above della Rovere's skin-and-bone-faced head than the tiara's heap of gemstones. Della Rovere's morality was also pessimistic, which of course was a consequence of his intellectual tragedy: he set at the center of theology not origins of being and the shaky Towers-of-Babel god-definitions, but *moral questions* — God Himself was a *moral* source, logical attributes were shed from him like a set of staves shed of their hoops. The one concrete factor was human action, not thought: the *magister* was history, not philosophy.

The source of that conclusion, of course, was embitterment, and its melody, if it had one, was nostalgia for a once tasted but — so it seems — impossible thought. His motto was always: "If we are to live in such a terrible world where we must act instead of thinking, then let us go deaf and blind in the effort of acting, which is baloney — let us pursue morality: with obliterated brains." And because that was how he thought, the concurrence between Renaissance, pope, the landscape of the area around Lake Garda (where he dwelled prior to his papacy), between pubes-lethal Brunelleschi, *&* the upstart Pazzis, could indeed be perfect.

What kinds of flowers, what kinds of trees, accompanied the General of the Franciscan Order on his way to Rome? Olive trees! Are those plants? Organic? Are they living?

Do they have love or sap? Color? None. Pale, linear, misty; the whole thing is a fine snow of problems trained into mundaneness, a formal showing-off of melancholy. Silver, silver — what is to be done with silver? Those mildew velvets, stifled-pusillanimous vegetations filtered della Rovere through forests — now he could see his ascetic questions again in the mirror of nature, he could see that he was undeniably the son of this soil, where the leaves and flowers are even bigger fakirs than him. Italy and the tropics know nothing about nature — the olive tree, too, is in part a nauseating, aggressive spice, in part a *calcul farouche*[76] as a Parisian poet put it. And what else? The cypresses? Once in Gardone I rambled around late at night to check whether I might retrace a memory and the mood of that acrimonious pope's wanderings in the unexpected fall of a bird or (with its tiny bubbles of breathing & wave beats chirruppier than a chirrup) in a fish's grief, whereat I landed by such a grove of tall cypresses. One could not even imagine anything more awesome, more evocative, of the *Toteninsel*.[77]

Low down the trunks were lighted silverish by the occasional lamp, but higher up only the reflections of the night sky reached their towering *pelisse* canopies[78] in the places where unrestrained darkness did not pour out of them like a mute waterfall. Those great poles had maybe been dipped by someone into the crater of the night, and now they were poked into the hillside like badges of triumph to let everybody see what stuck to them. The sort of thing that can be imagined of Assyrian kings.

Yet that is a simile — but those were cypresses! Those two kinds of darkness were mysterious: of midnight and of the giant cones of moss — both such kindred material, and yet the blackness of the cypresses stuck out so visibly from the blackness of the night as if they were standing in front of a white wall. When I describe those Gardone cypresses (what a ridiculous word "describe" is: all intellectual operations are possible, but never precisely to describe or delineate something — to write it down!), in point of fact I am working against myself, for what was splendid was precisely the fact that in them Italian abstraction achieved Teutonic frondescence, & from the direction of the stars they looked down with a calm pride at my petty patterns. What ricks of stillness those trees were: once again I can only think of those half-crazed Persian or Lydian despots who gathered together all the muteness in the world, then stored it in tall towers like that as a standing reproach to their chatterbox counselors.

An abiding caress lingered in their form: their striving for the heights was not a Gothic pose, as with the bonier specimens, but a charismatic coiffure — someone had combed and scraped the mass together upwards with the palm of the hand. That was indeed a good reality gesture on the part of reality. No man nor animal, no ants or Carthusians are able to be solitary and sociable in the way of cypresses — each alone so nobly, with such Acherontic aristocracy (is there any other?), yet the garden was nevertheless such a chorus, a synod of trees absorbed in murmuring anonymity.

How does the wind treat you; how do animals go through you; does the moon have a bridge to you? Here the breeze approaching at great seagull tempos from across the lake does not move the foliage, there are no boughs, branches, leaves — here the whole tree turns into a moan from the inside, as the wafer of the host turns into the body, or the inside of the statues of Memnon into music, according to some miraculous otherworldly transfiguration: they are philosophical trees inasmuch as they will not become instruments like the lindens in Bamberg (I have heard them!) but for a couple of seconds — from the wind's touch — they muse with even blacker emotion and even more funereal peace over their own tree nature. But the cowardly melody-smuggling of sentences is unworthy of them. Is that an evergreen? God knows where that color lurks between black and green, silver and brown. But I didn't expect anything different from you, reality: complete evanescence from between my fingers, the ultimate, victorious nuance, with which not only the *impuissant* intellect but also *impuissant* love is unable to catch up. How they stood there by the road! How are they lovelier: if they accompany a road, or if they form a freemasons' lodge on the hillside? Here each of them was a step, a step with perennial ambiguity: agreement, conquest, form attained — and restlessness, direction: on, further on. That melancholic "go on, go on" mood is so strong that it does not even spontaneously come to mind (is there anything which spontaneously comes to mind?) what is vertical and what horizontal, what is the tower and what the road? May you stay on, gloomy cypresses, perhaps forever: humming with all your great weight that every kiss' hook is folly, and yet, *malgre tout,* all this Nike-nothingness is worthwhile.

You stand before me like the Assyrian firebrands of a riddle, while silence furls a black sail over the lake — and you rendered me a riddle: my heart was alien like a powder-weight star, my memory incomprehensible like a fish, the name of which not even fishermen know. That is our perennial fate: great wonders appear in our wanderings like the awakening palaces of Atlantis; gods also flash before us their strumpet's hips and philosopher's eyes — but that all remains just a horror, a fake wonder, a pseudo-revelation: the secret of the cypress is everlasting, the mendacity in it more everlasting than its green.

(I mused about that too for a while: how can people be so impotent and theoretical that they see an analogy to the phallus in the slim hush-spines of the cypresses? I never felt such disgust and intellectual contempt for the whole phallus-sentimentality and myth-mendicancy as under those trees. One must break once and for all time with every variant of "sex + death.")

"What am I?" — della Rovere asked himself one morning, there, among the cypresses. "What am I? In no case anything to do with sex, or with death. I am simply a mirror of the world, and simply infinity. Life's 'basic laws' and 'basic facts,' like sex and death: they are just visions of the sick, bad hobgoblins of delirium. *Principium* is always *infernale.* Woman: mirage; coffin: mirage. And my denial of women is not even metaphysical: it is simply normal, common, or garden indifference.

Love for me means nothing; death means nothing. Things usually only have 'meaning' for the obtuse and sick. In my cell there hangs a lamp on a solitary cord, with a single flame. That is also how I see it. Once, however, I fell ill & feverish and I saw three cords with three objects, and they did not hang straight down but rotated like the spokes of a wheel. The analogy is set and unchangeable: just as a fever sees one lamp as three, the stationary as revolving, so only a fever can see meaning, symbol, sense, & — *horribile dictu* — a 'basic law' in an object!

Genitalia and mortalia are given emphasis *only* in illness. In that I am not giving an apology for down-to-earth health to my followers. After all, I too, am a nerve, only I have no spit. I am desiccated as a wizened mummy forgotten in the Sahara. This is what is decisive: endless sensibility, boundless impressionism, but no sentimentality and no thirst for *principium*.

(I cannot imagine a more perfect annihilation of Bachofen[79] and Lawrence than the play I saw the other day. There, sex and death had the most ideal roles. The subject: a murder takes place in the auditorium on an opening night in a vaudeville theater, and in the play one minute girls are leaping before the audience's eyes, the next one sees a detail of the criminal investigation. That is the maximum or optimum that can be brought out at all from sex-cum-death: sex is represented by half-naked mechanical girls, death by a mob of detectives, cops, and dactylographers fidgeting about a pistol shot.

How kitschy even the most poetic, most ancient, and most popular myth beside such a 'vulgar' film. Let us leave those secretive plans, beyond and outside apish accidents of death-and-sex: they are far better disentangled by a vaudeville show or film.

In time anyway everything with which myths & philosophies busy themselves is transferred to the vaudeville stage. Not in mockery or out of depravity or a citified taste for blasphemy or Lord knows what, but out of intelligence: it turns out that the so-called ancestral, central, and the most profound 'problems' — *quelle garde-robe!* [80] — were only masks of impotence for sick petty-intellectuals, and play was their sole chance of being processed.

Because life is made up of only two parts: of anonymous, irrational, and purposeless objects, and of events, i.e., play. The facts of sex and death are either indifferent, things that exist but have neither metaphysic, nor clinic, nor poetry, *facta anonyma et indifferentes,* as Sixtus IV put it — one can either play with them, style them up into vaudeville, apply them purely ornamentally and frivolously. Indifference or somersault: those are the alternatives for an intelligent person — symbolic cypress smuggling is only for degenerate slaves.)

And the stone pines and palm trees? Don't they too proclaim this ascetic standpoint around the birth of Sixtus? The stone pine is foliage & yet not foliage: Claude Lorrain would be able to make the most enigmatic, sweetly & autumnally languid, romantically cloudy and haunting round-midnight magic with them: and yet they are cold, like the emaciated, skeletal sibyls, who due to their prophesying are mystical actresses, but because of their bones, bitter aridness, are Florentine, which is to say, tartly rational & formal.

Form! Form! I read yesterday for the umpteenth time that "in decadent eras form predominates at the expense of content," when even the blind can see that the inverse is the case: great eras *in ultima analisi* are "devoid of content," they are only interested in form — it is the petty bourgeois baroquists and *fin-de-siècle* misery-guts who would give their last drop of blood (in all likelihood they never have more than one drop) for the cherished, terribly important content. Cypresses, Stone Pines, & Palms are those kinds of Renaissance trees: contentless, virtually anorganic.

When della Rovere learned that he was going to be made pope, it was those trees he saw — not a *Wunder des Lebens*, but a *Wunder des* Nicht-*lebens*, or to play around: a Nicht-*Wunder des Lebens*.[81] He was a Renaissance pope: not of the sensualists or naturalists.

The blue of the lake, which is never blue but either white as milk or foggy or a transparent ultra-green, combining mirror, lizard, and Madonna: never endless but simply and clumsily empty: that lake is also before him, sobered-up, cooled. (Is the masquerade I am making of Sixtus too simplistic? It could be — I must trust that the accumulated variations of sensitive whimsies elsewhere will compensate for the monotony of mania.) Is there anything lovelier than a balcony room opening onto such an empty, white lake?

Two beds with quilted coverlets, the large baptismal font of the washbasin, the oh-so-narrow Latin hardly-door, the balcony, a sunbaked straw armchair, grids in the big nothingness of water, sky and air, then nihil, auroral mist, more mundane than all of Gardone's women put together.

Stillness: evening is stillness' innards, pelt, lining, and warmth: morning is its exterior, its form, its Hellenic limitedness. On it, like minute meadow floral decorations or tiny little sketches in very thick hair, the protracted whine and bubbling of the washbasin in the room next door, the creaking of a strange chair leg on the stone flags of the balcony, the name of an Italian waiter down in the park grounds, an amalgam of tangos coming from two opposing directions like those of figures in a piece of fabric (the lacy edge of a petticoat and the smoke dahlias of the georgette dress over it!), the slight lapping of wavelets on the jetty, the tooting of an automobile unfamiliar back home, which is also willy-nilly a portrait of the strangers traveling in it, the champagne-bottle-like popping-open of a hose pipe, & afterwards the whispering of spray, which scarcely differs from a September breeze searching for roses, as the hand of an older lady's does toward the hair or lips of young boys: impatiently, but with the tight-lipped discipline of salon life.

Roses: they, too, are flowers that are absolutely in keeping here. In a German-language brochure on Gardone I read about "*wuchernde Rosen*":[82] true enough, but nonetheless they are not baroque phenomena. Points: white, melting into space. A rose is not made prickly by its thorns, but by the deportment, the whole 'mentality' of its flowers, its leaves, and its position. It has no 'contour,' no 'figure,' like women or the calla lily; and only the shape is erotic or vegetative. A rose is an isolated, naïve little point of splendor — branches and leaves do not crimp or snake it into the deceitful theater of 'nature.'

I never liked roses as much as there. What two kinds of worlds! For instance, a green pasture overrun by a yellow sun spurge or wolf's milk, a rose bush winding around the foot of a vase. Roses can be tea roses — "Ceylon Tea"-s, or "*Momie de Cléopâtre*"-s, undershot with blue or black, porcelaneous or incensing: all the same, through the fact that they are solitary, grow here and there, as a rule passing off badly as a woman, they are not in the least gorgeous or natural, but they always strike one as a still empty, sparklingly polished cold tea service on the table when one has already set the hopes of one's lips & fingers on the warmth of a cup of tea.

But perhaps even more decisively than by them, I was let loose on my one-sided Sixtus fiction by my travelling companion, a woman I encountered at the train station in Vicenza. I have always felt at ease at that station because, most amusingly, it resembles Déli Station in Budapest, which I dote on. I just happened to be quaffing a thimbleful of *birra* in customary Italian fashion, *hat on my head* (lest I be taken for a weedy young toff) in the small bar, where an Italian bloke at the very same kind of table was eating the very same kind of cheese under the very same kind of afternoon lighting, out of the very same kind of paper, as I had eaten with my father in Paris in a bistro near *Les Invalides* — at that time I thought that I was the only one who would do such a damned fool thing as not to eat a decent lunch out of my distaste for the masses & out of cowardice, but skulk in rundown dives with stone-hard scraps of Parmesan: & lo & behold, after ten years, I gained release: a 'normal person' (the one and probably only god of the nervous) eats exactly the same as I do, and what's more: heartily. In my ecstasy over that, and also refreshed by the beer, I walked back besides the rail tracks to my little zippered handbag of a coffin on which my green raglan overcoat was lying like a wreath.

On the asphalt platform I spotted a skinny woman in a linen beach outfit. For the time being, she was a tritonal scale: an awfully big black hat with a wavy kale-leaf brim; under that, flaming red or cinnabar hair — and holding a huge illustrated magazine with lilac pictures: on the cover, unsurprisingly, there was a naked boxer or water polo player.

I guessed she was French; only they tended to be spread in bread-and-butter fashion with that sort of brick-red paint. The fact that her magazine was Italian was irrelevant. I decided straight away: "You'll be a symbol if it's the last thing I do." I love (of course not in an amatory or sexual sense) those abstract women who no longer have either a body or soul, but are an Alexandrian hieroglyph, each & every one: just as out of a sailing, rowing, galley-slave boat only a single hooked line features in the script, so all that remained here of the whole of the woman's life were these few commas & splotches. The bare legs, sandals, red danger-fingernails sat uneasily together with the big black hat. No one is able to *not* look at someone the way those "women" do. Quite by chance, I ended up in the same compartment with her. She took her hat off and with great difficulty managed to ease it into the smaller of the luggage racks — obstinately, its bell kept on opening, and it would fall ripely onto the seat. I helped with hoisting up her trunk. She thanked me in perfect French & heavenly sweetness. More than once it was jokingly predicted of me that my undoing would be a woman who, as the hit song had it, would be "a bit of an angel & a bit of a devil." We got two middle places in the full compartment — to the right and left of the central armrest.

Next to her sat a sweaty, tubby, chinless Italian; next to me hunched a startled, little old dame with outwardly strabismical eyes who was praying out of a prayer book. Opposite her a clean, blue-eyed, sun-tanned, slightly balding German was reading the *Basler Nachrichten*, with the side of the newspaper that faced me being about a party rallying in Nuremburg, with photographs. Someone who also boarded with us was an Italian girl in mourning dress with an iron engagement ring, an unfriendly, serious one who later turned to solving crossword puzzles, and I ruminated on how it was possible that she was not ashamed of herself. For me the line between Venice and Milan via Verona will forever mean the journey, being underway — made so by the easy monotony of the countryside, the abstract arrow-straightness of the rail track. In this case a person does not travel so much as complete miles and hours in airless space. I am fond of that, so it is over quickly.

Maybe it is also important that Milan is not a center of art so much as of commerce, and when I travel there I don't have to be ashamed that I am not a salesman or an engineer: I rattle along civilly together with all the other civilians, as if I had business in Milan or Turin — the sole place where I manage to be a 'passenger' among the passengers.

With the shared armrest my head came eerily close to the woman's. What is red is red. I acknowledged the big news when with anti-philosopher impudence I examined her hair — "*wir wanderten durch Feuergluten.*"[83] It was a curious material: it was gathered in broad waves but every strand seemed separate, and the skin of the scalp beyond its deep-purple roots was not hidden. But that is not devilish redness and not the redness of life: there was no apocalyptic sin, no vitalist fire.

It was then that Sixtus IV was born, albeit a little illegitimately but definitively, and with him Brunelleschi and the whole alkali-and-acid-Renaissance. How that chignon twisted, streamed, and roamed beside me, and yet its every line was evident, deliberate, its weight, its direction, its supporting strength, its shadow — everything. It was red the way only the hair of dyed-in-the-wool whores is, but nevertheless remained in near-idyllic shape — sealed and 'neat' like a Venetian snuffbox heirloom.

And so it goes on: the eyebrows have been plucked out & in their stead is an eye-pencil scrawl arching to the ears, near the root of the nose it's still Indian-ink-dark anathema, but toward the temples it's already smeared like the tips of leaves in a pastel drawing by Manet, or like the signature on a postcard hastily thrown into the letterbox at a train station before setting off. She had no eyelids; her low and smooth brow simply swept round a quarter circle toward the inside of the skull. The area of the eyelids also seemed to be made of bone and immovable. Under that the eyes huddled together and bulged like a cherry pit between two fingers in the half-second before being flicked away.

At first sight they were wicked eyes, shifty, murderous, morphine-sleepy and harlot high-and-mighty. One of the most characteristic features of bar girls is that their eyes are just as much inferior organs as their nails or teeth: they paint and polish, gouge and grave them as if they were made of bone or horn. Is that not splendid — to trump the soul's mirror that way. Is this reduction not impossible to surpass: the hair a few sparse red lines, the eyes, single black shards of glass?

For a moment, I wavered: the whole thing was so absurd that I reviewed the women full of, or if not full of, then at least sprinkled around with a perfume of ethics, beauty, and emotion, to consider whether it was out of posing, of keeping my own weakness secret, that I was standing by this formula, this "Sistina"? Of course I thought of my mother, too. But no, there was nothing extraordinary: to my dying day I shall carry the two extremes — the "incandescent Sistines" from the Barbary beside the Adriatic, and the humanistic, pretty-kindly, Levantine girls from the East, *ex oriente nox*. Shuddering, torturing myself with those sadistic Florentine women who are beyond even the memory of anything human;

& shut in, lonely, repelled by the warmth of the idyll, the sensitive finiteness of love, when the Jerusalemites around me showed off their tragicomic swanking of humanity. Incidentally, the woman was also a symbol of fall: in her hair's unquenchable carmine, onto which the sun combed something of itself through the window, it was not just the stigmata of categorical damnation that glared, but those of something more placidly resigned as well: autumn leaves.

It astonished me: how could that flameless chemical fire also give expression to the warm, idyllic spleen of late September? Was I still too close to the Tintoretto exhibition to be able to forget the foliage-substituting autumn of his nude figures? In truth, in treeless, unwooded Venice those Tintoretto Susannas, Danäes, and Catherines substituted for the yellowing foliage, as the large, ivory-tinted linen curtain through which the afternoon light leant against the paintings made them even more waxily languid. Now here was that lipstick-red hair that also managed to express the Catullan fall no less than the Venetian painting canopies. Perhaps because she occasionally closed her eyes to let the September light reach her unhindered at right angles: that lent her entire being beastly simplicity and domesticity. My favorite pursuit is to observe how overly made-up women dissolve, crumble, and depreciate in trains — from troubled negligée all the way through to 'Murder on the Orient Express'-variety crime scenes.

I shall not forget that half second, somewhere around Trento, during which I caught a glimpse into a half-full

Italian first-class compartment: the window-shade had been half-lowered, but crookedly, a decapitated Thermos flask sat on the folding table, & papers were slowly shrinking back into their old position, the velvet of the seats was quite dark black-and-red, the painstakingly bleached lace on them in places stiff like a grille, in places crumpled and smeared into a sludge; on the seat, reclining, a woman who was putting on weight, all jewelry and make-up, all perspiration and the ammonia of dreams; in her hands, a hat and handbag, her blouse half-open, with a congealed petticoat froth; her shoes pointed like gondola-lines on foreign-tourist posters. But one of her stockings was sagging with a thousand wrinkles like a punctured air balloon; her coiffure was a sea of flat curls, but in some places it was so tousled as if she had been dragged by the hair down the corridor: the lighting, smell, and dress like a fantastic cross between a working-class toilette and a duchess' boudoir. One could track, inch by inch, the decay and holding-up on the woman's body: up to such-and-such a point evening dress, but there a complete rag; in one spot, gay abandon, but in another, a devastating disease; on the right, a *passable trotteur*, on the left, a dead body plucked from a car crash.

There is nothing wrong with the snoring and gorging peasants of third class; that is always harmonious. But that agonizing luxury-class at midday, in semi-darkness, with bits of body floating in eau de Cologne & cigar smoke was more ghastly than being eye witness to a killing. My present neighbor was as yet very far from the final stages of *agonia wagonica*: she was a pussycat, basking in the sun, all but purring, despite her great Babylonianness.

Now that I have already smuggled in one of the extremes beside "my Sistina," I will place the other by her side, too — the most perfect expression of a kindly, Ariel-light, poetically gleeful fall that I have ever seen: the bouquet that stands before me on the table.

Pale pink carnations held between pale red autumn leaves and the lot set between two pale-green tapers, their wicks still white. More than likely, put down in the text like this, the whole thing has a noxiously precious or æstheticist flavor, but then what business do I have with texts? For a start, I would not have dared to dream of such a triumph of pale colors: in women's dresses, automobile coachworks, Parisian skies, powders and book jackets, I always felt the unmistakable nausea that only those things elicit in me in which a gracefully wilting aristocratism & an absolutely elementary artistic gesture are united in a meticulously exact balance, but this outdid all of those: I have never known such harmony and such variegation. The carnations and autumnal leaves were almost uniform, yet they nevertheless stirred one with a well-nigh Mozartian dissonance. Spring and fall, in the end, became consubstantial; likewise elegant refinement & selfish primeval forest.

Is anything more needed? The spring of the carnations was virginally groping and childishly resigned, like the virginity of princesses who were engaged to black princes when still in diapers, and the fall of the leaves was easy and playful, with mortality being just a cosmetic device & lurking death, merely a *cachet de Lanvin* fragrance. And those prickly, stubby, spiky buds among leaves round as coins! It was that round coin shape and cold flatness, colder than a dog's nose, that made their yellow so unmelancholy: no curliness, no leafy grouping — each leaf separate, a monocle or medal standing haughtily on the youthful branches.

Carnation buds are the kings of buds: podgy & squashy as if a giant snake had devoured two wardrobes full of women's silk shirts — and what tips those padded, impish paunches end in, what smoked beaks! With no other buds can one sense that the flower is already fully formed inside, it is just packed in very tightly like those huge powder puffs in dinky compacts; diminutive bombs. And those tiny cartridges of spring are now swinging to and fro here between the lonely scales & lenses of the red leaves.

Finally, the candles: it's as if they, too, were plants, a completely translucent species of reed in which the slow rising of the green water was visible like an angelic blood circulation. How vernal, slim, and elegant. At the same time, they nevertheless represent the somewhat haughty inorganicity of objects among the flattering leaves round them, next to those chortling improvisations of vegetation. Candles are the most discreet objects: can an object be less than just a line? A church mood, breathed from afar by the candles, then the primeval fern mood, murmuring from afar by the unfolding carnations, quietly pour into one another: consecrated flowers and an altar turned by magic into a bouquet smile together on the naïve adventures of the pen scratching under them. As a matter of fact, this more muted, parlor-house, incense-like fall can do no harm as a respite next to the rigor of Sixtus IV's autumn. Since the propensity for grading & cataloguing is so strong in me that on pronouncing the word "autumn" I must strike the indispensable notes of myth-autumn, Tintoretto-autumn, harlot-autumn, and parlor-autumn, why should I not try to explain with hypocritical force, or at least suggest, that such autumn-variants were brought together not only due to my senseless compulsion for collecting, but also because they are the fatefully congenital features of the pope's portrait? Is not that my sole possible ideal? To come across a marvelous constellation in which, Lord knows how and why, the scatterbrainedness of a child's attention & a mercilessly monotonous concentration on each given subject coincide.

Arriving in Rome with a pessimism redder than Saints Cinnabarius and Carminius, della Rovere was for a while a guest of the Pazzis, where he immediately announced that his first act would be to organize a crusade against the Turks. The family took that fairly coolly; they had worries for their bank. Financing the pope was a posh amusement, but also life-endangering. The lipless pope nervously sipped must in the Pazzi vineyard and made inquiries about an artist to supply embossed armchairs for decorating the council hall in which the kings, princes, and princesses of Europe were to be invited to confer about the war against the Turks.

Pazzi knew one and showed him the letter Brunelleschi had written to the young patron of the arts at the time he was planning the Herodotus frescoes.

The letter flared up in weary Sixtus like a match touching a rough wall. The pope knew that this was the very man. He immediately withdrew to his cool room; alarmed, the servants carried after him his half-drunk glass of wine, but all he asked for was quill and paper. Though it was hard to find those sorts of items on a wine farm, something came to hand. By that time the pope looked very old; he was indescribably thin & his skin was roasted dark as an Arab's. On the black, Othello-ish skin the long, white locks of hair, reminiscent of a pianist's, made an odd impression. He always dressed in disorderly fashion, hurriedly; he went around in the borrowed purple of a cardinal, in a Franciscan cowl, or the uniform of a mercenary army captain. Now all he had on in the autumnal heat was a white shirt.

He wrote this letter:

"I read your plans, gained an insight into your imagination, & in you I found myself. You are a black mirror, but God binds the Old and New Testaments above the Dead Sea, and over the Mediterranean Sea He is silent. That is why I am turning to you. You will have to furnish a large council hall in the Vatican just like a church choir: with lots of massive armchairs. If you have time, you may also paint a fresco, a battle scene; with assistants to make it snappy; with scenes taken from Herodotus or Revelation, as your inspiration dictates. The important things are the armchairs. The outlines should be uniform, but each one should have a different carving, depending on who is to be seated in it: the king of Hungary or the emperor of Portugal, a Sicilian countess or the English sovereign. You catch my drift: study history. Feel that you will be bringing those lords to life: the world is in our hands, Brunelleschi. I make no stipulations; if you wish, you may carve sadly."

Brunelleschi sent the following catalogue to the pope, whose insignia of P.P. he always read as Parca Parcarum:[84]

Armchair I: a wall relief above the armrest — the death of Pius II in Ancona among five fellow-cardinals, on the brink of the planned crusade. A gorgeous young Adriatic, a single blue plate, for which it matters not whether it throws Venuses out of itself or swallows strutting Jerusalem kings, whether God's spirit is hovering above it, like a stray migratory bird, or whether it is two Venetian boats with spoiled nutmegs: indifference itself, azure cynicism, non-physical platitude. I wonder whether Your Holiness is of the same opinion? There is nothing more demoralizing, or stupider, than the sea: dumb water, which like every 'openness' and 'sincerity,' has nothing to say for itself.

That slays the highly-strung pope: not an apoplectic stroke or the storms, not the Turks, but the Adriatic's flat grin. Is the baptism of Jesus conceivable in the sea, or in other words, in emptiness and a line? Do you know that on the mosaics portraying the christening of Jesus in the baptismal chapels of Ravenna the god of water, the quasi-interreligious figure of Neptune, is many times larger than Christ himself?

So how big would one have to paint the puzzlegrass, reed mace-wielding fellow in the sea? I can paint sadly, but won't that make me worse than a hundred heretics? Sadness is a sin against the Holy Spirit; a mockery of Pentecost. Never mind — from a political and moral standpoint alike it is madness to decorate the walls and chairs of an anti-Turkish congress with pessimistic, almost suicidal images, but what am I to do? You told me to study history. Heroism is a solitary insanity, which carries death around within itself like a flower does its scent. It was your predecessor's, Pius II's, as well. He ran out of the two possibilities: worldliness in his younger days, sanctity in old age, and here he collapses unhaloed in the end.

He is supported by five stony-faced cardinals — no sign of the startled, bird-eyed excitement that one sees among the Franciscan friars in Giotto's fresco. One of them was a military cardinal, the second an attorney, the third a Mercury, the fourth a book theologian, the fifth a spy. That's the tragic bit — neither the merchants nor the heroes are necessary. But it might not be as gross as all that to carve that agony to serve up to the assembled rulers: it will be a reproach to the lazy princes.

On the back of the chair the following image from the history of Cyprus. The Frank regent who ruled there, the consecrated owner of three sacred coats of arms, sold his wife at a high price into the harem of the sultan of Egypt. When the bishop of Byzantium learned that and started talking of excommunication and death, the prince lied that his wife was a proselytizer and spy: within one year the sultan of Egypt would be paying homage to the pope in Rome. The Frenchman was a swindler; the princess for her part escaped, Cyprus fell into the hands of the Turks, and by the time the woman reached Rome, her clothes were more tattered than those of a beggar.

That is what will be depicted: Lusignan & the sultan are sitting together in a garden, with the French prince attired in Turkish dress out of politeness, but with the Christian insignia of his arms gleaming on the buckle of his turban, whereas the Turk, so as not to be worsted in the matter of diplomatic niceties, is garbed in the costume of a Norman crusader. They drink and laugh, but above all they point toward a flight of steps at the bottom of the back garden where the half-naked sold-off princess, bleeding from the whipping and drugged, is faltering toward a small Turkish sailing boat, supported on the arms of two tottering eunuchs. In order for the religious *giardinetto* to be complete, on the garden well there stands a wonderful statue of Venus, the ancestral goddess of the island. What became of Venus, and what of Mohammed and the religion of a few more inhabitants of Asia Minor? Garden party, diplomatic Orpheum theater, aqueduct, and harem deal. And no one is responsible for any of that; at the bottom of my soul, though I shall eternally rebel against blasphemers, I know that that is the disheartening order of things — the nub of even the holiest principle is perhaps, *de origine*, just an illusion of illusions, and conversely: there is an ineradicable sanctity in even the crudest compromises.

I feel, Holy Father, that my collision with history and the lives of men is so intensive here that with this I shall probably say farewell to history. But I believe and avow that only a blend of a despondent outlook and a limitless thirst for Catholic morality is capable of viewing history the way it should be seen. Perhaps I shall provoke your anathema with my letter: then I shall feel with inexplicable clarity that your excommunicative judgment is absolutely right, and for all that my complete apathy over or under history is absolutely right.

On the right armrest the image will be a portrait of the Holy Roman Emperor Frederick III, what is this German-Roman Emporium? A loony, the most highly masked-crater of turmoil. In the figure of Frederick III. I want to caricature (i.e., mourn) this extreme fiction. I do not judge but mourn European history like a professional or uninvited wailing woman. To judge it?

No one stood at a more absurd distance from passing judgment than I — no person loved a child with a more maternal embrace than I do Europe. For it is truly lovely, this Europe: in its grandiosity of hypocrisies and in the shamelessness of its self-contradictions. This Frederick III is partly a Tristan figure, the Germanic ghost of sensual idealism, partly a low-caliber despot, a by-now totally bourgeois-style unlawful lawyer & black-marketeer.

Empire, empire: who could here separate mystic ideal from boorish land ownership, the moon from sixpence?...[85] Every moonstruck poplar of midnight, glistening lizards and conspiratorial moles, glow-worms and closed-calyxed bindweed should be gathered around the water-sprite Frederick III, to the feet of this Oberon of the Nordic magic empire: but the narrow-minded Ghibelline, the crude laicism, should also be manifest in his features, in his scepter, his sealed letters and bags of money. Of course, the whole Reich-paroxysm is a much more complex fabric for me to drag it down into cabinet-making budgets of this kind.

On the left arm of the chair I will carve this image: a scene in front of the Parthenon of the Morea.[86] Of course, I shall carve, or order to be carved, a hyper-Parthenon of which the Greeks could not even dream. On the left will be a ruined torso statue of Mary, on the right a jagged, bashed-up crescent resembling a chipped scythe. In the middle a nude figure in the manner of St. Sebastian: an image of the last Palæologian emperor, as to his right a gorgeous Turkish woman takes off his jewelry with her right hand and passes it on with the left to the slave girl standing next to her, who is collecting it in a sack; on the left, a senile Venetian trader who is stripping the emperor of his clothes, sword, crown, and his scepter and handing them to the crew of an elegant Venetian boat. That is the ultimate mercantilism: the whore-odalisque and the superannuated San Marco rag-and-bone merchant are, if anything, even more agonized than the looted, naked emperor-skeleton. The emphasis here, too, is on the tragic, not the critique of ownership as a disease, a Midas syphilis. The heaven & hell of 'property' — it bears a lot of thinking about. That would be the first armchair, but I wonder who should be seated in it at congress? They will not be in high relief, never fear their being made uncomfortable! Although I may give up my ghost in the *Dispute of Europe,* I know that before all else I am a carpenter whose job it is to produce comfortable armchairs. We shall put big feather cushions on the seats, with velvet covers & braided edges.

Armchair 2: on the wall over the back of the chair a relief — a triple image portraying the canonization of Catherine of Siena by Pius II in such a way that Pope Gregory XI is also visible, whom St. Catherine brought back home to Rome from Avignon. I will portray the holy woman as old, although she died young, partly because when I paid a visit to Siena I ran across only old dames, but secondly because this is the only way I am able to render ascetic stubbornness and fierce obsession. The dead body is propped up, almost standing. Her face is Acherontic defiance & desperate loneliness; a true mystic always has a mercilessly martial, unmelting profile. I wish to convey on it all Pythian alone-ness, all feminine obstinacy on being confronted with male humbug — that rabid earthiness in which virgins & magna-maters concurred from time immemorial.

What does that grim cadaver have to do with the elegant figure of Pius II, author of *The Tale of Two Lovers,* a favorite of heretic popes, and Frederick III's boudoir lawyer? She is the vegetative source of morality, morality as destiny: she is killed by virtue as Midas was by gold. She is like Siena itself: a castle on a hill, full of heavy military-Gothic, twisting, broken streets, which are not serpentines of the senses but the natural agony of goodness — goodness which by now is already bile, so logical and consistent is it.

I used to know a young Arab stargazer — what can be seen here in the form of morality is his mathematical sadism. And the canonizing pope: I have painted him as a martyr in the sketch for the first armchair, as a symbol of the eternal barrenness of heroism in Ancona — his vast white beard a snow that suffocates everything in deafness. For the sake of contrast, I want to portray here the as yet unburied troubadour, equerry, anathematized heretic-agent and playboy. With a sweeping gesture of Adonic ease, he points to the sky: in that movement, too, some dream of empire glistens, with Fata Morgana naivety, like in Frederick III's portrait: but here I would rather like to create the enduring image of the political genre of diplomacy — the sweet, smile-raising faith a whole lot of people have, that everyday hypocrisy *&* *civitas dei* can be brought into harmony. The self-deluding butterfly of diplomacy in May self-satisfaction over the black mummy of Siena; the idyll of raw Gospel hunger and political interpretation. Catherine seems to be pursing her lips. Perhaps she is not pouting, but if she is, then it is quite certain that her gesture is unjustified.

And the last leg of the tritone? The pope of Avignon? Needless to say, he too will also be something abiding, eternal Avignonesqueness, eternal worldliness, Rome perfumed in Paris. From those two figures it becomes clear what conflicts worldliness encompasses. My favorite imagining is how wild

Catherine yanks, as on a dog leash, her reluctant, Frenchified guest from Avignon back to Italy: like a screaming wife pulling her husband out of a tavern. In the picture, he stands there shuddering, folding in his two hands two halves of a sundered Avignon castle, blubbering like a spoiled child whose favorite doll was broken.

Ought we not to seat the Princess of Portugal in this chair? I have heard that she has been to Siena to visit relatives, and she may have seen the sibyls on the cathedral's marble floor panels — one is driven to identify Catherine with those Saracen "Lybicæ" & midnight "Delphicæ," to associate her with citations from Euripides & the Erinyes, rather than with gentle nuns. It will do Portugal good, to be sure.

I shall depict a similar scene on the chair's armrest: my acrimony begins to take pleasure in those canonizations where the saint seems to detest the conferrer of sanctity, who in almost every case was a born blasphemer rather than the administrator of halos. Emperor Frederick II at the ceremony at the grave of Saint Elizabeth in Marburg.[87] Let the sovereigns see in this image what a caricature this art-loving demon & rag picker of the remnants of sultans & emperors was: an intellectual.

He sits on his tower-high throne in Marburg, clad in a baggy Roman toga, plagiarized with lamentable haste — the *imperium romanum* as a stage prop; on his head a massive turban with some exotic bird. Before his feet, the opened grave; next to it, the princess' dead body at the moment when the emperor's Sicilian Saracen slave girls wish to hoist her up. On the left side, an alarmed gaggle of cardinals, who express with gestures of pathos their terror at the sight of such blasphemy, but they are kept in check by Frederick, like wild game in a forest, with falcons, hunting dogs, and eunuchs.

On the right, symmetrically, is a similar group — a cluster of Franciscan monks on whom the emperor's soldiers are about to shovel bejeweled garments and headwear, as Frederick's august majesty is offended by the bohemian beggars. To the right and left of the emperor's throne can be seen two other, similar thrones: on one a sidelocked Maimonides, wearing huge eyeglasses, is reading something from a Hebrew codex, on the other an Indian leopard is tossing and turning amid a tangle of cushions. Those two are his true councilors and friends.

Europe could also come to this, to such a wondrous 'synthesis': let the sovereigns arriving in Rome see, in case there are still a few among them who, with similar upstart brashness, would call a zoological garden and an asylum for Jews an empire. The buffoon of illusion, an artificial demon patched together from intellectual paper labors, a despot loafing around in the peeling mask of humanism — all that will be written on the face of the emperor, who wished to raise Elizabeth into the jumbled Elysium of his own empire when he declared that what we also love about Jesus is that he was descended from the *royal* family of David. On that carving I want to finish off the unadulterated grotesquerie and comedy that threaten the secular layman if he liturgizes and mystifies himself — the result is invariably: a vapid, unecstatic Carnival in place of Apocalypse. A culture parrot is always ludicrous.

Oh, pope, laugh out loud and forever from your cathedra in Rome, from this armchair, in the face of Frederick II's dream of a Roman empire, his Nordic neurasthenia and Southern mendicancy, so that this naïve lyricism, which is on roughly the same level as the daydreaming of a teenager reading Julius Cæsar, should never again be made policy. And what are the Orient, Jews, & the secrets of nature for us? The poses of 'omniscience' — infinite understanding? (Though that is a tautology, as 'knowledge' and 'pose' are in any case synonyms.)

On the left armrest: St. Catherine of Alexandria's debate with a late-Gnostic philosopher in such a way that the philosopher's most important theological ideas can be seen embodied. Here, too, male coarseness and insatiable male romanticism are faced with female lucidity, with butterfly-like, Parisian-buoyant rationalism.

Maleness as quintessentially an eternal just-a-parody option. This heretic — let us call him Basilides — has three fundamental figures: the first is the very first and remotest source of all existence & every possibility of being, the unknown, anonymous, Creator X, pure, abstract reason, the bleached-out What in whatsit. The second is the primitive worlds radiating from that, & the primitive myth-vapors & god-fumes belonging to those worlds: one such vile myth-vapor, in Basilides' view, is the god of the Old Testament

& the god of the Jews, who thus becomes merely a distorted accident of distorted matter. Finally, the third: Christ as pure Nous, *intellectus belligerens byzantinus*, who came into the world in order to destroy that Jewish myth-vapor.

Behold, the incarnation of male frivolity! Behold, the three scoffing imps of Christian Europe, which for centuries, indeed millennia, have jested and sneered on the edge & bottom of all our history & thought: great ignoramus, great anti-Semitism, and great rationalism. According to them: the end-cause? — an unknown causal point. Jewish monotheism? — a material shadow or bud of *materia*. Christ? — the source of *raison*, raving barbarian scholasticism, pan-intellectualism. On the relief Basilides is pointing out, with philological narrow-mindedness, those three absurd hyperboles to ironic Catherine.

The unknown cause: that will be represented with hieroglyphs shrouded in clouds & the hocus-pocus signs of freemasonry — the ignoramus, the bankruptcy and burlesque of the ultimate abstraction, a caricature of whimpering or raging skepticism. The heretic notion of a Yahweh derived from dust & choking back to dust I shall model from a Jew twisted almost into a pretzel, whose limbs grow into sources, tree foliage, & basilisk tails, while his face is contorted into an agonizing, desperate grimace. The animals & plants also all suffer, for according to Gnostic doctrine they are crippled outcast æons. Finally, the symbol of intellectualism run riot, that blasphemed pseudo-Soter[88] posing as an Alexandrian professor? A thin-as-a-rake scarecrow with a transparent rag body, like a tassel-fish, which mimics to the point of looking identical, the decomposing plants at the bottom of the sea: only its head is gigantic, its cerebrum an unluggable puffball mushroom that is held up by three little Egyptian eunuchs with rods & gruesome efforts, lest it crush them to death.

Is my tragicomic relief not right? In Europe we are doubters to the bottom of our heart, but we feel that skepticism is an unworthy, cheap, slavish attitude; our morality has its source in the Old Testament, nothing better or fairer being found; yet still some invincible alienness holds us forever at bay from this people, suspecting in it the blindest earthliness; since the Neander Valley our brain has been our sole organ & instrument, yet we cannot laugh at anything louder than at such words as *Nous* and *Gnosis*.[89]

Feminine Catherine scoffs at this mediocre necromantic séance of tales. There is a youthful autumnal afternoon floating in her clothing and colors, but in her body and soul a man-mocking spring. Her bronze-hued hair is parted in the center and twisted up high to the temples at both sides; above her brow there are as-yet minute tongues of wildfire, which above the ears have become large flames — the curling is like September leaves or the shriveling of paper that gets too close to fire. A low brow (because the female intellect, as the one and only conceivable true form of the intellect, does not derive from the brain but from the whole being); below that are Chinese, Mongolian eyes that one can sense are now narrowing in the delirium of myopia, now unexpectedly opened:

at such moments it is not the swan pond of the soul docking in her, but the virgin-funereal light of a blind roe deer's black irises, nightless black, pure, reflex alarm.

How splendid those blind deer eyes, paralyzed in fear before the hunter, with their own electric ignoramuses, laid beside doubt compromised with Basilides-style, *cour-des-adieux* gestures. The eyebrows jump into sharply pointed triangles, but the tips of the triangles are far away from the root of the nose. The mouth is big, with healthy teeth: speech, argumentation in this mouth is truly a game of the mouth, not the brain — on those lips it is like lipstick, or the spume on a ripple lapping on a lake with no wind.

The whole figure is a mixture of the girlish & womanly: in part, she feeds milk to him, and in part imitates Basilides with a theatrical gourmandizing; her teenage-girl penchant is expressed in her every action, from scorn to motherliness. Her fingers, on which she counts her arguments, are translucent candles with barely visible joints; her nails are pale daytime flames — instead of the funereal lamps of the male *lumen*, the genuine brightness of life. And this whimsical adolescent cheerfulness vanquishes not only the deplorable God-masquerades of European thinking, but also the wraiths of morality, and love lost in the mazes of nonsensicalities. Just as the three theological puppets grow above the head & shoulders of death-Basilides, so on the right-hand side, under the feet of reasoning Catherine, wriggle the snake heretics, ophites,[90] who adored Lucifer and Judas, whose god was Cain and whose sole prayer text was perversity.

That rampant eroticism and absurd Satan cult is likewise male stupidity *par excellence*, and Catherine annihilates the lot with a coquettish-dismissive smile.

The ophites may have been adolescents and pre-menopausal women, or in other words, sick. Holy Father, I saw both at one and the same time: the unanalyzable stupidity of puberty, and all the beating-about-the-bush and long-drawn-outness of wilting women. Let me put here, before Catherine's feet, the whole of adolescence, in which I went astray, and from which to this day I have not found the way out: the main argument for the existence of Satan. *Pubes* and *climax*: that is all I know about love, *et nox est nomen eius.*[91] I do not believe that Catherine, with her own Nike-arching, could give me the least scrap of assistance — it's already too late ... You came, pseudo-autumnal fires in your hair, in swift-winged ships to doddery old Alexandria; and while many priests & philosophers raise altars to Nike, I, wildest of your believers, lure you to the harbor, and drown you deeper in the water than the anchor, because I came to know this on your second coming: knowledge is one thing, but force is only Nike's — loss ...

On the right armrest I sought an ultimate formula for woman's self-deification, which denies man, indeed, is all-denying. I thumbed through a codex that dealt with Frederick II, thinking that maybe some female whatnot might occur in it. I did not find any women's thing in it, but I did find something that helped me get very close to the matter. After the death of the emperor, there were many who did not believe that the *dominus mundi* really had disappeared from the face of the earth; there had even been a prophecy that had foretold for him a lifespan of two hundred and fifty years.

One after another, new bogus emperors arose in Sicily, Thuringia, and Egypt alike. There were plenty of swindlers among them, but some were not swindlers at all, and suddenly all my sympathy was drawn to them: figures who, out of tragic ambition, theatrical obsession, & the indomitable self-mythicizing instinct of their lives, promoted themselves to the living or resurrected *deitas solis* — they were great intellects, who saw that schooling was worth nothing, only actions and the human individual's rivalry with god. From time immemorial that dream has been living in me, too: the dream of a brain, which has ended up in a cul-de-sac, that one day I would wake up not as a scholar but as the Duke of Miravalles y Fior-di-Luciferas. That was the first step toward the figure of the *'ultima puella'*[92] that was to be created.

Then came a second, which I found in the Pazzis' immensely vast jurisprudence library. By pure chance I lay hands on the much later commentaries on the protocols of the Council of Rheims in 1148. There I came across a heretic who did not imagine himself to be a demigod emperor but a downright god, a Messiah in the true theological, not metaphorical sense. His deeds were also proportionally more colorful than those shadows of Frederick II: he plundered churches, burned down monasteries, and flung the rags and bones of the booty to the poor with the aim of boosting his popularity. By now I already had a suicidal intellectual who played the emperor;

I already had a mentally deranged slave who had himself worshipped as the god of gods. It was then that I glimpsed the marvelous marble bust of Eleanor of Aragon,[93] signora di Sciacca, which has been preserved in the Abbey of Santa Maria del Bosco di Calatamauro; I think it is the work of Francesco Laurana.[94]

People commonly say that something they do not understand is all "double Dutch" to them. Now, that female representation is the very essence of "double Dutchness." Her hair & brow, right down to the eyebrows, are tightly bound by a filet-woven cap like that of nuns, patients swaddled in gauze, or ascetic women lying on a cosmetician's table bound in skin-beautifying strips. There is no forehead, no ears, & no hair; or, in other words, no thinking, no overhearing of, or listening to, the outside world; no forest in the Ardennes.

The tight cap is a negative halo: a more stringent apotheosis of restrictedness. The eyes are slanting, spiky; the 'master' is always an exoticism, and for precisely that reason the national, inbred sovereign is not an absolute ideal — the true master is Atlantean, Chinese, or a star (and for precisely that reason the fable of Phædrus, in which the frogs start behaving impudently toward a log of wood as their king is incredible: a mystery like the log fetish was meant to awaken respect in animals not just at first but until the end of the frogs' world). The eyebrows can barely be made out — the whole thing a pale line; the edge of the skin of the cheeks underneath the eyeballs is much sharper — like an unshapely scar in the wake of its being split. There is something aggressive about the eye slits, as if originally there had been marble-smooth skin there, too, and just as there was no need for ears there was none for eyes either; everything beyond the woman is superfluous. Someone has nevertheless slit them (perhaps a republican or a man), and now she also has eyes, though one more readily imagines blood oozing there than light rays. The nose is straight as a rudder that has been frozen in place. I had not previously seen exoticism, Renaissance purism, female self-absorption, elegance, & feudalism combined in that way in one head. It was obvious for me to think of the Amazons and Penthesilea — and I immediately saw what I was going to carve on the armrest: the condemnation of the Sicilian female heretic Spasima d'Ansalone at the Council of Cefalù.

Spasima taught that the Holy Ghost really did invade the body of the Madonna, who was none other than herself, only she did not allow the Holy Ghost into her womb but drank it into her blood and thus herself became a Goddess, without having brought a Savior into the world. Mutilated, the Holy Duality bleeds in Elysium, as she described it in her madness; they yearn for the third, which has fallen into female slavery, *et nostalgiam cœli non concedimus.*[95] As a token of that, she carried a pigeon on her wrist at all times, like hunters a falcon: its legs were clapped into a golden bracelet like into handcuffs. Spasima succeeded in persuading women to murder their husbands — that was the most cultic deed of 'her religion,' the way to 'salvation.' Men were destroyed with poison, political betrayal, dagger, and by boring holes in ships.

She ended up being imprisoned & arraigned before a tribunal of the church council.

The background of the picture is formed of the bevy of bishops sprawling in their armchairs (ought one not to design reliefs for those?) — they are like rheumatics clambering out of their graves with great difficulty at the Last Judgment, or insomniac women in their ravaged beds. In the center, eyes closed so as not to see men, the Chinese Satan-mænad. A statue! At the moment the executioner was about to touch her shoulder to snatch her off she has turned into stone, and with the bird clinging to her breast, all its feathers already ruffled, is, if anything, even more frightening. In the foreground, three big figures of the council are grouped round the statue, which is askew like the Leaning Tower of Pisa: one of them has thrown himself on the floor, is tearing at his hair and immensely wrinkled purple cloak; the second has his arms raised to the heavens in execration and may even be on the point of smashing the statue; and finally, the third is in a skeptical, contemplative pose, stumbling out of the church with uncertain steps (the man submissive to women to the point of suicide; the man taking revenge on women; and the perpetual meditator).

I want to add a few more words in relation to the armchair. The subjects of two reliefs are certain: one has to be taken from *Revelation*, the second from nature: after so much historical circus, let the two extremes stand in conclusion — the inner tragedy of total metaphysics, & the similarly mysterious fiasco of total physics. Mysterious I call it, because as you will see from my ratiocination — although I will talk about comedy, failure, useless anarchy, & Harlequin tricks like a compulsively blasphеming, rabid heretic: in the end, I nevertheless see in all this grinning *mal-chance*, in the ungainly tumbles of what is ultimately beyond-nature &, in contrast to it, ultimately within-nature: a *triumph*, the sole triumph possible for man. If history, as you have seen it in the images so far, is a hodgepodge that is somewhat nostalgically spiritual and just as nostalgically bestial, never reaching a point of rest, then why should those two elements not stand here, in Satanic or conceptual nakedness, cleaned up & separated: the purely supernatural, i.e., the Apocalypse, and the purely intra-natural, i.e., an animal scene from the jungle or the sea bottom?

In any case, the opposition of metaphysics and 'small-scale history,' of big celestial backdrops and little-earthly tinkering, immediately brought to mind the prologue to *Revelation*: it speaks alternately of the seven churches & the seven Spirits. Is the opposition of those two not a magnificent *propositione thematis*? And are they not homogeneous to the point of inseparability in their own Semitic nature? Are they not most Oriental: the snuggling up to one another of the *tribus*, a murmuring swarming, it matters not whether in Laodicea or Jerusalem — and beside it, the 'Spirit': the cult of abstraction, of the hocus-pocus sources of feeling & thought (= sentimentalism & mole-rationalism)? John the Divine lists the names of the cities: Ephesus, Smyrna, Pergamos, and so on.

All that is far too this-worldly, too little and ephemeral, for amounting to restful excitement. The Semitic ghosts still hover above those, in a sky of chattering markets: the 'spirits' — spirits that are far too remote, disappearing into a triple murkiness of poetry, nerve, and phobia, for us to be able to hold on to them. *Terra deficit; cœlum deficit.*[96] After that unsettling prologue comes the deluge of facts or notions from which every neurosis & god, every play-acting history or begging art (my choice of those attributes is not accident but essential) has ever drawn nurture. (Small wonder that all this is stuck onto Asia — an Asia about which to this day we still do not know whether it represents the essence of our fate in Europe or if its mentioning there is merely female *chinoiserie.*) Jesus Christ is the 'faithful witness': the legal, mystic, & logical concept of the truth of *ex oriente*-thinking bubbles here in respectable hybridity.

What is truth in this oriental vapor? Bearing witness in a trial by the winning party, on the side of the truth of the prosecution, or on the side of the truth of the defense in a legal dispute: whichever way it be, it is a profoundly bourgeois, tribal affair rooted in the market, in Mercury, in petty law and forum. The 'heavenly' truth: of course, the eternally valid meaning of the world, the sole authentic explanation of all things, an impossibly large and lofty absolute. And mystical on top of being commercial and philosophical: the mysterious emanation of the truth, the bodily essence of matter & existence, a voluptuous, tangible proof. What has John to say about the Son? He is the first begotten of the dead.

The juxtaposition, in such an oversharpened formula, of the two myth-rostra of death and birth, already verges on affectation in a paradox.

But it is beautiful and credible only this way. Not only is he of the dead, but a prince as well. Again, the two divine comedies juxtaposed: the Orpheus comedy with the *psyche*-rotten underworld-flummery (that word is used literally here, in the gastronomical sense) and imperial comedy, the eternal magic and reality of secular power, the eternally seductive crown and scepter of despots and emperors, sultans & democrats that can never be eradicated from the world any more than death. The concept of "prince" is a human organ, an accessory brain or accessory heart, part of one's body.

After "underworld" and "empire" he speaks about *sin* — how enigmatic that sin is as well; how over-precise in its own Patmos contourlessness. Sin: in general the darkness of the world, some sort of black melancholy; next to the tree of life it is simply the physically inevitable shadow of the tree of life. Then the specific sins: fornication, murder, blasphemy, theft. Here the waves of practical morality & pessimism of the great *Primum Malum* collide. That Satanism is more attractive than Greek destiny. After sins, finally blood: that is the cheapest junk shop for symbols, an image of strength and humiliating death.

From the whole *incipit* it is evident that every metaphysics which takes itself a bit seriously spins off into a holy frenzy from its very first gesture. Anyone who sees in this any compromising of metaphysics is naïve. The sole justified and credible form of metaphysics is: the fantastic downfall — a flurry so insanely anarchic that in its startling, tawdry tragedy some god eventually makes its appearance. All transcendentalism starts with the rending of the garments, the tautening of the strings to breaking point, with delirious despair: because ready-made 'metaphysics' are drier than bone, but humankind's intoxicated, maniacal need for metaphysics & enchainment to myth is the purest theology. The theology of the future will no longer fiddle around with the micrometry of 'belief' & 'non-belief.' The great religious experience will be of a third kind — the fact that it is not immediately definable will not give much trouble in times that will at most acknowledge the anecdotic nature of the genre of 'definition.'

When Jesus Christ speaks about the keys of hell & death — I sense the inebriation with metaphysics, the delirium around the "end of all ends." That is true rapture — that Semitic & abstract ecstasy yields wilder wines, and gets more drunk from them than any platitude-sexed Dionysos. The Keys of Death: is it not the two fateful-fantasticalities of life that have free rein in those two words? Fear, evil, destruction, the inner sadism of being, the eternal negative, illness, and shadows: the source of superstitions, the eternal womb from which gods are born. And the key?

Knowledge, mastery over death, the medicine for sickness, "charming philosophy."[97] Nowhere is there such bitter rummaging in the earliest kitsches of life and fate. It is a mystery how the blood-death-Satan monotony does not become boring; no doubt because it is so wild, so scornful of literature, so common (in the holiest sense of the word). It is driven by the impatience of the mythical imagination, the hunger for vengeance of the God-demanding soul; it is so strange that sometimes it nevertheless stoops to literature.

Seven candlesticks? Who wants them? Neither symbol, nor object, nothing — and yet sublime. How can the miracle occur that the powerlessness of something is demonically convincing? Am I guided at times like this solely by my two basic elements — my boundless pessimism and my boundary-fearing æstheticism? Do I indeed readily accept something that is both representatively bad and nerve-tinglingly beautiful? Probably: *tant mieux pour le pessimisme.* And how is it that when I hear from John's lips the word "tree of life" I am struck with much more elemental force by the smell of flowers, the taste of meat dishes, the savor of spices, the inherent profligate liberty of the whole of nature, than if I were invoking (?) the wheat, water, and genitalia-dolls of nature religions? Again, it is just bad medieval neurosis grinding around inside me: does the background of Satanism *ad lib* awaken more unhealthy appetites? That, too, is possible, in which case again *tant mieux pour la névrose.*[98]

It may be that hitherto people never 'believed' in religion: neither in nature religion nor in Christianity. A natural religion knows nothing about belief — it is a simple merging into reality: religion just 'is,' it coincides without crises with people's lives, with their un-glossed, self-evident 'is.' Christianity (mine at least, that of Brunelleschi) eludes 'faith' in precisely the opposite way: its greatness consists in the fact that its boisterous absurdity tortures itself into such unrestrained doubt phantasms that the *furore* of doubt, its poxing-into-a-problem, becomes a new positive, one of the most pliant, most concrete stances in the face of being.

Partisan fanaticism is more sublime than philosophical omniscience. The difference is intriguing: how unenjoyable the Quran with its execrations of its own enemies, yet how magnificent Revelation with its own revenges on the hostile. You, Holy Father, will naturally say at once that I am playing with words. The Quran is a partisan book, Revelation is God's... How come a book seems unacceptable in every detail to my doubt-mechanical brain, yet in its entirety it is nevertheless the thesis of all theses? Party or God, or both of them together? ... I have never seen anything more antagonistic than Jezebel, the licentious woman and false prophetess who worshipped idols in Thyatira. Why? One would have expected that I, an adolescent artist, would take the woman's side, but I didn't. Perhaps I cheated again: in Jezebel I did not see the heretic denizen of bordellos or in John a true messenger of the true God, but merely some provincial feminism, left-wingery thinned out with æsthetic — whereas in John it was an enraged King Lear, pessimism incarnate, a rendering of every myth ultimately impossible, a frenzied Anti-myth.

What I like in the Thyatira section is the part of verse 24 that runs "... & which have not known the depths of Satan."[99] I have always associated "depths," whether spiritual or bodily, religious or amatory, philosophical or political, solely with

Satans; I saw in them the false tricks of the simulacra of the Semite 'soul' (curiously, until my dying day, I shall not rest content that maybe I, the John-blasphemer, am more faithful to John than the faithful.) John does everything possible to place the 'soul,' that fruit of Oriental hypochondria that is tougher and more secular than the idols, above all, while I can only see in it a black panorama of the inner sterility of the 'soul,' of 'psychology.' That grandiose Minus & Negative — that is my belief, my spiritualism, or what you will. (At the risk of repeating myself: the 'soul' is to blame, my torturer and savior, my unsolicited Asiatic dowry.)

When I get to the Four Horsemen, I am quite festively moved by the greater mystery of the impossibility of myth. Nowhere does the internal meaninglessness, poverty, and withering of symbol and myth cry out and weep so loudly as here (no doubt I am committing a mortal sin to put such distant, indeed opposed, entities as 'symbol' & 'myth' under the same hat) — and for that very reason do they appear so monumental. Do I content myself with 'monumentality' when it ought to be truth — or reality? What if it is impossible to get more? I see in the galloping of the Four Horsemen the flight of myth, the eternally craven and eternally ignominious escape of all metaphysics from the world. Leaving the truth below them: destruction.

They may indeed always punish sins, but, as I wrote before, that punishment is so universal that one forgets its ethical quality and simply picks up on the *l'art pour l'art* everlastingness of suffering & destruction. Myth declines, violence flourishes. I have nothing to do with either Poseidon or Pegasus, or with myth *x*'s horse *y*, which symbolized everything imaginable from eroticism to anti-eroticism, from victory to ghost horror (or to put it more grandly, in the argot of *Sein*-slobbering: they shared in Being). It is only those horses that I like, even though they may be nothing more than the emaciated remnants of Jewishly-abstracted great horse mythologies. Whence the unexpected nature of this turning away from Greek myth toward distorted myth and phony-myth? Right now, at the dawn of the *Rinascimento*, in the center of Florence, where people beribboned the legs of ancient stallions and Venuses with their own bodies, in the manner of nostalgic ivy? I don't wish to go into this at length, but I think they do that because what stands at the core of Greek myth, in spite of all its anthropomorphism, is the whole of *nature*, whereas in John, in spite of all its cosmic ornaments, it is mankind, character, the private *spiritual person*. In my view, the chasm between *mankind* and *nature* is vast, unbridgeable; only someone who never looked in their own mirror, never smelled a flower, can seek analogies between mankind & nature.

Mendacity and ignorance — to seek a link between the frigidity and carnage of virgins on the one hand, and the selfish snowfields of high mountains, the bleeding pigs of deep forests, on the other hand; or in other words, Artemis is a left-handed metaphor torso. It is mendacity and ignorance to see fraternity between the labor pains of mothers and the wheat and flower crop of fields, to slap Demeter

Earth and Demeter Mother together into one: man and nature are *separate* lonelinesses, and those two damnation-autonomies perform their aimless dance of death *far* from each other. In John, that is the thought at the bottom of everything: mankind's man-directedness and mankind's loneliness, & around that human solitude, nature is just a tatter of an ornament, which can never be of any assistance to us. The monumental insensitivity to nature: that is the most anthropomorphic attitude.

Sin is not Midnight; solitary yearning is not Moon-Narcissus; theft is not the streets' Hermes dance in the dizziness of distance; death is not the cockleshell lap of hetæras. Sin, adolescent meandering, stealing, death are one's most personal, unmodeled inner pains & joys — the world, the "whole of existence," the "reality of nature," and other Alexandrian nonentities of that sort never bothered with it, and they reject the kinship projected on it from without. It is of hair-raising significance when Paul mentions with undiluted European obstinacy in his letter to the Romans: "to the Jew first, and also to the Greek"[100] — that being Europe's internal tension, the inability ever to poise between Jewish "*reductio ad* hominem" & Greek "*reductio ad* naturam." One's soul is filled with a special rapture of agony by the knowledge that that duality, that Jew-Greek opposition, can in reality never be resolved — we shall go to the grave not knowing at the very last moment whether with one's death an autumn leaf fell with the other acacia and aspen leaves into the leaf mold of a seamless cosmos, i.e., whether we were *nature* at one with the other natures, or a lonely, banished *soul*, a persecuted, accursed foreigner, a Jewish psyche-orphan in the hostile prison of nature, a writhing morality clockwork that is now finally leaving the enemy camp. And no one knows better than I how much that is not a problem of "the history of ideas" (to throw in a bit of modern jargon), but the most practical issue of everyday life. That Paulian bifurcation sweetens & sours my every kiss: I separately kiss 'Jew' & 'Greek'; separately as a *flower* inclining to a flower, and separately as a flower-charring *soul* demon.

Now that I have my grips on abiding tensions, here is another, just as strong and tragic as the first: the difference between the Christ Lamb & the dreadful, world-subverting God the Father, the overlord destructive even in Creation. This is one of the most unsettling of Revelation's double-edgednesses. For me, at that, who only sees double around myself in Florence: the tiger arrogance, dazzling elegance, and murderous perfection of the dukes, everything that medieval heraldry-romanticism & physical harmony together can give, the redeeming drunkenness of power, the fraternity of poetic beauty and resonant gold (a thousand times more resonant than Palestrina), the weapons' logic a thousand times more logical than Plato.

For me no other way of life is conceivable than the aristocratic, the mystic solitude of money and health hallowed by style: a peacock, a high, evergreen-clad castle wall, a fountain, a thousand-year-old coat of arms, a harem, and sarcophagi with a hundred alabaster statues — that, or nothing.

Notwithstanding that I also see and live something else in Florence: with the poor in cellars, with patients in hospital, with outcasts in forests sodden into mud — I am a demos with every demos, scarlet-fevered with every child with scarlet-fever, & it is only squatting beside the bean soup of proletarian kitchens that I feel my reality — for me man and destitution will be inseparable to my dying day: my fate is the slums.

I probably carry that duality in my blood; I know whose child I am; I am familiar with my father's red-flowered and red-leaved family tree, the entire colorful legacy of Ghibelline poses & preening deportments; I am familiar with my mother's black genealogy, the dark relay of modesty, humility, self-consuming sympathy, & God-secreting hypochondria. From my mother I have in me the blood of the Lamb of St. John, from my father the blood of the Prince in the royal seat of St. John — and just as it is a perennial European thing to go fruitlessly to ruin between 'nature' & 'humankind,' it is a similarly European thing to be unable ever to choose between "moralizing gentleness" and "barbarian despotism." If I spot tender-hearted sympathizers, necrophobics, and sugar-light humanists — I flee panic-stricken to the Machiavellian dominies, to tyrannical soldiers, to the Colleonis, & to the pirates with the death's head sails.

When the robbers' Bucentaur sets off with me, I slip among the hypochondriacs, the good, and the slobbery humanists. Of course, Holy Father, it does not take your sharp-sightedness for someone to say to me: why do I associate the Meek of John straight away with saliva, with hypochondria, and with the pettifogging neurasthenia of the ghettos? Equally, why do I associate the Prince of John with the robberies of pirates and the butcheries of rabid despots?

Because for me the goodness of the best is a bit not morality but the withering of a wilted frame, against which even the most wilted neurasthenic frame for me is not a sickness but morality; if you will, *"gratia semi-plena"*[101] — in short, even in the frazzling of nerves I sense concrete gods, and in the concrete sanctity, a few wandering nerves. As a result, "slobbery humanism" is neither a compliment nor a judgment: it is a matter of mood whether I see the divine in sickness rather than sickness in the divine. (Needless to say, after all that, a few aulic blind fogeys around you will ascribe to me some stereotyped determinism, but then the blind are outside.) And just as sick Orient and living God merge in the Lamb, so the blood of history and holy kingship merge in the Prince: in all Teutonic sadism there is something of the heavenly spirit of divine rule, of the eternal metaphysics of the *dominus sacralis,* just as in every crown, scepter, and emperor or burgrave legalized by mysteries there remains some essential, unmaskable bestiality, beastly selfishness, penetrating evil. Hence when I spoke about the fight of the Lamb & Prince in relation to Revelation and, above all, my own soul, I so readily identified the lamb ideal with compromising the lamb, the loftiness of the Prince with the prince's depravity.

Incidentally, I think I have not yet been entirely honest in my confession to you. When I sketched to myself the equal presence of the lamb world and the *dominus mundi* world, I only informed you of a temporary state. For if I have to choose, I will choose the Lamb, and the untouched crest of *fleurs-de-lis* are very withered beside the embers of goodness. It is a mysterious moment when an artist who has entwined all the colors and forms of the world with the vine tendrils of his nerves suddenly realizes that the essence of his life is *not* beauty but morality — moreover, a morality which he knows to be a variant among the other ephemera, and it is precisely in its tragic intermezzo-nature, in its historical evanescence, that he senses what to others is the stimulus of the 'absolute.' I cannot be anything other than moral, & I cannot be moral in any other way than John the Divine in Revelation. The colors of flowers made me drunk, but the poverty of the poor maddened me; Nike-footed girls morphinized skies onto me, but I myself became a martial goddess if I saw the humiliated good on the threshold; I grimaced if, instead of a miracle, I was given tedium by a concert of violins, but I was driven to murder by the slightest whiff of human arrogance; if I heard a mistake, words poured from my lips with rhetorical *furore*, and I wanted truth, but even the greatest truth became a funfair clown if suffering and happiness, assistance and stone-heartedness, goodness & wickedness, importuned me on the street.

Beauty is *not* a problem, as *all* things are beautiful; beauty is a given, omnipresent; distinctions between accident and substance are useless; the world is beautiful and that's that.

Nor is truth a problem: insofar as beauty is a vulgar public masquerade, the impossibility of truth is just as vulgarly evident. If, therefore, beauty is nothing other than the truth-vapor of truth, a simple intimation, withdrawal, or underlining of the features of existence, or in other words, not much more than a cliché — truth is nonsense, even to speak about it is an absurdity; it's classical non-existence *per se*, pure nowhere and pure never: then we should not fritter away even a second on either. *One* thing is concrete, the rest is all *flatus vocis:*[102] a person wanting happiness. That's what morality is concerned with. "Eudaimonia?"[103] you ask, pulling a wry face.

What can the very last of things, a word, have to do with the very first of things, with happiness, with fever asking for water, a hand searching for a sibling? The most terrible thing about it, however, is that although beauty is a platitude, truth a nonsense and only morality, the goodness of the Lamb is the sole something: we shall always have much more art & philosophy than morality. Nothing is more gnawing than the knowledge that my goodness-ecstasy is totally futile — it is a natural law that there are ten thousand bad people for each good one. If I had to bring up children I swear I would bring them up to be scoundrels. Why should they be good? Whatever assistance they could give would amount, parodically, to nothing in a sea of evil. And they themselves would be unhappy to their dying day because they could see the difference between their own goodness and the wickedness of others, so they would be forever alone & laughable.

Holy Father, you know that the world around us resounds with the slogan "*Rinascimento*" — you cannot take it amiss from me that although I wish to express the 'truth' (to be more precise, just some sort of truth) & 'myself' (there's no point in even ironizing on that obscure point): nonetheless, forms, literary style and other such matters, which exclude 'truth' and 'personality,' also go round in my head.

I commentate — the tragic thing is that I am convinced that there is no other sensible & exciting genre in the world than commentary, which is to say, following a book, a human face, a million-celled flower, or a ten-act series of events from one element to the next — but at one and the same time, out of an ineradicable 'artistic sense' (what plebeian chicanery!), out of my formal & histrionic inclination, and maybe also due to editorial cunning, I am tormented by the fact that such following of reality (whether of a text by St. John the Divine, or a stranger's face) is the greatest denial of art, the greatest trampling of form, and editorial anathema.

Because it is part of the tragic essence of commentary that sometimes the climax will be at the very beginning, and last of all (where the *fortissimo* of the effect ought to be) stand quite mild, small-scale philological, relatively uneventful parts. I wonder whether before I die I will be able to reconcile the 'form' superstition of my age, the Renaissance, with my own form-trampling pursuit of reality, my stubborn taking of 'aphorism' & 'truth' as next of kin (something that is most likely no more than another superstition as opposed to the former, Florentine one). Maybe one day I shall write in more detail about this: the elemental denial of form and the murder of editing at work in every 'truth'-natured thing.

Anyone who has not experienced all the paradisiacal rapture of 'form' and at the same time not lived through the Satanic denial of form and the wrecking of composition of some "truths relating to reality" does not know what a back-breaking struggle between the two is building up in me: between the truth, which is by its very nature the absolute torso, and form, which owes all its beauty to the fact that it is a fiction, an empty illusion, nothing but a radical, nauseating lie.

The 'depth' & the 'key' in Revelation will forever be exciting to me. 'Depth': is it not curious that depth always signifies evil, devilish, death, and the rhetorical negative paradise of being? How did this immutable connection between depth and evil, between height and good, arise? Is it not natural if I identify man's depth, the 'soul,' likewise with dross, the devil, with death, with the ever-vindictive zest of kitsch? But what will be the consequence of this identification of the 'soul' and 'Satan'? Because I cannot stop: once I have accepted this depth-demonism, then my deepest feeling, nostalgia for God or love for Sappho, my profoundest thought, my every moral feeling, my kharis,[104] and my utmost doubt (the latter two are roughly the *pièce-de-résistance* of the soul): all of them are uniformly unnuanced, Satanic caricatures, continuous death burlesques. And the angel king of all this destructive depth is the Greek Apollyon, who brings destruction.[105] Here myth postulates itself, almost ceremonially & provocatively, as an absolute mishmash: the 'soul' as impotence, superstition as nonsense *in absoluto*, myth as immediately obvious anti-myth manifest themselves here, as it were, *ex cathedra*, citing all the metaphysics bundle (to put it in St. Paul's style) in the spine-chilling Aristophanes of compromise — "to the Jew first, and also to the Greek."

The destruction & triumph are complete: Greek Apollo & Semitic devil; matter-agitated religion & psyche-ruminating mentality get mixed up; Semitic abstractions and Hellenic concretions drunkenly drink each other into synonyms; with all their waxen-malleable, naïve or refined traits, the skies are drenched in a single suicidal orgy: relativism at last reaches its no longer relativizable, 'absolute' boundary — metaphysics devours itself in guffawing agony, and again, as this tone has sounded out so many times from my monotonous letter, at this very moment Venus rises from her foam: that is where post-metaphysical metaphysics begins.

This absolute relativizing-apart has a historical counterpart, when, in chapter 11, verse 8, we read: "And their dead bodies shall lie in the street of the great city, which spiritually is called Sodom and Egypt, where also our Lord was crucified." "Spiritually": in the pessimistic language of my 1408 Florentine argot, that is tantamount to saying, "in no way at all"— meaning, anarchical-ly, phantasmatical-ly, whatever-ly, Narcissistical-ly.

According to symbolist gourmandism, last but not least, Sodom, Egypt, & the land of the Jews will be one, "meaningly," in a symbolic moral sense. But the symbol is nothing but dream, unfixedness, & lack of outline, the most grotesque symptom of the soul's natural frivolity. Yet it is only by that that Sodom gets its due: it shook off the rain of ashes & the fires of brimstone as a dog shakes off water from its fur, but it was destroyed for good, made impossible and ludicrous, when it was turned into a symbol. What gnawing one's own hide is to a wretched outcast starving in the Sahara, stooping to symbols prior to death (if indeed it may still be termed prior to death) is to human so-called thinking. What if I do *not* take that geographic parrot stage symbolically? Then it is simply confusion, an unmarked chaos, for which no soul or body is responsible, simply the paradox-ostentation of history, the eternal rankness & bragging obscenity of every geographic, ethnographic, and historical phenomenon.

Historical events & sites have no escape from the trap: as symbols they get lost in just as much confusion as in their actual outlines. One is well aware: the mystic interpreter of woman, in the fumes of love, annihilates her just as much as a physician, who follows the minutest atoms of reality with a magnifying glass, does under the surgical scalpel. A Sodom *symbol* is nihil-sacrifice; but Sodom as a thousand-electron tissue of *reality* is just as much a nihil-sacrifice. Reality (whether a woman or Sodom) cannot bear *two* things: its *interpretation* into sense, meaning, or symbol — and the copying, anatomy of reality, its *self-identity* down to its last atom. *Zwei holde Spiele der Erkenntnistheorie* ...[106] All this is *ad antica acta* "depth."[107]

But, as I have already said, my other favorite is the "key." I am barely thirty (my nihilism is proof enough of that),[108] but I acutely sense an aging, maturing process within me.

Perhaps that is an illusion, but that process is always identified in my imagination with the key. In point of fact, the older I become, the simpler, downright startlingly primitive, the thoughts or principles through which I 'explain' the world as best I can (needless to say, that 'explanation' is not philosophical, but merely a physiological reflex, given that we are not privy to philosophy — *de philosophiis quae non sunt* ... etc.),[109] in parallel with which the sentiments, moods, and impression perfumes, whether of the body or soul, become all the more colorful, made up of a millionfold million elements: and that logical simplification, indeed, the thinning into simple-mindedness and the emotional *non plus ultra* of complication do not in the least interfere or intersect with each other. Two large-scale futilities that you could sum up as: introibo ad altarem realitatis cum clave *simplicissima*, sed qui cum ista clave venit avicella est pardisiace et *multiforma* cordis scintillantis.[110] That's the way it is with the depth & the key, those two ends of the parabola that trail off into infinity. Because this is the human feature of man: that parabola character everywhere. There are only directions, with no target. Only tendencies, intentions, foci; but neither a true center nor a true end exists. This mere tangentiality, mere intentionality, is expressed marvelously (only for me, of course, for the commentator I am: arbitrary to the point of absurdity, or if you prefer: *forgery*) in these two lines from Horace: "*... te Priape, et te pater Silvane, tutor finium.*"[111] The god of ends, sensible goals, boundaries providing logical satisfaction is now Silvanus, Priapus' most-blood relative:

that is, something natural, chaotic, drunkenly lethal. And since it's the target, the end, and the sense, then: Priapus, Silvanus, madness. So there is no 'key,' no 'depth' either, only in their stead one's *instinct* for keys, one's *impression* of depth, which one can signal artistically maybe, but never complete, never live to the end.

The Revelation (as I indicated earlier) was written for me particularly because it equally annihilates reality for being reality — or deduces that, since it is reality, then for live thinking man it can only ever appear in the form of irreality — and it annihilates all the 'names' relating to reality: philosophies, myths, gods, & symbols. That consistent killing of two flies with one stone makes for extraordinarily attractive reading. Is not something like "... and seven thousand *names* of men were slain in the earthquake"[112] a brilliant Brunelleschi line? Incidentally, no deliberate emphasis is placed on the word "names": the Revelation is mine, not John's. If the wine permits itself to be poured into water, then it must surely accept becoming mixed up in it: if it is written for humans, it must accept the chemical changes that take place in them, in me. Is it not a *delight* to read that for once *names* were slain, not bodies? That the height of sadism for the vengeful Inquisition was not so much coating the incriminated organs with wax & burning them like candles, not gagging the mouth with dog excrement, but the slaying of *names*: the part of us which is literature, intelligence, interpretation, and mundane culture. My whole life is nothing other than a yelping declaration of war against the *name*, against all real & disguised nominalism, against definitions, language fetishisms, sciences, and bogus precisions (there is no other, to be sure), so it is understandable that I snap up a sentence like that (however chancy it is).

Anyway, what is one's position on those chancy sentences that only I interpret as being one thing or another? What is one's position on such subjective autocracy as makes a mockery of all boundaries of morality? Does it not follow even more readily than naturally from all I have written so far in the margin of John the Divine that there is not, nor can there be, any real difference between just and unjust, philosophically or pneumatically founded, & impressionistically whimsical interpretation?

But since one sole reality and one sole truth is "the irrational utmost-foreignness of reality," then one sole thing is important: that I signal this *"plenitudo alteritatis"* as intensively as possible. If misunderstanding intensively offers the sole experience worthy of existence, then misunderstanding is the greatest possible understanding. The well-known academic accusation: "I shall unleash the hysterias of the lyric, the 'gourmand Hebrew dead' of æsthetics (in the phraseology of an English poet)[113] on the chilly corridors of logos" — means nothing.

The matter is the other way round: logos is, by definition, precisely the hysteria of imprecision, & the intensive irrational experience of reality is *suprema ratio*. One can *imagine* a rationality a thousand times more rational than the latter, most certainly; but that is not how it is — it is never granted to us. The misunderstanding starts with academic logicians imagining by "irrationality" or all experiences untouched by *nomen* some fantastically naïve bogeyman, a romantic prehistoric animal that will devour cathedras and *Grundrisses*[114] with ferocious teeth lock, stock, & barrel.

All that imagination shows is merely the naivety and romanticism of 'logicians,' not the experience of irrational reality. Words like 'irrationality,' 'reality,' & 'experience' can be smeared with as much marsh journalism as suits an insatiable marsh — but who on earth is bothered about whether any given label is dirty or clean; whether one should have made a top hat or a glass coffin for an as-yet-unborn child, and whether the measurements are right? Beneath the names, reeking of sentimentalism, of the "experience of irrational reality," an absolutely exaltation-free thing, radically alien to chaos programs, comes into being — a more sober & simpler classicism than all classics, the sole *bon sens*.

Since in the end I wish to carve a relief & not philosophize, I have carefully read through the passages about the woman of Babylon and the other woman persecuted by the dragon.

Eros in apocalyptic regions is either dark perversity, a foulness that in no way differs from the ugliness of the butcheries meant to punish it, or the symbol of spiritual things: engagement and betrothal feature as symbols. In truth, one cannot make anything else from the Eros Cross: either a bodily agony that does not differ at all from sickness and death, or an exalted symbolism, a metaphysical mannerism, which shows not the slightest difference from falsehood & psyche. *Corpus mortis, anima fraudis est calix impatiens.*[115]

The involuntary dialectic of distortion & apotheosis flits through the whole book: before the great triumph of the 'Soul' of Chapter 22:17 in all its Orientalism, two other superb verses resound in their un-oriental purity, where all the merchandise that shall be bought no more from the merchants of the earth is listed: gold & silver, fruit, all manner of vessels, spices, horses and slaves, and after going through the whole catalog it finally mentions the "souls of men."

Oh, would that I could visibly paint or carve this invisibility: the 'soul,' the oriental quality of psychologizing, ragbaggier than the accidental splash of perfume of a woman of Smyrna; Plato's & Horace's greater barrenness in comparison to the residue of the sweat of a eunuch galley slave on his chains. Everything, absolutely everything in the world, is more than that sort of 'soul.' And an equally peculiar voice sounds in the verse, declaring that death delivered up the dead. Right, quite right, that confusion between sea, death, and hell (i.e., between reality, soul spleen, & myth ship) — if slaves & horses are more than 'souls,' then the matters of death are just as much the remains of reach-me-down finery: god of death, empire of death, sense of death, & the venery of death, through typical narcissizings of the soul.

Getting lost in the eschatological ignominy of soul-searching is at one and the same time also the ignominy of death, that's only natural. That is where metaphysics manifests itself with the most perfect gesture: it is not divine by reason of offering something positive after physics, but because it takes the inner negativity of physics (of course, that continual and absolute negativity is always only a negativity from the point of view of *cogitating* brains) *ad absurdum*: in point of fact, it is the highest possible degree (*mutatis mutandis!*) of "Luciferian philosophy." Death? Sea? Hell? Where those infinitely disparate entities are synonyms, there is no border between the Lucifers & Medusas; where the morality of hell and the immoral naturalness of the sea are simply all the same, there everything is all the same, the world is all the same, even the cosmos may be no more than a cynical shrug of the shoulders — and this, but most certainly and exclusively this, is the threshold of metaphysics.

And after all that, the Oriental conclusion, the two scary dramatis personæ of 'Soul' and the 'Bride,' with whom, in accordance with my acerbic-intricate bent, I would like to prelude nascent Florentine humanism. The 'Bride' is an erotic symbol; Eros, on the other hand, is a constant ritual expression of the body's physical nature. Nobody knows the physicality of the body, the sickeningly sensual bios part of biology, better than the inhabitants of Asia Minor. But at the same time, nobody perverts such psychological debauchery & analysis-baroque out of and into themselves like that same Levantine people.

That shows that 'Bride' and 'Soul,' which is to say, physicality and spirituality, physiology and psychology, anatomy & psychoanalysis, cannot be two entities but only one: after all, the glittering golden ribbon called "neurosis" indistinguishably binds together the body's internal juices and the soul's external ideologies. I see all too well what blooms or withers from a body tortured into being a body, or a soul harried into being a soul.

Biology, and the person living in accordance with it, is as much lost in the purposeless blindness of vegetation and instinctiveness as psychology and the person living in accordance with that is destroyed in the absurd fiction-automatism of thoughts, words, & gods. The Oriental peoples are forever the chosen tribes of metaphysics because they preach with theatrical self-display the two versions of man, the eternal and uniform sterility, beyond-inferno infernal negativity, of body and psychologizing. That is why I wrote my last marginal note *ad notam Fiorentinae humanitatis.*[116]

3. TUSCAN ARIAS

(MONTEVERDI)

I.

Can song bloom in the absence of these two Muses
In the golden midnight of Tuscany?
Was not *Landscape* the source of all music?
Did not sylphic *Time* carry it to me?
Space's secret is now lasting made,
The earth and all distant: enclosed in paradox,
'Here' and 'there' around me: senseless, tinged with black;
And from my home town I fell into the dust
As the wretched fruit falls from a tree.
Landscape: Giorgione shape for where and for nowhere,
Striding and running, tree-crowns and town gates —
Wish there were a sundial in my mountain-water chaos,
And in this blind silence somewhere, a North den;
A star that did not tack in haste in hellish zodiacs,
Somber cypress, which to me beckoned with its shade —

But no: than spaceless wormwood, there's no more bodiless orphan.
Every horizon has faithlessly taken wing.
And with it, *Time*, more heretical yet, inquisitive devil-angel,
Bodiless and aimless, nameless and storm-raging;
One moment by sword it ousts me from my instant-Eden,
The next, it's an annunciation drowsy from peace-moss:
If *Space*'s many mourning figures accused me only,
Time as shrieking Cherub has me already condemned;
If by a green bay's apology I was appeased,
In an instant, Time opened a blood wound.
Where is the naïve age which knew past and future,
Yesterday's waters on a twin day's step,
The sleepy ship, 'one year,' and the whistling heart-slayer:
The Minute, turning on partitioned time's clever wheels?
'When' has fallen out of my soul forever —
The bud of the moment shot a century's apple,
And I don't know: was it infinity, or fleeting need,
That on me the gates of this landscape opened?
I saw many gods, giant myths, and puny flies —
White-bosomed cities, the real shredded into bits —
I could gaze at them forever (rich memory-catafalque),
Like my proto-picture, the girl Lot begets for me.
But in vain did the beam, like death's liana, on Marian shoulders glint,
In vain did the lido's foam wither at my feet:
As a final lesson, only midnight-lapped *Space* and the slender
Puzzle, chameleon-souled *Time*, were left;
In my wanderings, at one weary threshold or other
I would sometimes chide myself for them,

Saying: How come, thou masked Fate-siren,
That this lute only for abstractions sounds?
Ragusa's Venus-valleys, ascetic Tuscan soil,
Blood-colored goldfish that in nymph-thermæ swim,
Ornate sculpture bigotries of aged Saxons,
And the bubbling chanting of castrati choirs:
Did all that merely tempt me, latter-day St. Anthony — the *concrete?*
Deceptive dew, that fever-lipped South steams on its own lips?
Did fate sketch its anguish-atomed portrait in vain:
For the face — is dead? While the two mænads, *Time* and *Space*, thrive?
The Mænad-Muses answered me in canon;
Landscape, this Danaë combed to horizon, responded;
Time, too, answered, two-faced procurer of seraphs,
Yet I don't know if ever such a cynical whoop of joy
Resounded on earth, on this suspect thicket of gods and flowers.
What did I hear then, subdued, pillaged pupil?
"You no longer have a home, a mother and family hearth,
And misty remotenesses are not magic groves either:
From your worshipped home my treacherous love expels you,
You're also bored with this fairy tale realm: your weary hand;
The earth is finished, the concept of 'place' by now a ruin:
Neither home nor Asias will bewitch you any more —
Every pose of creation is a market junk heap,
From wonder to habit Fate has plundered you outright.
You are bored by every terrace on Florence's jaunty branch,
Disgusted by the Alps' Artemis snows:
Only *Space*, pure Here, blind, unfleeced Jason,
Haunts you in your Lent-soul, from this Tuscan today on."

As in a watermill blade falls on blade,
So did *Time*'s girlish curse fall on its heels:
"The calendar can burn in delusion's bad fire,
Sages and star-gazers can all go by turn;
If for our soul's inner secret, or for the outside Time
Chants: on it I will quarrel no longer.
Eternity? A moment? Memory? Soothsaying from dreams?
Old age? Centuries? *Perdu* or *Retrouvé*?
What is your future in the stars? Where's the earthly offset?
You never know, because, like my sister Danaë:
I am a riddle, blue-boughed anonymity entrancing,
In whose rumbling shade Zeus himself is a dumb beast;
Deaths and strokes of luck come to me in a tangle,
And to measure long or short for lessons: I haven't the power."
That is what the canon voiced, and I lost heart
To attempt to caress Tuscany's body in verse —
When lizards, Marks, and Byzantiums,
Arab garden lairs and frayed papal ramparts
In their wilder-than-abstraction canons called down
Curses on watery *Space* and still waterier *Time*-Io,
Asking for form, for the kiss-shackling word.
Thus, like an apostle, who whisks from his head the Soul,
The paths of inspiration to seek at brushwood fire:
So did I secretly sorcer a Tuscan garden,
Cheating on the philosophical Muses both.

2.

Oh, beauty-torment and wonder-command:
When will this curse of sight come to an end?
When will it be that I am not I, yearning for tree-being,
But all the cypresses will be just amiable friends?
How many times did we laugh at the Titans of romance,
For not sniffing out Iris' wild hila:
They would rather themselves turn into gods,
Thus into pushy Pride's altars they turned their lives.
The curative silk lament of scent
Never again touched their mournful nose;
Desire to be deified is only poor wretches' dream,
Never yet carried anyone into the skies.
What a pack of buffoons is every gang of Titans:
Here the flower threads spring into a pearl,
There a god clouds over his snow-silver chest —
Tow-haired Titan perceives neither wonder nor smell.
And yet, in vain: when before my eye Lake Garda
Her azure and her needle-leaved bayonet stretches,
I feel, straining in labor, that she alone exists,
And all humanity and poetry is but a trashy mask.
In vain does a crummy Titan saunter on kitschy bridges,
Morbid Romanticism's Breughel priestlet —
Neither Christian scripture nor Olympic lyre will sound:
He has no dogma or victor's law — the tree alone has.
Just once, oh, Fate! *To be* just once and not express:
Could I but rustle as a masked bird on bounteous branch-slings;

Could I but be the crystal ring on the garden pond's belly,
I, a shadow shaggier-coated than a sick dog;
In Ravenna's quiet me, and me the stray comet Cain;
To be a razor-necked swan on Venice's waters;
I, the strict, semi-circular Florentine Marian thesis:
In Ferrara to not peek at the Borgia grave's hushed secret —
With Realized Object Reality my poetic delusion.

3.

As Jesus (Apollo!) into the depths I, too, have descended:
A Satanic porch awaited me: my 'individuality,' my ego, my soul —
The blue clovers of solitude: a selfish end-in-itself pulled me down,
And like the Count of Orgaz in my I-silence's lap I lay.
I knew there was but one damnation: the *Self,*
That no word would throw a shadow on someone *else;*
No kiss could sketch me on a stranger's face,
No *Kharis* hug will be fruitful in *another's* hands.
That was why I, drunken daredevil theologian, descended,
Thinking some petal-sprouting miracle I could make:
All that *for me* is merely reason and Eros color
I shall redeem: let there be law *outside me* as well.
How that limbo rejoiced in its cliffs and strumpets,
Mud-spattered qualms, pagan cæsars, stray birds!
I was offered blonde-haired love, a snake-head crown:
For escape from the *Self* life was not too wild a price.
As this parrot panorama scampered into view,
My hand unthinkingly clasped the 'way back' handle —
On the old Psyche swing of yore little did I suspect

That under a gentle wave it was all: drunken corpse cauldron.
But instead of a handle a Magdalen hand
Coiled round my bone-wrist, like a feline-supple ray;
In her eyes a hummingbird dream, in her ears a Capri conch,
All that allure-whole: frothy over-promise and intimation of love.
In her hair a Cyprus dawn spotted wheat;
On her brow glided a Byzantine Moon;
The dew on her arched breasts had a Siena glitter —
And my redemptive intent died a double-quick death.
Had I come to redeem my Ego, or for a wedding feast?
For male order, where female chaos had narcissized in its own mirror;
To be a triumphant Orpheus— or an oafish bridegroom,
In adversity now choking, like a hunchback Icarus?
But all these thoughts straightway took flight
Like a breeze-tickled shadow on a garden path.
"Thank goodness you've come down (Christ mask or Apollo's runaway?);
For your fate-cast muscles in limbo I would forever wait:
Take me by flight from this accursed marshland,
Where Lethe deathly crabs sires from its blind loins —
Let not green ashes sodomize in the wake of my kiss:
Let my desire reach goals *outside* me: give me over to being."
Around her lap rosy and golden fumes whirled
(Buoyant flowers rebelling against their stem) —
From her eyes a request pined like a faintly sloping stairway,
And I was expected to win over 'soul' or Ego's filth.
But, alas! Instead of taking her body, in gold weeds, to wing
And ripping open a door, as a surging well, on poem-hell:

Dazedly, with a feeble "*In nomine Christo*" mutter,
I lost myself in her swan-plumed lap.
"When are we going? shadows here are longer than a tautened string,
My blood spins like poppy seed ground in a bad millwheel:
I'd had enough of *myself*, of being Sun and its sundial-shadow:
Would I could slip a long way from this *ipse ad ipsum* bordello."
But all this female entreaty fell on my heart
Like rotten fruit into the shabbiest of baskets:
Albeit with burning self-reproach, I sought only her kiss valley,
And in the end forgot my pride-key in the lock.
And while her falling hair all bestrode my body
Like lead-weighted fog does echoing Engadine,
An old fogey with the Prophet Jeremiah's book drew nigh
And exhorted, his withered arm to forgotten skies raising:
"Look! My book's thousand pages are packed with resined knowledge,
But in the darkness of the soul my words rebound on me alone:
Let us go from the deaf, echo-proof hall of the Self,
What I have given myself, to *others* (sacred word!) let me pass on."
I gazed through the Eve octopus' tatter of green-lace
Foliage, doltishly, at this rhetorician's gestures,
And while the colors of an amorous tableau stuck to me,
My lips I began moving to the rhythm of his voice;
With these wild-sad lines gathering in an anthill on its pages,
I went around as with that round-bosomed woman:
I did not turn to the world but burrowed into myself more deeply,
Thus my infernal auction ended up — a grotesque stratagem.
"Oh, don't declaim my book so, wizened-brained wanderer!
Don't chant my Ego back with yet more egotistical *furore*:

Bring me closer to the stranger, indeed, *into* him,
Let so my crumpled-flamed hopes be fulfilled at last."

I then saw how foolish was the intention
To rebel against Me, while immersed in myself:
Now that I'd stepped into this filthy madness,
I'd have to sit in it forever, scoff-orphaned, and stock-still.
And I, with my Christ-like pose, a cheap market Christian,
In the depths of Me, can part from my beloved Christ:
Whoever had once his love let fall into the My-well,
Can never see God, and woe! can think only of himself.
Mother, that dear oak tree, tent of the golden age,
The object of my life, buzzing harbor of my love:
Mother cannot see me either, my kiss' arrow twists far from her —
Sinking-into-*Me* has killed her into naught.
Father? The silver-mossed norm; of my pride,
Of my humility the cowardly commander —
My father, that all-purpose bride, I can also not see:
Ego's pirate ship took his son over into verse.
Spouse: smiling fire at the crypt gate of my fate,
Fairy me-understanding, more malleable than water:
For whom whatever does not mirror you should be thrown away —
You too learn one sole lesson: that he lived in vain, and in vain
Did toward you his bad heart wrestle,
In vain did he toss a craved cord round your calling stake;
Although your body's and virtue's secret he may forever seek,
Of the yachting in Eden he understands himself at most.
The news of a grim angel speaks, the hand of death holds the chilled sky:
"Your venturesome Orpheus is perpetual captive in hell."

4.

We drank Tuscany's wild wine from broad glasses,
So that the Muses might, perhaps, blithely assist us:
These grapes of the underworld should make every line of our work
Bubble up to the heavens, and Florentine gods
Of their immortality all secrets and holy powers cast
In such final forms as this woman here,
Who smilingly offers me her drinking cup.
The bedraggled locks of this wild harvest
Unbidden poured out the blood-flirting juice;
Looking with rounded eyes, we watched as the Muse
Threw into us a moon-true song like a flower.
What useless hope, what puerile let-down,
To await inspiration from wine's fire:
The Muse is one: just a shortsighted, mole-ish prose-wretch,
Who makes music of *life*, not of heavenly *works*.
There's just one 'inspiration': that lures you to money and skirt,
To hunting deer or swimming wild rivers;
It drives you to breed at most, & may halt the boundaries of the instant,
But your work it steams into kiss with such greedy snigger
That you forget forever all the plans you had,
To surpass (so you believed) your rapture veil.
Here it must finally be settled what you desire —
To feel, what a declining star or Milky-Way spiral feels,
Feel the life that spring brings and begetting cries of lust,
Where every strength and joy attests to being screamingly alive.
But all this wild game of the real is shaded in deadly pace
By the tiara of passing in funereal ebb;

Or your dance-craving fingers on the gloomy *opus* you press,
In whose vein throbs the stillness of blue and death:
In such realms no kiss-poppy ever bloomed,
Beside it, every siring swoons into the grave:
But for all these unreflected Narcissi that *non*-existence offers,
To an exchange you're tempted by twin god-faces:
⌊memory, and the "abiding immortal."
Oh, dreadful bifurcation, Hercules' lousy heel:
Either all life and after it funereal ash,
Or eternal life, but such that the face of life is dead —
Who in Florence needs such a fret on the lute?
My Ego-fate is darkest, its face and reverse a poltroon;
Like a scruple-dry soul, it drifts between life and work:
Startled by work in life, my fate in work is: being —
My epitaph be this: "no heavenly work, nor earthly life."

4. PALAZZO GRIMANI

The longing awoke with irresistible intensity in Monteverdi: to go to Venice, his native city, to go to himself. He was well aware what that sort of thing betokened. Those highly strung, agonizingly hare-brained hankerings tended to obliterate themselves: a person inclined ever so little to thinking or spleen never fulfills them, since he is scared of them, and a thousand other things. A sunflower turning to the sun has a big shadow. Nothing in the world can be worth us hankering for it so much. Since he therefore knew that the longing would be a wilted lunacy before long, a bad mush of guilty conscience & phobia, he jotted down in his notebook, in inventory fashion, what it was that in those moments, after the disappearance of the Nike-girl, and on the eve of All Saints' Day, what it was that had attracted him to Venice, according to the humiliating scheme of "above all else: thus, in vain."

1. St. Mark's Basilica — a copy of a church in Constantinople. Thus the city's essence is another city: what is the most personal in her is yet not her. *Raffinement,* eh? Vulgarity? Affectedness in dizziness? Delight in history's inexhaustible games? It doesn't matter: the blood of one thousand and one nights in the heart of Italian culture, a Latin-devouring Byzantium on the Italian peninsula, and above the corpse of an Orthodox apostle every drawing of the 'heretic' Paris. There is no city in the world, no focus, the *essence* of which is not something *foreign,* something utterly hostile to it. The apple of the Greeks' eyes is Egypt. The ethos plinth of the warriors of the Golden Fleece is Palestine. China's root is India. The foliage and *raison d'être* of the Nordic Reich is Sicily. So will it be forever. Venice is Constantinople, and Constantinople, Mecca.

2. St. Mark's dead body was 'stolen' to reach Venice. Culture and theft are synonyms. Who did the 'stealing'? Two merchants, Levantines. Although a monk and a priest were also present when the sarcophagus was opened, the two Venetian merchants no doubt hoped to make a business transaction of the matter. If I go into the Basilica (Monteverdi writes), I adore stolen goods. Roving Mercury and masked Hermes guided the body there. When the body was smuggled through the streets of Alexandria in a basket, the grave-robbing Argonauts called out, "Pork! Pork!" — so Mohammedans avoided the impure meat. The customs and excise men tapped all over the consignment and the body, failing to find it, just as they failed to find smuggled perfume and

crepe romaine[117] in the trunks of ships from the Orient. That was destined solely for a Tuscan princess. This? For a republic, for history, the orthodoxy of a whole millennium!

3. Among the reliefs that run in Romanesque semi-circular bands above the gate, there is one that represents May: a gentleman is being garlanded or crowned by two girls. We have grown accustomed, in the imagination or in reality, to the scene when a pope or Holy Roman emperor is crowned: it will be like the magic circle inside a *nymphaeum*, with the pope a budding young man, the crown, profligate Ophelia foliage, as if it was not a matter of politics but of young girl æsthetics. Here the reverse is the case: the topic of "May" itself is idyllic — yet the whole is like a Roman legal ceremony: the man is old, his knees doddery, the coronation girls are Germanic vicars or Frankish bishops, and the crown is also heavy like a chunk of congealed European history. That will perennially attract me: that Romanized May, that non-æsthetic rigor of ceremony.

4. "August" is also wonderful. A young man rests in his armchair (almost an archiepiscopal throne). I don't know whether he is a weary peasant or a hypochondriac castle seigneur. And I don't know whether he is weary or sad, musing or awaiting his death. This notion of eternal "melancholy": where death & thought, intellect & respectable impotence, so self-evidently run into one another. A resigned prince? Is that August indeed? After all, could burning-hot summer really be this philosopher, this decadent, sick man? ... Or a drowsy peasant?

5. One mosaic in the Zeno Chapel[118] shows the capturing of St. Mark by the Saracens while he is celebrating mass. And yet, one of the most lovely ornaments of the basilica of his body is an Arab *"archivolte"*[119] — and here I have to use the French term because there is none finer or more expressive: one takes it to mean a bouncing archangel, leaping into the heavens. Was he killed by a Saracen? Then nothing could be more natural than to have Saracen motifs decorate his tomb and to make its name.

6. A French friend, in a letter recounting his impressions of Venice, once wrote the following genial sentence to Monteverdi: "*Cet ensemble ornemental a une certain charme, mais est un peu tourmenté.*"[120] "*Charme*" & "*tourmenté*" at one and the same time: is not that the classical formula for life? Beauty? Delight? Dionysiacs and art? Those are long gone. There is only "*charme*" — that is all we have, which somehow still resembles impossible beauty and even more impossible delight. But pain, death, apocalyptic damnation, and absolute sickness are likewise exaggerations — nowhere on earth do you find such great wrong and hell: instead of it, just "*un peu tourmenté.*"

7. In the same style of flattened embossing in which coin-minting lambkins symbolizing the apostles press to the wall, there is an image of Alexander the Great raised into the sky by two griffons or winged lions. How odd you got together! Gentle lambkins of the Jewish Holy Land and a megalomaniac despot. Out of the diminutive Oriental animals, a

whole culture, a whole mythology sprang up — and from that Macedonian tyrant, a saint rising skywards, a ceremonial ascetic. How many actors there are, how many roles.

8. In the atrium, mosaics of the Creation. First and foremost, the marvelously true and sculptural representation in which the days of the creation are symbolized by angels (cf. St. Augustine's *De Civitate Dei*, Book 11, Ch. 9, concerning the creation especially of unfallen angels): the first day — one angel, the third day — three; the seventh — seven. For Monteverdi there was no other reality in the world than 'one' day.) That time, too, he wished to travel to Venice for *one* day in order that the inter-growing of time and space should at last be mystically fulfilled: every single hour with a stone of the church, every single minute with a wave of the sea. Just as one day an angel embodied Creation, so Venice would become embodied time. Leaving aside the intention to be there on All Saints' Day, since All Saints in its wild 'polytheism' is in any case an accumulating triumph of sculpture, of the figure, of physical concreteness over everything abstract, all psyche-futility. One day — one angel: a Byzantine girl, togaed, with legs and a crown of hair. One hour — a toga on her knees. One minute — an eyelash. Yes, that is time: space becoming ever spacier, simply the best perspective from which to view objects. Perhaps a bit of semi-cheap eroticizing does not unduly spoil the matter: time & the nude are one. Accordingly, to play the chain of equations right out: one day — one angel — the whole of Venice.

9. A young, almost feminine Christ instead of the old Father — Lord God. In Byzantium the world is not created by a nonagenarian Jewish sage or a nepotistic Colonna pope[121] but a young poet, almost a girl. As in the Good Shepherd of the Mausoleum of Galla Placidia,[122] in Ravenna. How senile Adam & Eve are next to the otherworldly freshness and youth of Christ the Creator. How angelically transparent and breath-like Jesus is in his toga; what clod-hopping peasants are the first human couple in their nakedness. This marks the break-up of the Byzantium superstition: of the "rigid icon," "hieratic gold," and other such nonsense. Maybe only in Byzantium was Christ & the ever-living God-wind-wing since time immemorial a Mediterranean angel.

10. Here, too, the soul is a butterfly-winged embryo in the Greek manner. This *awkward* notion of psyche is the sole thing that was worth anything over the course of time. 'Spiritual life' — could it be that? Something embryonic, foetus-like — and then a butterfly. Is that too much or too little? ... 'Soul': the missing bridge between life's pathological roots & free illusions, between the fœtus & the butterfly. *Laissons ...*

11. Human forms stand for rivers just as much as they stand for time, the days. Why is the river so important as to be symbolized by a figure of equal size and weight as God and the first human couple — to be one of the dramatis personæ in the same vein as the other three? The water in Ravenna is also 'divine'; the water in which Christ is baptized is bigger than Christ himself. Water and time thereby

become kindred. That is a tad more important than mere Neptune routine or decoration.

12. In the interior of the church, on the cupola depicting the Ascension, the four rivers of Paradise — according to the French tourist guide: *le Guihon, le Pischon, L'Euphrate, le Tigre.*[123] Each of those words bears a resemblance to something: the first — a giant, the second — lowly nature, the third — a fellow, and the fourth — a tiger. Those are generally written off as doltish associations, and most probably, indeed certainly, they are. But anyone who has only clever associations will not know till his dying day what history is and what its main driving forces are. Outdated gods, empires, myths, and physical humans sprang from little else than "doltish associations." For the time being, not even the remotest possibility suggests itself that one day we might yet be able to reconstruct or otherwise produce such things. It is another question, of course, whether there is any necessity for myths & living people. But then, on the other hand, what did clever associations ever give rise to? Modesty forbids me from writing obscenities.

13. Those two point-like nothings, candles or lamps that are lighted every evening on the southward-looking side, by way of appeasement, in memory of a young man who was innocently executed. That bit of rural humanism is so unexpected and so touching in the huge chaos of history and its almost caricature, danse-macabre self-contradictions (which is what Venice is in essence): unexpected in principle & unexpected for the eyes, formally. Venice is by excellence

history turned worldly, underworldly, and otherworldly — mendaciousness, sadism, genteel & aulic Apocalypses that time envelops with its autumnalizing-into-æsthetic ivy.

Its essence, however, is always a doing without man, a great self-serving function, astro-chemistry — whereas those two lamp points are human, something of the now, actual, and familial, something non-feudal and non-gesticulating. How on earth did they end up there? The cooking spoon of mercy in the European heraldry of mercilessness? And why is that particular unknown young man granted them? Here on world history's altar of Lucifer and Gabriel, in the capital of Europe? How do those two candle flames, provocative in their modesty, relate to the grandiose flowering in stone of mausoleums from Rhodes to York, from Cyprus to Moscow? Which one makes more sense? My feeling is that those two candles are not being burnt by Venice, that being history, but only by two senile priests or some little old lady. Why is that allowed? It is the crisis of my entire life: should I stand by *humanity* or *history*? Nowhere else can those two be seen in eerier opposition. Virtually in a shared vase of hell & pietism.

14. And to see the Palazzo Grimani di San Luca again![124] Right now I am sitting here, among the hills in late November, in driving snow, and somehow I have the impression that no greater enemy than snow is imaginable either to constructed stone or to lagoons splayed like eyeballs without pupils. Snow distorts forms, deadens the sharp music of Lombard lines. Besides, snow is always of the earth & not of the

water; if one were to play out the Danaë-myth with snow in place of gold, it could only ever fall on earth, never on water.

At this moment the whole of the Grimani grid of lines and *laguna desnuda* is simply not-snow; it is the tormenting question as to how is it possible for idyllic snow and cruel stone form to coexist in one and the same world, indeed Italian world? Mute white flurries of flakes and hard, jangling waves of water? Shall I one day have to leave a world in which there are such extremes as snow and Venice? Must this cerebrum one day be filled with the darkness of death as a jar with thick black plaster? As when a negative is made of them instead of flowers growing out of them? This brain, capable of simultaneously imagining such impossibly distant worlds as snow and Venice? Like those bundles of diminutive dry leaves with the froth toupee in front of my window, and the sun-shaved classical outlines of the Grimani? It is so mysterious: on the one hand, in the angelic monotony of snow and against the backdrop of its weaving loom of silence, Venice appears to me even more sculptural than usual; on the other hand, the matchless stupefying presence of snow molds this thesis straight into my soul: "If you have snow, Venice is impossible; it ceases to be, it's a nonentity." Snow is the sole narcotic, the sole chaos, worthy of the name. But let me nevertheless break through this scurrying-dallying net (which is the more apposite for snow?) to the architecture. I know that for me architecture has a radical, central secret. Just *one*? Yes, it is increasingly my experience that there is just one feature of every phenomenon that excites me:

even as I am wallowing in the millions of nuances of impressionism, the *idées fixes*, simplifications, and stripped-off dogmas treacherously ossify.

In architecture, this mature *one* mania is the following: the decisive element in the beauty of a building is always the sort of thing that the architect did not reckon with, never even dreamed of, and could never have dreamed of — something essentially new and surprising, an almost heretical +, in the enjoyment of which, however, I am sometimes upset to the point of despair by the knowledge that that was not the artist's intention, and yet I would never find that particular chance with another artist. That +, that unfair & unjustified + with architecture, is not even two or three inches of an accretion of historical time, nor the possibility of milieu, *plein air*, and varied points of view around it: there is something in the very structure, one senses, that that concept or plan is something much more primitive, more naïve, or clumsier, for the demonic majesty that it nevertheless radiates to be natural. The greater the analytical precision with which I formulate the component elements of the Palazzo Grimani, and their relation to each other, the more clearly do I express the naivety, the negligence, of this building, its tinkering with petty *bibeloterie*, its vulgar kitsch-classicism. The realization, all the same, is uniform, pure, great art, and entrancing. What is going on here? What makes this possible? From where does the architecture draw its celestial authenticity, its hidden capital, that of all the works of art it is able to accommodate the greatest fantasticality, tastelessness, self-contradiction, and distortion? Sometimes for precisely that reason I have the impression that it is ridiculously easy for a building to be beautiful. (And I look through a sea of ugliness...) What is architecture made up of? Undeniably, it has about it something of an animal lair, nest, or molehill, therefore, of a primitive substitute womb: a shelter, a defense, some enveloping mass. Then there is the other extreme: completely geometrical architecture, the whole thing an abstract composition of space, a counterpoint of ratios and apportioning. True architecture, which usually yanks me by the roots, is, of course, somewhere between those two — unconsciously, needless to say. It has no inkling of biological compulsion, no inkling of "pure composition."

My homesickness for the Grimani is an unproductive longing for those kinds of unconsciousnesses. Because that is the one & only possible life — that of a Michele Sanmicheli, its designer. Anyone who sees principles and opposed poles is dead. Sanmicheli would sometimes construct like Euclid and sometimes decorate like a fishy lowdown confectioner; there were times when he expressed one of his dreams, and also times when, with the greatest of ease, he attended to his customers, cutting frames for three windows instead of two — but he remained completely untouched by such brainy inanities or idiotic "essence-spotting" intellectualism as the idea that life is made up of the competing principles of "dream," "practicality," "construction," & "blind *bibeloterie*." The most essential feature of any true life and any true understanding is absolute blindness to its own components, a quite absurd ignorance of one's own elements, an incompetence at self-analysis. Although this thesis, too, is just playing with words: after all, elements never existed in the real world, just analyzing brains — the concept of "complication" itself is a neuro-pathological term; "analytic vision" is just as much an illness as a persecution mania or moral insanity. Sanmicheli, then, was not at one and the same time a cake decorator and a Euclid, a classicist and a mole: those terms are not components, because such a thing as a component never existed in the world. That is all just *"luxe d'interprétation"* — and who the hell needs that.

The Renaissance was nowhere ghastlier & more haughtily self-serving than in Venice, above the waters. The Arab Gothic grew out of the water: the slender columns, tendrils, roses, and *fioriture* x-ing and y-ing into each other were embodiments of light falling on the waves, more watery than the water: all spume, bubbles, & chattering-chirping foam. The Gothic was Triton and Neptune from the very beginning. But classicism? It sends a chill down the spine just to pronounce the sentence: a row of Roman pillars floating *on water*, hard arches hovering above a swampy sea. The expression of everything fixed, eternal, juridically ascertained, here — on the water. That is already a long ways away from the simplistic notion of opposition (is there any phenomenon in the world that is not a long way past the simplistic notion of opposition?). The mystery is further intensified by the fact that the classic palace rising in the middle of the choppy, storm-tossed sea is as much of a riddle as the Renaissance towering above the mute and mirror-smooth water of the lagoon. Why? After all, the smooth water is seemingly something 'classic.' How false that statement is! The water is a dream, a mirror, psychology, Jewish Narcissism, and Greek instrument of chaos, a treacherous trap where sick Nereides kiss one into damnation. How imposing: Sanmicheli and Co. were *not* familiar with those lousy myth-suggestions & death-hedges of the water — how triumphant the limitedness of the classical architect not caring a continental whether he built a palace on a plain or a mountaintop, on water or a bridge — there was no 'milieu'; the whole world was closed off at the contours of the façade. We shall never be so redeemingly limited — so provocatively *non*-conformist.

Venice is a dry-land city built on water — no question of that. The water is just an uncomfortable accident, nothing more. True art and true sense are only to be found where accidents pop up from ancient myth-topics: not from myth-destroying naïve rationalism (that kind of thing would be no more than myth B replacing myth A), but from an indifference that can never reach formulation, thank God! Just imagine a Venice that *accommodated* to water — water classicism, snorkeler baroque, or aquarium Byzantium: what wretchedness would come of that! That not caring a continental about the water is superbly expressed by the hue of Palazzo Grimani: the black and white shadings, in contrast to the motleyness of Gothic and Arab palaces. That motleyness is somehow still aqueous: a relative of the rainbows of colored fishing boat sails, soaked lampions, & frayed sunlight.

But that is stone, here blackening, there whitening, into bone. That is inner London, northern fog, the earthly weight of a northern bank. How come it ended up here? There is no resolution of the tension resulting from the fact that the *impression* that "the water of Grimani is grey, anti-stylistically grey," may last for hours, but the *sentence* that asserts that impression is delivered in a flash of time. Why, in the course of cultures, did a link arise at all between an "impression" and a linguistic or any other kind of "expression"? Who was the infernal scoundrel who hit upon the idea of putting those accursed alien oddments together? Why could they not have sunk forever in the eternally fermenting freshness of an impression, not even dreaming of Freudian nightmares of "expression" — or why don't they busy themselves with 'expressing' subjective hallucinations of logic and sensation from dawn till dusk, never as much as suspecting the otherworldly sensations of the "impression gained about reality"?

The Proustian mask, the acrobatics of analysis, seemed for a moment to show that setting 'impression' and 'expression' into a well-balanced parallel, and both intellectually and poetically justified linkage, would be possible, but that was just the magic of the moment. Afterwards, reality flourished before us in ever more inexhaustible richness (*"plus oultre"* even than the Pillars of Hercules, as Emperor Charles V had it engraved in his coat of arms), and the autonomy of the lonely thought, together with its predicament to be forever remote, *off* reality, also flashes its characteristic grin in our direction. After all, here at the grey color of the Grimani, anyone might assign a *"moment proustien,"* for Proust's diplomatic tricks and the features of his analyzing mask are by now easily accessible — but would that be honest? And when one protests against it, out of unexpected morality, is one not already swamped in it since long past? ... That Grimani, of all places, was the one granted those smeared, Manet-like black and white moltings — of all things, the house of pillars, arches, & severe balustrades became a victim of that sort of "shadow wash" and aquarelle cosmetics. Who wanted revenge here in rigor of form? Perhaps water with its vapors reaped a greater triumph here than anywhere else in the world: the fully external shades of color (color! and shade! — those hyper-frivolous words alone must be humiliating to the quick for a Palladian idol) penetrate the palace like an *inner* flame, the cell sap of flowers, organ-depth currents of wind: they force into it all the shame and ignominy of psychology.

Let us look at the footstones; in the end, that is the massiveness, the toughest part, the most robust *"festgemauert"*[125] part: all white mist, steam, flour-dust fraying and powder gloom — fate so willed it that most of the uncertainties should intersect here to the point of total mockery. Not even the heads of columns on the ground floor fare better: in places where as a rule scaly lions struggling under the weight, the flattened heads of slaves, & large stone griddle cakes put on flab — there, too, you find snowy porousness, melting, peeling sugar. I am surprised myself that when a moment ago I mentioned snow, that simile did not automatically occur to me.

Still, there is a less ironical, less anti-construction whitening and blackening — indeed, a downright propagator of geometry, emphasizing structure. It is a special pleasure to note how that whitening and blackening passes through the stages from destruction of form to intensifying of form, until finally the game is accomplished in a strident white band around the roof. How come that black-and-white contrast, glaring like a chess-table, does *not* speckle, *not* break up the building? Because, despite its all-imbibing, spongy shading, it cannot be said that it is a matter of a discrete greying. No: the white is very snowiness, the dark parts very leaden and deep evergreen. All the same, the building is not blotchy and not mottled. The adding up is deception: after all, the entities to be added up yield either no sum of any kind, or a quite unexpected sum. As if the whitening were itself a timid ivy that readily adopts the shape of each more suggestive form, while with gentle forms it freely opens its shade lianas. And where are half-piers more plastic, with their thousand channels of fluting — where they are all black, or where they are all white, where they have cooled, or where they incandesce? What a superb game: the upper story's highly strung Mont Blanc-whiteness above the soaked-bronze hue of the ground floor, like a crown, the resplendence of rapture.

In that snow rapture one no longer expects form, yet since *notwithstanding* there is form: it produces more delight than with hard contours drawn in ink. By the end, there's no knowing which is whiteness of light, which whiteness of stone, where it is optics, and where raw mosaic — is it not a priceless jest that stone can be confounded in the last act: with light! Much has been spoken about the Gothic ethereality of stone: there is none. Here there is, though: in whiteness silted on classical forms. But that stone color is not a color; indeed, perhaps it is not even primarily color, but time. That was all Sanmicheli and the whole rigor of space lacked: the mystery of time, its chemical paradoxes which know no boundary, the forbidden poison of all hesitancy. Nowhere does time as syphilis, as skin disease, as lethal destiny, glare so loudly as on the Palazzo Grimani. With the best will in the world, ruins, fractures, or distortions of form do not mean or suggest time. Only those rainy stripes signal passing, time as giddiness, time as opium, the delirium of history breaking up from wave to wave. A ruin is simply nothing: neither space, nor time: useless junk. But those shadows on the Roman mask of Palladio — they are transience itself *in statu volandi*. Time here is nausea, seasickness, the most original inner secretion of human existence.

I do not believe anything until it is in the shape of a disease: that is the most philosophical form, the most reassuring style. Time as god? Time as clock? Time as "*à la recherche du*"? No, no, those are dilettantisms. Time as a tangible physical disease — that is a valuable beginning. Again unable to withstand my lousy instinct for wordplay: apotheosis is tedious, apo-*pathosis* is devious. Of all things it is the classical, most anti-hypochondriac Grimani that does this. Serves it right, serves it right. It wished to be form and yet it yields time, non-form.

I keep on mentioning architecture: but then, is Palazzo Grimani a building? After all, its essence is just a façade. As with the other palaces in Venice, incidentally all ordinary houses, apartment blocks, onto which a façade has been stuck in naïve isolation like an ornamented relief roof on a worthless Romanesque baptismal font. Is that architecture? Or blown-up embellishment in stone? For here it is a matter of the opposition of Christ and Antichrist when I am confronting pure façade with "thinking in terms of a whole design." For me thinking only in terms of a façade is just inconceivable; for me to build is expressly identical to a denial of the plane; little more than the enjoyment of three-dimensionality (or more!) for its own sake. The Grimani and the whole of the Renaissance, my instincts tell me, is anything but architecture. Even with 'monumental' forms, the emphasis is not on the modeling of space but on certain ratios.

'True' architecture cannot even exist; the Renaissance 'apartment + façade' is not yet architecture, just a game of proportions on the plane, backdrops, sheets of drawing paper with sketches; on the other hand, my kinds of 'space for space,' organic space sporulations rippling out of *one* space vortex, are beyond architecture: they are dynamic combinations. But how is it that after so much relativism such scarecrow nullities as 'true architecture' still bloom with elemental force with me; indeed, all my reflections on architecture are due to that stubborn obsession of mine. It is a curious and quite incalculable historical experience that great art was born in places where there was *no* uniform conception, where people did not even dream about the essence of art, and where dynamic features (whether in the sensory or technical sense) were lacking. I can only imagine a building, and plan it, so that everything, from the shape of the very last cellar keyhole to the overall impression from five miles away, is an outward rippling-off of a central thought: a tenth-rate ornament and the ground-plan are born in absolute simultaneity. Is that a 'dynamic space gesture'? Which, as it becomes clear forthwith, is of course nothing but a straying into the asylum of life's poverty. Great woks of art are not born that way — in those cases a ground plan is valid only up to a certain point, & thereafter come newer autonomous brainwaves, ornaments, fillings-in, omissions. In that way, in its ignorance of space and its flatness of façade, it nevertheless photographs the vibrations of inner space in a much more refined way than a space-conscious architecture, in which a homogeneous concept of 'space' prevails alone.

The Grimani façade shows, with the harshness of a bitonal chord (a second, moreover! a second!), that it is, in essence, a geometrical backdrop: columns, arches, vertical and horizontal lines seek to express some proud, puritanical and haughty, aristocratic and tragic order — but just as forcefully, it is decoration, ornament upon ornament, tiny local inflorescence on tiny local inflorescence, like a garden in spring, or a tapestry. There is no more exciting chapter in the history of architecture than the game starting with Michelangelo, which consists of some sort of combination of geometrical over-rigorousness & luxury of decoration; more accurately, an unexpected unanimity. As with the Grimani. Something ornamental with virtually the fragrance of decadence? Indubitably. Something strict, darkly arithmetic, multiplied and divided, simple? Verily. How does that squaring of the circle come into being? Because one cannot dismiss it with a wave of the hand as a chicane of impressions, a routine game. One must put one's finger with a certain 'physiognomic tactfulness' on a positive. That is none other than a formula that is inexpressible, root and branch: not a flower and not geometry, and for that reason in no way a mixture of the two, but a fortuitous, unanalyzable positive, to which one responds with a homogeneous yes-mimicry of one's whole sensory, emotional, and intellectual being. The more definitively and precisely something can be depicted, the more fictive, arbitrary, & ephemeral the impression that it makes: the more elusive it is, the more positive & more real its effect. Reality is every inch nameless and forever unnamable, so individual, self-serving, unconnected is it, mystically and scientifically, artistically and mathematically such a 'useless' and a 'hopeless case' from A to Z, that one can save one's breath when it comes to making exceptions, seeking nuances, piecing together infantile scales from the comprehensible & manageable phenomena to the 'biggest problems' (it would be much better to give the name of Suzanne de Beaujeu[126] to the latter): the world is unceasingly, seamlessly untouched by truth, untouched by god, and untouched by beauty.

My Grimani mania is not a stylistic analysis because there is no style, and analysis is self-deception; the Grimani is a station I have seized on merely to symbolize my boundless sense of reality: my theology, to use what is maybe an anachronistic word. An analyzable nuance is no longer a nuance. The strange thing is that such "refined," or if you will, "over-refined delicacies of style," to which supposedly only decadently over-refined nerves (?) react: make a dreadfully elementary impression — the more unfollowable the nuance of nuances is for the brain & the skimpily valved heart, the stronger and more accessible the effect on one's whole body, the more at home, the surer, instinctively livelier one is in it. For it is utterly illusory to make a distinction between decadent over-refinement and the primitive health of primeval animals. The essence of reality is that in every moment it is absolutely new, absolutely individual, incommensurable with any kind of apparent precedent in the world, and by the time one has found it, or deemed to find it, some self-deceptive 'expression' of it has long since become something else. Well, then the sense of nuances grabs *that* from reality, i.e., precisely the most real part of reality, which is what makes it reality. One should see in it not a neurotic disquiet but, on the contrary, a sick animal's keen nose for medicinal herbs, the bee's flower-locating instinct, the owl's night vision, and the successful hunting implement of electric rays.

One is at the pinnacle of irrationality, and can only be there. An odd tack for the world to take: in times of old the '*theos*' was the eternal anti-nuance & anti-ephemeral over a thousand slivers of detail: nowadays precisely that ephemeral & ultra-nuance elicit the effect that the manifestations of God had on saints in times of old.

A perfume bottle is standing in front of me, next to an engraving of the Grimani. It is a squat, round bottle, with a round paper label. As it lay there, a circular air bubble formed in the pale, golden-green liquid, its outline almost coinciding with the outline of the paper label. But only almost: it had slipped a little to the side. In that little 'flaw,' that motionless internal shivering of the bubble, that eternal tension of effervescence and infinitely determined contour, in the counterpointed coquetry with the label, I see such an "absurd ephemeral," or as I anachronistically termed it just before (though purely from a linguistic point of view): a sole possible "god." An absolutization of accident? Cumbersome words — a sole redeeming fact. At the sight of such an accidental, momentary constellation, whatever mystic, superstitious, theologizing instincts (and what else is there in me if not those kinds of things) suddenly pour into an absolutely reassuring form. Even there the network of dimensions, weight, lighting, smell, and proportions is unfollowable: on the other hand, precisely because of that I feel that I am on more reliable ground, wading up to my neck in gods.

It is possible to adore only an absolute and a reality: the notion of absolute reality, however, is only given by those surprise cross-sections. What out of arrogance you call neurasthenia and out of laziness call art here turns out to be a religion of animal impulse. The inner paradox of the Palladian style also serves for this, for this sort of surprise attack, with it becoming clear that there is no 'ornamentation' or 'geometria' — things like that are insipidly smart hallucinations, behind which there appears some reality, to which we respond with our entire lives as to the blood of our blood. In the end, one has heard more than once in the form of a classy or cowardly phrase that "reality is unapproachable": but no one took the issue seriously. Those hyper-analyses were a very good school for gaining awareness of the irrationality of reality stretched to breaking point. They accustomed one observing the "insignificant," "senseless details": that is to say, to the one thing that is significant and sensible. Because there is truly nothing other than an insanely heterogeneous mass of 'insignificant' and 'senseless' details, and the rest is silence. (It is truly superfluous, and would not be pertinent, to quote the hit tunes from the operetta of skepticism — it makes no difference whether it is for me or against me, I am not disillusioned, don't have 'scruples' about anything — I don't even know what that means.) Since time immemorial man is a textbook example of individuality and originality, but even so it was not suspected that individuality had to be understood in the eeriest literalness, & originality with the most insane radicalism, and not just as art-critical praise or an excuse for poor learning.

Individual: that is to say, everything that is not precisely himself is completely useless nonsense to him; it would be futile to force links with the outside world, with other people; all they could yield would be grotesque fiascos. And they did duly yield them, those torsos then being fitted out with nicknames like "historical fate" or "German philosophy," and similar verbal inventions. The sole mystic happiness (and obviously we want mystic happiness and nothing else) for such an absolutely clueless individual or "origo" (originality!) could be to see in each unexpected constellation, object, or time segment of the outside world, right to the infinite depths of the whole thing like some proclaimed law, a feature of the divine self-servingness of reality, victoriously unpredictable, individual in every electron, new & foreign with hysterical exaggeration. A typical grandiosity of nonsense of that kind is myth, or 'god.' For me, here is the Palazzo Grimani.

Why not a flower or landscape? For one thing, there are plenty of flowers & landscapes as well; for the second, that is to some degree a matter of low-minded piquanterie: in an object prepared with a conscious brain and with very finite human imaginative power in whatever extreme forms, there is a greater pleasure in the animal gobbling up of totally unpredictable nuances that are flagrantly extraneous to intention, denying of intention, than in a nature without humans. I was always disposed to write my confession of rehabilitating reality in Vicenza under the title *Palladio*. What antitheses stemmed from one and the same principle, or rather, to be more frank: what kind of caricature to pretend, even for one moment, that as much as a shadow of principle could ever have existed. And ... to carry on spinning the 'frivolous' wheel of my inconsistency: in the end I nevertheless felt that a row of columns of the starkest simplicity and the most orientally variegated Teatro Olimpico[127] are somehow of one nature: the classicism of death and romanticism of life are natural siblings.

On the other hand, the same nevertheless happened for the destruction of every kind of principle. Drunken baroque and set-square Romanization were able to be inner relatives because, in point of fact, it was not a question of "drunken baroque" and "set-square Rome": those are just concepts and intellectual clichés, the paradox of which (a crippled substitute for *solid* nonsense and *total* irrationality) I sought to avoid, confessing the never-expressibility of the phenomenon. What is one doing, talking about mundane theatricality and geometry, rococo petty bourgeoisdom and basilica posture, epigonism and eclecticism, elegance and despair — in short, that kind of essay sludge? It would be more honest for me just to say "Palladio," thereby signaling a group of novelty & anonymity which I can only comprehend with wordless internal yes-mimicry, never any other way.

The vulgar prank intended to *épater*[128] that I saw in a Surrealist magazine, or dreamed up myself in my callow temper, that under various senseless disturbances on the line and typewriter tests were written, as captions, the names of well-known towns and works of art, whereas under photographs of well-known towns and works of art quite absurd groupings of letters and words, possibly the names of *other* well-known towns and works of art: it better expresses the essence of things than an essay playing Narcissus with — *horribile dictu* — art-historical concepts. If I were consistent, I ought to have described the Palazzo Dolfin Manin on the Grand Canal for myself as well. I don't think it will take a long time until such things cease to count as bluff but will come to be seen as the only possible stance toward reality. But since I have begun in this old-fashioned way, and the 'modern age' is only episodically ahead, let me stay by the Grimani, my fetish and totem, by my recollection of when, immediately upon arriving to Venice with a friend, we took a gondola ride in a side passage next to it.

We arrived at noon, the most impossible of times to arrive. The morning and the evening, with their own mythic weight, are simpler, more accessible — noon, with its vegetative flatness and laziness, in a mix of sharpness of outline and slimy spreading, is much more mysterious and absurd. The contrast and yet entwinedness of artistic marvel and mundane new life is most critical at that hour: lunchtime, the mood of eating and dozing, is so intense that it makes the Palazzo all but evaporate; on the other hand, its outlines become even more positive in congealed isolation.

Since my youth a healthy and natural distaste for vegetation always overcame me most strongly around noon, irrespective of the redeeming lack of stomach and of the inorganic chemistry of the palazzi. The greatest curse of warmth is that it brings the stomach right outside the skin — in our eyes and fingertips and on our tongue we sense, with a vulgar indiscretion, the tastes and decay of our forgotten breakfast. There is something humiliating, depressing, & deeply ignoble in that. Nature's vindictive denial of form. Its compromising of art, its plebeian nature. That was always the way I saw Venice at first, the forms & the polar opposite of vegetation. If only I could be a stone, could set myself free forever from the unbearable prepotency of 'life'! The opposite of the body, it is clear, is not the soul — the soul is a much worse, more intricate stomach. The body's opposite is the Palazzo!

Those Venetian noons: thrown among the senseless hills of luggage, I peek waif-like in a gondola, between my vegetating blood & foreign stones that will never open up to me, feeling the classic aimlessness, the precise uselessness of my whole life. There is only body and stone: the body is the stupid fermenting of death — stone is the perpetual muteness, the lethal aristocratism of foreignness. Tiny bridges are coming up: we are going so *slowly* in an unknown rhythm that does not resemble walking, or swimming, or bumping along, or standing still (the timeless humor of the gondola: between swan and outcast cadaver, time silk and time knot) — and yet, whenever one ends up under a little bridge like that, the bridge's stale-smelling, sludge-colored, mold-exudate arch glides so *swiftly* over one's head into unexpectedly smoothed-out time, as a wafer, a second ago still brittle and white, was immersed in a trice in a glass of water, to instantly become a grey slush. A host of closed window shutters, longer than ironing boards and more crumbling than the coffins of the Etruscans would have been, had they been made of wood: that tremendous uncertainty between monument & wash-house, Veronese pomp & proletarianness, aimless proliferation and Italian rationality-art. And the sole utterance for hours: "Look! ... Look at that there! ... Look!" And finally out onto the Grand Canal, bound for the corner of the Grimani. The canal is very broad, without shape, a true southern scale — sunshine as snoring tedium. The black Grimani stands alongside that. That is a corner.

Lying on our backs in the gondola, we look at its edge. It is quite close. That is the big joy of life: what was very distant for so long is suddenly right beside one. On a large scale! And the game of games: "quite different from what was imagined" and "I recognize its every atom." Within a trice the opposition of the words "different" and "identical" melts away: we exist. Where else is a palazzo so much a palazzo if not in Venice? Nowhere can one feel the fairytale difference between house and palace as one does there. That is a palace. And gentility, unbridled *feudal* solitude, is one & the same in this palazzo atmosphere as *poetic* solitude, a Shelley-style "poet hidden in the light of thought":[129] only craziness would be able to distinguish here between *dominus* and *artifex* — the thirstiest dream of that union in my life.

Two incomprehensibilities: the Grimani reverie and the Grimani reality. Which is the more impossible impossibility: the Grimani which right now is swimming alive besides our gondola, or the one that stretches into our dreams like a branch of a weeping willow bent there by seductive winds? Whence this naïve obsession that we attempt to imagine a 'true,' approachable Grimani between the Grimani as an absurdity of reality, and the Grimani as an absurdity of dreams? The multitudinous channels of fluting are quite close: & big. Everything is big, big! They are like the lines of rain in the Great Flood of the mosaic in St. Mark's.[130] And above us the Corinthian capitals, and perpendicular on them, the cornices separating the floors. Yes, yes! To use a Pascalian turn of phrase: *la véritable description se moque de la description.*[131]

Channels of fluting? Corinthian flowers? Hard ribs? Annihilating religions, philosophies, bite-shaped responses. It all floats, the gondola does not halt for even a second: those devastating positives and "metaphysical portraits" (the sole definition of this architecture) hover, changing from one moment to the next. How high it is from here, from the surface of the water, which is deeper than the depth of the water. How peculiar to perceive a turreted-like structure & water simultaneously: a tower is always land, castle, a parched Iran. Meandering lines run past the oars: teemingly and sharply, in the same way as that whole paradox of classicism is *négligée* and *geharnischt*[132] at one & the same time. No unstylish windows or crowdedness distort the sight — in reality the reality atmosphere is so boundlessly strong that next to it everything is dwarfed. At those moments it is virtually incomprehensible that there is such a thing as a "bad" building, where the experiences of "close," "big," and "I have got it now" do not prevail. What a journey has been taken by the line of the flat roof — not long ago it was still a sluggish finish, a clumsy flattening, later the upper yardarm of a skew sail, but now, seen from directly underneath, it is almost vertical. And how much the zebra-striped canvas roller blinds belong to it, with their bathing-pool flapping in the wind — like stray butterflies stuck in a deep-sea cave. And now it is already disappearing, and one observes how *feebly* a wooden curlicue supports the gondolier's oar on the edge of the skiff.

That rather loose, uncertain hook symbolizes the laxity of the South and its biological self-disgust.

A French expression buzzes between my teeth like a passing fly in autumn: "*nihilisme articulé*" — I want to express my melancholy as the inner sadness of the world's objects, articulated, one by one: the *precise* sadness, nonsense-anatomy of oars, flowers, tiddler fish, big fish, stone, style, time, letters, history, passivity, the gods. Everything but "*en bloc*" pessimism — that is nothing, it's the 'soul,' Byron, frippery. Just once to describe Palazzo Grimani in such a way that it be proven mathematically that fluting, meander, balcony, and flat roof as such are pure *primum malum* ...

5. REVELATION

Snow was gently covering the branches, as the wakeful gaze of a boy does the lashes of a slumbering girl; in the kitchen the melting fat sizzled one last time under the turkey's ruddy body; on the velvet dress that you were given for Christmas, the last wrinkle under the bosom trains the way you wanted, and the last cassock-style button has also found its own little toggle-eyelet: nature, kitchen, tailors glance with mute consent our way, we priests and scholars — God can be born.[133] We all prepare for an idyll, for some ultimate intimacy, an innermost innerness and warmth, *non plus ultra* dream and childishness; we are preparing for the complete forgetting of history, truth, and love, for forgetting God, for ostentatious indifference toward theology: from the first, and now decisively triumphant-looking reality of the *home* — and thereby we supplicate the Madonna to not bring Christ into

133. Passage from a letter (from between 1545 and 1550) by the learned tutor of Elizabeth Tudor to the young princess. Its author is a young Cambridge don in whose soul, nervous & prone to immoderation, branches of Reformation that were either overblown, overcritical, or romantically overphilosophized, blossomed into wild flowers. He tries to look more heretical than the heretics since, being in love with the princess, he thinks that in that role he will better stir the imagination of young Elizabeth.

the world: let the idyll beyond God and man carry out the satanic strangling: let nothing remain apart from the essence — in other words, the air steams around the nostrils of cattle and horses, the quiet intestinal rumbling of ruminating goats, and the glittering Arabian Nights gifts of the three magi (magi or kings? politicians or opium dreamers?). Lay people now finally want to have flings — not in the form of a Dionysiac frenzy, nor a passionate heresy or militant atheism. No: with bed feathers, with challah milk loaf, hot coals, and money. Knowing that I must deliver a Christmas talk to you, young princess, I gave a lot of thought to whether I should leave you in the greatest poison and greatest tenderness of evanescent time, or else stir you in line with the perennial indecorum of theologians and show that what is settled here is the no longer separable unity of tragedy and life. Like orthodoxy has done so many times before, I think I shall choose some middle course.

I shall give you a commentary on Ch. I of the *Revelation of St. John the Divine*. I shall do that so you can see in the idyll's denial of faith, more fateful than every open conciliar rebellion, the impossibly great tussle of divine things, the eternal strife & metaphysical enmity of God & humanity; the entirely incalculable struggle of nature and the supernatural; suicidal deities and deifying atheists — and I also picked it because (you will perhaps be surprised that after this flaunting of demons I suddenly refer to such a gentle reason), while your eyes fall on snowy forests, icy lakes, and clock hands tripled by icicles: your imagination will go around the islands of the Ægean Sea, the parrot-garish Archipelago, the palms of Asia Minor, the red-sailboats of Lesbos, the white-leaved olive trees of Corinth that chirrup more marvelously than birds — the whole mood of Asia Minor, whose minor fills the soul with as melancholy a sweetness as the minor-key variations of music. Those two starting-points will lead to what is nowadays usually referred to on the continent as the "Reformation," but which both politically and theologically is just a vulgar caricature of what I understand by it, and that I (despite my knowing that this might lead to fateful misunderstandings on the part of a rather young girl) am going to impart to you, Princess.

Who are the two protagonists at the beginning of Revelation, before even John appears on the stage at Patmos, which is so characteristically a "minor" stage — half ascetic-karst, half orange-smirking tropics, an idiosyncratic mixture of European 'southernness,' rigor, and vegetation at one and the same time, as in Sicily, Portugal, or Avignon? But more about that later. The two heroes: Jesus, whose badge is blood, the dead, nails — and God the Father, who is first and foremost the basic principle of all basic principles, the Alpha & Omega, and besides that a creative source, such a demonic life (how, siding fully, he shouts out, making it even more conspicuous with a broken rhythm at the start of Verse 18: "I *am* he that liveth ...") that one can sense anger in the creation of lilies and hummingbirds, in the blowing of spring breezes, so unbridled are his energy, creative *furore*, and his vegetation insatiability. My pretty, auburn-haired girl, there is plenty for you to contemplate in this beginning of all beginnings. Jesus the victim, suffering, melting for others, infinitude of *Kharis* — in short, all that is moral: identifying with blood, with the dead (he is "the first begotten of the dead"!), with complete annihilation. That passivity, that perpetual offering of the self for sacrifice, that perpetual powerlessness against all: a ceaseless solitude & barrenness of every moral feeling or thought, a state dreamier than any dream.

Morality seems to be the sole practical earthly thing, the sole important and true lay religion: when I look at that first Jesus *introit* in Revelation, I see morality as being forever outside the world, a dream condemned to die — drunken slaves (by that, to be frank, I mean the whole of society, along with its feudal cream), flourishing nature, and the demon creator by the name of Alpha and Omega himself will uniformly wreak destruction & pose the greatest impossibility.

It can find no shelter anywhere; by its very nature morality cannot be expansive — it is the amorous mirage of secret silence, fantasy's most self-consistent zone for living things through. There was a heretical sect somewhere between Attica and Syria (the sole human soil on earth, mark you, Queen of England), that the Byzantines called the Theopaschites, who held that with the crucifixion of Christ the divine nature was also crucified and, bloody & nailed, God also died inside him. An understandable heresy — in the way in which the surest criterion of a dogma is: if orthodox — incomprehensible, if heretical — then understandable.

Christ is at one and the same time God and morality, and therefore God also had to die within him, because morality is condemnation to death *in excelsis*.

Morality is the quiet incandescence of poetry and enchantment, somewhere clouded through the mirror of tears: you, too, felt that, when you kissed your mother, or when you gave a gift to a child, or prayed for English soldiers, or invited the poor to a banquet: you, too, undoubtedly felt filled by something endless, a *melancholy* ranging beyond all horizons, by spleen and by renunciation of life, you felt that here was something impossible, something heartrendingly frightened & deforming that would otherwise be so magnificent if something was to be added to it, but that unknown something would be missing forever. That almost cosmic depression is your solidarity with Christ, your instinctive feeling that morality is powerless, that there can only be sacrifice, the first begotten of the dead.

Therefore when now, at Christmastime, you pass before the manger & you see the infant Jesus Christ's curly-locked wax head, think of this: something that was the greatest was born there, and he came into the world only in order to be annihilated with mathematical completeness. How many thousands of times does one say with one's bit of housekeeping pessimism: we are only born in order to die. There, by the manger, it truly is a matter of that; one bears witness to morality, being the first impossibility, really is an impossibility, & murders even God: "All kindreds of the earth shall wail," John writes: & truly — dogma is one thing: the non-entity of Christ (i.e., the earth did *not* want the life of Christ) and the liturgy to go with it is another: endless mourning. Let that be the first topic of your Christmas self-searching: in Jesus' place — a "*lacuna sacerrima*," as a scholarly friend of mine from Flanders put it. Picture a park with a marvelous well in the center; then the same park with no well. From one moment to the next. That is how crudely real the annihilation of divine morality is in Christ, in the most complete sacrifice. It exists not.

Now raise your eyes to the Father — what was it one said about him? He has two features: first, that He is the reasonable cause and goal of everything, the philosophy of philosophies; secondly, that he "liveth," & is so much alive that He appears to be destruction, the most extreme romanticism of energies. As a matter of fact, here too for the human brain it is a question of some kind of renunciation. The "Alpha and Omega" quality compromises Plato and Aristotle alike, every church father & Parisian skeptic alike — in any case God knows everything better, anyway, and on high roars with laughter about 'thinking.'

It remains an eternal secret whether this Semitic primordial-principle was born in such a way that a people thought right through the last still possible thought and, in the end, found that thought-annihilating 'One,' or whether a people, living in the most hysterical thinking phobia, were covering up their cowardice & intellectual impotence with this 'One.' I always felt that that identification of God with a prime mover was something like lumbering troglodytes in the history of thinking & life as Stonehenge-style Cyclopean stones in the history of art. God as Alpha and Omega: that is a logical monolithic style and more idol-like in its overblown abstractness than a bunch of leaping Venuses (in accordance with my own English sobriety and my own hyperbolically inclined games of poetic playfulness). It seems there is just as little place in the world for thinking thought as for loving love (morality): for I never felt worse anywhere than in the company of thinkers, big & petty intellectuals, skeptics and atheists, scholasticists and logicians jumping from one idea to the next — on the other hand, that haughty, tableau-like, Semitically simple counter-poison, that "Alpha and Omega," trampling everything with its mammoth clomping, is likewise foreign. But *hic, hic, semper hic incipit metaphysica, pietas et deus.*[134]

What about the other side? The *creative* destruction, how to put it, is the perennial source of fear, the constantly glittering keys of hell and death; the chill of a wraith in the May sunshine, the infinite proximity of damnation in forest kiss-clicking, the flowery mimicry of death in birth. About vegetation, people were never wrong: now in the form of kitsch-myth, now as medical-dryness, but they always knew precisely that where big stores of vital energy lay, it was pointless talking about anything but death.

So, you saw Christ as ever-annihilating morality; you saw the Father, in part, as a chaos-era lump of logos; in part, as a dreadful death-fermenter in the vastness of vegetation: that is to say, three excruciating apparent negativities, which would be cause enough for you to take your life here, on the eve of Christmas. But let me quickly add why one should do precisely the reverse, and why we should rejoice till drunk after chapter 1 of Revelation. Because, in a miraculous and unsurpassable way, God succeeds in accomplishing two things at once: first, in showing the most complete & most valid *status quo mundi* — and secondly, in throwing open in the most abundant torrent the sole source of inspiration for belief in God and living in accordance with God — that is, the all-out, inevitable absurdity of all theologies from start to finish.

'Doubt' in humanity is not a problem for God, nor should it be for you: faith is a divine gift, this or that way — if you have your gift, then the giddinesses of doubt, the orgiastic wines of blasphemy, all serve only to exaggerate the *heightening* of belief, the awful delight of a notion of God by the most direct and most natural route.

All morality is sterile, all thinking, willy-nilly, is downright anarchy — the whole of nature lives in such a vegetative frenzy that it cannot be bothered for even a moment with the health, love, or salvation of each individual person: is not that the triple impression of the world, that any person, however little good, contemplative, and nature-watching, will always inevitably have? Is not that the pessimistic, indeed 'nihilistic' trinity of the Apocalypse: the eternally dying Christ; the eternally logos-slaying Omega; and the Father eternally-creating in a spring hurricane? That is the picture of the world.

Yet, at the same time (this is the marvel in this scripture), through the totally discordant picture of God being the most tragic and most faithful projection of this world, precisely through that demonic self-annihilation, paradox, and absolute torso: it is the image of God's being which most compels devotion; God is remoteness, conflict, secret, problematic ecstasy, life-threatening crisis, pre-eminent restlessness.

If there is a Reformation in Europe, then this is it: that we have discovered that our former prayers are blasphemies with their own over-familiar security in God, and in their place the problem, the crisis ('blasphemies' like my own here, before you): are the greater fondness, the greater respect, because they are a thousand times better at expressing the genuine situation: the quasi-impossibility of God for human morality, the human mind and human nature. To overplay the affair in a literary manner: blasphemy defines, definition blasphemes. That Reformation (that is to say, my personal, lyrical Reformation) is not a merit; it contains not a scrap of a touchstone of any kind of development or progress — it may be that it is death and chaos; the fact is that at the present historical moment I cannot think and feel in any other way).

The world is a torso, for me the various '*theions*'[135] are likewise torsos; intoxicated and intoxicating tragedies of self-contradictions. The world's fragmentary character is unquestionably tormenting, but no pacific, heavenly ideal, no Platonic kitsch of Elysian classicism, is a remedy for that torment, only an even more distorted myth-absurdity (an absurdity *for us*), the permanent orgy of the impossibility of Nous. If in my fantasy-life I have reached the concept of "heavenly Nous = infernal nullity," then I have found the 'divine.' Of course, criticism can tag on a great deal to that thought: Satanism redolent of literariness; the restyling of long-known heresies with more words and less inner compulsion; the frivolous, bluffing temper of the court theologian; the wish on the part of a thinker jealous of Luther to say something more astounding at all costs, a psychological, lyrical game, etc., etc.

But that is of no interest, as every human thought or deed is a pose or obsession, a tissue of morality and falsity, and 'causes' don't count anyway: only for dockworkers is there a difference between face & mask. Of course, now I have opened the sluice-gates of the whole partition for you: *virgo infelix, tu nunc in montibus erras* — if I may use your favourite Virgil to describe your position.[136] Can there be a more comfortable state, my enemies will say, than for a theologian to declare that the more depraved your disgraceful fantasies about transcendencies, the more pious a lambkin you are in the flock of the faithful?

I know that I am playing with life and death, that there are many hazards; indeed, that my entire theology consists of risk. It may be pedantic of me to emphasize it, but I did *not* give a program, I only characterised a subjective state. *Seeking* that state (a state of apocalyptic crisis finally fixing God as God) would be a ridiculous game, cretinism, infantilism. My 'Reformation' is the retrospective pathological finding, a recognition of one possible (& in the modern age perhaps ever-more possible) spiritual state: no more, no less. My theologian colleagues are going to write bulky tomes, most of which will be produced with a tacit or openly declared ambition of drawing up a counterpart to St. Thomas' *Summa* to replace the classic geometry-theology with the standard work of romantic anarchy-theology. I can predict that will never succeed because the plan in itself is a laughable self-contradiction.

My kind of theology (let no one take it as arrogance that I am high-handedly aggrandizing my scrawny thoughts into a 'theology' — we are much more deeply embedded anti-intellectuals to suppose that a 'theology' implies something peculiarly sublime) cannot take the form of a book: as it is the essence of Thomas' that it is a book, mine is a text, Queeny (am I permitted to address you so on a Christmastide day?), its essence being that it plays out only in the mind, comprising an infinite network of unbroken associations, an 'undisciplined' infinity of images and ideas that only death will bring to an end without any inner reason: I confess it is you, you, I want, young princess, to confront with the *Summa*, your fantasy, the million shades of your mind between the poles of your nihilism and your blind trust — *flevere myricae:*[137] weeping spring flowers, I have that Virgil picture of the content of your psychology and all psychologies. In the course of world history there have always been lay kings who demanded ecclesiastical authority for themselves & wished to signal dogmas in much the same way as the upkeep budget of the Cloaca Maxima. A naivety. However, you, too, will be a lay sovereign, and for that reason you will nevertheless be able to be a dogmatic authority, because simply with your human nature, your logical and amatory fiascos, your roving half-heartedness, your virgin cynicism & circum-menstrual morality embolism or "*humanum divinum*" — reformation and humanism are united here, & you will be the main work of my life if my teaching succeeds.

I said at the beginning of my letter that my croaking out the problem (written down in its most splendid form, this kind of thing can only be grotesque) is just one of my aims — the other is to carry you off in your imagination to the Ægean Sea, among the islands, which stick out of the southern waters like big stones on Pompeii's streets used to, so that, with their skirts pulled up, Latin girls could wobble their way along in the event that rainwater were flooding the street.

Just like those *fin-de-siècle* young ladies were able to totter in their high heels about on those stones over there, on those islands, so culture was able to tramp over from Hellas to Asia and Asia to Hellas. True culture and that kind of jumbled insular world: those are kindred concepts. If one takes a bird's eye view of it all, the picture is like part of an animal's or a human's body in enlargement — as if I were seeing plasma & bones, cells & blood, folds of tissue & bacterial colonies — it is all a sporulating, dividing, breeding, uncontoured and ossifying entity with all of "life's" self-contradictions and experimentation in a duality of *joie-de-vivre* and laziness. That culture is exclusively a physiological notion, and to mix intellectual elements into it doesn't even make the cut for a bad joke, that's clear. The main thing, as always, is if the subject of 'life' comes under discussion, then by 'life' one should *not* mean simply some erotically undercoated, romantic impulse, but simply a *non*-Dionysiac, prosaic, inventory item of organic existence.

The other thing: here, besides its being a matter of histology, commerce blooms; fussy junk dealers, Jews, Persians, Greeks, and Armenians tell fibs, cheat, and steal pirates — the whole of insular Hellas is one big stock market, a thief's paradise. It is a true Mercury panorama, where the road, a new region of the world, the discovery of nature & the immorality of profit (in other words, the mask of 'holy work,' which is misleading for so many) so colorfully prosper together.

There are no 'big commercial routes' (which is just a decadent commercial pose, given that trade and retailing are clear-cut things: wholesaling is no longer trade, but an entirely different physiological torso): tiny ships plod from island to island, and Apollo did not move on huge ritual triremes along the Ganges, nor did Aschir-M'Hatta-A'Cholchem immigrate to Corinth in the golden fleet of the *pontifexes* — the former was smuggled through customs between two sacks of cloves by a hump-backed little Jew, the latter god was accidentally left in the pocket of a Persian pirate, a Hellene harlot stole him from there, though only because she thought there was money in the pocket. This little trafficking of myth is the sole healthy mixing of cultures; it existed in celestial freshness there, between Greece & Asia.

The third important feature: at the time when Revelation came into being, everything there was already debris — trash Greeks had dealings with trash Jews, trash Persians humbugged trash Romans. *Hic Rhodus, hic salta* for the intellect. Intellect is always synonymous with the turn of the century, intelligence and decay (truth and death, if you prefer) are closely related phenomena. Anyway, here a 'truth' resides in every blade of grass & tree ("*in questo prato adorno ogni selvaggio nume sovente ha per costume di far lieto soggiorno...*," as my friend Monteverdi has them sing in *L'Orfeo*).[138] Naturally. Where three such charming Graces as organic chemistry, junk-dealer immorality, and folk-trash meet, it takes a superhuman effort to be orthodox — that is the world's garden of relativities & heresy.

Heresy is the topic of the greatest style that can present itself nowadays, Queeny, since from a certain standpoint we, too, are heretics, albeit not in relation to Catholicism but *per se*.

Those sterling heretics from Byzantium & Naxos strove to force all that emotional swirling and intellectual chaos of the brain that does not stem from the subject of the emotions or thinking, merely from the *physiological* affectation of the emotional and intellectual life: they strove to force all that back to the subjects themselves, and even proceeded to fix those nonsensical acts of aggressiveness in polished thought, pointed text, & dogma. Those first-century heresies are the eternal Meccas for a brain living in the struggle of all human thinking, every absolute and relative, every objectivity and lyrical relativity — that is where I direct you and everyone: the only place.

What is the perennial charm of heresies? The fact that in those days men did not yet know the difference between a dogma and a poetic figure of speech, they were not familiar with the ambiguity of an impressionistic soothing of nerves and a logical precept. If a person is every inch a poet, but equally a philosopher through and through, is not the archipelago where heretic bindweed flourishes, paradise itself? If one speaks nowadays about an unknown deity, the whole thing remains a salon-slogan for a salon sect: in those days nothing could stay as simple gossip or as a social watchword — priests could not have private metaphors: the most carelessly uttered epithet straightaway became a precept, dogma, or council resolution, and people never said what a "nice watchword" or the like was, but right away ten or twenty of them would gather together in a coastal cave or snow-capped mountain peak, found a sect, start scheming, improvise rites, swap wives, and (sweetest of all) kill the emperor: and all that in salvational token of some "*hagia agnosia*" or who knows what kind of "Cretan ignotism."[139] Was that sort of honor ever lavished on a metaphor? Were such casually dropped attributives ever taken that seriously? The intelligence has no sphere of action that does not become perceptible in eerie daylight there; there is no possible object that has not been talked about there.

After such blossomings of heresy, European thinking came to a close once & for all time. Its legacy is, in point of fact, the most statuesque expression of the sole realistic question of all thought: a sterile picture of inevitable irrationality and yet ever-recurring longing for sense. Never did the world's horrendous tension between mystery and myth and the human brain's logos-obsessiveness rush at each other so nakedly. And never did both fail so uniformly forever. Every subsequent mythicizing inclination has been only rural petty romanticism, every subsequent intellectual desire just parvenu pedantry. It is also clear that once the matter comes to a desperate head, neither heresies nor orthodoxy can offer anything — the glaring one-sidedness of those sects will keep one's brain far from heresy, however much that one-sidedness may be the most essential feature of human nature, adorned with every peacock feather of poetry & logic. However, we shall equally pull away from orthodoxy until our dying day, because we shall always feel it is merely a compromise, a notion lying outside of truth: and even if it is not deliberate harmonization, and not a feigned middle course, it only raises an impression of the impassive vapidity of the brain and the senses. It is useless saying to oneself that, after all, the truth has nothing to do with hysterical women's melodramas and parrot colors: not so deep down one suspects that those are just empty words — if there is anything at all like truth within this worldly existence, that is indeed something melodramatic, and a parrot affair. Thus, if heresy and orthodoxy leave one equally unsatisfied, because we have in us an original unassimilability for the human soul: there is no need to mess around with them for even a second but (*à propos du vieux jeu 'humanisme'*) leave them; inner problems, all kinds of 'problems' in general, are of wholly the same rank as bodily secretions: putrid, decayed, useless — out with them, and at worst suffer on account of them.

Just one more remark on heresy. Studying them (above all Marcion)[140] led me to the thought that in fact 'tragedy' is only possible on a lower intellectual level — the so-called "tragic view" of the world is possible at most on the part of a naïve Spartan doughboy: if one looks over the matter even just slightly (always bearing in mind, of course, that the 'over' is quite 'inside,' indeed 'underneath,' at the end of the analysis), one can see only comedy. The fact that supercilious idiots or petty barrel-organ cynics laugh uproariously makes the gods themselves guffaw: zerœs cannot compromise the number.

To start with I, too, saw the "tragic" struggle of the human spirit in those island heresies and Asian council amphitheatres, but I later came to realize, for good, as I now see it, that the intellect, the brain, can never know tragedy. Because the brain looks with involuntary cruelty and the most supreme, compulsory indifference, on this or that tendency in man — will it achieve its goal? Fair enough if it does — if it doesn't: it is a ludicrous, useless, tendency, tantalizing boredom or tantalizing burlesque. Nostalgias that turn out to be directed at something totally, semi-, or relatively impossible do not constitute "human tragedy" but human stupidity. Heresies illuminated the two pillars of human life with blinding moonbeams (we know by now that the two are one): the life of the emotions and that of the intellect. Heresies are eternal:

because human hearts, hence exaltation, and human brains, hence the ornamentation of rationality, will be around forever.

Emotional life has a certain tendency, let us speak in quite broad generalities (and in this case quite accurately as well): finding happiness, some kind of vegetative peace, ignorance of death and suffering, a proto-zoological dream. There is also such a tendency and nostalgia in intellectual life: the recognition of certain truths, a definite and undying truth without the remotest whiff of relativism. Those two basic tendencies, two nostalgias, threw up sky-scraping waves of red around the problematic person of Christ: at the time there was a greater Apocalypse, a greater dance of death, than ever there was in John's imagination. It is questionable: can emotional life reach its goal of complete happiness, animal harmony? And can intellectual life reach its own goal of complete truth? If I look around the world in search of answers, I see dead beings in place of smiling animals — and in place of the truth: only a million thought maladies. There is no sign to indicate that that perfect failure of the most ancient tendencies of the emotions and the intellect is just a temporary state — all the signs permit the opposite conclusion.

In that way the flop of the emotions and the flop of the intellect immediately become *comical*, the classic farce of *parturiunt montes*.[141] Physical pain or disease is just as much a farce, a blunder to chuckle at, only pain shuts off the elastic functioning of the laughter nerves, which is why one doesn't laugh out loud.

The subject of laughter easily leads us onward to Chapters 2 and 3 of my commentary — the chapters in which the mistakes of various congregations in Asia Minor are highlighted. It will not be untimely, I think, if in particular I underline for you the comedy of love in those places: from the comedy of myth to the comedy of the psyche, from the inner impotence of lewdness to the bankruptcy of moralizing. The first divine epistle is addressed to Ephesus.

If you want some historical decoration for the affair, then you can set up Artemis first & the Madonna last: as if that city were betrothed to all of nature's chaos of virginity and maternity, virgin motherhood & frugal sterility. With the Phoenicians, it began with some Semitic myth and was carried on with Artemis, poeticized in Greek fashion, only to come to an end with the dogma of virgin birth at the Council of Ephesus. At the moment, I am not in the mood for any kind of measuring or relativizing of myth, so I shall refer to the three historical states purely as European lessons: to start with, just animal myth, in which rumination and myth are still just a single bovine reflex; then Greek myth, where the animal roots and the effloresced statue mix (however much of a simplification that may sound to your sensitive ears); finally, pure abstraction, intellectualized dogma. That is the triad of Ephesus. Can one be more destitute than in being between a winking lard mouthpiece, an ideal statue, and a paradox beyond dialectical peaks? Yet that was the status quo at Ephesus.

Right now the backdrops are of no interest, it is more the actors: the Nicolaitans, the heretical sect of Nicolas,[142] a deacon of Antioch. What is known about Nicolas? He was accused of jealousy, whereupon he made his attractive wife everyone's prey, allowing any of his adherents to marry her, from which point onward, all of his adherents lived holding their wives in common. What is that? For me, love is a perennial fluster, somewhere between a so-called "spiritual delicacy" and a golden age of total freedom. Jealousy is the most flagrant symptom of the inner impossibility of civilized love: if such a thing as "jealousy" may be a human reality, then there is something very wrong with it, bad and absurd.

Jealousy made this Nicolas, in my eyes, a martyr to "spiritual life" in the sense of a Plautus or Aristophanes. How much internal conflict, weeping, thinking, & struggling must have gone on in him before giving way to that wild theatrical gesture of making a whore of his wife. A fine *salto mortale*: from psychology to the bordello. It is important not to forget that the same leap in reverse would have been just as much a sentimental journey out of the frying pan into the fire. In that Nicolaitan somersault, undying love also makes a somersault — sex as a caricature of life, Eros as a permanent grin.

That Nicolas teaches you, Princess, that the affairs of love are so murky, so much a disorganized flea market of cultures and zoologies, and for that reason so impossible and unusable, that you can never take up any position in relation to it, have any feeling that could be called a feeling, or any thought that could be called a thought, have no moral or scholarly opinion, nothing. You have to come to terms with that infernal nonsense from moment to moment: nothing is good, nothing bad, there are a billion situations, with not one of them following from another. Nicolas is one of the purest comics — how could he not be, once he had flute-played himself to death on the subject of Eros. Of course there is no buffoonery in the world better or worse than what writers are in the habit of grinding out on their barrel organs as "sexual reform." Whether the person in question is a physician, prophet, or a writer, they preach their irrationalities with an astounding "*candeur naïve.*"

Sex exists in the world, it is clear as day, in order to compromise & be compromised, that we should be able to feel in our very blood impossibility as a positive component of the world, not just at the tail end of pretentious contemplation. Eros is elementary rottenness, a printing error, a misunderstanding, & correcting it with institutions, myths, injections, and spiritual pedagogies is the same as revealing water from fire, establishing a mathematics on "no = yes." Nicolas' jest was coarse, and for that very reason healthy — it is a parody at one & the same time of the two extremes of spiritual life and free groping-and-grazing.

Even a child knows full well that spiritual life, in its own nuance-amassing aimlessness, will never reach a resting point, at best lyrical sophisms — a society living in polygamy is impracticable in practice in the foreseeable future (given the European lessons to date); there is no uglier grimace of original sin than utopia. We are banished from the *aurea aetas* — to waste even a thousandth of a second in longing to be back there, in search of some sort of free love: that is a cheap and rotten carnival jape. The queen of England can never play tricks in that fashion.

Look at the other stage, Pergamos, where John does not lash at the Nicolaitans, but at those who hold the doctrine of Balaam — here we see fornication mythicized, unlike at Ephesus, where Nicolas' neurasthenic shadow figure coats everything with the decadent fragrance of the 'soul.' If something had a deity in the world, that can have meant nothing other than that something flopped, it was a fiasco. God of the forest: dissatisfaction with the forests — God of the moon: the memory of a wretched flirtation-torso with the moon — god of war: a blunt dagger, or an arrow that has missed its mark — Balaam and the entire holy whoredom, the *"sacral-Hurerei"*[143] that surrounded him: despondent mourning for love's ultimate absence, ineffectual narcosis for proletarians. If laughter had by chance still been lurking in Nicolas' tussle with death, it would unmistakably have roared in the carving of idols.

Never forget this, young Princess: Whatever pleasure, whatever physical or spiritual exaltation it affords, do not create out of it a poppy-haired or lilac-bodied Aphrodite for yourself, because sick scarecrows like that will kill your pleasure — may you never in life be tormented by any pain in love lest you knead for yourself some erotic mask for the region of Akheron.

The Christians hounded idols in the name of the soul & a God — I hound them in the name of the body and the ultimate godlessness of reality. Love is always a crisis of reality; life within it identifies so much with paradox that at every second one has to reckon with the chance that it is no longer life. Love is not a manifestation of a part of life but, on the contrary, the *whole* of life, or even more precisely: life when it presents itself to us as a *whole*. Every amorous moment is a "masked marriage," as I was in the habit of saying to my old pupil: the connection of an indefinably special, over-shady, & absolutely transitory image of the soul, and the shadow of an unknown electricity of cell, secretion, numbness and death and inner taste of the body: the marriage of a nameless soul atom & an unknown rustling of cells — what has all this to do with idols, virginity or fertility, death vitamins, or obsessions with snakes and bulls? Every so-called pagan nature religion is an indissoluble marriage of *abstraction* with masturbation or *castration*: Dionysus or Baal do not mean suffering — not the vegetation of death, not forest love in the form of foliage, but the isolation from all of nature of one single open nerve (the word "open" is used here in the sense that violinists say an "open" G string), hanging a host of intellectual trappings on it. Don't forget that those ghastly clods of pagan gods first scraped mankind at a time when there was still no love in the world, and for that reason, the enigmatic, ignoramus fragrance of body and soul had not tickled the peoples noses.

Besides that, you can learn from Pergamos' idol hysteria that religion always has a big chance when it is foreign and exotic, not one's own. The Jews concerned themselves with Baal and the Romans with Isis because they were strange; after all, if you go abroad, you perceive even the most common customs in each place as ceremonies; the other's business is always metaphysics. If something is colorful and incomprehensible, then it is surely something divine & salvation — that's the primitive logic. Then the desperate, greedy aggregation of gods begins — as poachers, people sneak into nocturnal gardens and steal foreign gods off the altar, even forbidden game — they organize veritable metaphysical dives & mints of religious counterfeit money, because what others have, the foreign, is unfailingly truer.

That gesture, needless to say, is a thousand times more congenial than the Pasiphaë type of bull-*abstraction*. That is: the trading-in of the world's huge capital of unknownness for the small change of irrationality of children's rooms: in place of the silence of a god-phobic ignoramus are the bells of a donkey-ignoramus, & therefore, there is at least some vulgar polyphony and carnival gaudiness in it.

Have you noticed that those who are the most sweepingly skeptical about everything European still blithely believe in Asia? Those ostentatious apostates in your entourage who inspected the plunder of Drake's ship, the Ceylonese divinities, and Yang-tse-kiang devils — all of a sudden, with mysterious miens on their mugs, they started praising the profundity of those religions. Phobia and snobbism trifle with people in those regions — what need would you have of such democratic effusions?

Don't forget that only *one* saint functions for the human mind: realism, understanding by that the unceasing prying into reality, the excited groping for its criteria — and the greatest enemy of that is the idol, a Greek or Persian myth. Not because there are no gods and there are plants, but almost the reverse: there are no plants — *sed numina turbulentes adsunt.*[144] Yes, ritual intercourse or the carving of phallus stones is such a hair-raising and ludicrous simplification of the divine reality of love as the number 5 is to a storm of five apples, five maidens, five seas, & five muslin shirts. It is incomprehensible that even clever evangelizers hounded the "modeling," the materiality, and the sperm-curse in Greek deities, yet that gallery of gods is the most pedantic store of ghosts of indifference to reality and denial of reality.

Reality and nature have two lethal poisons and enemies: ecstasy of the instincts & artistic modeling, the demon-ape and Aphrodite-*littérature*. Two Greek deceptions, the same Balkan trick as today, when in Chios you are given malarial water instead of wine. Irreality in place of reality.

After castigating 'soul,' disgraced as a cult, & our instinct for idols castrated as cults, John mentions a specific woman's name in Thyatira, that of Jezebel, the prophetess who likewise absconded with her believers into "idol-cum-fornication" impotence.

I likewise see a big danger concealed in this, something that lies between Nicolaitan over-psychologizing and Baal-type myth: which is to say, the constant temptation of a specific human being, another person, a flesh-and-blood fellow being. I am not only thinking of love; you may have noticed that people are only interested in another person, another woman's dress or love life, another priest's property or training in asceticism, another king's crown — only one thing stirs them up in elemental fashion: what does that most divine of divinities get up to behind closed doors & windows — the other? The humanist ceremony of that heresy is gossip. Of all play-metaphysics that is the least game-like — the sort of thing that it costs me the utmost effort to fight down & condemn, I confess. I would have been incapable of believing in psychology or Greek counterfeiting of reality, but gossip could often count on me as one of its believers. As a matter of fact, we do not have any true feeling for animals, nor gods, nor thoughts, nor flowers — only for the other. How many times have I prayed hard in the morning and afterwards philosophized and drank, then gone out on a stroll to the crocus fields around the college, then finally, after lunch, seen a face that I loved: though God gave my whole body an "aerial hue,"[145] though thinking somehow changed my blood into blood, & the chill freshness of the crocus giddied me into the most Aranjuez of paradises: the power of *it is*, of the positive, the worthwhile, of transformation, I found only in the arriving *face*, a *face* that is not God's and not an animal's, but one of my own kind. What happiness, black repose, after the barbarous hallucinations of gods & animals — another person.

That is humanism's perennial guarantee, that stupefied acceptance which, denying animals and denying gods, wants only another face, the sole language that is comprehensible to me. I don't analyze it; it does not have a separate dark-blue velvet dress, a separate maidenly-womanly body, a separate unicorn-wild spiritual life, a separate social role, and a separate rayon for poetry. No, the essence of such a human-like notion of a human is that it is not constituted of parts but is homogeneous from costume to soul.

Here everything is reconciled: here the flowers bloom without 'nature's' tremendous remoteness being felt on the cool shoulders of the pea flowers — here the soul mirrors its own goldfish now & then, without my having to get lost in the analytical nooks of those Semitic traps — here sensuality first sprinkles a pair of blue-smutted poppy seeds like Ariadne, without my having to annihilate myself in the idol nothingnesses of vegetation — here the dress subtly signals that the mask is just as ancient on man as the face, without falling into the awkward "world as lie" Manichaeism — here æsthetics may open its impatient February-buds, but without being attended by art of 'beauty' vilifications — here idyllic peace hums like a beetle spontaneously whirring its wings in sleep, without its becoming a suffocating incest of family and morality — here the inability to meet is also present (from which one knows that a man & a woman are face to face), but that depth, too, is gentle like the concavity of a rocking dinghy. But *on that account,* the other is the greatest temptation: because nowhere else but in another face can you find such leaving suspended, unresolved, and yet intelligible, of the gentle melting into each other of everything to do with reality and thought.

I shall be quite frank & reveal a struggle. For one thing, I would have liked to tell you, Princess: may your face always be to England that which, with a few sorry metaphors, I have generally characterized as a face — secondly, with the dour theologian gaining the upper hand in me, I must also trample on that cult of the other person, as it is not a 'definitive' solution. And anything that is not a 'definitive' solution is bad, quite clearly bad. In my childhood, I always identified the figure of Jezebel, fashionable in Thyatira, with the description of women in the *Song of Solomon*. Now, in my adulthood, that impossible association comes in very handy: I see ever more clearly how much the 'face,' 'the other person' as the third superstition-panorama after the soul and the idol, is not like the description, or rather *non*-description, of women in the *Song of Solomon*. Whether I look at the shepherd or at the women, what happens to them in the *Song*? Her love is better than wine; she is comely like tents and curtains; like Pharaoh's horses, the hanging cones of the cedars of Lebanon, clusters of camphire, and bundles of myrrh; the gaze swaying out from her eyes like doves ... If ever there was something that is not a face, not human, not a portrait, it is that. There is something 'everlasting' in it, an everlasting & colorless nostalgia for nature. Whereas the essence of the heresy known as the 'the other' is that it is always just a single portrait in a flash of a single historical second. Something that, in any case, cannot resemble Pharaoh's horses and the tired-scented fruits of cypresses going back millennia — it is a solitary wonder that has no premises, its conclusion unknown.

ENDNOTES

The work of classical scholars Péter Somfai & Ábel Tamás has been invaluable in elucidating and translating the Latin and Greek quotations in Szentkuthy's novel. Pierre Senges had a fair share in throwing light on one particularly obscure reference. The translator & editor wish to express their gratitude for everyone's generous help.

1. Osbern of Canterbury, an 11th-century Benedictine monk who wrote a Life of Dunstan, fixed the date of his birth at "the first year of the reign of King Æthelstan," 924 or 925, which cannot be reconciled with other known dates of Dunstan's life. Historians therefore assume he was born c. 910 or earlier.
2. Bloody Ass, or Bloody Donkey (Véres szamár), is the title of the 9th volume of the *St. Orpheus Breviary*, which was published in 1984. It received an Excellence Award from the Hungarian publisher Magvető.
3. Edgarius Cæsar, Augustus of the Albion of Anglia, patrician, patron & consul of Britain, the kings of the Saxons …
4. Exekias (active in Athens between ca. 545 BCE – 530 BCE), famous ancient Greek vase-painter and potter working in the black-figure technique, one of the first major representatives of that art, whose prestige is corroborated by the fact that fragments of several of his works were found on the Athenian Acropolis. His best-known extant signed works had been exported to Etruria and were found in the Etruscan tombs of Vulci & Orvieto, hence the reference to his "Etrurian" cup.

5. Viz. Edward the Martyr (974–978).
6. Æthelred the Unready (circa 968–1016), King of England 978–1013 and 1014–1016.
7. In English in the original. All further words, phrases, or sentences in English in the original will be set in Legacy Sans. This passage is seemingly a quotation from "Elves' Hill," a lied by Carl Lœwe (Op. 3, № 2, ed. 1825): "One fondled my white chin, / one whispered in my ear: / 'Merry young man, arise, arise, / let there by dancing here!" See *The Fischer-Dieskau Book of Lieder*, with English translations by George Bird and Richard Stokes. Lœwe used Johann Gottfried Herder's translation from the original Danish.
8. Mihály Vörösmarty (1800–1855), one of the foremost Romantic poets of Hungarian literature, creator of influential national myths of romantic inspiration, of several verse epics and verse dramas, histories and romances. He was also the author of the canonical translations into Hungarian of Shakespeare's *Julius Cæsar* and *King Lear*.
9. Author's note. See p. 24.
10. Source not verified.
11. Cf. Book 6 of *The Annals*: "Et sæpe in propinqua degressus, aditis iuxta Tiberim hortis…" "He would often come to the neighborhood, visiting the gardens by the Tiber…"
12. Without anger & partiality — a phrase used by Tacitus in the introduction to his *Annals*.
13. Presumably a reference to a now vintage Art Deco graphic style developed by Franz Lenhart in commercial posters (e.g., for Modiano brand cigarettes) during the 1920s & '30s.
14. A porch on the Agora in Athens from where the philosophy of stoicism (derived from the Greek word *stoa*) is said to have been expounded. Zeno lectured to his followers from it.

15. To each his own.
16. To shower them with glory.
17. From the Latin text of the Creed: "was made man."
18. Desecrated pen, ungodly speech.
19. The novel *I, Claudius* by English writer Robert Graves, which uses Suetonius as a source to tell its story, was first published in 1934 and almost certainly known to Szentkuthy, who actually met Graves in the Sixties.
20. Marcus Salvius Otho was Roman Emperor for three months, from January 15 to April 16, 69 AD; he was succeeded by Aulus Vitellius Germanicus, who ruled for eight months from April 16 to December 22, 69 AD, but here the reference is probably to Lucius Vitellius the Elder (before 5 BCE – 51).
21. Ah! let's leave it ... freeborn youths.
22. Defiled with perversity.
23. Nor was it only the figure and the beautiful bodies [to kindle his desire.]
24. The effigies of the ancestors.
25. According to regal custom.
26. Tag end of a quote (the phrase is given in English in the original) from Act V, Scene ii of *King Lear*: "Men must endure / Their going hence, even as their coming hither: / ripeness is all."
27. The *Iliad* records Patroclus, the son of Menœtius and the grandson of Actor, as being honored in death by his friend Achilles, who organized an athletic competition including a chariot race.
28. "Christus, from whom they take their name, had been executed in the reign of Tiberius by the procurator Pontius Pilatus." Tacitus, *Annals* (15.44).
29. The original sculptures on the Harpy tomb (5th century BCE), which overlooks the modern-day town of Kınık, Turkey.

30. Seneca, *Moral Letters to Lucilius*, tr. Richard M. Gummere, Letter 26 ("I was just lately telling you that I was within sight of old age. I am not afraid that I have left old age behind me...")
31. Greek for "He has lived." Seneca, ibid., Letter 12: "Pacuvius, who by long occupancy made Syria his own, used to hold a regular burial sacrifice in his own honor, with wine and the usual funeral feasting, and then would have himself carried from the dining room to his chamber, while eunuchs applauded & sang in Greek to a musical accompaniment: *bebiotai, bebiotai*! Thus Pacuvius had himself carried out to burial every day." Seneca concludes his letter by advising that we transvaluate Pacuvius' debased motive into a good one and return to sleep "with joy and gladness," saying as did Pacuvius, "*Bebiotai*; the course which fortune set for me is finished. And if god is pleased to add another day, we should welcome it with glad hearts."
32. "An attempt at a mythology," a reference to Ernst Bertram's 1918 monograph, *Nietzsche: Versuch einer Mythologie*, arguably the most influential intellectual biography of the philosopher to be written in the first half of the 20th century, which is a perspectival view of Nietzsche that casts him & his philosophy in a mythic perspective.
33. Letter IX from Seneca's *Moral Letters to Lucilius*.
34. Ibid.
35. Partial quote: "Claudius further added to this sacrifices after the ordinances of King Tullius Hostilius, and atonementsto be offered in the Groves of Diana" ["... Dianæ per pontifices danda, inridentibus cunctis, quod poenæ procurationesque incesti id temporis exquirenrentur."]
36. The punishments and expiatory rituals of incest.
37. Court-of-farewells, a recurring phrase in the *St. Orpheus Breviary*, sometimes subject to wordplay & portmanteauing: in volume 9, *The Bloody Ass*, it metamorphoses into "Courtoisie Dieu" for instance.

38. The loveliest of Rome's youth.
39. Here is love, jump here: variation on the Latin phrase "*Hic Rhodus, hic salta*" ("Rhodes is here, jump here!") taken from the Latin version of Æsop's *Fables*, where an interlocutor challenges an athlete who brags to have jumped from one foot of the Colossus of Rhodes to the other, to demonstrate his bravura by repeating the feat.
40. Byzantium was founded by the Greeks, in the extremity of Europe, upon a strait which disjoins Europe from Asia.
41. At the summit, a whore.
42. The philosophical degree / stairway of angels.
43. Her body was not cremated, according to the rites of the Romans, but after the manner of foreign Monarchs, embowelled, and replete with spice ...
44. Embalmed with a stuffing of spices.
45. A hundred ways to cook the dead.
46. Incessant variations on no theme at all.
47. But let's leave the idiots and let's see the nuances.
48. Thlibia (testicles) is from the Greek *thlibein* (to press hard or confine), deriving from the practice of tying up the scrotum to sever the *vas deferens*. *Kazimazia* is probably Szentkuthy's distortion of *kartzimas* (*καρτζιμάς*), Byzantine eunuchs who had their genitalia entirely removed.
49. *The Land of Heart's Desire* is a play (first performed in 1894) by W. B. Yeats.
50. A number of religious traditions and groupings throughout the 4th to the 6th century AD opposed the doctrine asserted at the Council of Chalcedon (451) about Christ's dual (divine and human) nature, stating that, in spite of his taking on a human form, Christ's nature remained altogether divine, with no inmixture of the human.
51. Not romanticism in the least.
52. William of Champeaux (c. 1070–1121) taught in the school of the cathedral of Notre-Dame, Paris. Among his pupils

was Pierre Abélard, who figures prominently in Volume I of the *St. Orpheus Breviary: Marginalia on Casanova.*

53. In the Lydian mode.
54. I'm hurt.
55. The rest is censored. — "*Ceterum censeo Carthaginem delendam esse*" ("Moreover, I consider Carthage must be destroyed") was a saying used in the Roman Senate by proponents — most famously Cato the Elder — of any policy aimed at destroying Rome's aggressors.
56. To me chance has charismatically promised a picturesque dementia forth-glowing with red from Paris' syphilitic shade.
57. Source unidentified.
58. The decision of William of Champeaux, Archdeacon of Paris, to retire to a small hermitage near Paris in 1108 was connected with the foundation of the Abbey of St. Victor, Paris.
59. Gentile Bellini's portrait of Sultan Mehmet II (1480).
60. Szentkuthy recorded elsewhere that in this figure he "tried to immortalize... a full-scale portrait" of János Horváth (1878–1961), Professor of Hungarian Literature, who "had a demonic impact on me." Horváth in Hungarian denotes 'Croat' (hence the "de Illyria").
61. The featuring of these two Venetian churches underlines the novel's elaborate game with anachronism. Whereas the three-domed interior of San Salvatore (San Salvador), an example of early 16th-century Venetian Renaissance, bears the imprint of architects Giorgio Spavento, Tullio Lombardo, and Jacopo Sansovino, and is thus distantly derived from Florentine models, its ornate baroque façade (designed by Giuseppe Sardi, 1663) could hardly occasion associations as described in the passage. The iconic Baroque façade of San Moisè (Alessandro Tremignon), on the other hand, was completed in 1668, more than twenty

years after Monteverdi's death (1643), who could thus not possibly have seen it.

62. Bartolomeo Colleoni (1400–1475) was a famous condottiero, one of the foremost tacticians and military leaders of 15th-century Italy. He became captain-general of the Republic of Venice; his equestrian statue, by Andrea del Verrocchio — one of the iconic equestrian public monuments of the Italian Renaissance — stands on the square in front of SS. Giovanni e Paolo in Venice.
63. Latin for "trembling."
64. A betrothed woman, bride.
65. Painter Jacopo Bellini (1400–70) is best known as the father of Gentile (1429–1507) and Giovanni (1430–1516), and the father-in-law of Andrea Mantegna (1431–1506). One of his sketchbooks is in the British Museum, the other in the Louvre.
66. Herodotus, *Histories* I, tr. Aubrey de Selincourt.
67. This particular Adrastus was the son of Gordias, king of Phrygia, and features prominently in Herodotus' story of King Crœsus of Lydia.
68. Metic: a resident alien in a Greek city.
69. From Herodotus, *Histories* I, tr. Gregory Nagy, Claudia Filos, Sarah Scott, and Keith Stone.
70. Lycurgus (9th-century BCE) is considered the founder of the Spartan constitution and educational system.
71. Now extinct long-horned cattle tribe *Bos primigenius*.
72. Alyattes (c 609–590 BCE) established the Lydian empire.
73. German for "in itself," reference to Kant's concept, "*das Ding-an-sich*," or the Thing-in-itself, the object independent of observation, and therefore of subjectivity.
74. Sixtus IV (1414–1484) was born Francesco della Rovere.
75. The naturally a-theistic evidence of things and the conceptual world of abstractions are naturally mendacious.
76. Ferocious calculation.

77. *Toteninsel* (The Isle of the Dead) is the title of a painting by the Swiss Symbolist artist Arnold Böcklin (1827–1901).
78. A silk gown often lined or trimmed with fur.
79. Johann Jakob Bachofen (1815–87) was a Swiss jurist and anthropologist, who developed theories of the role of ancient "Mother right" or Hetærism (matriarchy) & the Dionysian (patriarchy).
80. What a wardrobe!
81. Not a miracle of life but a miracle of non-life ... a non-miracle of life.
82. Rampant, raging roses.
83. "*Wir wandelten durch Feuergluten*" ("We wandered through the fire's glow") is a line from a duet between Pamina & Tamino in Act 2 of Mozart's *The Magic Flute*.
84. Parca of Parcæ.
85. *The Moon and Sixpence* is a 1919 novel by W. Somerset Maugham about a fictional English painter (Charles Strickland) loosely based on Paul Gauguin.
86. The Morea was a name given to the southern (Peloponnese) peninsula of Greece. The Morean War is the name for the Sixth Ottoman-Venetian War (1686–99) between the Republic of Venice & the Ottoman Empire, in which the Parthenon in Athens was destroyed.
87. Elizabeth (1207–1231) was a princess of the ruling Árpádian dynasty of Hungary but raised by the Thuringian court in central Germany. Married at the age of 14 and widowed at 20, she then gave her wealth to the poor, building hospitals, where she herself served the sick. She was canonized by Pope Gregory IX. Marburg became a center of the Teutonic Order, which adopted St. Elizabeth as its secondary patroness.
88. Greek for "savior, deliverer."
89. Nous: mind, reason; in Neoplatonic philosophy, divine reason regarded as the first emanation of God. Gnosis: revealed knowledge of a spiritual truth.

90. An ophite (from Greek *ophis*, "snake" via Latin) is one of several greenish rocks (e.g., dolerite & diabase), the mottling of which resembles the markings on a snake.
91. And night is his name.
92. Very last girl.
93. There are numerous Eleanors of Aragon, but this particular one was most likely the granddaughter of Frederick of Aragon, King of Sicily, who died in 1405, long before the bust was made.
94. Francesco Laurana (c. 1430 – 1502) was born in Vrana in Dalmatia, and adopted his native town's name (La Vrana yields Laurana). The bust allegedly portraying Eleanor of Aragon is now in the Palazzo Abatellis in Palermo, Sicily.
95. We shall not concede nostalgia for heaven.
96. Earth vanishes, heaven darkens.
97. Cited in English in the original, this is a reference to a phrase in John Milton's *Comus, A Mask* (set to music by Henry Lawes, this was presented at Ludlow Castle in 1634 before John Egerton, 1st Earl of Bridgewater, at that time the Lord President of Wales): "... How charming is divine Philosophy! / Not harsh, and crabbed as dull fools suppose, / But musical as is Apollo's lute ..."
98. Too bad for neurosis.
99. Revelations 2:24 (KJV).
100. Romans 1:16 (KJV).
101. A pun on a phrase from the Hail Mary: *gratia plena*, "full of grace."
102. Literally, "breeze of words," a term used by Roscelin of Compiègne in the debate between nominalism and essentialism: the naming of things is "bare word."
103. Greek for "happiness, welfare," from "eu": good, and "daimon": spirit; term used for the highest human good in Aristotle's ethical and political works.

104. Kharis, a word that frequently recurs in the Greek Scriptures, is variably translated as "that which causes joy, pleasure," "kindness, goodwill," "grace," "bestowed favor." One of its most well-known occurrences is in Ephesians 2:8: "For it is by God's *loving-kindness* [*kharis*] that you have been saved…" (The Twentieth-Century New Testament).
105. Revelation 9:11: "and they had a king over them, which is the angel of the bottomless pit, whose name in the Hebrew tongue is Abaddon, but in the Greek tongue hath his name Apollyon" (KJV).
106. Two of the sweet games of epistemology.
107. So much for the antique record on 'depth.'
108. Szentkuthy was born on June 2, 1908, and the first Hungarian edition of *Black Renaissance* came out in 1939, so he almost certainly was still 30 at the time when he wrote the book.
109. "Of philosophies that exist not…," a play on a dictum by medieval Hungarian King Coloman the Bookish (c. 1070–1116), who prohibited the prosecution of witches: "*De striges vero quæ non sunt, nulla quæstio fiat*" ("Of witches who exist not, let there be no record").
110. And I go forth to the altar of reality with a most simple key, but whoever comes with that key is the paradisiacally multiform little bird of the scintillating heart. The text plays upon the incipit of the Catholic Mass, "*Et introibo ad altare Dei…*" ("And I go to the altar of God"), taken from Psalm 43 (42 in the Vulgate).
111. The quote is from Horace's 2nd Epode (English translation courtesy of John T. Quinn): "… *Autumnus agris extulit, / ut gaudet insitiva decerpens pira / certantem et uvam purpuræ, / qua muneretur te, Priape, et te, pater / Silvane, tutor finium…*" ("… As Autumn hoists its head, adorned with / fleshy fruits, through fields, / he gloats, gathering

prize pears / & grapes purpler than the pigment / to pay you, Priapus, & you sir, / Silvanus, protector of property.")

112. *Revelation* 11:13 (Darby Bible). In the KJV, the same passage is translated as: "... and in the earthquake were slain of men seven thousand."

113. Quoted in English in the original, the phrase is from verse 20 of Andrew Marvell's *Daphnis and Chloe*: "And I parting should appear / Like the gourmand Hebrew dead, / While he quails and manna fed, / And does through the desert err."

114. Fundamentals, a word that features in the title of a range of works of German philosophy, most notably, Marx's *Grundrisse der Kritik der politischen Ökonomie* (*Fundamentals of Political Economy Criticism*).

115. The body is a chalice unable to bear death, the soul one unable to bear duplicity.

116. To the tune of Florentine erudition.

117. *Crepe romaine* is an airy woolen fabric produced from fine single crepe yarn.

118. Built as the tomb of Giovanni Battista Zeno (died May 7, 1501), who was made a cardinal by his uncle, Pope Paul II, in 1468.

119. The continuous architrave molding of the face of an arch (also known as the *intrados* or underside of an arch).

120. This ornamental ensemble has a certain charm, but it's a bit tormented.

121. Reference to Odo (or Oddone) Colonna (c. 1368–1431), who was elected Pope Martin V from 1417 to 1431 and in effect ended the Western Schism.

122. The Mausoleum contains three sarcophagi, one of which is that of Galla Placidia (d. 450), daughter of the Roman Emperor Theodosius I. The lunette over its north entrance shows a mosaic of Christ as the Good Shepherd tending his flocks.

123. According to Genesis 2 (KJV), the four rivers flowing through the Garden of Eden are the Pison, Gihon (these first two have not been identified), Hiddekel (most plausibly the Tigris), and the Euphrates.
124. The Palazzo Grimani di San Luca is a mid-16th century Renaissance building in Venice, located on the Rio di San Luca at the point where it flows into the Canal Grande. It is based on a design by Michele Sanmicheli and was completed after his death by Gian Giacomo de' Grigi ('il Bergamasco').
125. The German word, meaning "solidly built, immured," is evocative of the opening verse of Friedrich Schiller's famous poem *Das Lied von der Glocke* (*The Song of the Bell*, 1799), celebrating the intellect which creates form from matter: "Fest gemauert in der Erden / Steht die Form, aus Lehm gebrannt.' In Margarete Münsterberg's translation: "Walled in fast within the earth / Stands the form burnt out of clay."
126. Suzanne de Bourbon-Beaujeu (1491–1521), Duchess of Bourbon, was famously painted as a small child by Jehan de Paris, Master of the Bourbons, in a picture entitled *Child in Prayer*.
127. Andrea Palladio's last (unfinished) design, the Vicenza Teatro Olimpico (1580 – 1585), became a model for theater architecture; its illusionistic scenery giving the appearance of long, receding streets, by Andrea Scamozzi, is the oldest surviving stage set.
128. From the French for "to shock, to offend" — a reference to the French decadent poets' and European æstheticists' programmatic rallying cry, "*épater les bourgeois*" (offend the bourgeoisie), expressing their rejection of the philistinism of their contemporary middle-class society.
129. The 8th verse of Shelley's "To a Skylark" runs: "Like a poet hidden / In the light of thought, / Singing hymns unbid-

den, / Till the world is wrought / To sympathy with hopes & fears it heeded not ..."

130. Noah releasing the dove from the ark is a mosaic from before 1220 in St. Mark's Basilica in Venice.
131. This is based on a quote from Blaise Pascal (*Pensées*, № 513. *Mathematics. Intuition*): *La vraie éloquence se moque de l'éloquence, la vraie morale se moque de la morale* ... (True eloquence has no time for eloquence. True morality has no time for morality) English tr. by Honor Levi.
132. Armored, armor-clad.
133. Author's note. See page 252.
134. Here, here, always here begins metaphysics, piousness & god.
135. Divine qualities.
136. In line 52 of Virgil's 6th *Eclogue*, Hylas (from the Argonaut saga) consoles Pasiphæ: "Ah! unhappy girl, now you roam the hills ..." (tr. H.R. Fairclough). One perhaps need not add that one of Elizabeth I's best-known nicknames was the Virgin Queen.
137. A phrase taken from the beginning of Virgil's 10th *Eclogue* essentially meaning "a garland of flowers or tamarisks."
138. From a duet by the Second and Third Shepherds in Act 2 of *L'Orfeo* (text by Alessandro Striggio): "On this adorned meadow / every god of the woods / has frequently been wont to spend happy hours."
139. A mistake made in ignorance.
140. Marcion, founder of the Marcionites, an ascetic Gnostic sect, was the son of a bishop of Sinope on the Black Sea. The gospel of Christ, according to him, consisted in free love of the Good. He entirely rejected the Old Testament and all but a few epistles plus a bit of the gospel of St. Luke in the New Testament.
141. A reference to Horace's *Ars poeticae* (line 139): "*Parturiunt montes, nascetur ridiculus mus*" ("The mountain laboured and brought forth a laughable mouse").

142. An early Christian sect that advocated a return to pagan worship (mentioned in *Revelation* 2:6,15).
143. Sacred strumpeting.
144. But perturbed divine powers are present.
145. A phrase used in Shelley's "To a Skylark": "Like a glow-worm golden / In a dell of dew, / Scattering unbeholden / Its aërial hue / Among the flowers & grass, which screen it from the view ..."

COLOPHON

BLACK RENAISSANCE

was handset in InDesign CC.

The text & page numbers are set in *Adobe Jenson Pro.*
The titles are set in *ITC Galliard.*

Book design & typesetting: Alessandro Segalini
Cover design: István Orosz

BLACK RENAISSANCE

is published by Contra Mundum Press.
Its printer has received Chain of Custody certification from:
The Forest Stewardship Council,
The Programme for the Endorsement of Forest Certification,
& The Sustainable Forestry Initiative.

CONTRA MUNDUM PRESS

Dedicated to the value & the indispensable importance of the individual voice, to works that test the boundaries of thought & experience.

The primary aim of Contra Mundum is to publish translations of writers who in their use of form and style are *à rebours*, or who deviate significantly from more programmatic & spurious forms of experimentation. Such writing attests to the volatile nature of modernism. Our preference is for works that have not yet been translated into English, are out of print, or are poorly translated, for writers whose thinking & æsthetics are in opposition to timely or mainstream currents of thought, value systems, or moralities. We also reprint obscure and out-of-print works we consider significant but which have been forgotten, neglected, or overshadowed.

There are many works of fundamental significance to *Weltliteratur* (*& Weltkultur*) that still remain in relative oblivion, works that alter and disrupt standard circuits of thought — these warrant being encountered by the world at large. It is our aim to render them more visible.

For the complete list of forthcoming publications, please visit our website. To be added to our mailing list, send your name and email address to: info@contramundum.net

Contra Mundum Press

P.O. Box 1326

New York, NY 10276

USA

OTHER CONTRA MUNDUM PRESS TITLES

Gilgamesh
Ghérasim Luca, *Self-Shadowing Prey*
Rainer J. Hanshe, *The Abdication*
Walter Jackson Bate, *Negative Capability*
Miklós Szentkuthy, *Marginalia on Casanova*
Fernando Pessoa, *Philosophical Essays*
Elio Petri, *Writings on Cinema & Life*
Friedrich Nietzsche, *The Greek Music Drama*
Richard Foreman, *Plays with Films*
Louis-Auguste Blanqui, *Eternity by the Stars*
Miklós Szentkuthy, *Towards the One & Only Metaphor*
Josef Winkler, *When the Time Comes*
William Wordsworth, *Fragments*
Josef Winkler, *Natura Morta*
Fernando Pessoa, *The Transformation Book*
Emilio Villa, *The Selected Poetry of Emilio Villa*
Robert Kelly, *A Voice Full of Cities*
Pier Paolo Pasolini, *The Divine Mimesis*
Miklós Szentkuthy, *Prae, Vol. 1*
Federico Fellini, *Making a Film*
Robert Musil, *Thought Flights*
Sándor Tar, *Our Street*
Lorand Gaspar, *Earth Absolute*
Josef Winkler, *The Graveyard of Bitter Oranges*
Ferit Edgü, *Noone*
Jean-Jacques Rousseau, *Narcissus*
Ahmad Shamlu, *Born Upon the Dark Spear*
Jean-Luc Godard, *Phrases*
Otto Dix, *Letters, Vol. 1*
Maura Del Serra, *Ladder of Oaths*
Pierre Senges, *The Major Refutation*
Charles Baudelaire, *My Heart Laid Bare & Other Texts*
Joseph Kessel, *Army of Shadows*
Rainer J. Hanshe & Federico Gori, *Shattering the Muses*
Gérard Depardieu, *Innocent*
Claude Mouchard, *Entangled, Papers!, Notes*

SOME FORTHCOMING TITLES

Adonis, *Interviews with Pierre Joris*
Pierre Senges, *Ahab (Sequels)*
Carmelo Bene, *I Appeared to the Madonna*

THE FUTURE OF KULCHUR
A PATRONAGE PROJECT

LEND CONTRA MUNDUM PRESS (CMP) YOUR SUPPORT

With bookstores and presses around the world struggling to survive, and many actually closing, we are forming this patronage project as a means for establishing a continuous & stable foundation to safeguard our longevity. Through this patronage project we would be able to remain free of having to rely upon government support &/or other official funding bodies, not to speak of their timelines & impositions. It would also free CMP from suffering the vagaries of the publishing industry, as well as the risk of submitting to commercial pressures in order to persist, thereby potentially compromising the integrity of our catalog.

CAN YOU SACRIFICE $10 A WEEK FOR KULCHUR?

For the equivalent of merely 2–3 coffees a week, you can help sustain CMP and contribute to the future of kulchur. To participate in our patronage program we are asking individuals to donate $500 per year, which amounts to $42/month, or $10/week. Larger donations are of course welcome and beneficial. All donations are tax-deductible through our fiscal sponsor Fractured Atlas. If preferred, donations can be made in two installments. We are seeking a minimum of 300 patrons per year and would like for them to commit to giving the above amount for a period of three years.

WHAT WE OFFER

Part tax-deductible donation, part exchange, for your contribution you will receive every CMP book published during the patronage period as well as 20 books from our back catalog. When possible, signed or limited editions of books will be offered as well.

WHAT WILL CMP DO WITH YOUR CONTRIBUTIONS?

Your contribution will help with basic general operating expenses, yearly production expenses (book printing, warehouse & catalog fees, etc.), advertising & outreach, and editorial, proofreading, translation, typography, design and copyright fees. Funds may also be used for participating in book fairs and staging events. Additionally, we hope to rebuild the *Hyperion* section of the website in order to modernize it.

From Pericles to Mæcenas & the Renaissance patrons, it is the magnanimity of such individuals that have helped the arts to flourish. Be a part of helping your kulchur flourish; be a part of history.

HOW

To lend your support & become a patron, please visit the subscription page of our website: contramundum.net/subscription

For any questions, write us at: info@contramundum.net

Lightning Source UK Ltd.
Milton Keynes UK
UKHW04f0701161018
330624UK00001B/188/P